AVENGERS
NO MORE BULLYING

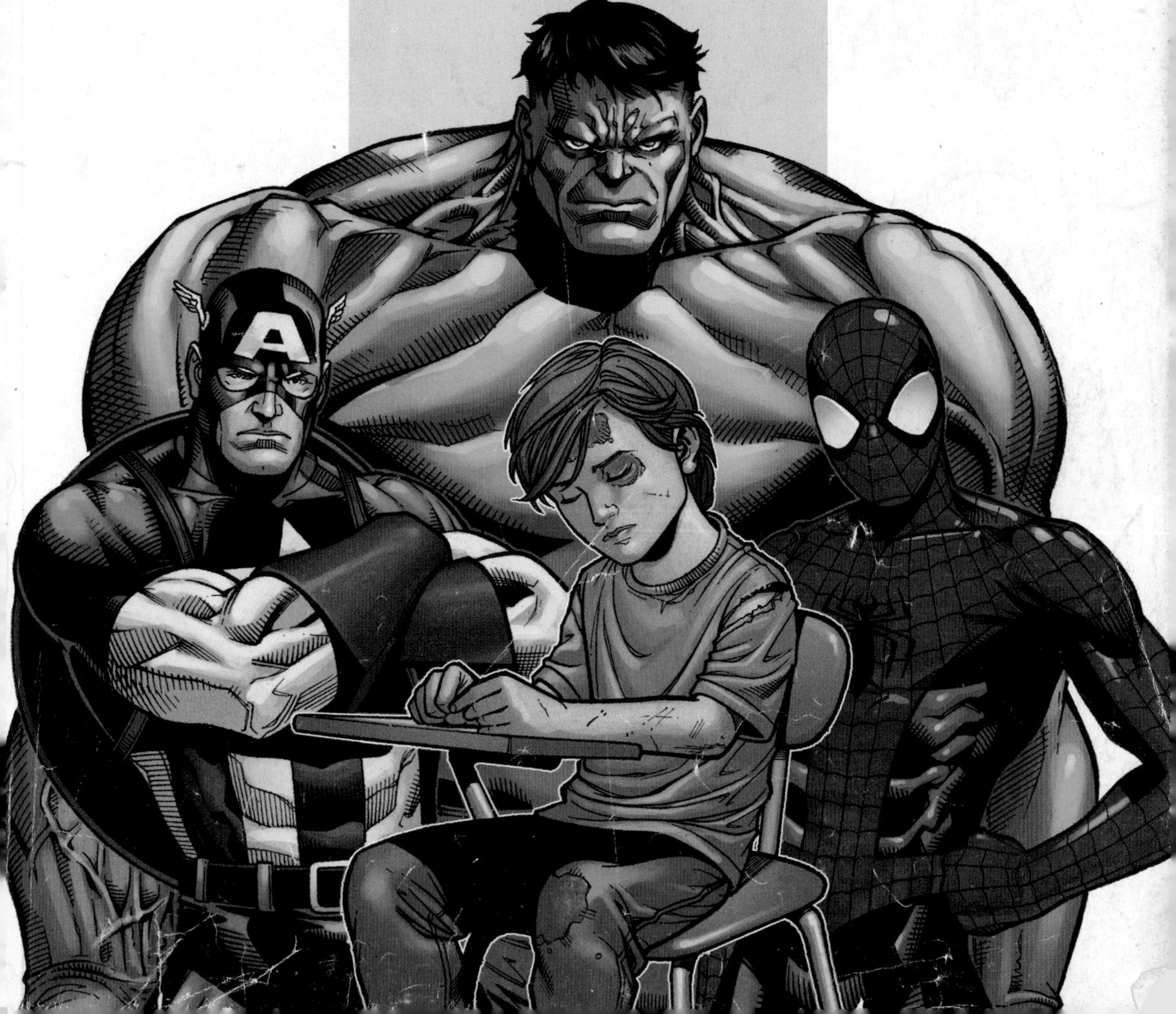

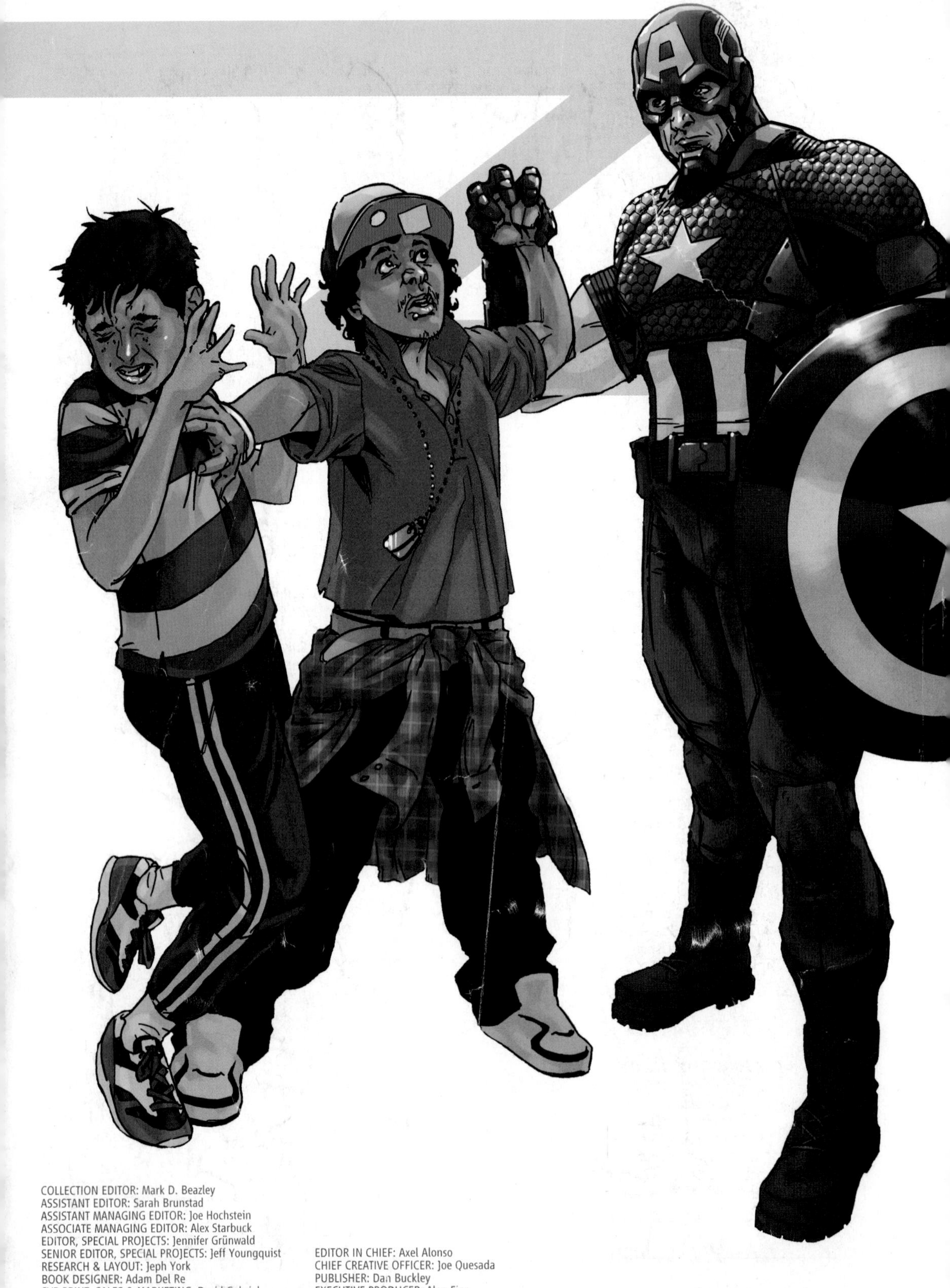

COLLECTION EDITOR: Mark D. Beazley
ASSISTANT EDITOR: Sarah Brunstad
ASSISTANT MANAGING EDITOR: Joe Hochstein
ASSOCIATE MANAGING EDITOR: Alex Starbuck
EDITOR, SPECIAL PROJECTS: Jennifer Grünwald
SENIOR EDITOR, SPECIAL PROJECTS: Jeff Youngquist
RESEARCH & LAYOUT: Jeph York
BOOK DESIGNER: Adam Del Re
SVP PRINT, SALES & MARKETING: David Gabriel

EDITOR IN CHIEF: Axel Alonso
CHIEF CREATIVE OFFICER: Joe Quesada
PUBLISHER: Dan Buckley
EXECUTIVE PRODUCER: Alan Fine

AVENGERS: NO MORE BULLYING. Contains material originally published in magazine form as AVENGERS: NO MORE BULLYING #1, THOR #356, PREVENT CHILD ABUSE AMERICA PRESENTS: AMAZING SPIDER-MAN ON BULLYING PREVENTION #1, AVENGERS VS. #1 and DAREDEVIL #28. First printing 2015. ISBN# 978-0-7851-9851-2. Published by MARVEL WORLDWIDE, INC., a subsidiary of MARVEL ENTERTAINMENT, LLC. OFFICE OF PUBLICATION: 135 West 50th Street, New York, NY 10020. **Printed in the U.S.A.** ALAN FINE, President, Marvel Entertainment; DAN BUCKLEY, President, TV, Publishing and Brand Management; JOE QUESADA, Chief Creative Officer; TOM BREVOORT, SVP of Publishing; DAVID BOGART, SVP of Operations & Procurement, Publishing; C.B. CEBULSKI, VP of International Development & Brand Management; DAVID GABRIEL, SVP Print, Sales & Marketing; JIM O'KEEFE, VP of Operations & Logistics; DAN CARR, Executive Director of Publishing Technology; SUSAN CRESPI, Editorial Operations Manager; ALEX MORALES, Publishing Operations Manager; STAN LEE, Chairman Emeritus. For information regarding advertising in Marvel Comics or on Marvel.com, please contact Jonathan Rheingold, VP of Custom Solutions & Ad Sales, at jrheingold@marvel.com. For Marvel subscription inquiries, please call 800-217-9158.
Manufactured between 8/7/2015 and 9/14/2015 by R.R. DONNELLEY, INC., SALEM, VA, USA.

10 9 8 7 6 5 4 3 2 1

AVENGERS: NO MORE BULLYING

AVENGERS: NO MORE BULLYING #1

AVENGERS: STRAIGHT SHOOTER
WRITER: Sean Ryan
ARTIST: Carlo Barberi
COLORIST: Israel Silva

GUARDIANS OF THE GALAXY: QUOTIENT
WRITER: Jody Houser
ARTIST: Tana Ford
COLORIST: Ruth Redmond

AMAZING SPIDER-MAN: FRIENDS ON THE WEB
WRITER: Gerry Duggan
ARTIST: Marcio Takara
COLORIST: Lee Loughridge

WEIRD
WRITER: Jeff Loveness
ARTIST: Gustavo Duarte
COLORIST: Lee Loughridge

LETTERER: VC's Travis Lanham
COVER ARTIST: Paul Renaud
VARIANT COVER ARTIST: Pascal Campion
EDITOR: Devin Lewis
SUPERVISING EDITOR: Nick Lowe

THOR #356

THE POWER AND THE PRIDE!
WRITER: Bob Harras
PENCILER: Jackson Guice
INKER: Bob Layton
COLORIST: Christie Scheele
LETTERER: John Workman
COVER ARTISTS: Bob Layton & Jackson Guice
EDITOR: Mark Gruenwald

DAREDEVIL #28

HELP WANTED
WRITER: Mark Waid
PENCILER & COLORIST: Javier Rodriguez
INKER: Alvaro Lopez
LETTERER: VC's Joe Caramagna
COVER ARTISTS: Chris Samnee & Javier Rodriguez
ASSISTANT EDITOR: Ellie Pyle
EDITOR: Stephen Wacker
SPECIAL THANKS: Tom Peyer

AMAZING SPIDER-MAN ON BULLYING PREVENTION #1

FEAR PRESSURE!
WRITER: Brett Lewis
PENCILER: Mark Bright
INKERS: Scott Elmer & Rodney Ramos
COLORIST: Transparency Digital
LETTERER: Chris Eliopoulos
COVER ARTIST: Mark Bright
ASSISTANT EDITORS: Mackenzie Cadenhead & Nick Lowe
ASSOCIATE EDITOR: C.B. Cebulski
EDITOR: Ralph Macchio
SPECIAL THANKS: SuEllen Fried

AVENGERS VS. #1

WRITER & LETTERER: Joe Caramagna

AVENGERS VS. RED SKULL: THE ART OF WAR
ARTIST: Andrea Di Vito
COLORIST: Laura Villari
COVER ARTISTS: Tom Raney & Tamra Bonvillain

AVENGERS VS. LOKI & FROST GIANTS: ASGARD ON ICE
PENCILER: Wellinton Alves
INKER: Anderson Silva
COLORIST: Carlos Lopez
COVER ARTISTS: Michael Ryan & Javier Mena

AVENGERS VS. ATTUMA: TO TURN THE TIDE
PENCILER: Ron Lim
INKER: Scott Hanna
COLORIST: Carlos Lopez
COVER ARTISTS: Ron Lim, Scott Hanna & Wil Quintana

AVENGERS VS. M.O.D.O.K. & A.I.M.: BROS BEFORE FOES
ARTIST & COLORIST: Dario Brizuela
COVER ARTIST: Kalman Andrasofszky

ASSISTANT EDITOR: Mark Basso
EDITOR: Bill Rosemann

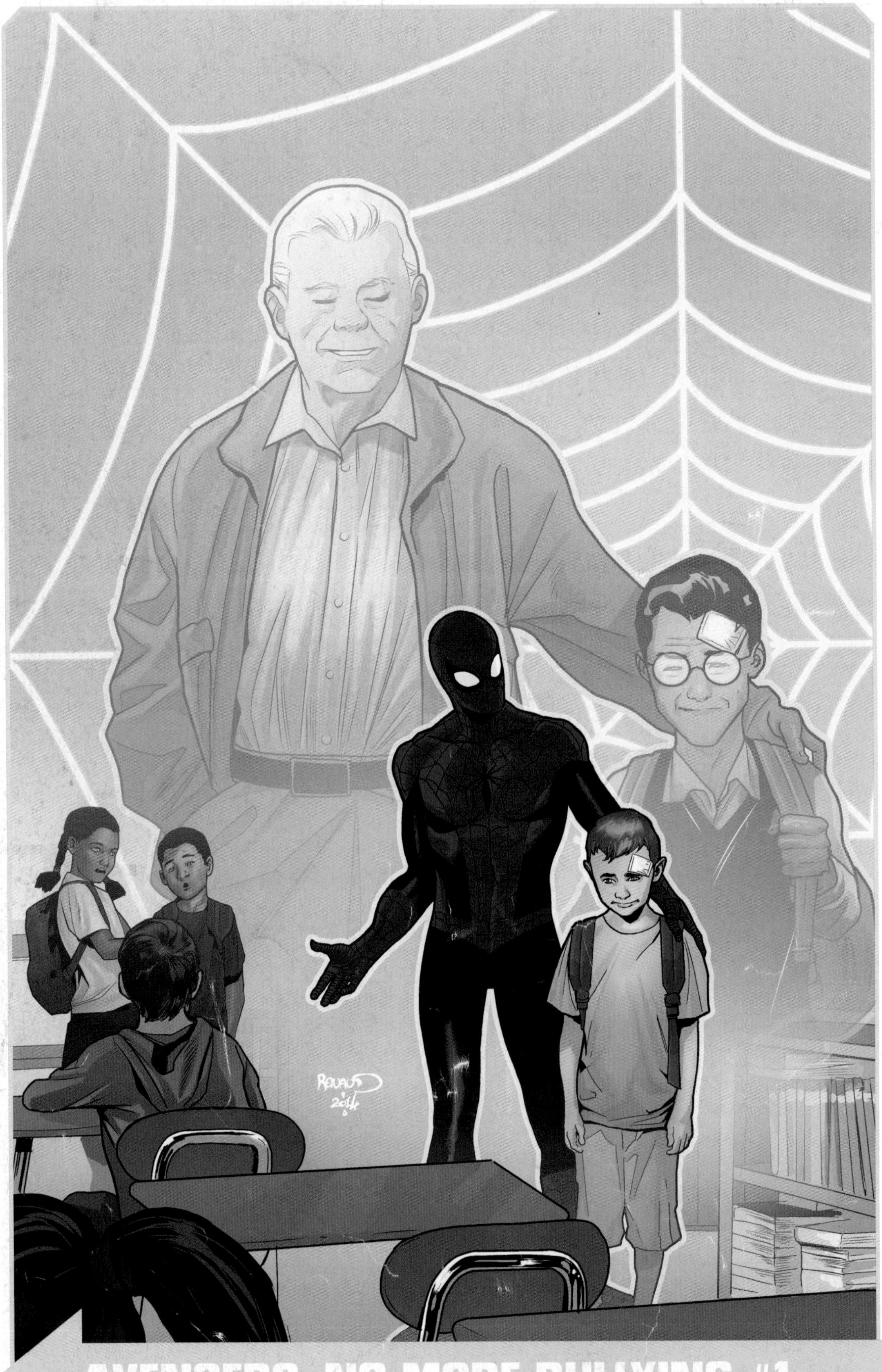

AVENGERS: NO MORE BULLYING #1

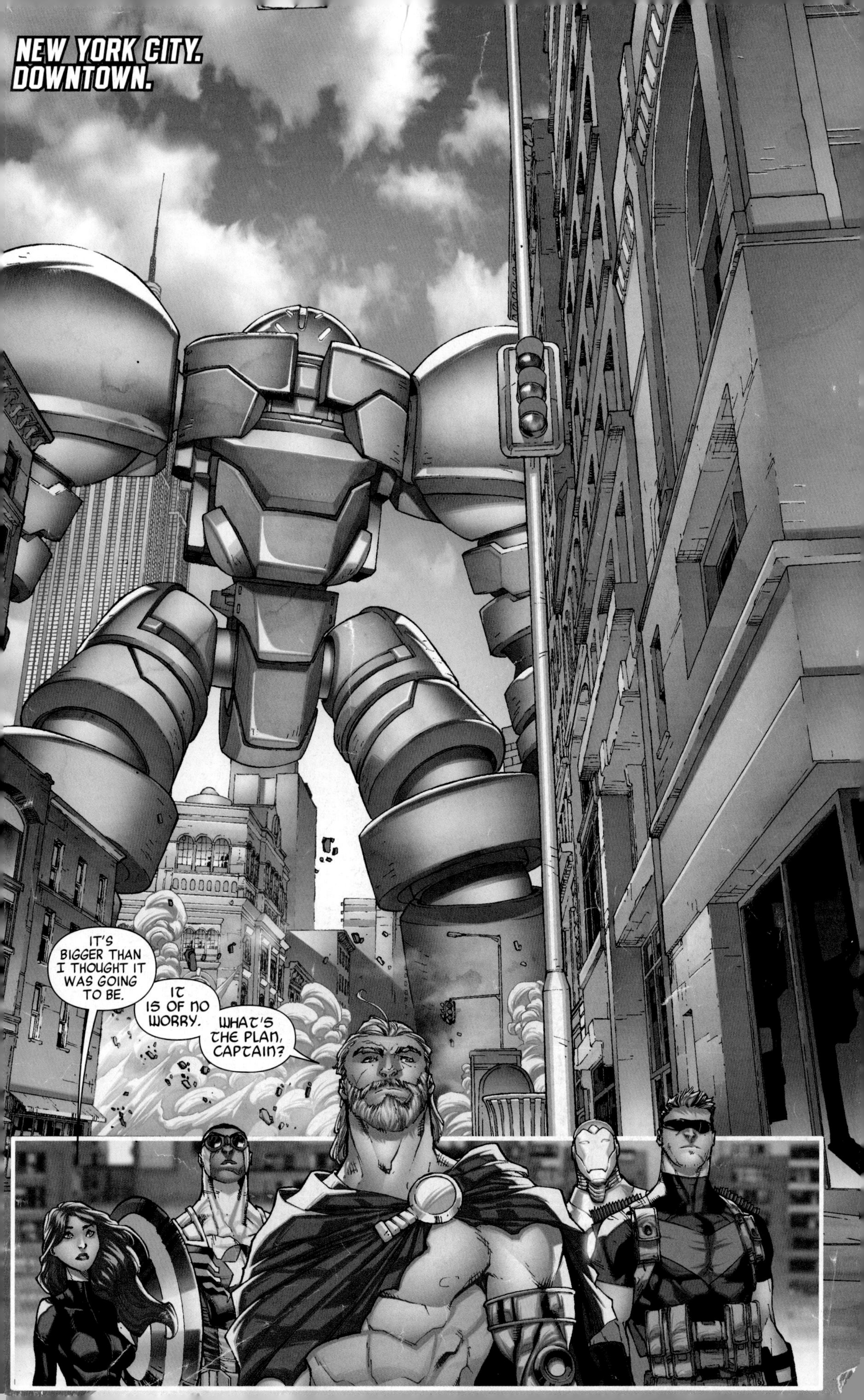
NEW YORK CITY.
DOWNTOWN.
IT'S BIGGER THAN I THOUGHT IT WAS GOING TO BE.
IT IS OF NO WORRY.
WHAT'S THE PLAN, CAPTAIN?

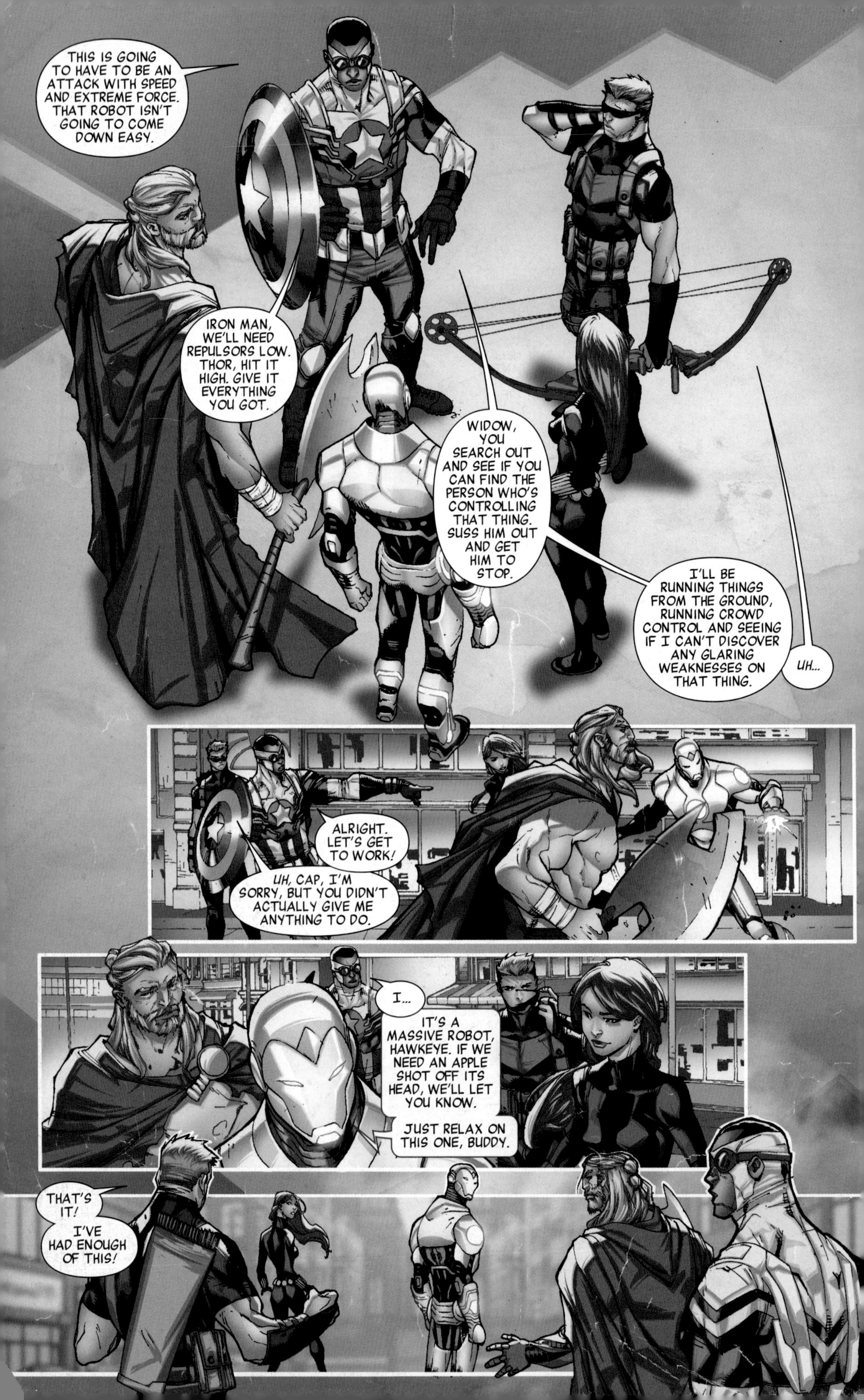
THIS IS GOING TO HAVE TO BE AN ATTACK WITH SPEED AND EXTREME FORCE. THAT ROBOT ISN'T GOING TO COME DOWN EASY.
IRON MAN, WE'LL NEED REPULSORS LOW. THOR, HIT IT HIGH. GIVE IT EVERYTHING YOU GOT.
WIDOW, YOU SEARCH OUT AND SEE IF YOU CAN FIND THE PERSON WHO'S CONTROLLING THAT THING. SUSS HIM OUT AND GET HIM TO STOP.
I'LL BE RUNNING THINGS FROM THE GROUND, RUNNING CROWD CONTROL AND SEEING IF I CAN'T DISCOVER ANY GLARING WEAKNESSES ON THAT THING.
UH...
ALRIGHT. LET'S GET TO WORK!
UH, CAP, I'M SORRY, BUT YOU DIDN'T ACTUALLY GIVE ME ANYTHING TO DO.
I...
IT'S A MASSIVE ROBOT, HAWKEYE. IF WE NEED AN APPLE SHOT OFF ITS HEAD, WE'LL LET YOU KNOW.
JUST RELAX ON THIS ONE, BUDDY.
THAT'S IT!
I'VE HAD ENOUGH OF THIS!

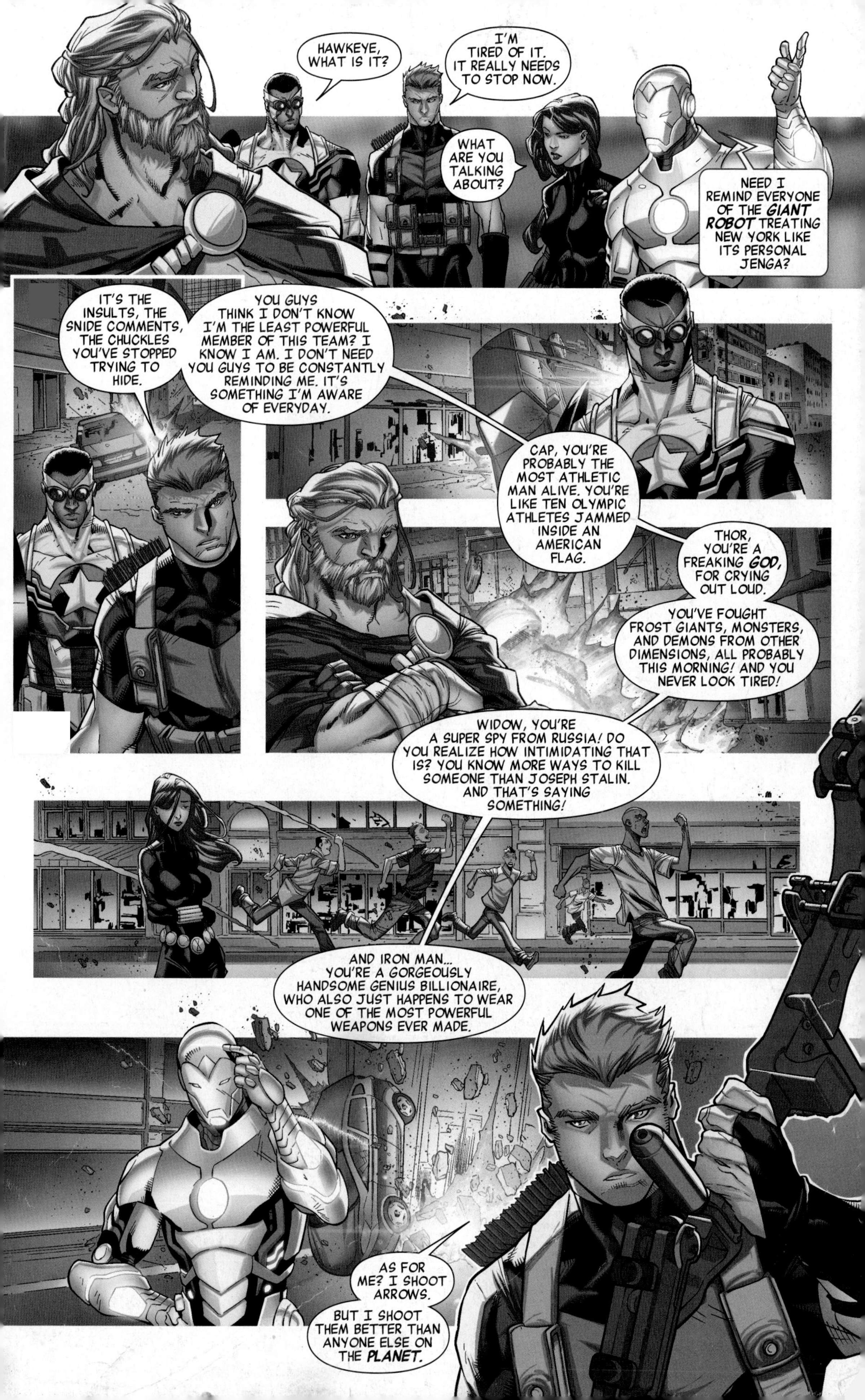
HAWKEYE, WHAT IS IT?
I'M TIRED OF IT. IT REALLY NEEDS TO STOP NOW.
WHAT ARE YOU TALKING ABOUT?
NEED I REMIND EVERYONE OF THE *GIANT ROBOT* TREATING NEW YORK LIKE ITS PERSONAL JENGA?
IT'S THE INSULTS, THE SNIDE COMMENTS, THE CHUCKLES YOU'VE STOPPED TRYING TO HIDE.
YOU GUYS THINK I DON'T KNOW I'M THE LEAST POWERFUL MEMBER OF THIS TEAM? I KNOW I AM. I DON'T NEED YOU GUYS TO BE CONSTANTLY REMINDING ME. IT'S SOMETHING I'M AWARE OF EVERYDAY.
CAP, YOU'RE PROBABLY THE MOST ATHLETIC MAN ALIVE. YOU'RE LIKE TEN OLYMPIC ATHLETES JAMMED INSIDE AN AMERICAN FLAG.
THOR, YOU'RE A FREAKING *GOD*, FOR CRYING OUT LOUD.
YOU'VE FOUGHT FROST GIANTS, MONSTERS, AND DEMONS FROM OTHER DIMENSIONS, ALL PROBABLY THIS MORNING! AND YOU NEVER LOOK TIRED!
WIDOW, YOU'RE A SUPER SPY FROM RUSSIA! DO YOU REALIZE HOW INTIMIDATING THAT IS? YOU KNOW MORE WAYS TO KILL SOMEONE THAN JOSEPH STALIN. AND THAT'S SAYING SOMETHING!
AND IRON MAN... YOU'RE A GORGEOUSLY HANDSOME GENIUS BILLIONAIRE, WHO ALSO JUST HAPPENS TO WEAR ONE OF THE MOST POWERFUL WEAPONS EVER MADE.
AS FOR ME? I SHOOT ARROWS.
BUT I SHOOT THEM BETTER THAN ANYONE ELSE ON THE *PLANET*.

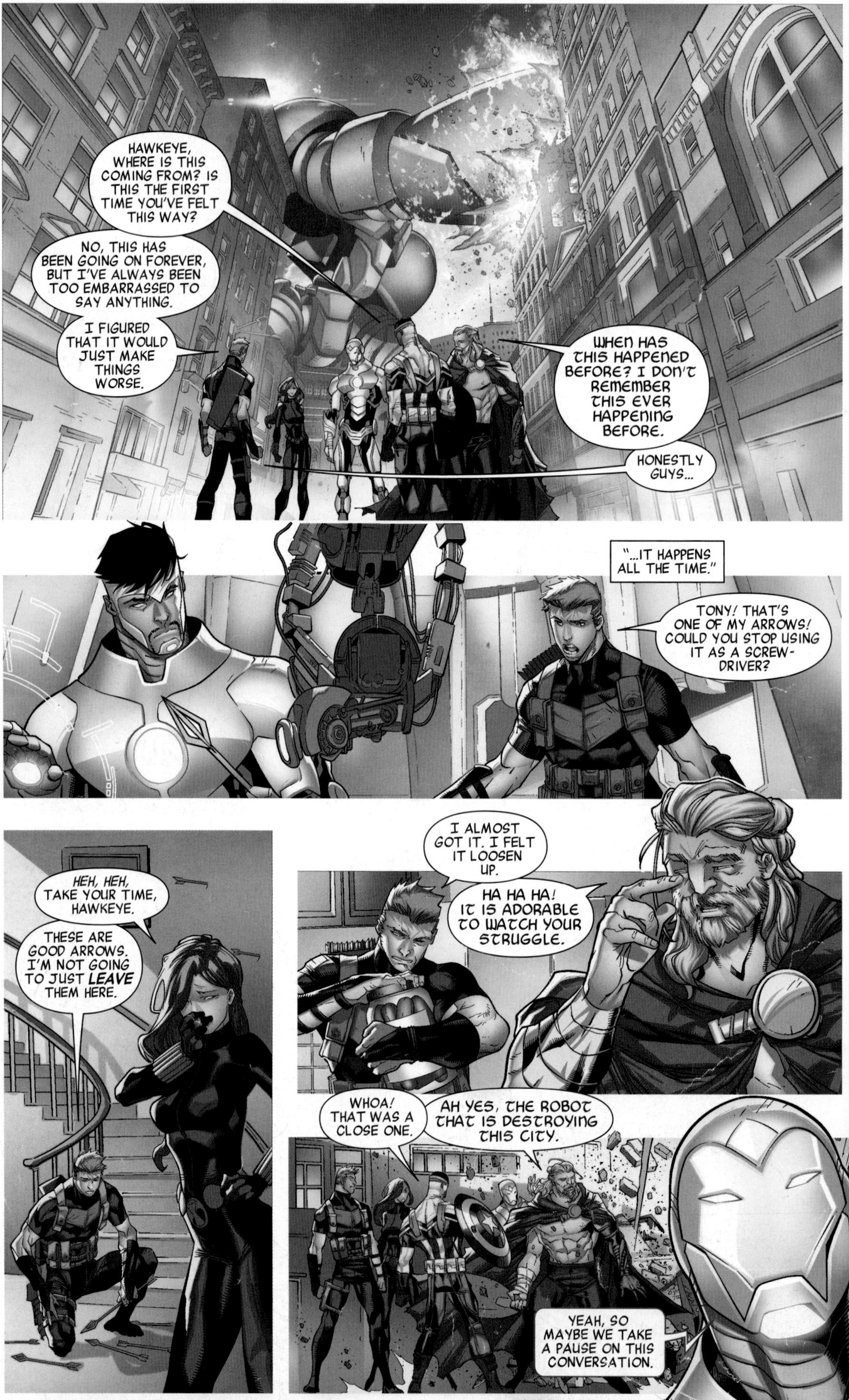
HAWKEYE, WHERE IS THIS COMING FROM? IS THIS THE FIRST TIME YOU'VE FELT THIS WAY?
NO, THIS HAS BEEN GOING ON FOREVER, BUT I'VE ALWAYS BEEN TOO EMBARRASSED TO SAY ANYTHING.
I FIGURED THAT IT WOULD JUST MAKE THINGS WORSE.
WHEN HAS THIS HAPPENED BEFORE? I DON'T REMEMBER THIS EVER HAPPENING BEFORE.
HONESTLY GUYS...
"...IT HAPPENS ALL THE TIME."
TONY! THAT'S ONE OF MY ARROWS! COULD YOU STOP USING IT AS A SCREW-DRIVER?
HEH, HEH, TAKE YOUR TIME, HAWKEYE.
THESE ARE GOOD ARROWS. I'M NOT GOING TO JUST LEAVE THEM HERE.
I ALMOST GOT IT. I FELT IT LOOSEN UP.
HA HA HA! IT IS ADORABLE TO WATCH YOUR STRUGGLE.
WHOA! THAT WAS A CLOSE ONE.
AH YES, THE ROBOT THAT IS DESTROYING THIS CITY.
YEAH, SO MAYBE WE TAKE A PAUSE ON THIS CONVERSATION.

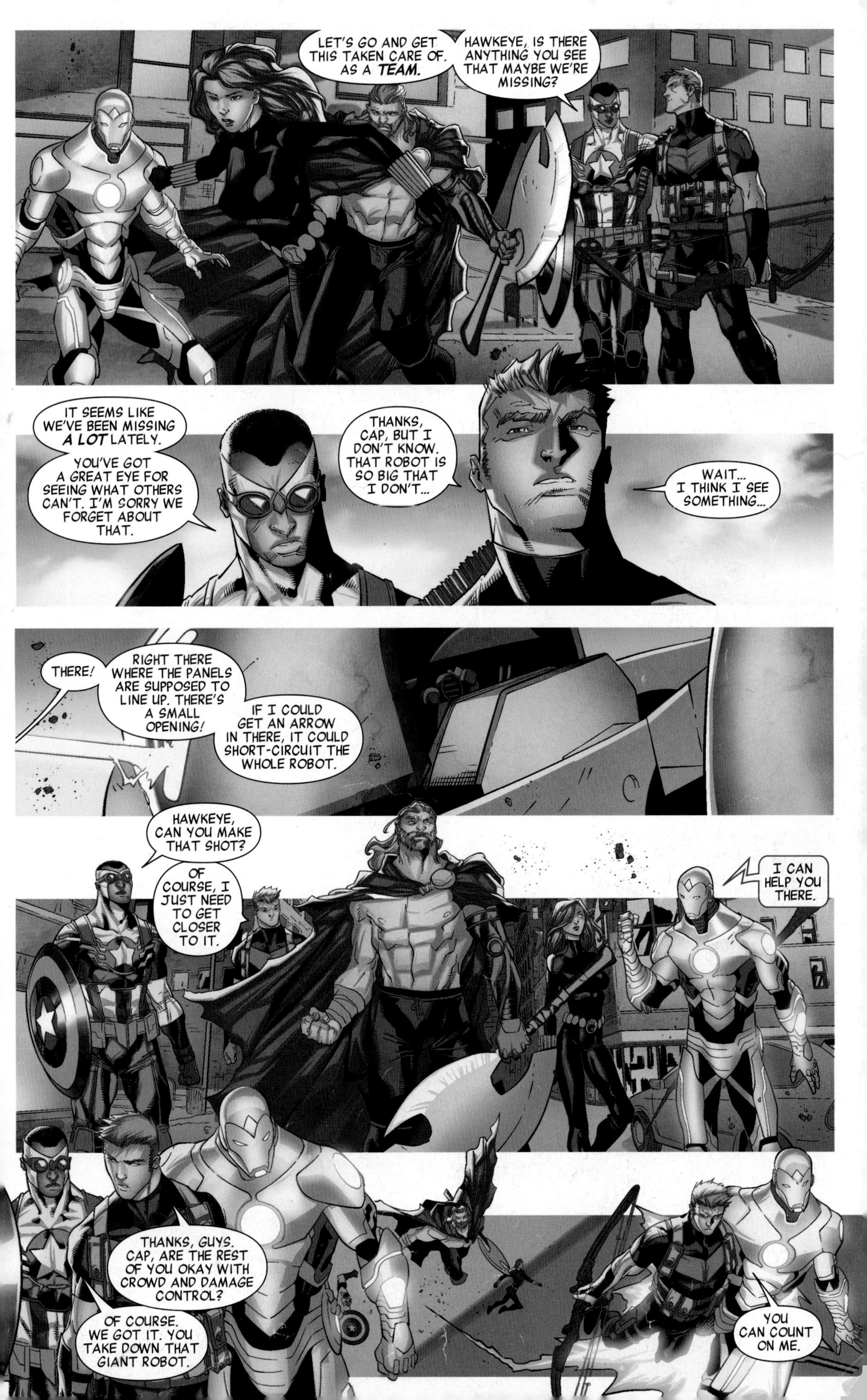
LET'S GO AND GET THIS TAKEN CARE OF. AS A TEAM.
HAWKEYE, IS THERE ANYTHING YOU SEE THAT MAYBE WE'RE MISSING?
IT SEEMS LIKE WE'VE BEEN MISSING A LOT LATELY.
YOU'VE GOT A GREAT EYE FOR SEEING WHAT OTHERS CAN'T. I'M SORRY WE FORGET ABOUT THAT.
THANKS, CAP, BUT I DON'T KNOW. THAT ROBOT IS SO BIG THAT I DON'T...
WAIT... I THINK I SEE SOMETHING...
THERE!
RIGHT THERE WHERE THE PANELS ARE SUPPOSED TO LINE UP. THERE'S A SMALL OPENING!
IF I COULD GET AN ARROW IN THERE, IT COULD SHORT-CIRCUIT THE WHOLE ROBOT.
HAWKEYE, CAN YOU MAKE THAT SHOT?
OF COURSE, I JUST NEED TO GET CLOSER TO IT.
I CAN HELP YOU THERE.
THANKS, GUYS. CAP, ARE THE REST OF YOU OKAY WITH CROWD AND DAMAGE CONTROL?
OF COURSE. WE GOT IT. YOU TAKE DOWN THAT GIANT ROBOT.
YOU CAN COUNT ON ME.

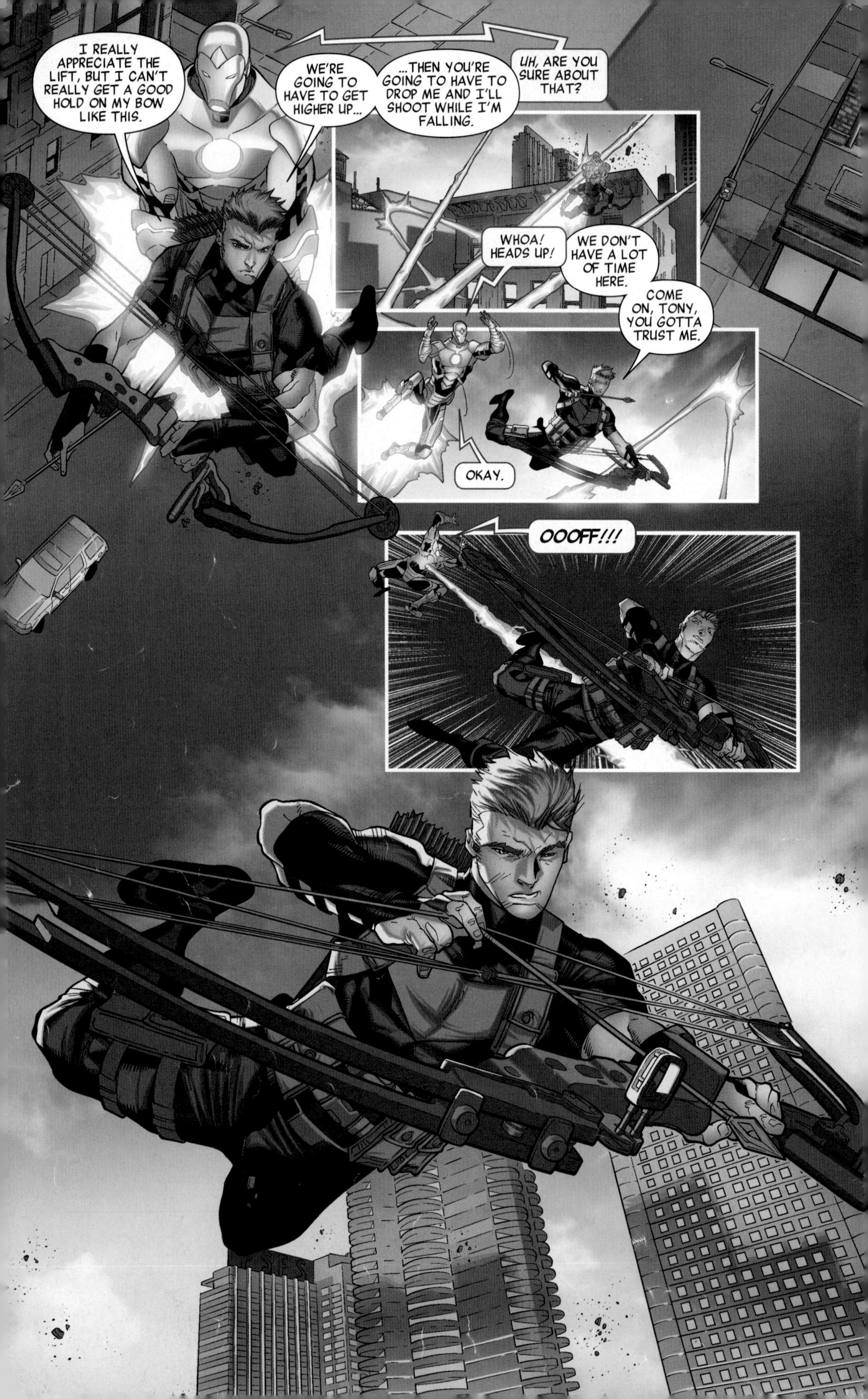
I REALLY APPRECIATE THE LIFT, BUT I CAN'T REALLY GET A GOOD HOLD ON MY BOW LIKE THIS.
WE'RE GOING TO HAVE TO GET HIGHER UP...
...THEN YOU'RE GOING TO HAVE TO DROP ME AND I'LL SHOOT WHILE I'M FALLING.
UH, ARE YOU SURE ABOUT THAT?
WHOA! HEADS UP!
WE DON'T HAVE A LOT OF TIME HERE.
COME ON, TONY, YOU GOTTA TRUST ME.
OKAY.
OOOFF!!!

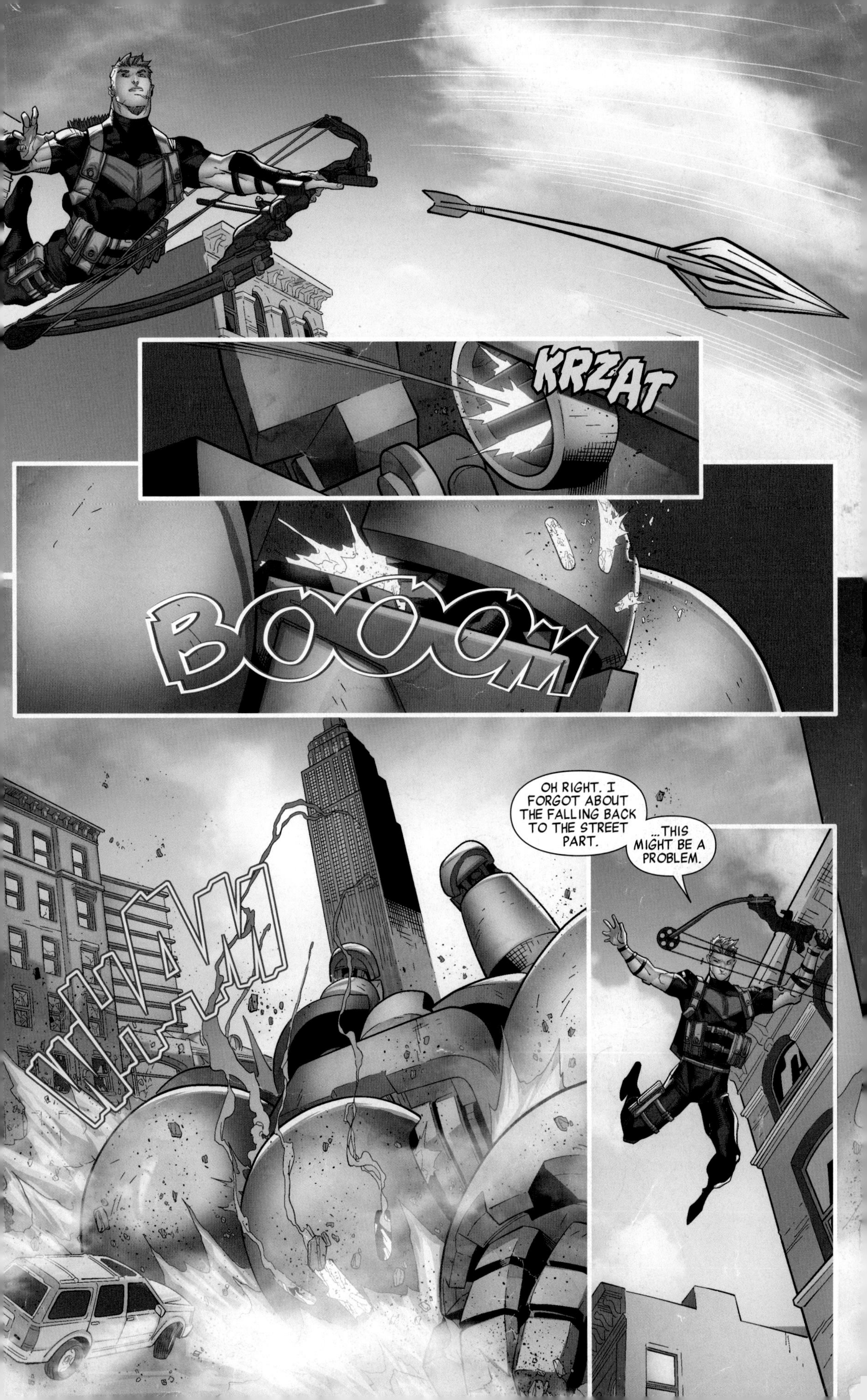

KRZAT
BOOOM
WHAM
OH RIGHT. I FORGOT ABOUT THE FALLING BACK TO THE STREET PART.
...THIS MIGHT BE A PROBLEM.

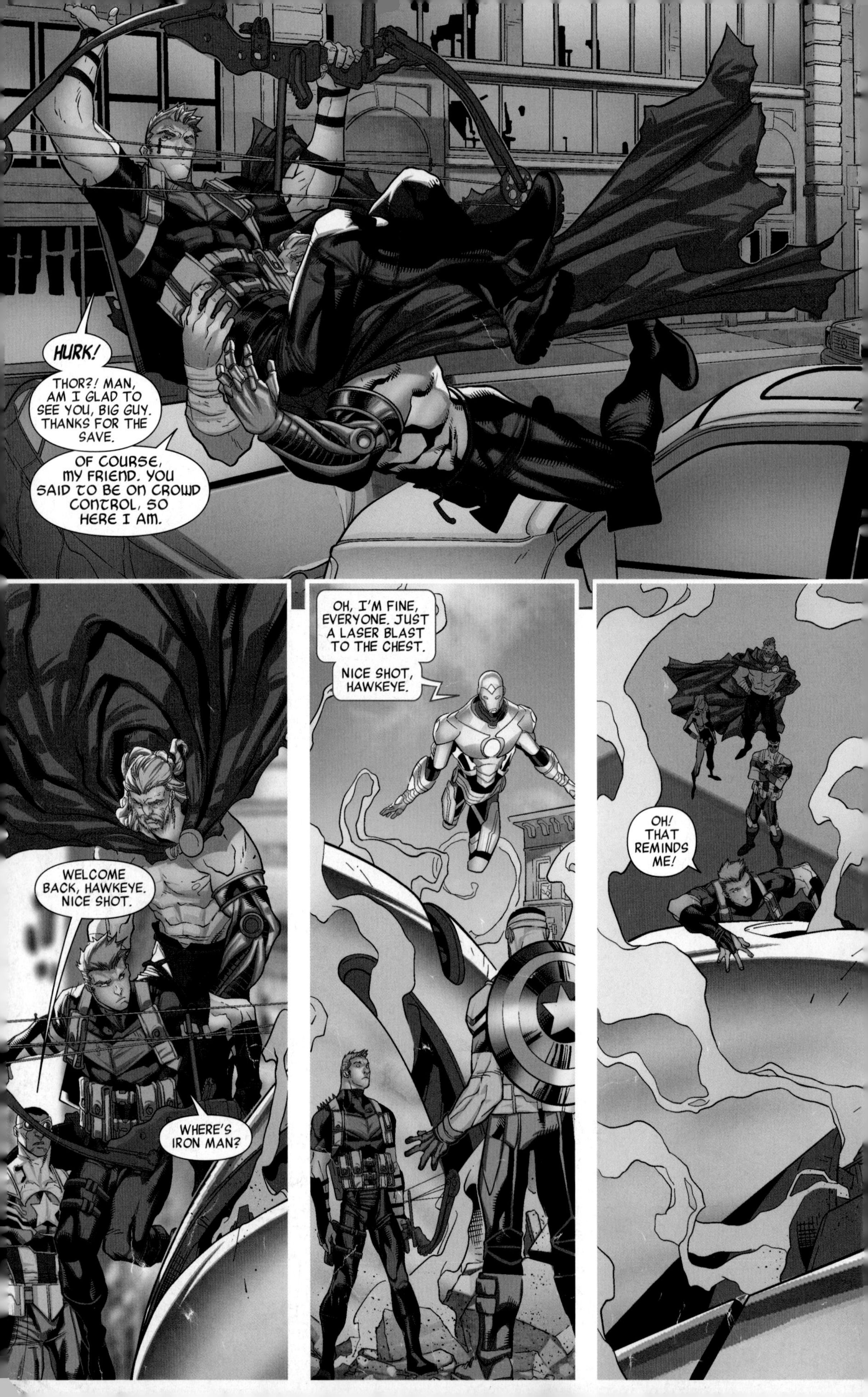
HURK!
THOR?! MAN, AM I GLAD TO SEE YOU, BIG GUY. THANKS FOR THE SAVE.
OF COURSE, MY FRIEND. YOU SAID TO BE ON CROWD CONTROL, SO HERE I AM.
WELCOME BACK, HAWKEYE. NICE SHOT.
WHERE'S IRON MAN?
OH, I'M FINE, EVERYONE. JUST A LASER BLAST TO THE CHEST.
NICE SHOT, HAWKEYE.
OH! THAT REMINDS ME!

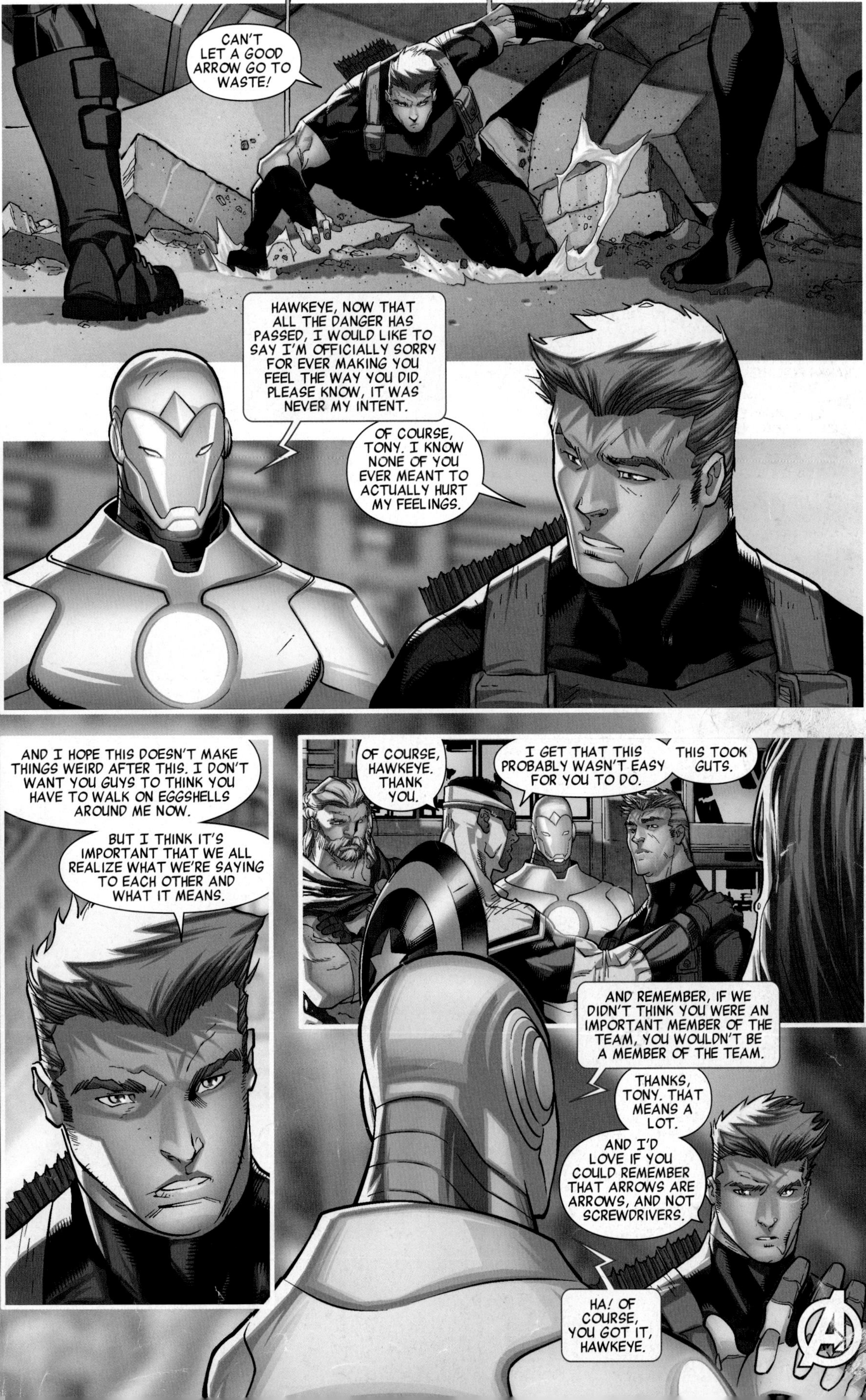
CAN'T LET A GOOD ARROW GO TO WASTE!
HAWKEYE, NOW THAT ALL THE DANGER HAS PASSED, I WOULD LIKE TO SAY I'M OFFICIALLY SORRY FOR EVER MAKING YOU FEEL THE WAY YOU DID. PLEASE KNOW, IT WAS NEVER MY INTENT.
OF COURSE, TONY. I KNOW NONE OF YOU EVER MEANT TO ACTUALLY HURT MY FEELINGS.
AND I HOPE THIS DOESN'T MAKE THINGS WEIRD AFTER THIS. I DON'T WANT YOU GUYS TO THINK YOU HAVE TO WALK ON EGGSHELLS AROUND ME NOW.
BUT I THINK IT'S IMPORTANT THAT WE ALL REALIZE WHAT WE'RE SAYING TO EACH OTHER AND WHAT IT MEANS.
OF COURSE, HAWKEYE. THANK YOU.
I GET THAT THIS PROBABLY WASN'T EASY FOR YOU TO DO.
THIS TOOK GUTS.
AND REMEMBER, IF WE DIDN'T THINK YOU WERE AN IMPORTANT MEMBER OF THE TEAM, YOU WOULDN'T BE A MEMBER OF THE TEAM.
THANKS, TONY. THAT MEANS A LOT.
AND I'D LOVE IF YOU COULD REMEMBER THAT ARROWS ARE ARROWS, AND NOT SCREWDRIVERS.
HA! OF COURSE, YOU GOT IT, HAWKEYE.

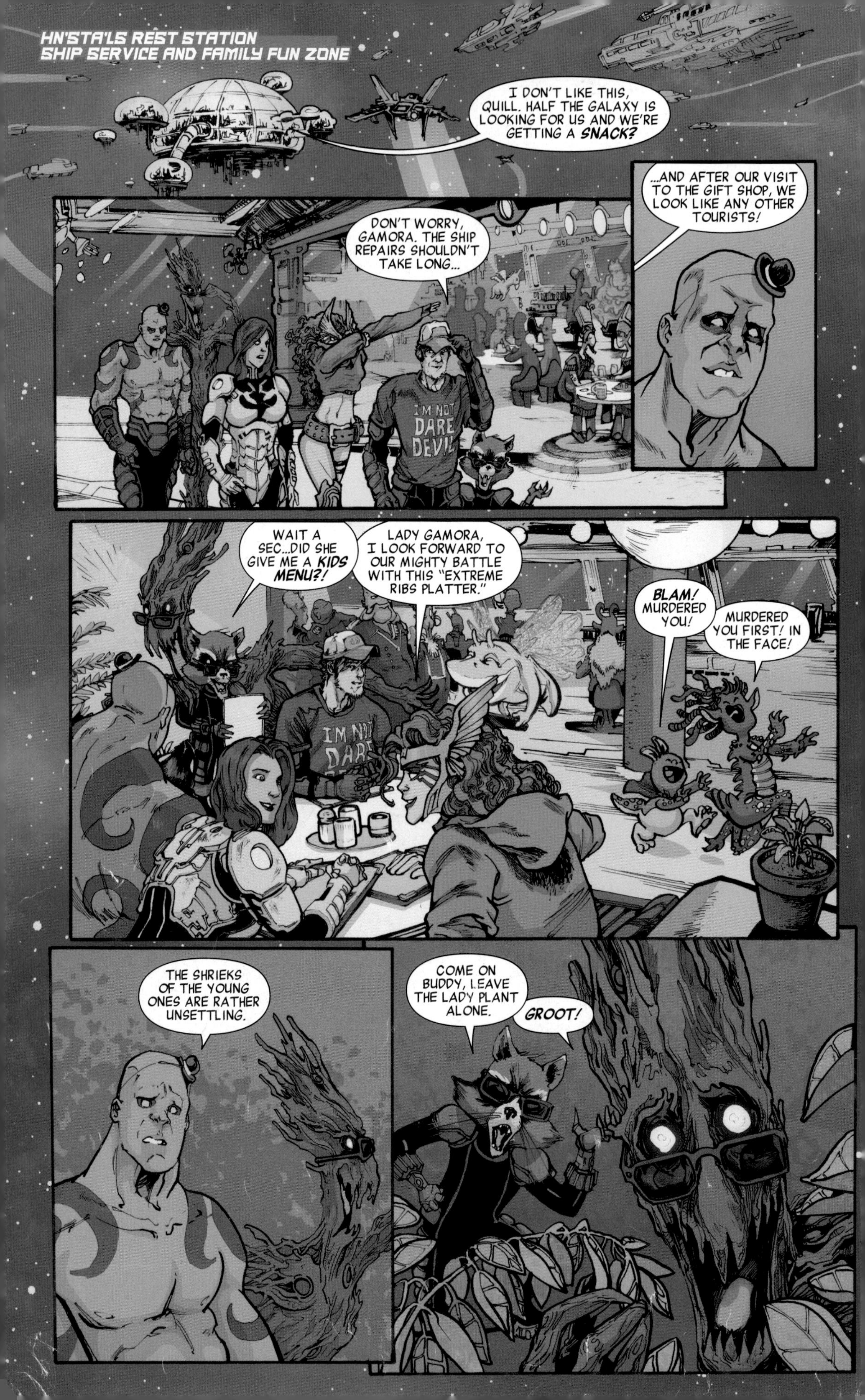
HN'STA'LS REST STATION
SHIP SERVICE AND FAMILY FUN ZONE
I DON'T LIKE THIS, QUILL. HALF THE GALAXY IS LOOKING FOR US AND WE'RE GETTING A **SNACK?**
DON'T WORRY, GAMORA. THE SHIP REPAIRS SHOULDN'T TAKE LONG...
...AND AFTER OUR VISIT TO THE GIFT SHOP, WE LOOK LIKE ANY OTHER TOURISTS!
I'M NOT DARE DEVIL
WAIT A SEC...DID SHE GIVE ME A **KIDS MENU?!**
LADY GAMORA, I LOOK FORWARD TO OUR MIGHTY BATTLE WITH THIS "EXTREME RIBS PLATTER."
BLAM! MURDERED YOU!
MURDERED YOU FIRST! IN THE FACE!
THE SHRIEKS OF THE YOUNG ONES ARE RATHER UNSETTLING.
COME ON BUDDY, LEAVE THE LADY PLANT ALONE.
GROOT!

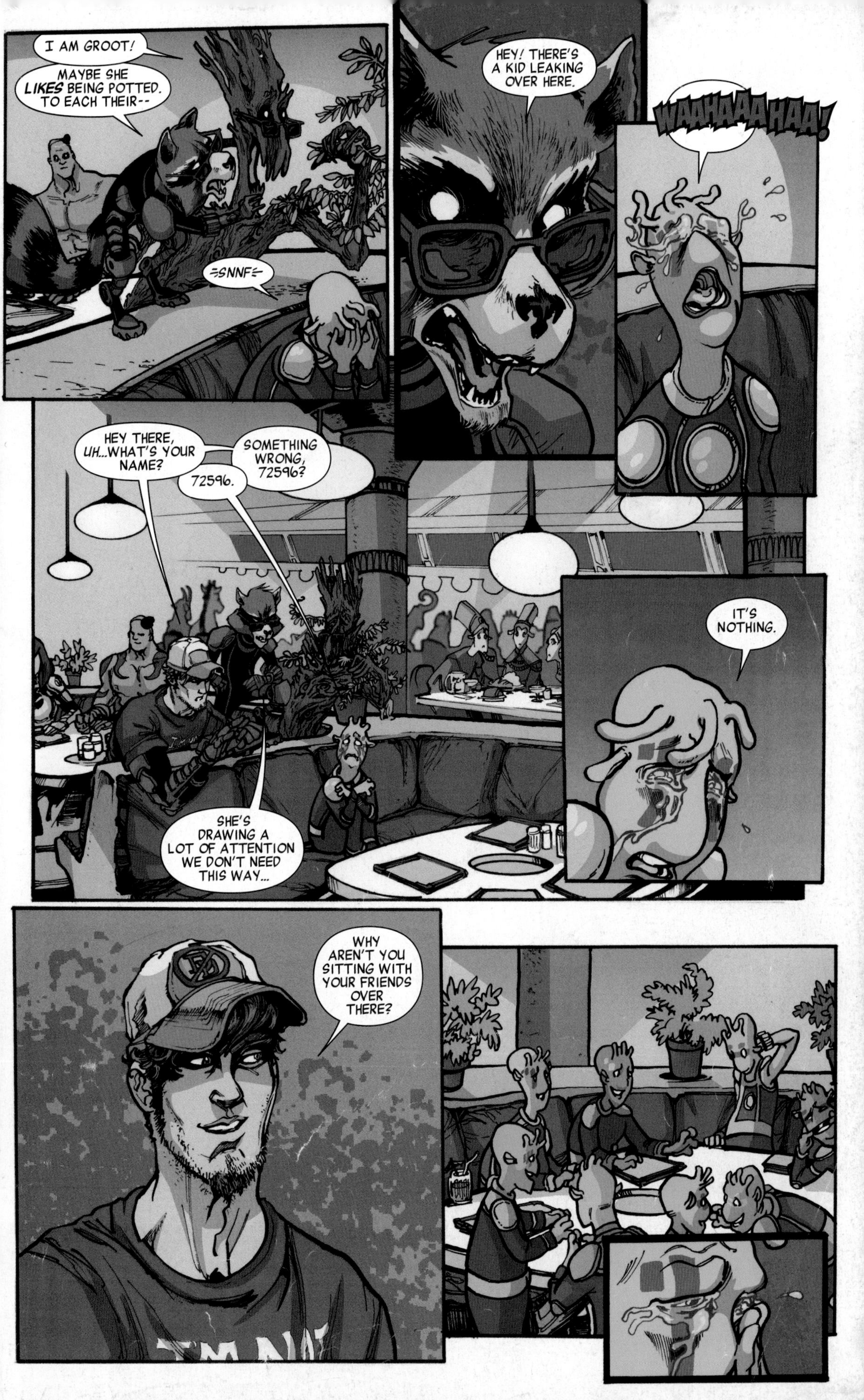

I AM GROOT!
MAYBE SHE LIKES BEING POTTED. TO EACH THEIR--
SNNF
HEY! THERE'S A KID LEAKING OVER HERE.
WAAHAAAHAA!
HEY THERE, UH...WHAT'S YOUR NAME?
72596.
SOMETHING WRONG, 72596?
SHE'S DRAWING A LOT OF ATTENTION WE DON'T NEED THIS WAY...
IT'S NOTHING.
WHY AREN'T YOU SITTING WITH YOUR FRIENDS OVER THERE?

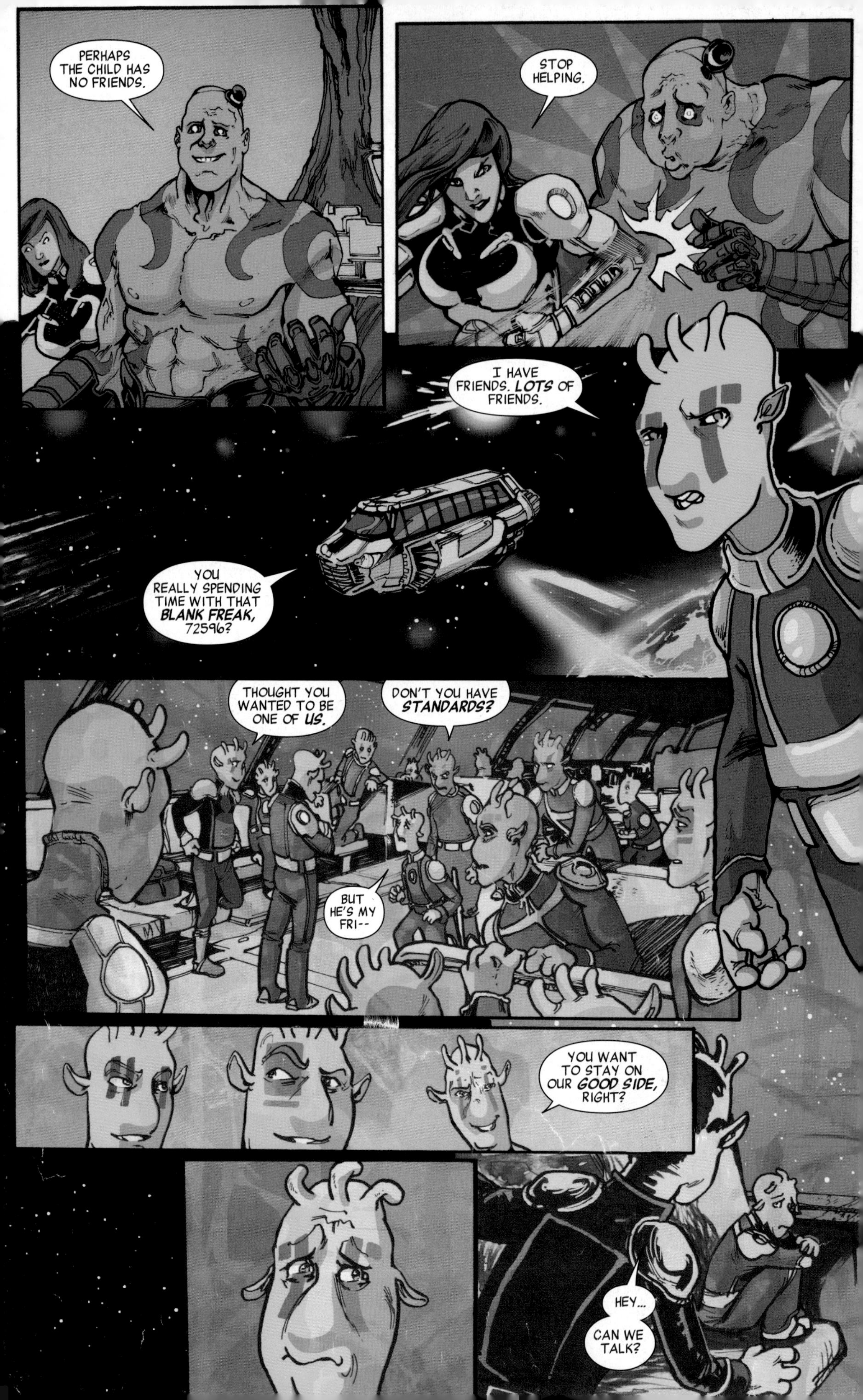
PERHAPS THE CHILD HAS NO FRIENDS.
STOP HELPING.
I HAVE FRIENDS. **LOTS** OF FRIENDS.
YOU REALLY SPENDING TIME WITH THAT ***BLANK FREAK,*** 72596?
THOUGHT YOU WANTED TO BE ONE OF ***US.***
DON'T YOU HAVE ***STANDARDS?***
BUT HE'S MY FRI--
YOU WANT TO STAY ON OUR ***GOOD SIDE,*** RIGHT?
HEY...
CAN WE TALK?

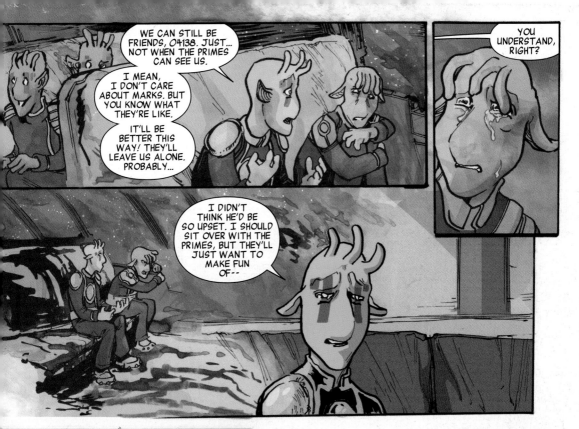

WE CAN STILL BE FRIENDS, 04138. JUST... NOT WHEN THE PRIMES CAN SEE US.

I MEAN, I DON'T CARE ABOUT MARKS. BUT YOU KNOW WHAT THEY'RE LIKE.

IT'LL BE BETTER THIS WAY! THEY'LL LEAVE US ALONE. PROBABLY...

YOU UNDERSTAND, RIGHT?

I DIDN'T THINK HE'D BE SO UPSET. I SHOULD SIT OVER WITH THE PRIMES, BUT THEY'LL JUST WANT TO MAKE FUN OF--

04138!

HAS ANYONE SEEN 04138?

I TOLD THE SPAWNERS NO ONE WOULD GET EATEN ON THIS TRIP...

04138!

HEY! NUMBER KID!

QUILL, BEFORE YOU GO BEING ALL NOBLE AND CRUD, I GOT A COUNTERPROPOSAL FOR YOU...

DINNER!

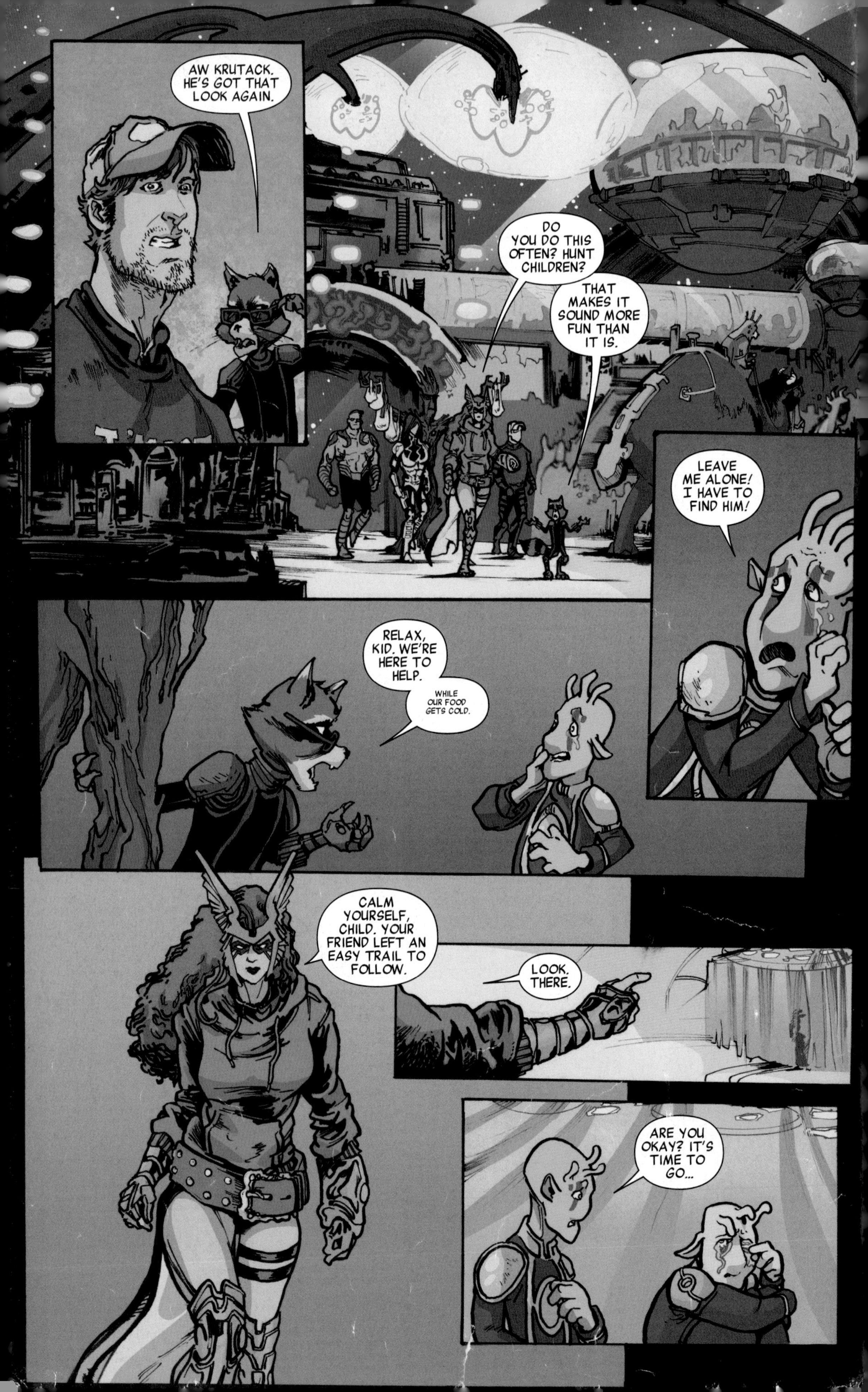
AW KRUTACK. HE'S GOT THAT LOOK AGAIN.
DO YOU DO THIS OFTEN? HUNT CHILDREN?
THAT MAKES IT SOUND MORE FUN THAN IT IS.
LEAVE ME ALONE! I HAVE TO FIND HIM!
RELAX, KID. WE'RE HERE TO HELP.
WHILE OUR FOOD GETS COLD.
CALM YOURSELF, CHILD. YOUR FRIEND LEFT AN EASY TRAIL TO FOLLOW.
LOOK. THERE.
ARE YOU OKAY? IT'S TIME TO GO...

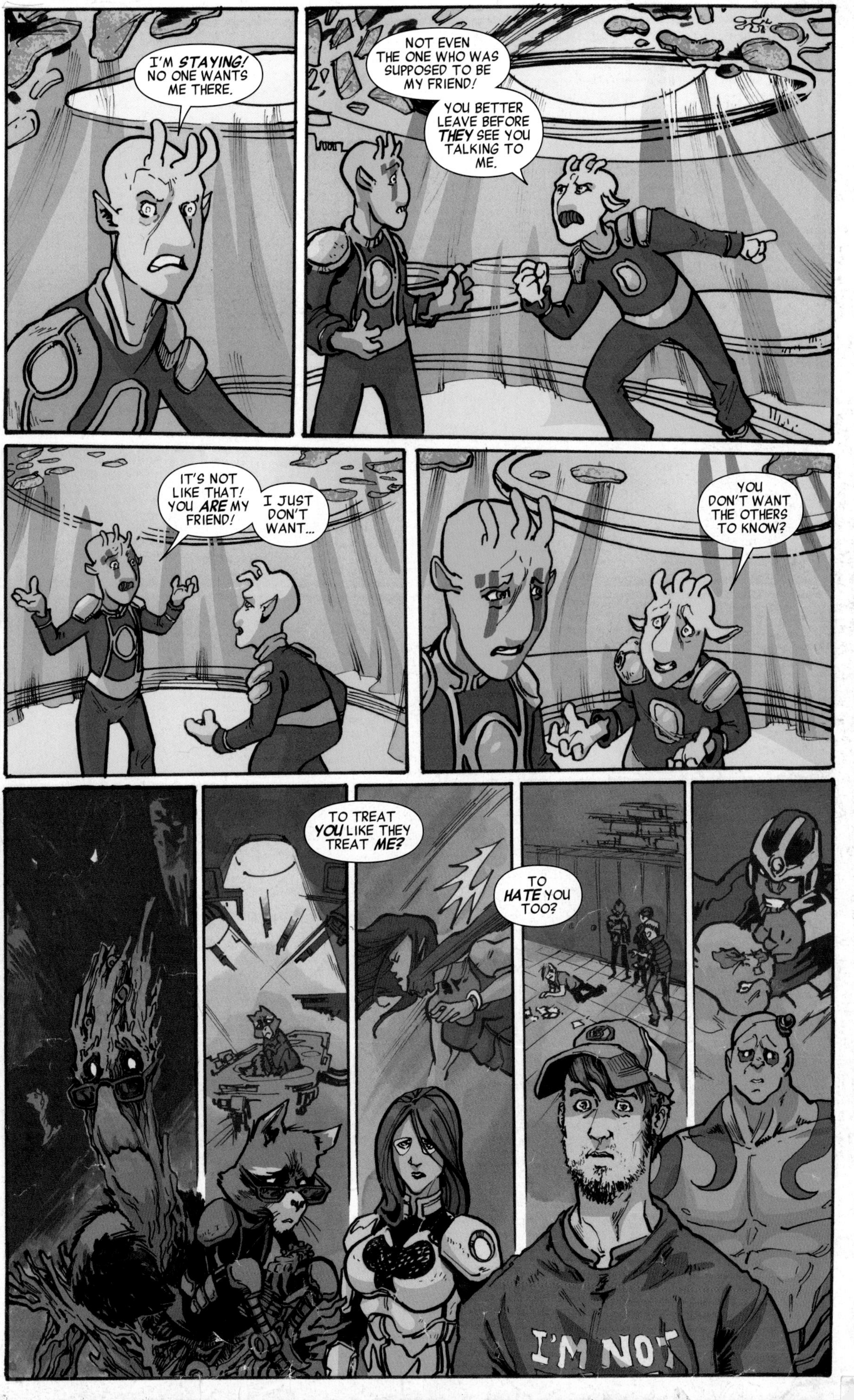
I'M STAYING! NO ONE WANTS ME THERE.
NOT EVEN THE ONE WHO WAS SUPPOSED TO BE MY FRIEND!
YOU BETTER LEAVE BEFORE THEY SEE YOU TALKING TO ME.
IT'S NOT LIKE THAT! YOU ARE MY FRIEND!
I JUST DON'T WANT...
YOU DON'T WANT THE OTHERS TO KNOW?
TO TREAT YOU LIKE THEY TREAT ME?
TO HATE YOU TOO?
I'M NOT

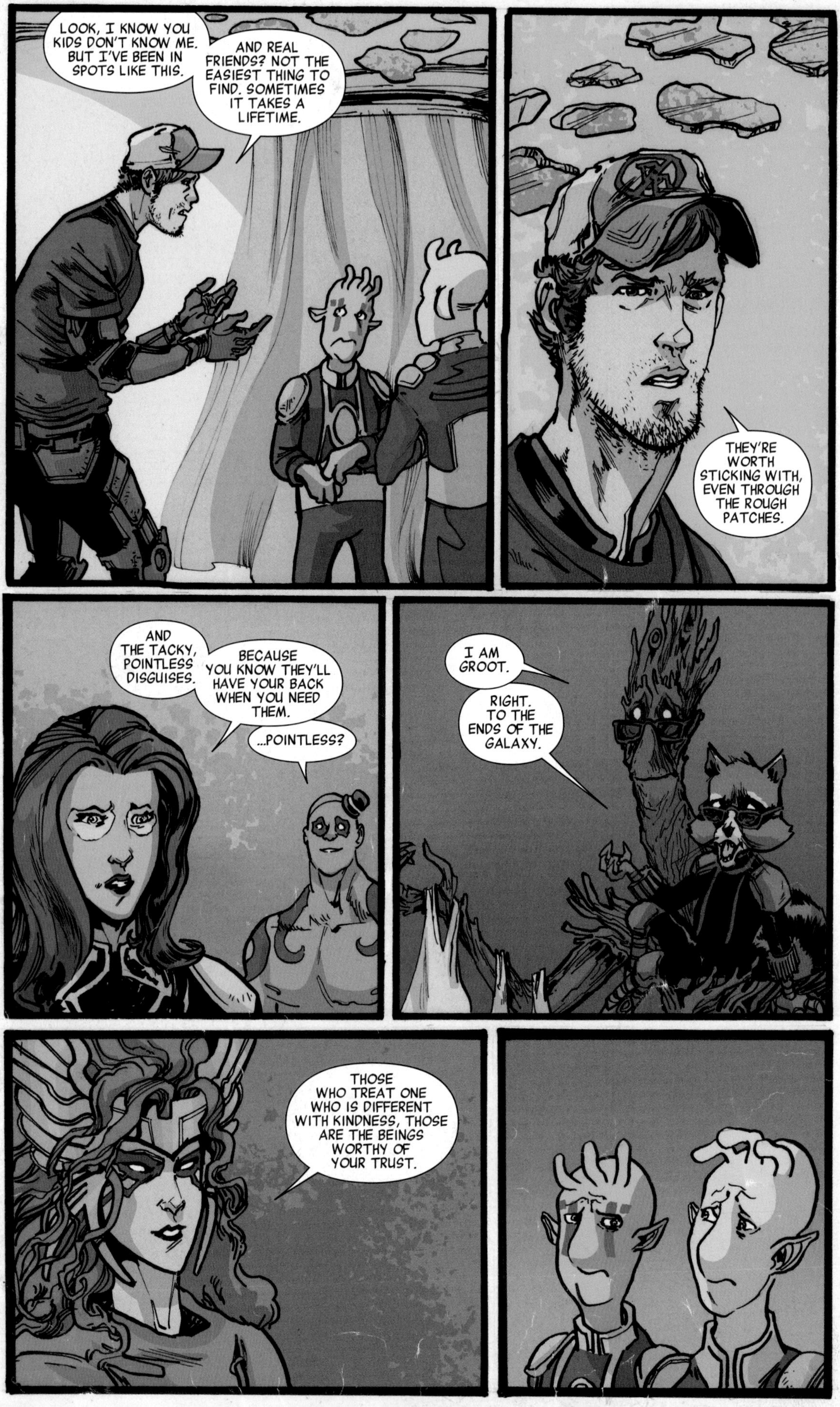
LOOK, I KNOW YOU KIDS DON'T KNOW ME. BUT I'VE BEEN IN SPOTS LIKE THIS.
AND REAL FRIENDS? NOT THE EASIEST THING TO FIND. SOMETIMES IT TAKES A LIFETIME.
THEY'RE WORTH STICKING WITH, EVEN THROUGH THE ROUGH PATCHES.
AND THE TACKY, POINTLESS DISGUISES.
BECAUSE YOU KNOW THEY'LL HAVE YOUR BACK WHEN YOU NEED THEM.
...POINTLESS?
I AM GROOT.
RIGHT. TO THE ENDS OF THE GALAXY.
THOSE WHO TREAT ONE WHO IS DIFFERENT WITH KINDNESS, THOSE ARE THE BEINGS WORTHY OF YOUR TRUST.

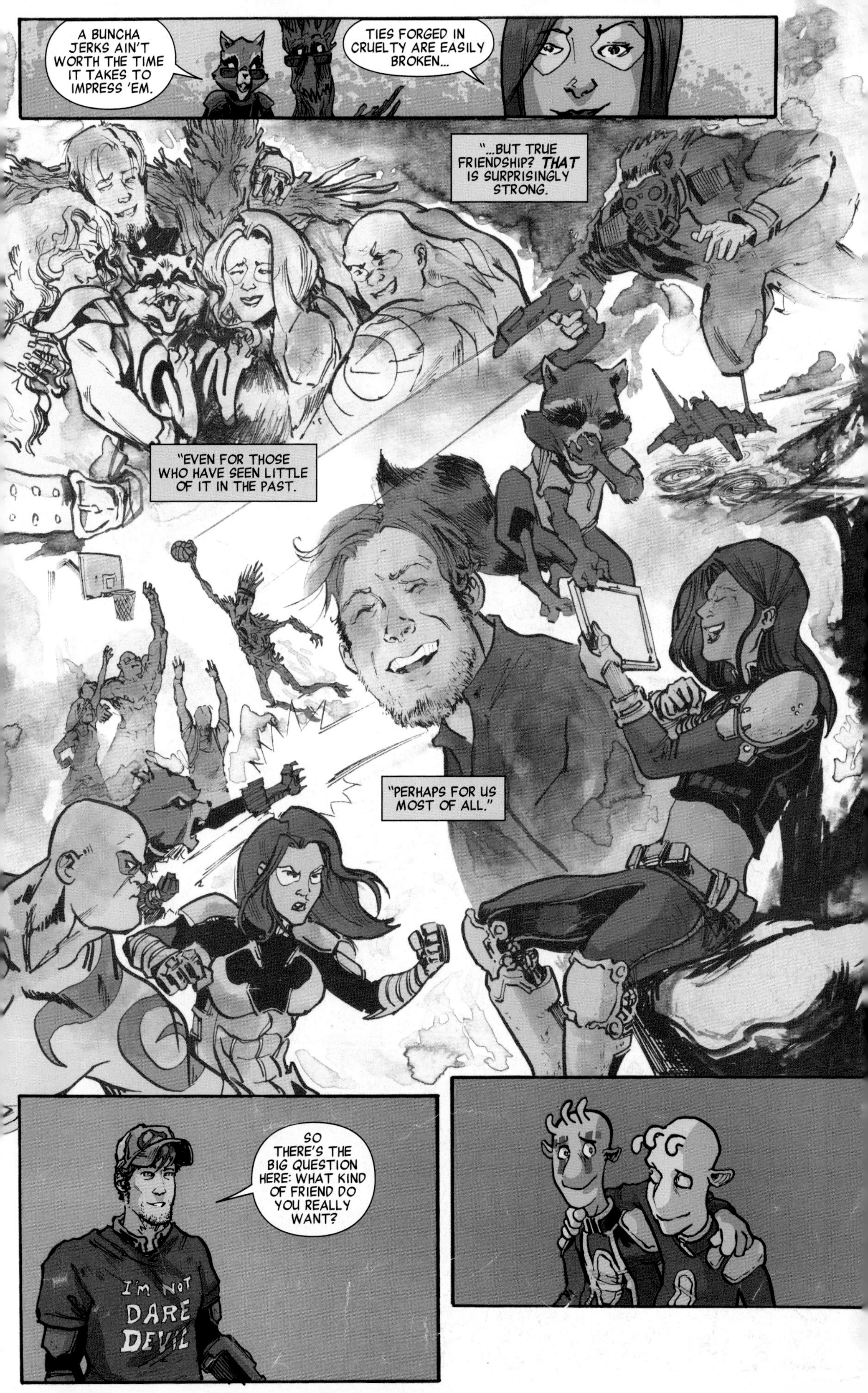
A BUNCHA JERKS AIN'T WORTH THE TIME IT TAKES TO IMPRESS 'EM.
TIES FORGED IN CRUELTY ARE EASILY BROKEN...
"...BUT TRUE FRIENDSHIP? THAT IS SURPRISINGLY STRONG.
"EVEN FOR THOSE WHO HAVE SEEN LITTLE OF IT IN THE PAST.
"PERHAPS FOR US MOST OF ALL."
SO THERE'S THE BIG QUESTION HERE: WHAT KIND OF FRIEND DO YOU REALLY WANT?
I'M NOT DARE DEVIL

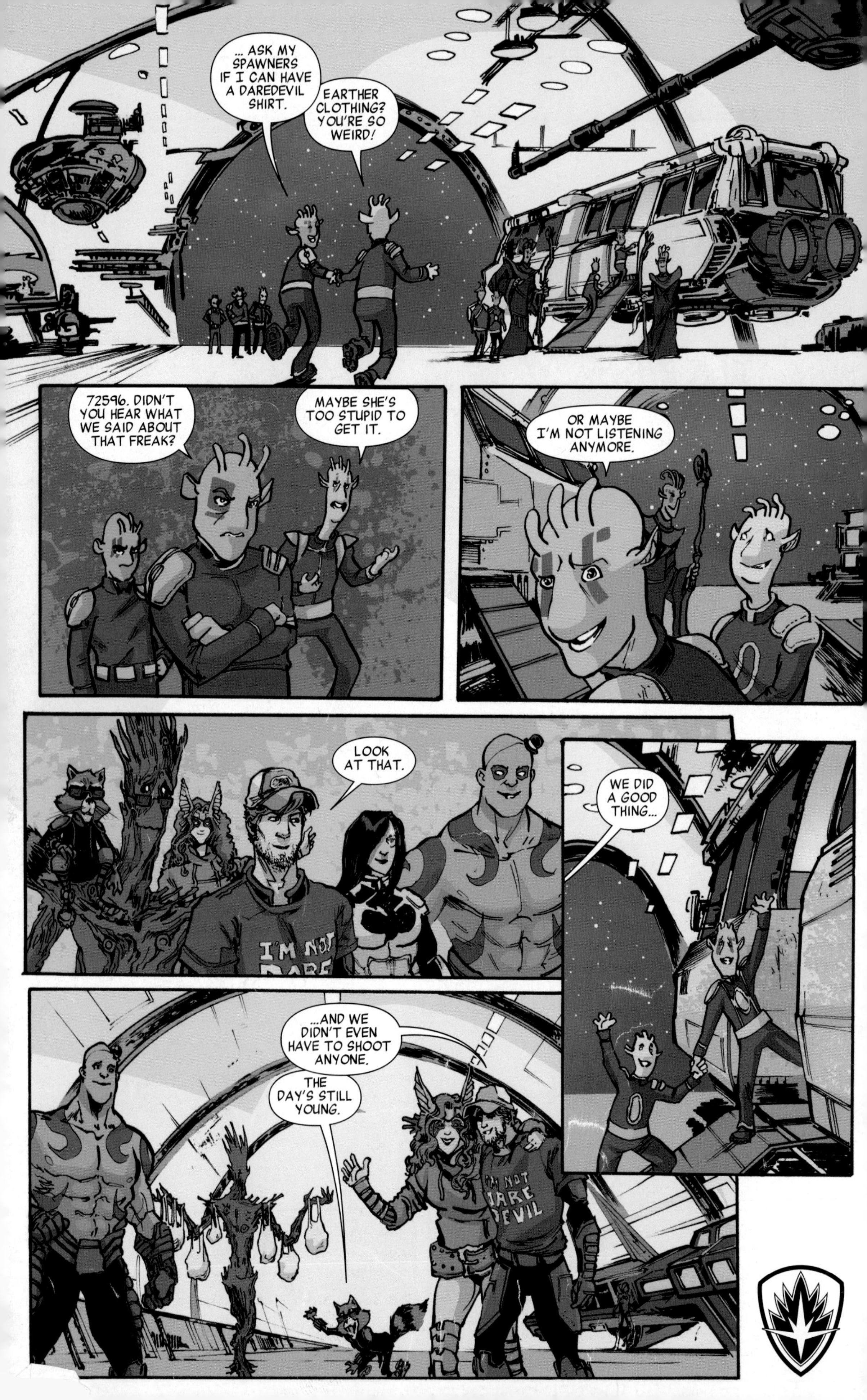
... ASK MY SPAWNERS IF I CAN HAVE A DAREDEVIL SHIRT.
EARTHER CLOTHING? YOU'RE SO WEIRD!
72596. DIDN'T YOU HEAR WHAT WE SAID ABOUT THAT FREAK?
MAYBE SHE'S TOO STUPID TO GET IT.
OR MAYBE I'M NOT LISTENING ANYMORE.
LOOK AT THAT.
I'M NOT DARE
WE DID A GOOD THING...
...AND WE DIDN'T EVEN HAVE TO SHOOT ANYONE.
THE DAY'S STILL YOUNG.
I'M NOT DARE DEVIL

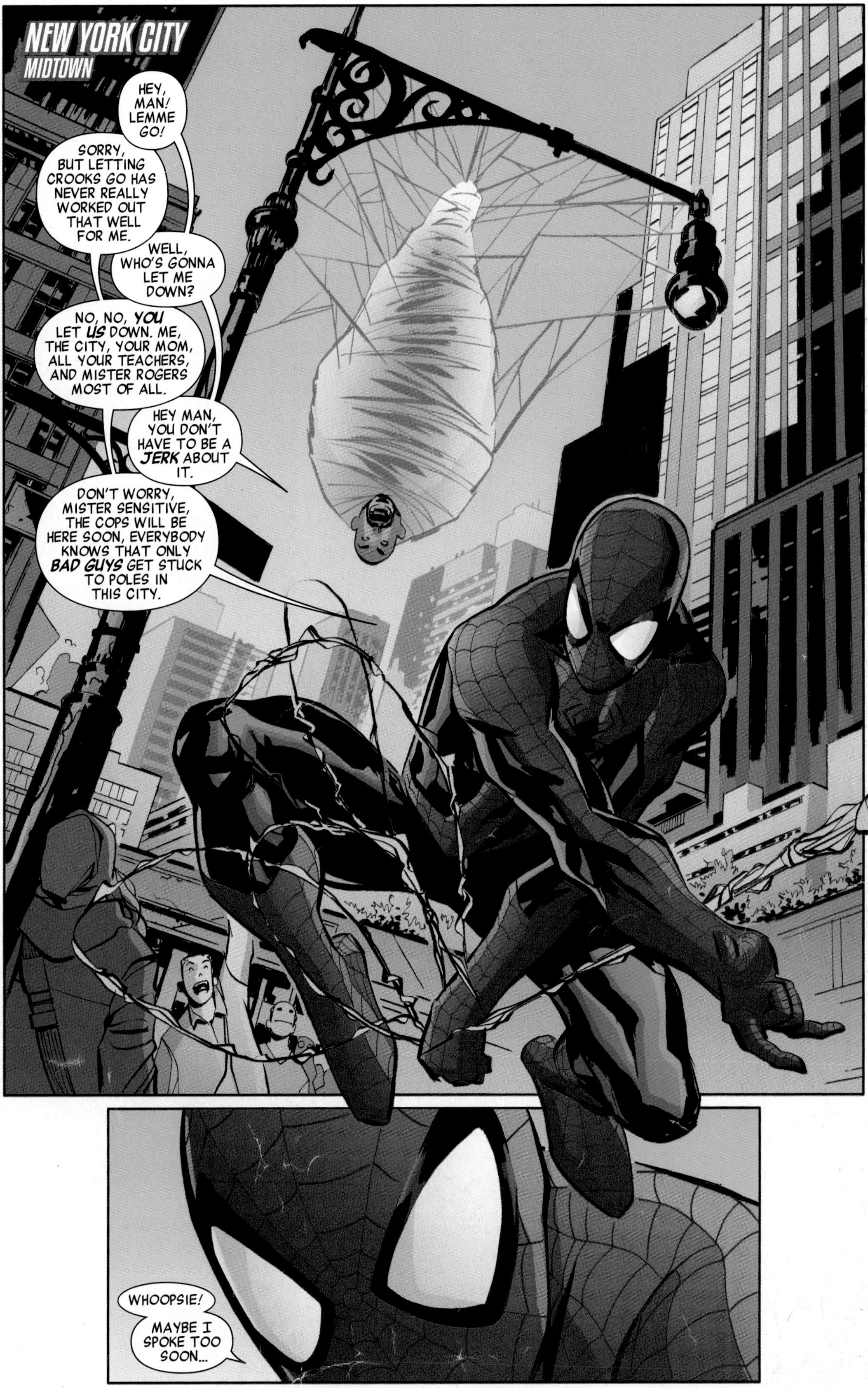
NEW YORK CITY
MIDTOWN
HEY, MAN! LEMME GO!
SORRY, BUT LETTING CROOKS GO HAS NEVER REALLY WORKED OUT THAT WELL FOR ME.
WELL, WHO'S GONNA LET ME DOWN?
NO, NO, YOU LET US DOWN. ME, THE CITY, YOUR MOM, ALL YOUR TEACHERS, AND MISTER ROGERS MOST OF ALL.
HEY MAN, YOU DON'T HAVE TO BE A JERK ABOUT IT.
DON'T WORRY, MISTER SENSITIVE, THE COPS WILL BE HERE SOON, EVERYBODY KNOWS THAT ONLY BAD GUYS GET STUCK TO POLES IN THIS CITY.
WHOOPSIE!
MAYBE I SPOKE TOO SOON...

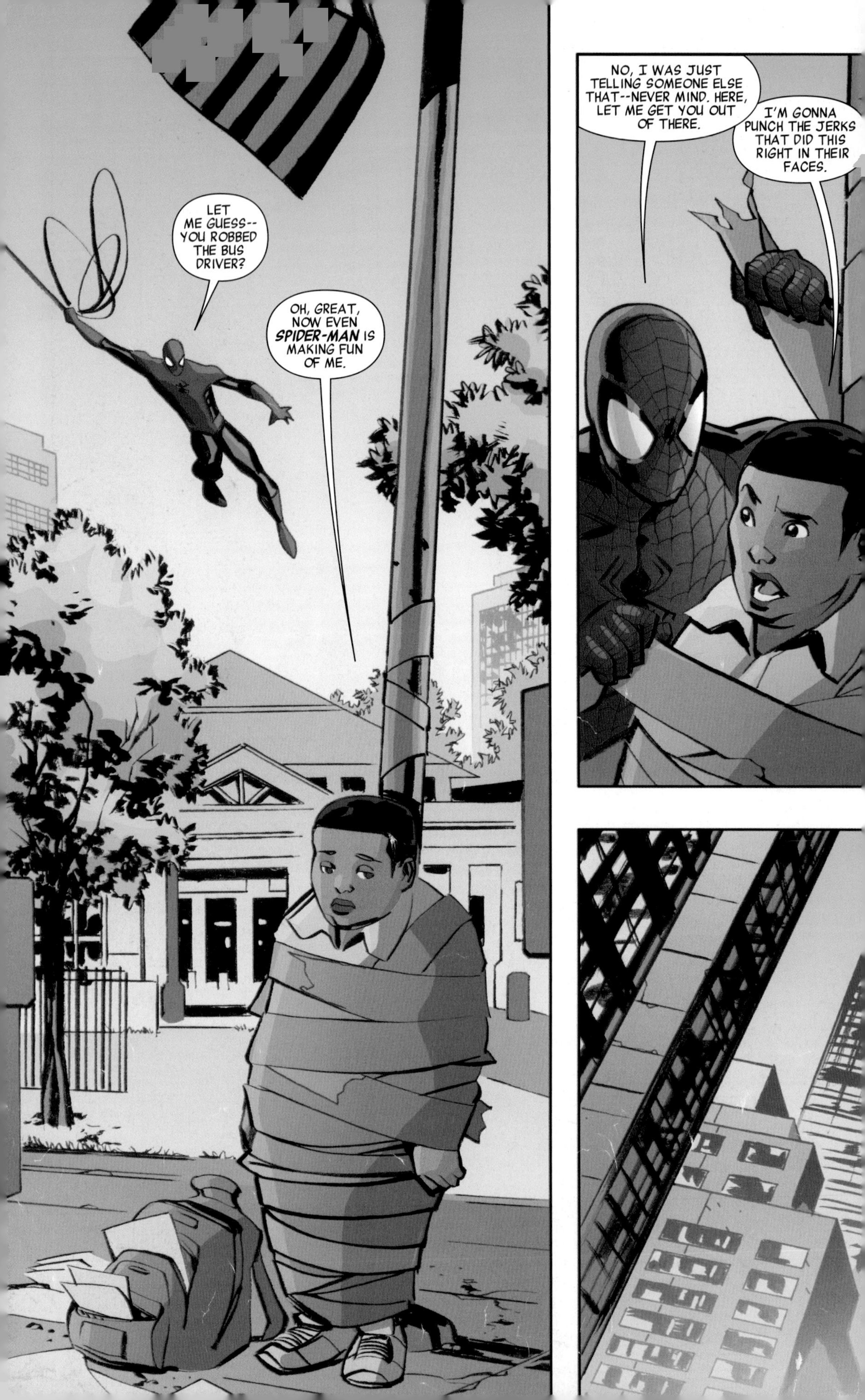
LET ME GUESS--YOU ROBBED THE BUS DRIVER?
OH, GREAT, NOW EVEN SPIDER-MAN IS MAKING FUN OF ME.
NO, I WAS JUST TELLING SOMEONE ELSE THAT--NEVER MIND. HERE, LET ME GET YOU OUT OF THERE.
I'M GONNA PUNCH THE JERKS THAT DID THIS RIGHT IN THEIR FACES.

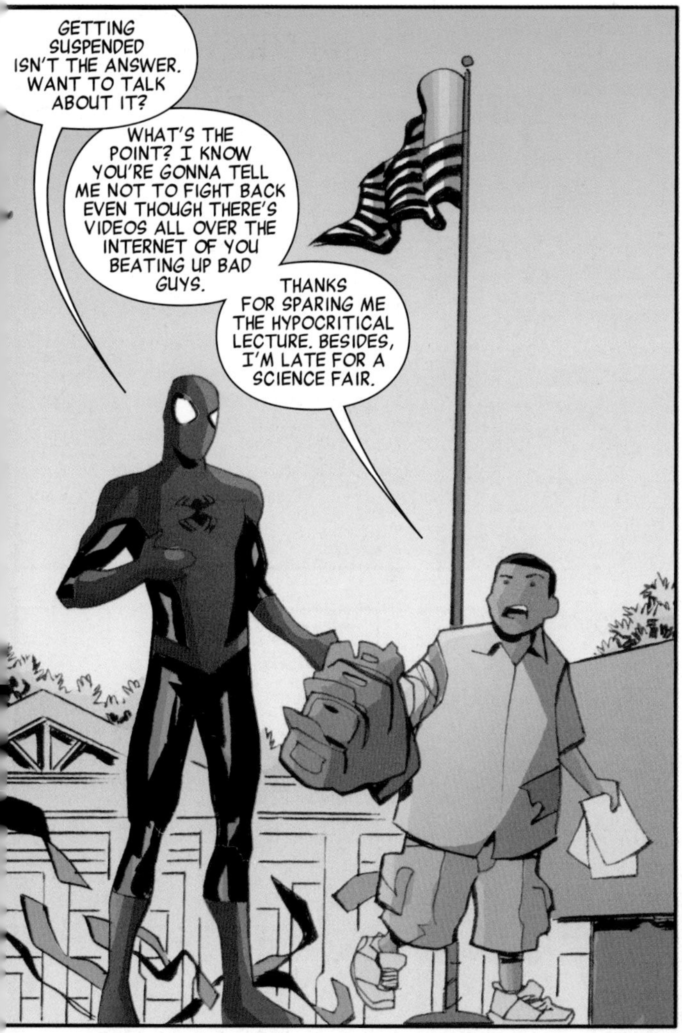
GETTING SUSPENDED ISN'T THE ANSWER. WANT TO TALK ABOUT IT?
WHAT'S THE POINT? I KNOW YOU'RE GONNA TELL ME NOT TO FIGHT BACK EVEN THOUGH THERE'S VIDEOS ALL OVER THE INTERNET OF YOU BEATING UP BAD GUYS.
THANKS FOR SPARING ME THE HYPOCRITICAL LECTURE. BESIDES, I'M LATE FOR A SCIENCE FAIR.

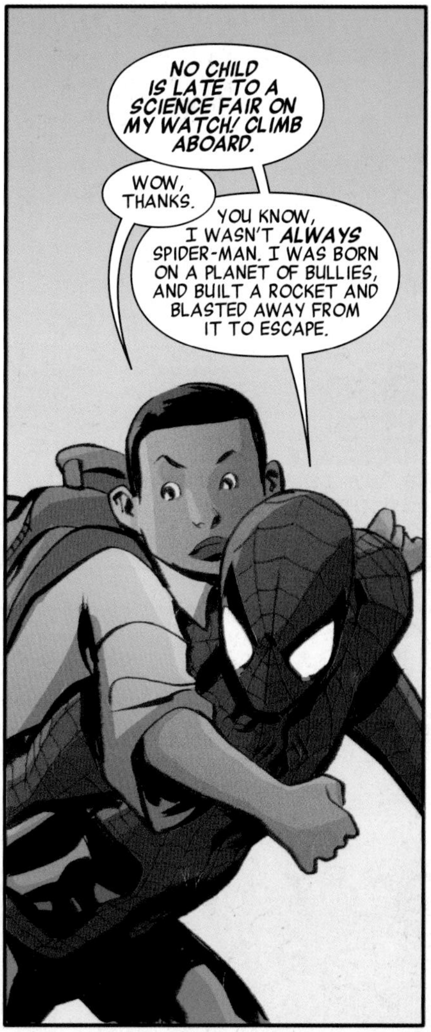
NO CHILD IS LATE TO A SCIENCE FAIR ON MY WATCH! CLIMB ABOARD.
WOW, THANKS.
YOU KNOW, I WASN'T ALWAYS SPIDER-MAN. I WAS BORN ON A PLANET OF BULLIES, AND BUILT A ROCKET AND BLASTED AWAY FROM IT TO ESCAPE.

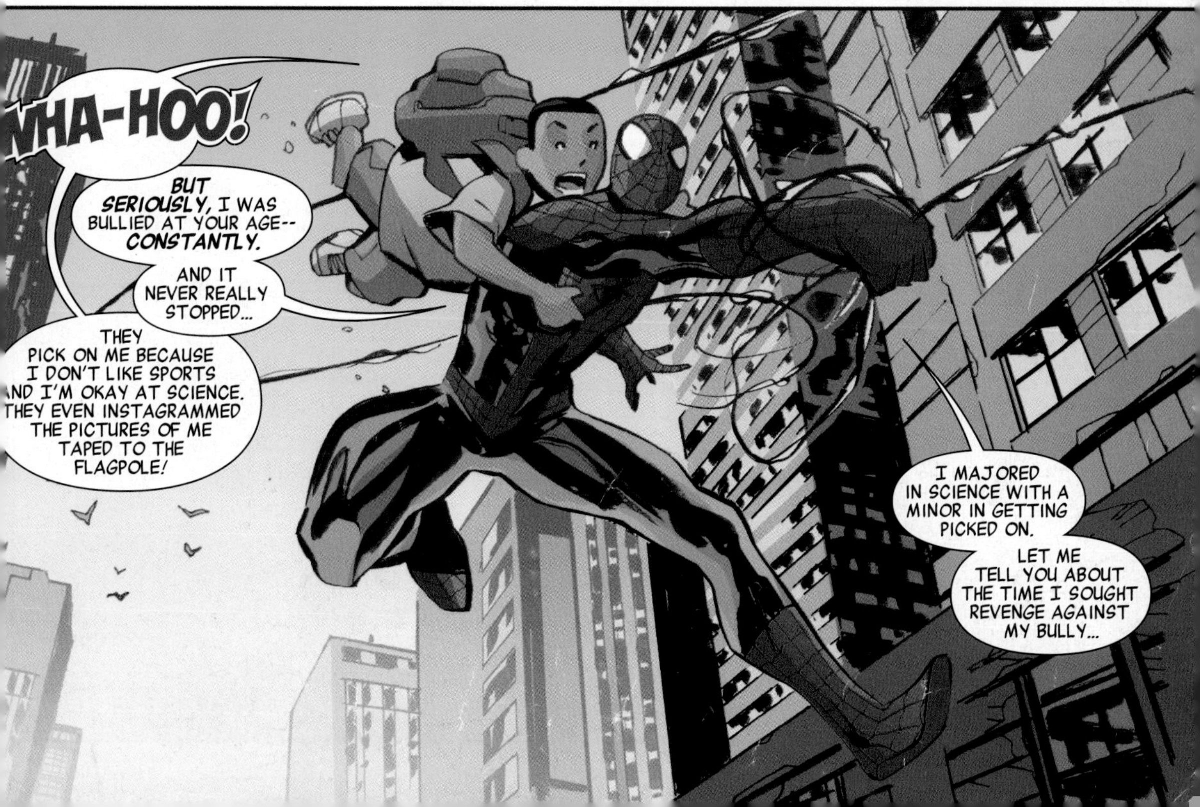
WHA-HOO!
BUT SERIOUSLY, I WAS BULLIED AT YOUR AGE-- CONSTANTLY.
AND IT NEVER REALLY STOPPED...
THEY PICK ON ME BECAUSE I DON'T LIKE SPORTS AND I'M OKAY AT SCIENCE. THEY EVEN INSTAGRAMMED THE PICTURES OF ME TAPED TO THE FLAGPOLE!
I MAJORED IN SCIENCE WITH A MINOR IN GETTING PICKED ON.
LET ME TELL YOU ABOUT THE TIME I SOUGHT REVENGE AGAINST MY BULLY...

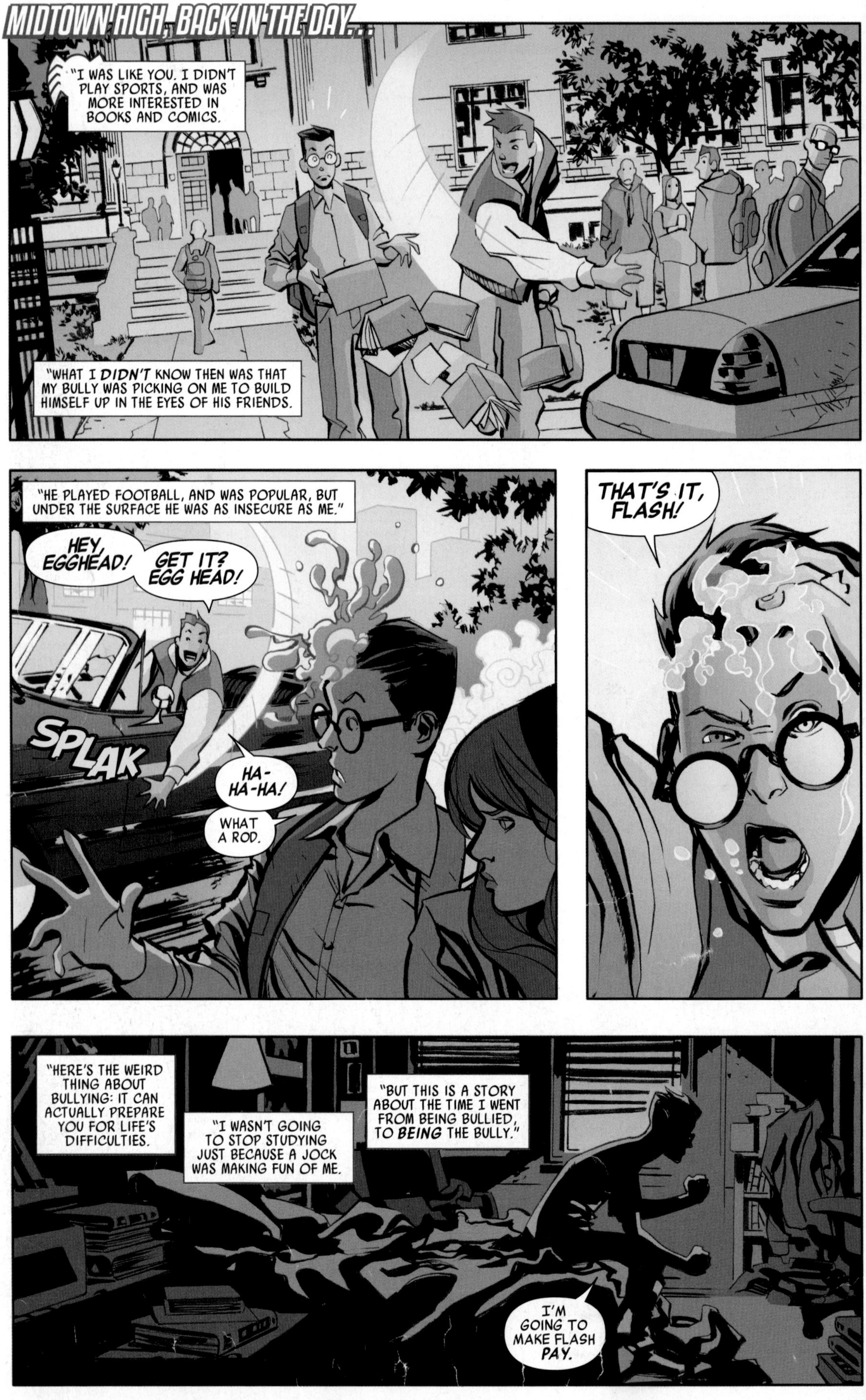
MIDTOWN HIGH, BACK IN THE DAY...
"I WAS LIKE YOU. I DIDN'T PLAY SPORTS, AND WAS MORE INTERESTED IN BOOKS AND COMICS.
"WHAT I *DIDN'T* KNOW THEN WAS THAT MY BULLY WAS PICKING ON ME TO BUILD HIMSELF UP IN THE EYES OF HIS FRIENDS.
"HE PLAYED FOOTBALL, AND WAS POPULAR, BUT UNDER THE SURFACE HE WAS AS INSECURE AS ME."
HEY, EGGHEAD!
GET IT? EGG HEAD!
SPLAK
HA-HA-HA!
WHAT A ROD.
THAT'S IT, FLASH!
"HERE'S THE WEIRD THING ABOUT BULLYING: IT CAN ACTUALLY PREPARE YOU FOR LIFE'S DIFFICULTIES.
"I WASN'T GOING TO STOP STUDYING JUST BECAUSE A JOCK WAS MAKING FUN OF ME.
"BUT THIS IS A STORY ABOUT THE TIME I WENT FROM BEING BULLIED, TO *BEING* THE BULLY."
I'M GOING TO MAKE FLASH *PAY*.

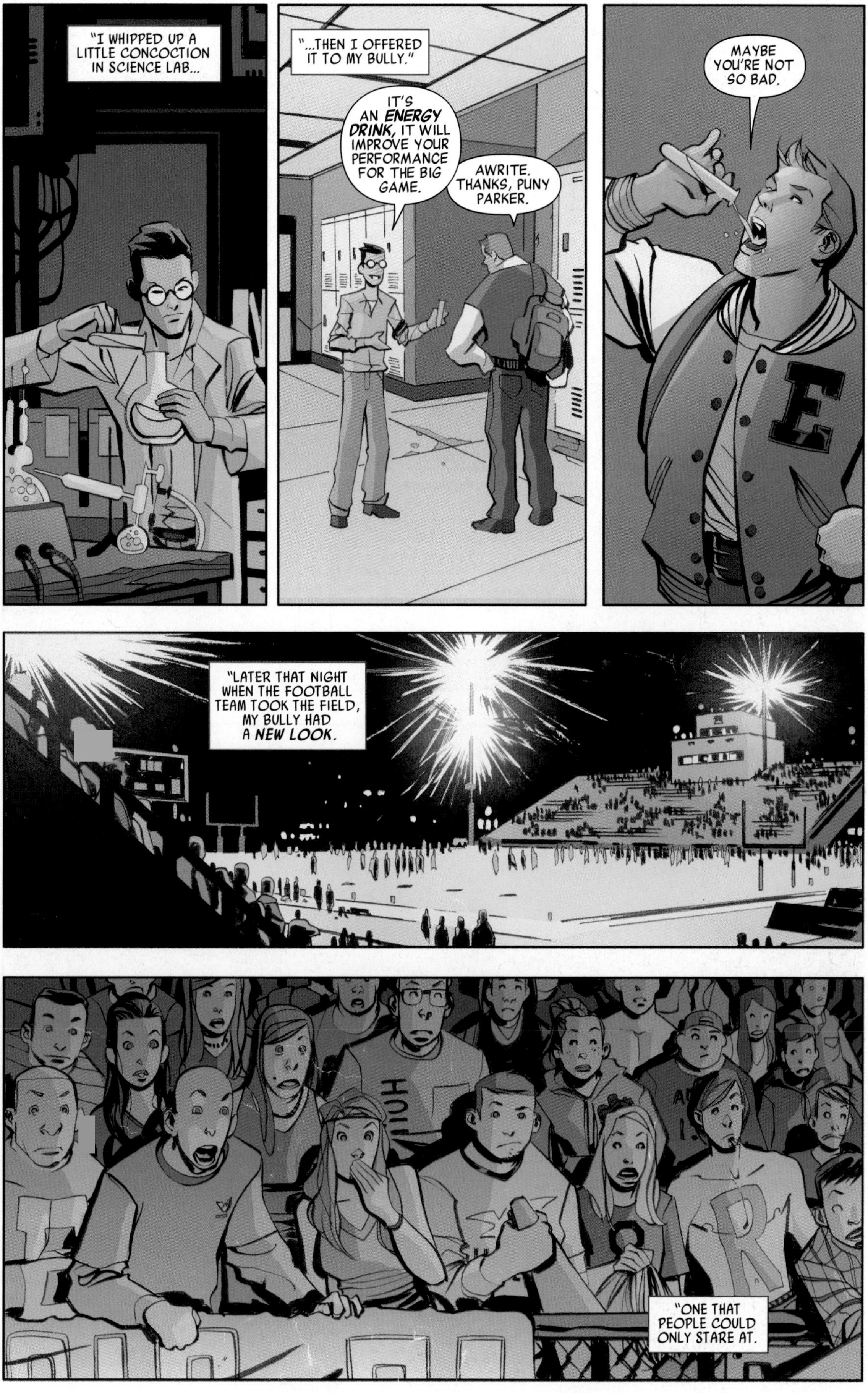
"I WHIPPED UP A LITTLE CONCOCTION IN SCIENCE LAB...
"...THEN I OFFERED IT TO MY BULLY."
IT'S AN ENERGY DRINK, IT WILL IMPROVE YOUR PERFORMANCE FOR THE BIG GAME.
AWRITE. THANKS, PUNY PARKER.
MAYBE YOU'RE NOT SO BAD.
"LATER THAT NIGHT WHEN THE FOOTBALL TEAM TOOK THE FIELD, MY BULLY HAD A NEW LOOK.
"ONE THAT PEOPLE COULD ONLY STARE AT.

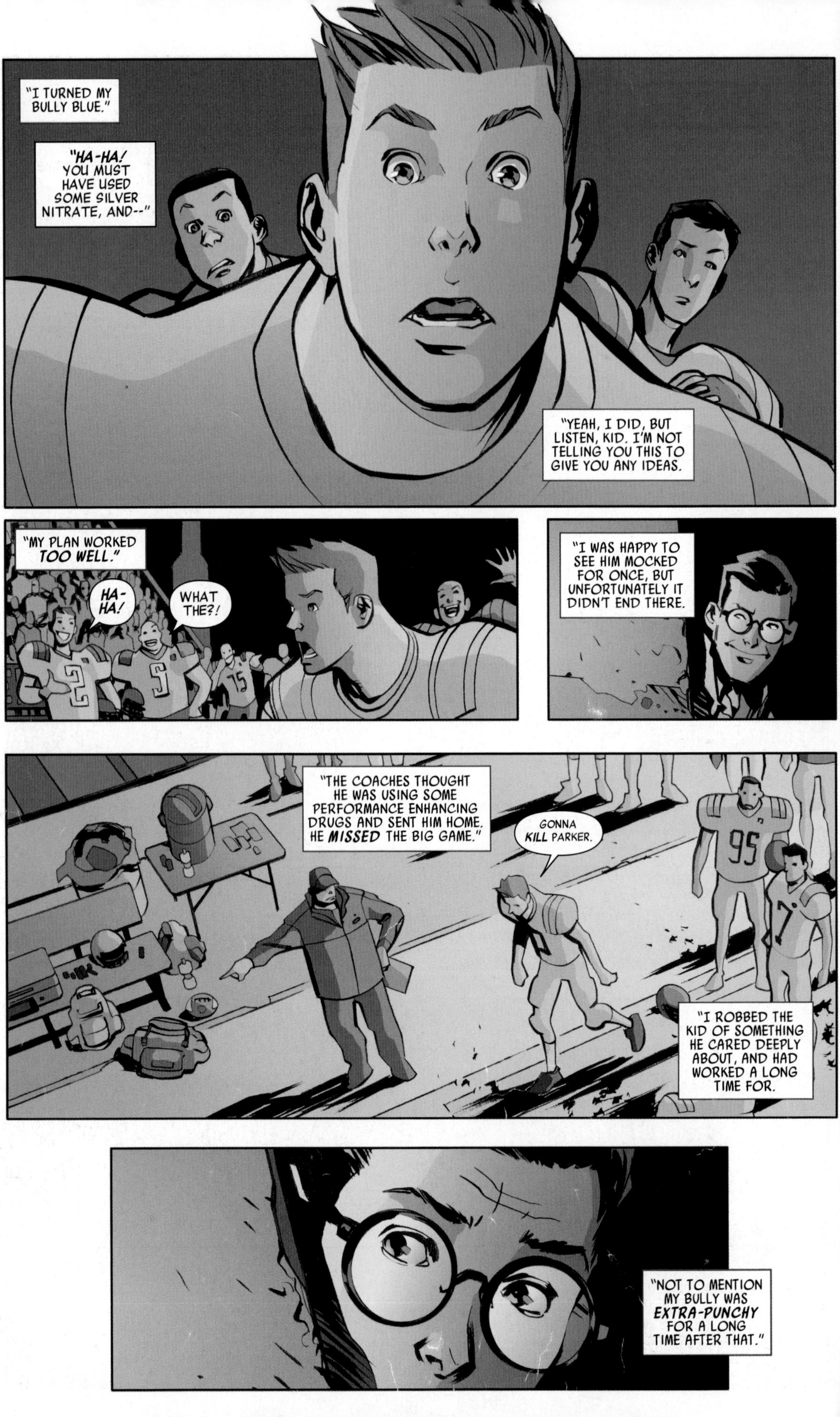
"I TURNED MY BULLY BLUE."
"HA-HA! YOU MUST HAVE USED SOME SILVER NITRATE, AND--"
"YEAH, I DID, BUT LISTEN, KID. I'M NOT TELLING YOU THIS TO GIVE YOU ANY IDEAS.
"MY PLAN WORKED TOO WELL."
HA-HA!
WHAT THE?!
"I WAS HAPPY TO SEE HIM MOCKED FOR ONCE, BUT UNFORTUNATELY IT DIDN'T END THERE.
"THE COACHES THOUGHT HE WAS USING SOME PERFORMANCE ENHANCING DRUGS AND SENT HIM HOME. HE MISSED THE BIG GAME."
GONNA KILL PARKER.
"I ROBBED THE KID OF SOMETHING HE CARED DEEPLY ABOUT, AND HAD WORKED A LONG TIME FOR.
"NOT TO MENTION MY BULLY WAS EXTRA-PUNCHY FOR A LONG TIME AFTER THAT."

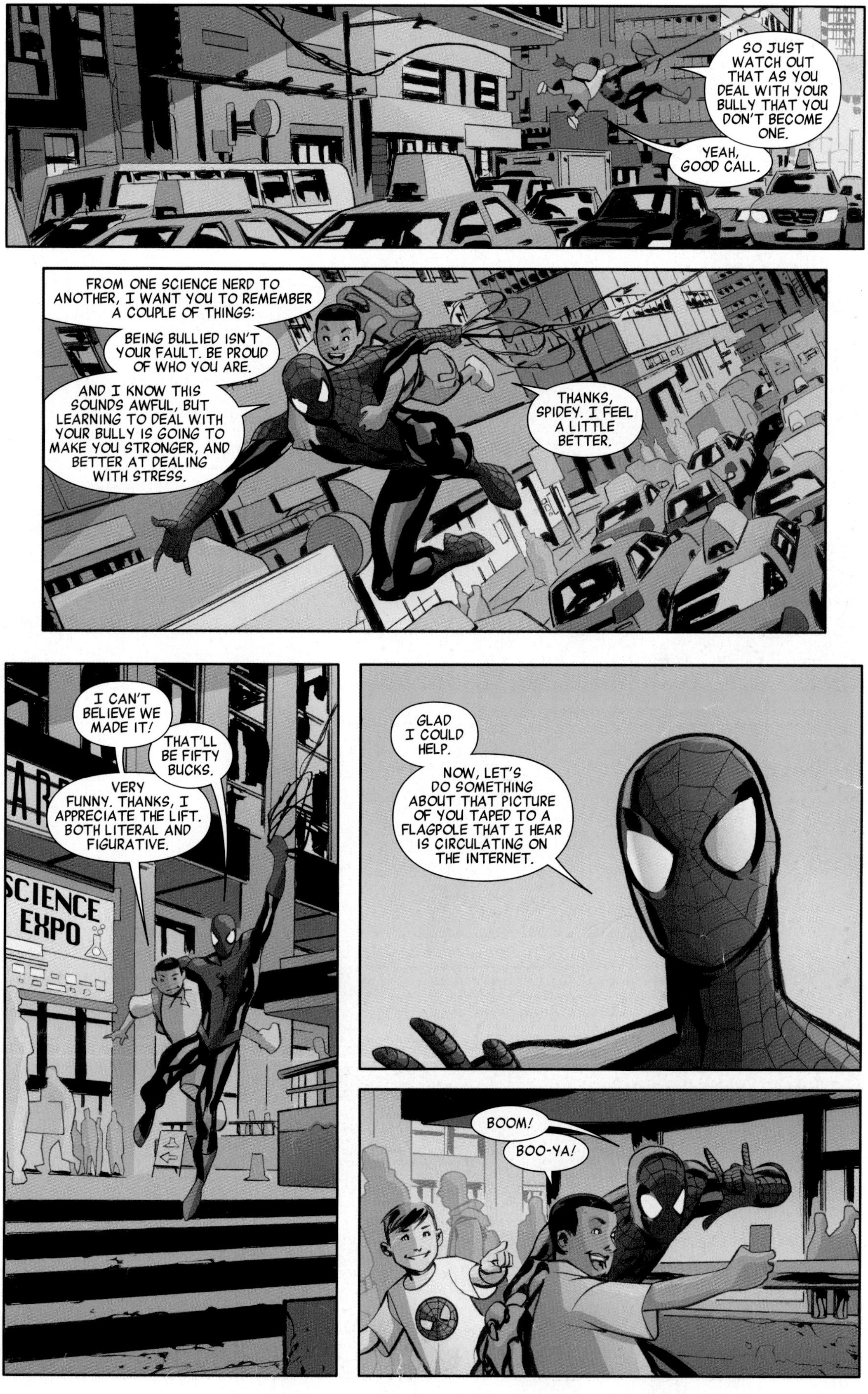
SO JUST WATCH OUT THAT AS YOU DEAL WITH YOUR BULLY THAT YOU DON'T BECOME ONE.
YEAH, GOOD CALL.
FROM ONE SCIENCE NERD TO ANOTHER, I WANT YOU TO REMEMBER A COUPLE OF THINGS:
BEING BULLIED ISN'T YOUR FAULT. BE PROUD OF WHO YOU ARE.
AND I KNOW THIS SOUNDS AWFUL, BUT LEARNING TO DEAL WITH YOUR BULLY IS GOING TO MAKE YOU STRONGER, AND BETTER AT DEALING WITH STRESS.
THANKS, SPIDEY. I FEEL A LITTLE BETTER.
I CAN'T BELIEVE WE MADE IT!
THAT'LL BE FIFTY BUCKS.
VERY FUNNY. THANKS, I APPRECIATE THE LIFT. BOTH LITERAL AND FIGURATIVE.
SCIENCE EXPO
GLAD I COULD HELP.
NOW, LET'S DO SOMETHING ABOUT THAT PICTURE OF YOU TAPED TO A FLAGPOLE THAT I HEAR IS CIRCULATING ON THE INTERNET.
BOOM!
BOO-YA!

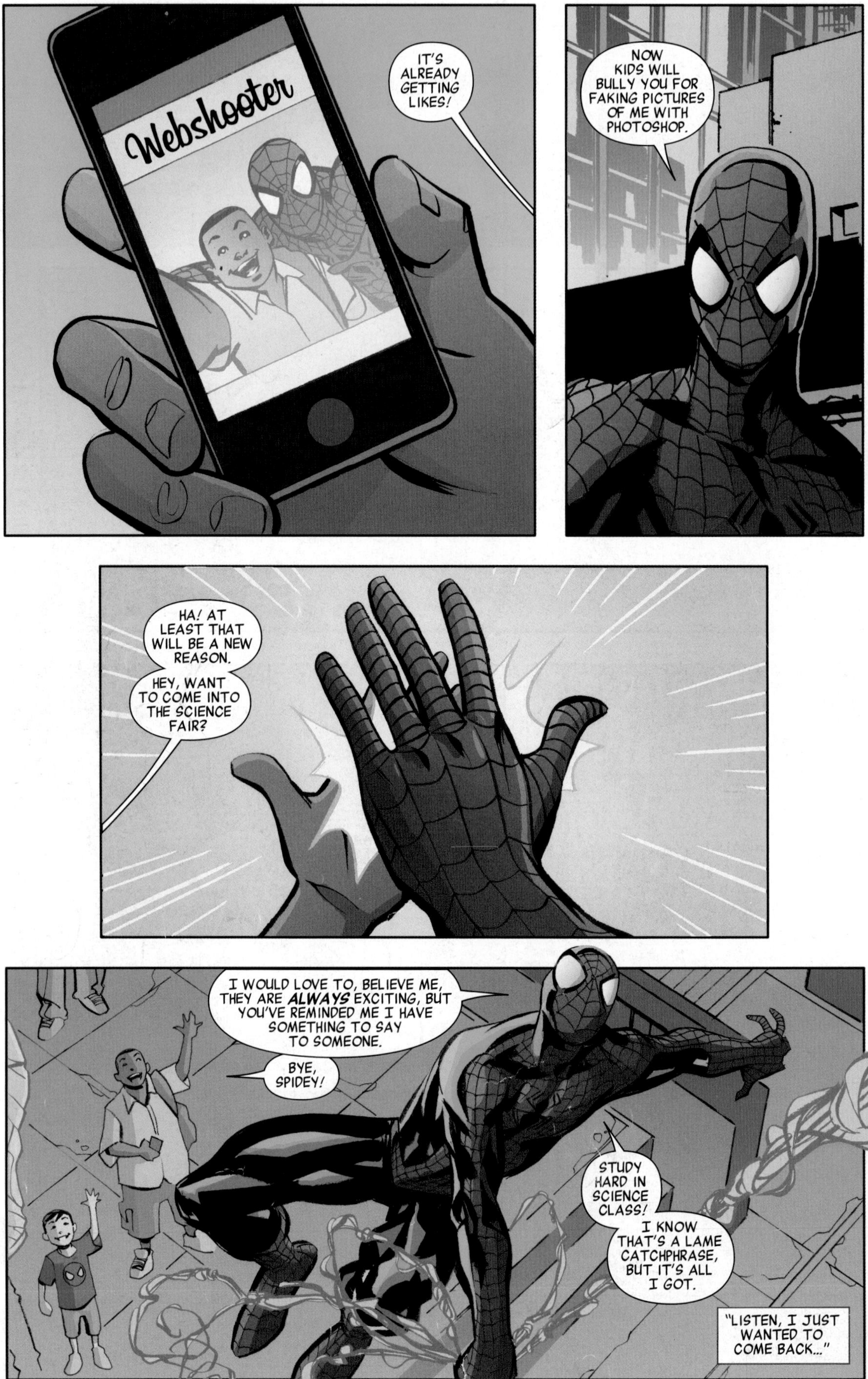
Webshooter
IT'S ALREADY GETTING LIKES!
NOW KIDS WILL BULLY YOU FOR FAKING PICTURES OF ME WITH PHOTOSHOP.
HA! AT LEAST THAT WILL BE A NEW REASON.
HEY, WANT TO COME INTO THE SCIENCE FAIR?
I WOULD LOVE TO, BELIEVE ME, THEY ARE ALWAYS EXCITING, BUT YOU'VE REMINDED ME I HAVE SOMETHING TO SAY TO SOMEONE.
BYE, SPIDEY!
STUDY HARD IN SCIENCE CLASS!
I KNOW THAT'S A LAME CATCHPHRASE, BUT IT'S ALL I GOT.
"LISTEN, I JUST WANTED TO COME BACK..."

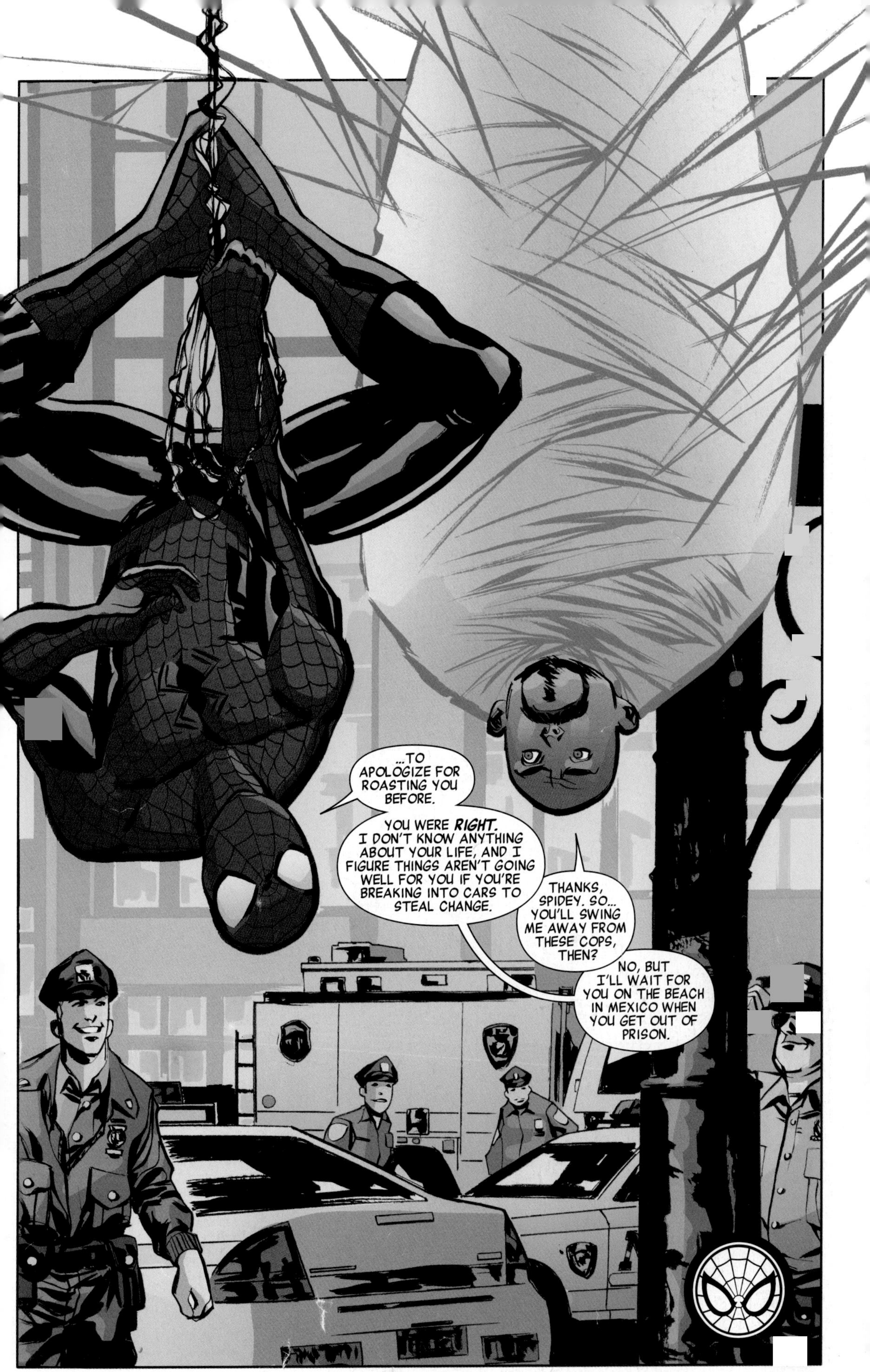
...TO APOLOGIZE FOR ROASTING YOU BEFORE.
YOU WERE RIGHT. I DON'T KNOW ANYTHING ABOUT YOUR LIFE, AND I FIGURE THINGS AREN'T GOING WELL FOR YOU IF YOU'RE BREAKING INTO CARS TO STEAL CHANGE.
THANKS, SPIDEY. SO... YOU'LL SWING ME AWAY FROM THESE COPS, THEN?
NO, BUT I'LL WAIT FOR YOU ON THE BEACH IN MEXICO WHEN YOU GET OUT OF PRISON.

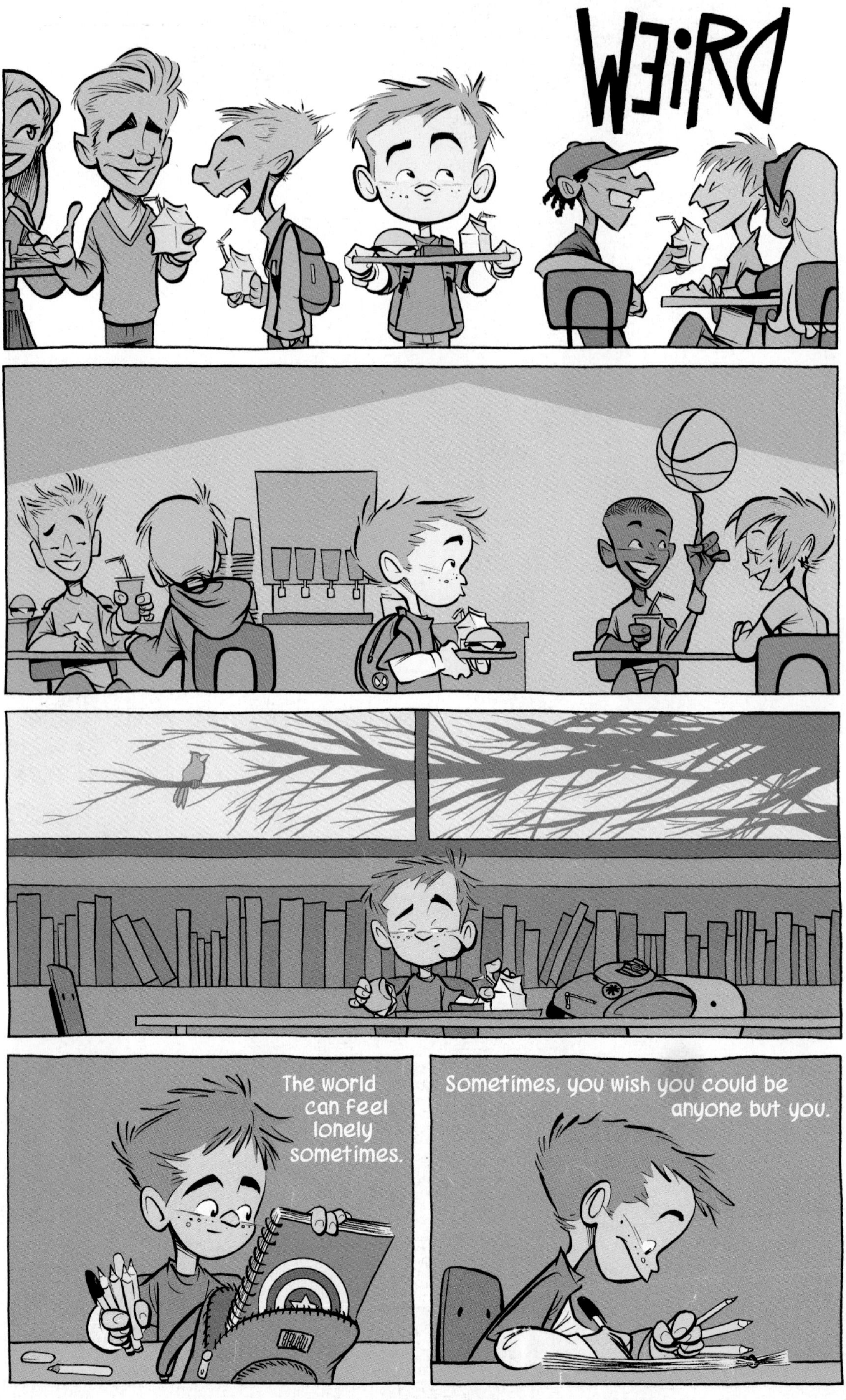
WEiRD
The world can feel lonely sometimes.
Sometimes, you wish you could be anyone but you.

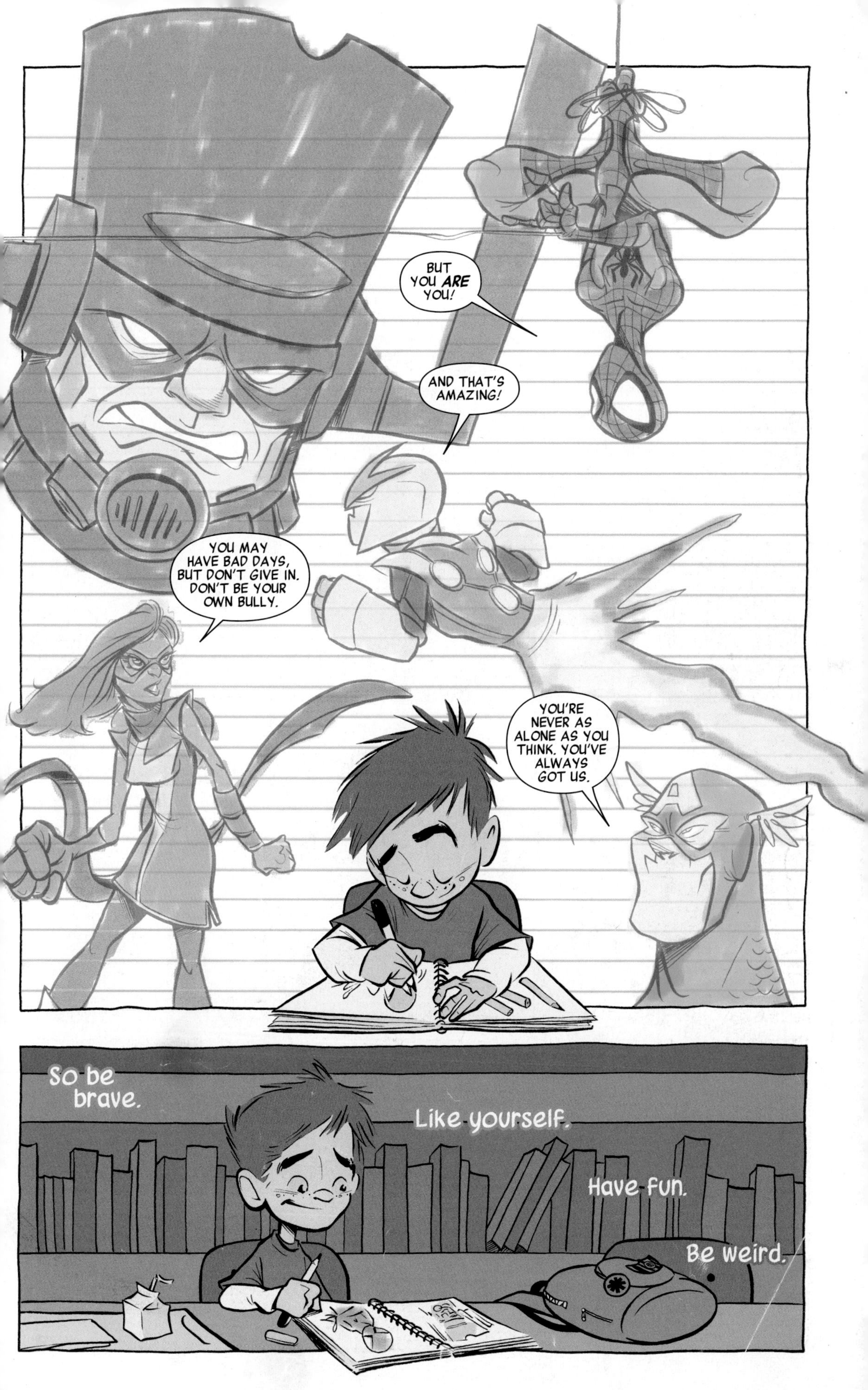
BUT YOU **ARE** YOU!
AND THAT'S AMAZING!
YOU MAY HAVE BAD DAYS, BUT DON'T GIVE IN. DON'T BE YOUR OWN BULLY.
YOU'RE NEVER AS ALONE AS YOU THINK. YOU'VE ALWAYS GOT US.
So be brave.
Like yourself.
Have fun.
Be weird.

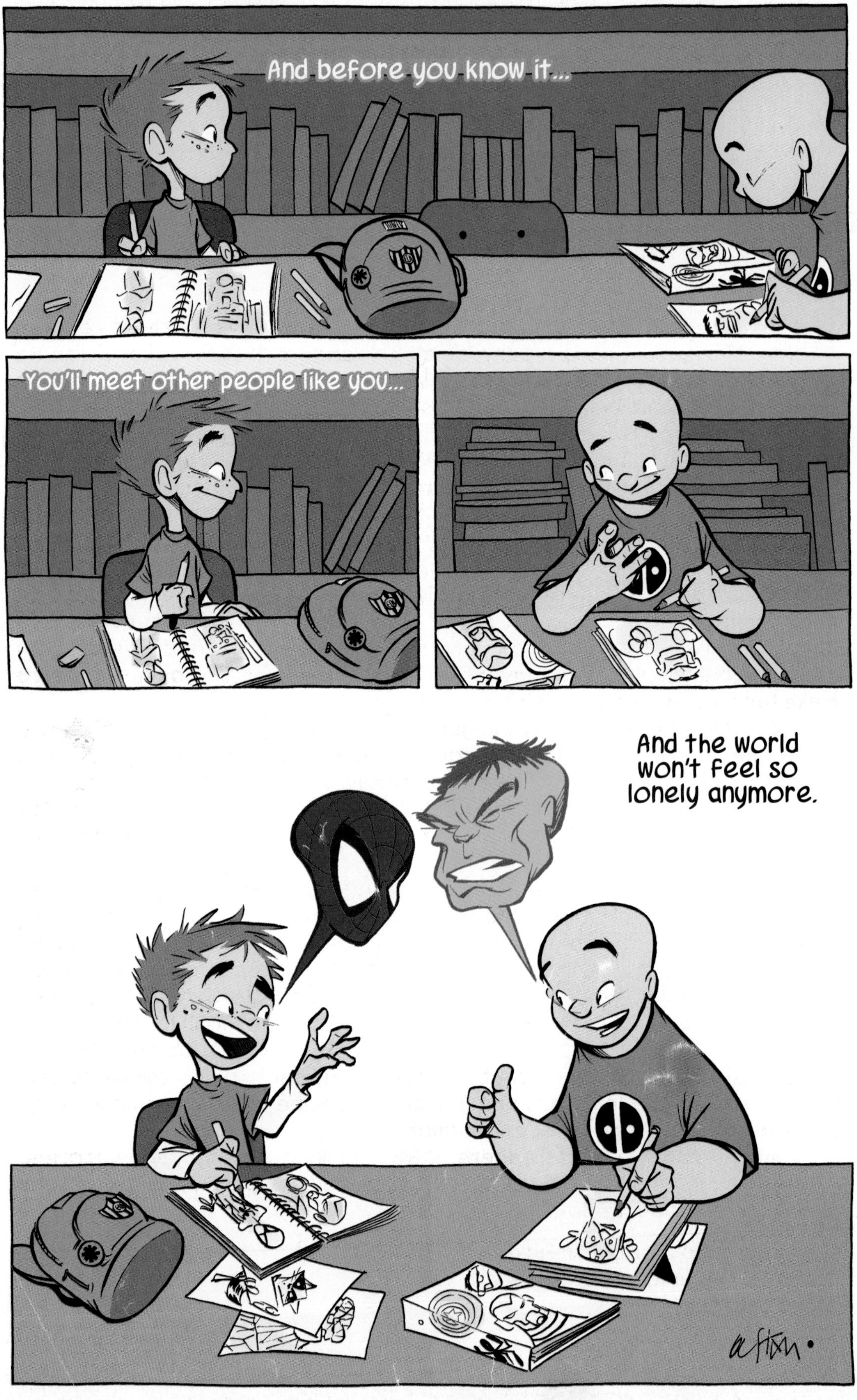

And before you know it...
You'll meet other people like you...
And the world won't feel so lonely anymore.

AVENGERS: NO MORE BULLYING

Hello, readers!

From the concrete canyons of New York City, to the furthest reaches of the galaxy, bullying is a pervasive and dangerous force. That's why we decided to get some of Marvel's best and brightest together to tackle the problem head-on.

Every story that you've read in this issue was carefully and deliberately put together by a team of folks dedicated not only to telling the best super hero story they could, but also to bringing aspects of bullying right out into the light--whether it's the harmful consequences of offhand "jokes," the corrosive effect those comments can have on a group of friends, or how people can become bullies without even knowing it.

In an age of computers, text messaging, and social media, it can be even more difficult to root out bullying where it lies, as sometimes bullying can take place on our phones or over our favorite websites-- called 'cyberbullying,' this invention of the 21st century only serves to make bullying as easy as using an app.

But those affected by bullying must take heart, because they are not alone. It is important, when someone is faced with bullying, that they do not remain silent. They need to speak up, to a counselor, parent, guardian, or teacher to help stop bullying at the source. And, though violence is never the solution to bullying, asking for help can be. Reaching out is the first step.

With that, I want to take an opportunity to thank everyone involved in this story. Gerry Duggan, Jody Houser, Sean Ryan, and Jeff Loveness all wrote stories that had super hero action to spare, but also genuine, human moments. Those moments were brought to life masterfully by our wonderful artists, Marcio Takara, Tana Ford, Carlo Barberi, and Gustavo Duarte. This was a team effort, though, and the art in this special was beautifully colored by Lee Loughridge, Ruth Redmond and Israel Silva. Add to that Travis Lanham, our tremendously patient and skilled letterer, and you have a recipe for a comic unlike anything Marvel has done in recent memory.

And thank you, readers, for picking up these stories. Hopefully, they gave you some insight into how bullying can take on many forms, even those we don't expect.

Here's to a brighter future.
Catch you in the cosmos,
Devin Lewis
Editor

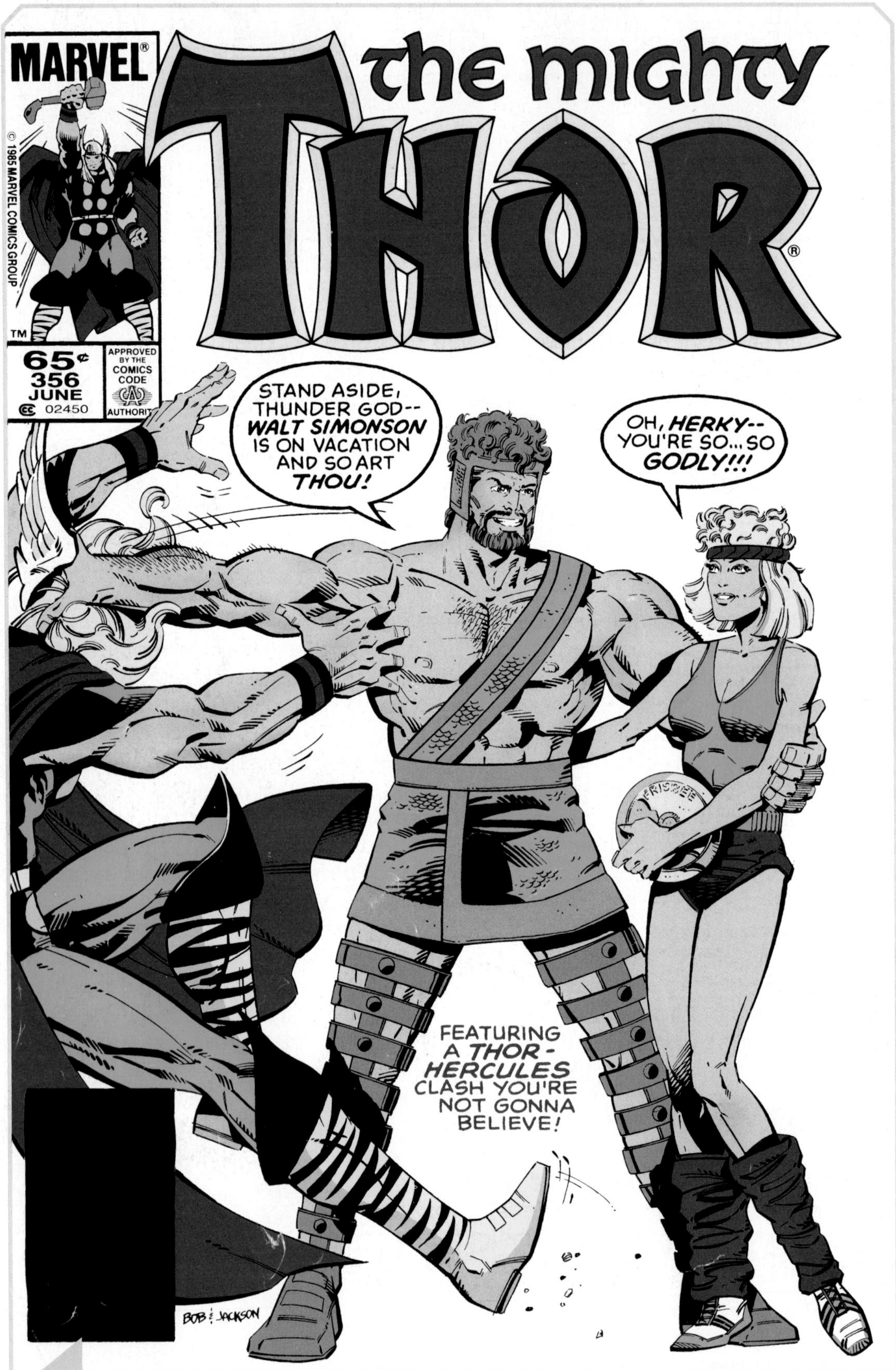
MARVEL
the mighty
THOR
© 1985 MARVEL COMICS GROUP
65¢
356
JUNE
02450
APPROVED BY THE COMICS CODE AUTHORITY
STAND ASIDE, THUNDER GOD-- WALT SIMONSON IS ON VACATION AND SO ART THOU!
OH, HERKY-- YOU'RE SO...SO GODLY!!!
FEATURING A THOR-HERCULES CLASH YOU'RE NOT GONNA BELIEVE!

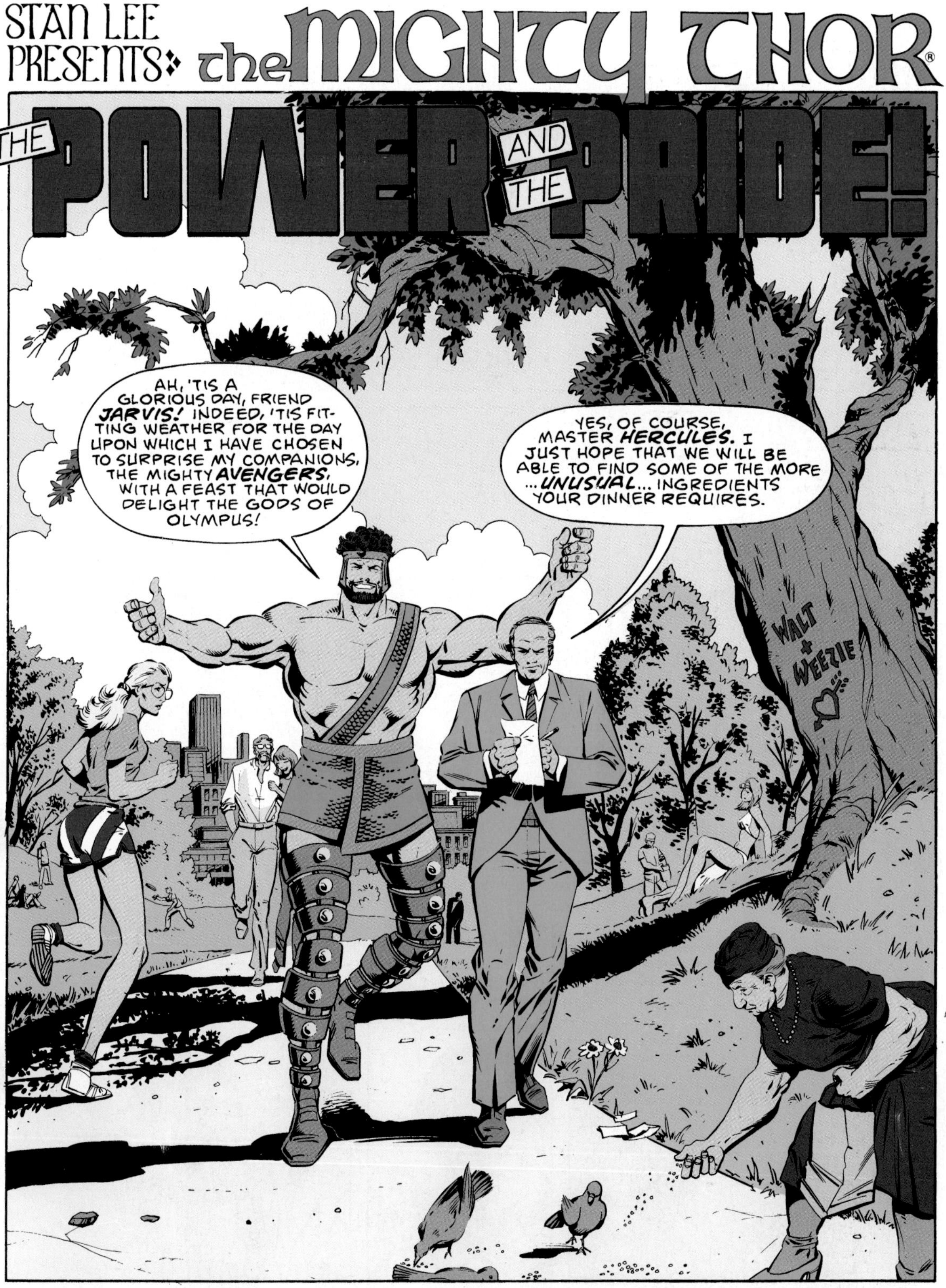
STAN LEE PRESENTS: the MIGHTY THOR®
THE POWER AND THE PRIDE!
AH, 'TIS A GLORIOUS DAY, FRIEND JARVIS! INDEED, 'TIS FITTING WEATHER FOR THE DAY UPON WHICH I HAVE CHOSEN TO SURPRISE MY COMPANIONS, THE MIGHTY AVENGERS, WITH A FEAST THAT WOULD DELIGHT THE GODS OF OLYMPUS!
YES, OF COURSE, MASTER HERCULES. I JUST HOPE THAT WE WILL BE ABLE TO FIND SOME OF THE MORE ...UNUSUAL... INGREDIENTS YOUR DINNER REQUIRES.
WALT + WEEZIE

BOB HARRAS WRITER | JACKSON GUICE PENCILLER | BOB LAYTON INKER | JOHN WORKMAN LETTERER | CHRISTIE SCHEELE COLORIST | MARK GRUENWALD GUEST EDITOR | JIM SHOOTER EDITOR IN CHIEF

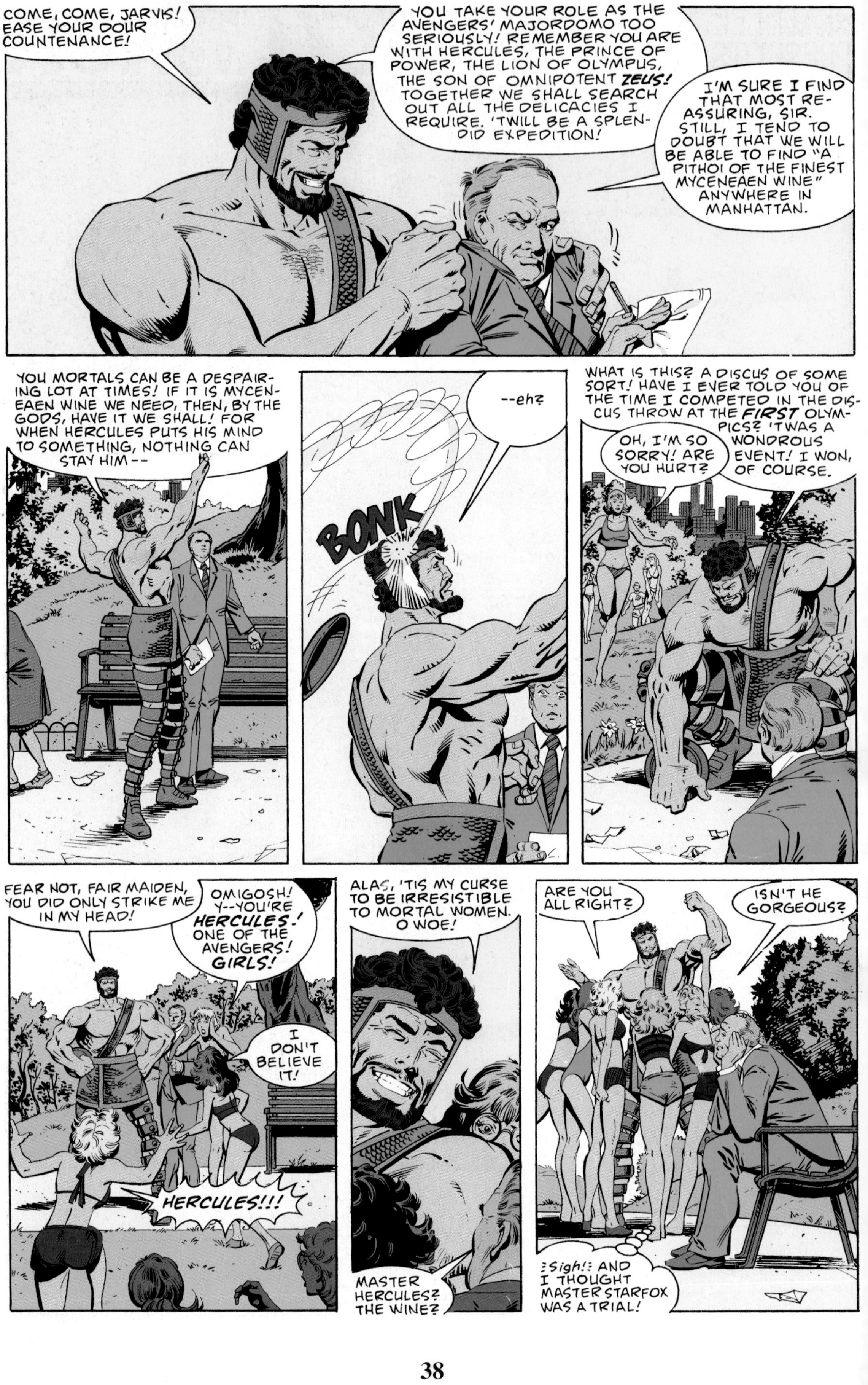
COME, COME, JARVIS! EASE YOUR DOUR COUNTENANCE!
YOU TAKE YOUR ROLE AS THE AVENGERS' MAJORDOMO TOO SERIOUSLY! REMEMBER YOU ARE WITH HERCULES, THE PRINCE OF POWER, THE LION OF OLYMPUS, THE SON OF OMNIPOTENT ZEUS! TOGETHER WE SHALL SEARCH OUT ALL THE DELICACIES I REQUIRE. 'TWILL BE A SPLENDID EXPEDITION!
I'M SURE I FIND THAT MOST REASSURING, SIR. STILL, I TEND TO DOUBT THAT WE WILL BE ABLE TO FIND "A PITHOI OF THE FINEST MYCENEAEN WINE" ANYWHERE IN MANHATTAN.
YOU MORTALS CAN BE A DESPAIRING LOT AT TIMES! IF IT IS MYCENEAEN WINE WE NEED, THEN, BY THE GODS, HAVE IT WE SHALL! FOR WHEN HERCULES PUTS HIS MIND TO SOMETHING, NOTHING CAN STAY HIM--
--eh?
BONK
WHAT IS THIS? A DISCUS OF SOME SORT! HAVE I EVER TOLD YOU OF THE TIME I COMPETED IN THE DISCUS THROW AT THE FIRST OLYMPICS? 'TWAS A WONDROUS EVENT! I WON, OF COURSE.
OH, I'M SO SORRY! ARE YOU HURT?
FEAR NOT, FAIR MAIDEN, YOU DID ONLY STRIKE ME IN MY HEAD!
OMIGOSH! Y--YOU'RE HERCULES! ONE OF THE AVENGERS! GIRLS!
I DON'T BELIEVE IT!
HERCULES!!!
ALAS, 'TIS MY CURSE TO BE IRRESISTIBLE TO MORTAL WOMEN. O WOE!
MASTER HERCULES? THE WINE?
ARE YOU ALL RIGHT?
ISN'T HE GORGEOUS?
:Sigh!: AND I THOUGHT MASTER STARFOX WAS A TRIAL!

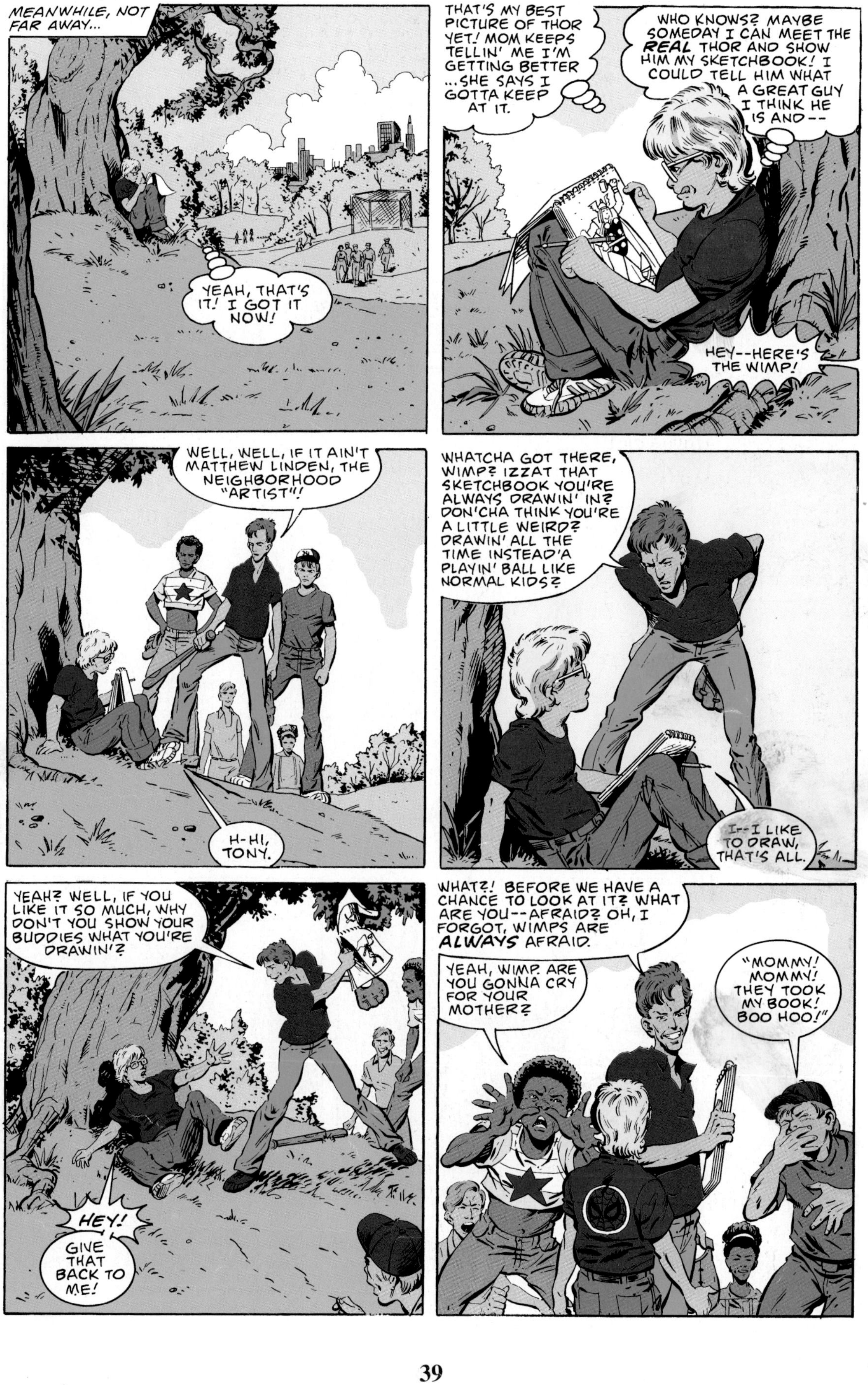
MEANWHILE, NOT FAR AWAY...
YEAH, THAT'S IT! I GOT IT NOW!
THAT'S MY BEST PICTURE OF THOR YET! MOM KEEPS TELLIN' ME I'M GETTING BETTER ...SHE SAYS I GOTTA KEEP AT IT.
WHO KNOWS? MAYBE SOMEDAY I CAN MEET THE REAL THOR AND SHOW HIM MY SKETCHBOOK! I COULD TELL HIM WHAT A GREAT GUY I THINK HE IS AND--
HEY--HERE'S THE WIMP!
WELL, WELL, IF IT AIN'T MATTHEW LINDEN, THE NEIGHBORHOOD "ARTIST"!
H-HI, TONY.
WHATCHA GOT THERE, WIMP? IZZAT THAT SKETCHBOOK YOU'RE ALWAYS DRAWIN' IN? DON'CHA THINK YOU'RE A LITTLE WEIRD? DRAWIN' ALL THE TIME INSTEAD'A PLAYIN' BALL LIKE NORMAL KIDS?
I--I LIKE TO DRAW, THAT'S ALL.
YEAH? WELL, IF YOU LIKE IT SO MUCH, WHY DON'T YOU SHOW YOUR BUDDIES WHAT YOU'RE DRAWIN'?
HEY! GIVE THAT BACK TO ME!
WHAT?! BEFORE WE HAVE A CHANCE TO LOOK AT IT? WHAT ARE YOU--AFRAID? OH, I FORGOT. WIMPS ARE ALWAYS AFRAID.
YEAH, WIMP. ARE YOU GONNA CRY FOR YOUR MOTHER?
"MOMMY! MOMMY! THEY TOOK MY BOOK! BOO HOO!"

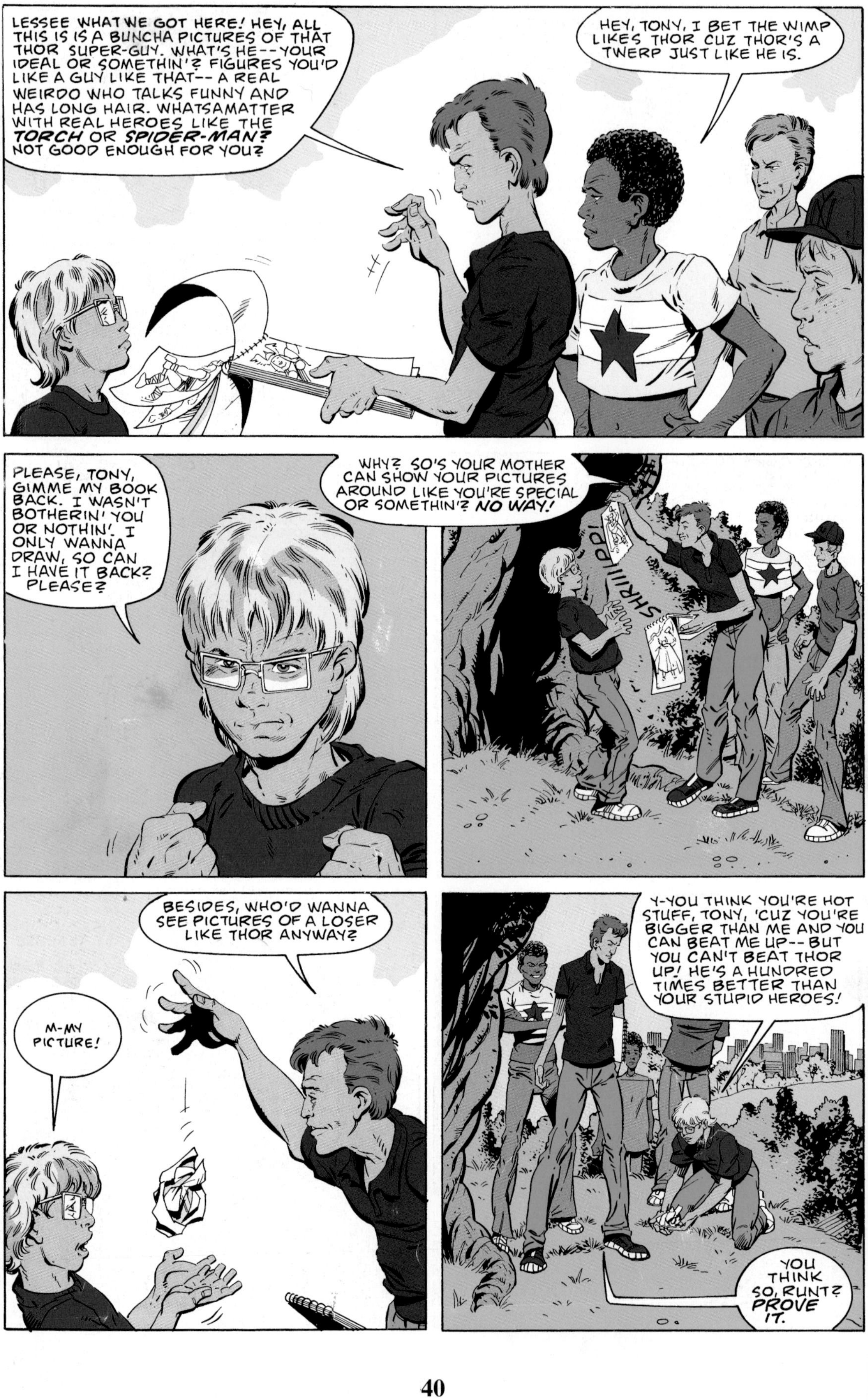
LESSEE WHAT WE GOT HERE! HEY, ALL THIS IS IS A BUNCHA PICTURES OF THAT THOR SUPER-GUY. WHAT'S HE--YOUR IDEAL OR SOMETHIN'? FIGURES YOU'D LIKE A GUY LIKE THAT-- A REAL WEIRDO WHO TALKS FUNNY AND HAS LONG HAIR. WHATSAMATTER WITH REAL HEROES LIKE THE TORCH OR SPIDER-MAN? NOT GOOD ENOUGH FOR YOU?
HEY, TONY, I BET THE WIMP LIKES THOR CUZ THOR'S A TWERP JUST LIKE HE IS.
PLEASE, TONY, GIMME MY BOOK BACK. I WASN'T BOTHERIN' YOU OR NOTHIN'. I ONLY WANNA DRAW, SO CAN I HAVE IT BACK? PLEASE?
WHY? SO'S YOUR MOTHER CAN SHOW YOUR PICTURES AROUND LIKE YOU'RE SPECIAL OR SOMETHIN'? NO WAY!
SHRIIIIIPP!
BESIDES, WHO'D WANNA SEE PICTURES OF A LOSER LIKE THOR ANYWAY?
M-MY PICTURE!
Y-YOU THINK YOU'RE HOT STUFF, TONY, 'CUZ YOU'RE BIGGER THAN ME AND YOU CAN BEAT ME UP-- BUT YOU CAN'T BEAT THOR UP! HE'S A HUNDRED TIMES BETTER THAN YOUR STUPID HEROES!
YOU THINK SO, RUNT? PROVE IT.

I DON'T HAVE TO PROVE ANYTHING TO YOU, TONY--

SURE YOU DO, KID. THAT IS, IF YOU DON'T WANT YOUR LITTLE PICTURE BOOK TO END UP IN TOMORROW'S TRASH.

HEY, TONY, WOULDJA GET A LOADA THIS!

HOLY COW! IT'S THAT HERCULES GUY FROM THE AVENGERS!

MY APOLOGIES FOR OUR DELAY, JARVIS! BUT, IN TRUTH, WHAT WAS I TO DO? TO ABANDON MY ADMIRERS WOULD HAVE BEEN CONDUCT UNBECOMING AN AVENGER! AH, THE PRICE OF FAME IS WEARYING!

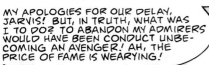

I'M SURE YOU FIND IT MOST DEBILITATING, MASTER HERCULES.

THERE'S THE WAY YOU CAN PROVE YOUR BUDDY THOR IS SO STRONG. YOU CAN ASK HERCULES. EVERYBODY KNOWS THEY'RE REAL TIGHT.

I--I CAN'T TALK TO HIM--HE'S AN AVENGER!

WHAT ARE YOU, CHICKEN? GO ON, GET OUT THERE!

HEY, HERK! MY BUDDY WANTS TO ASK YOU SOMETHIN'!

DON'T PUSH!

WHAT'S THIS?

A YOUNG BOY APPARENTLY AWESTRUCK IN THE PRESENCE OF MIGHTY HERCULES. TUT, TUT, LAD, COME, YOU HAVE A QUESTION FOR THE LION OF OLYMPUS? SPEAK!

Um--er--WELL--er--WHO'S STRONGER, MR. HERCULES, SIR, YOU OR THOR?

41

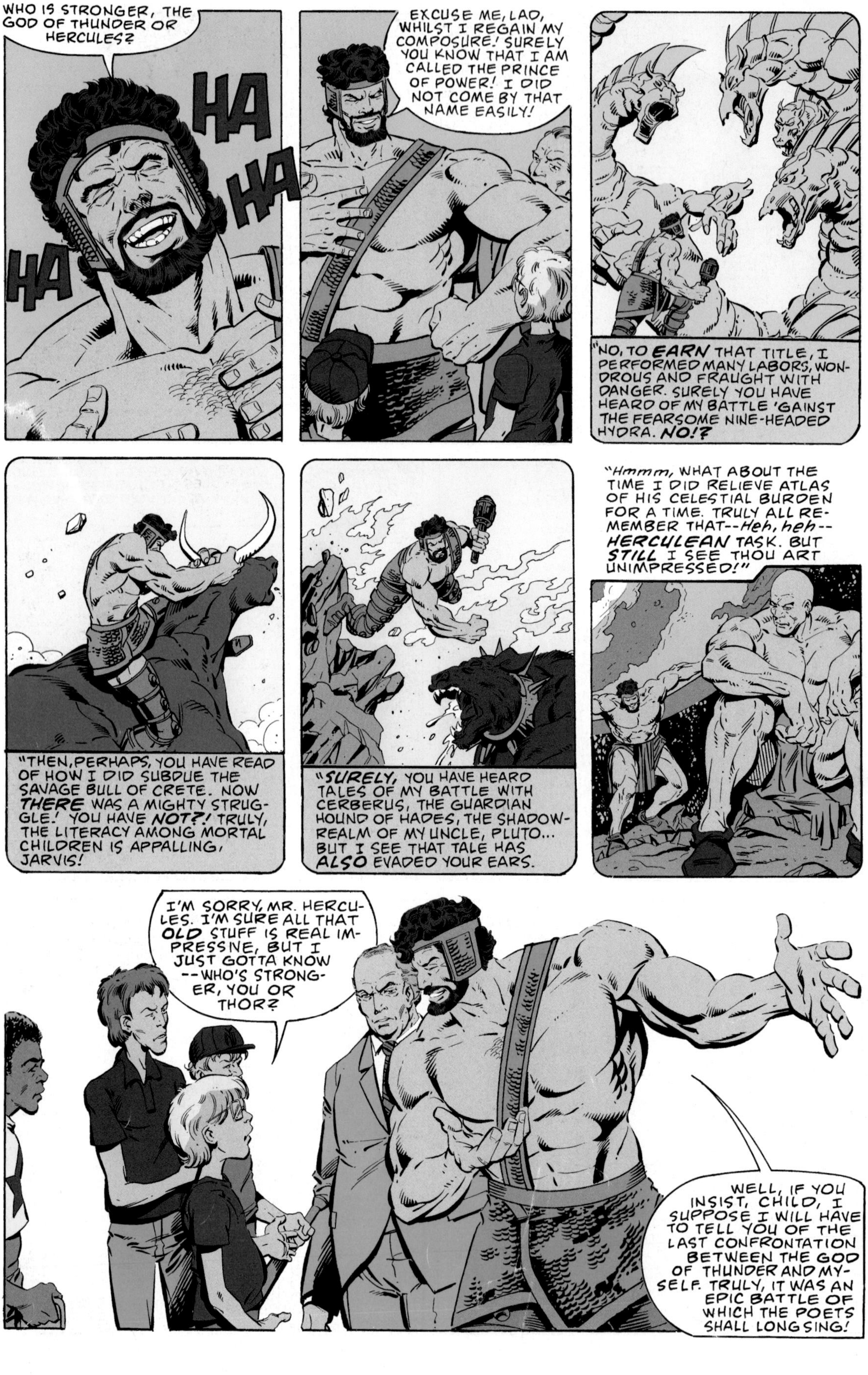
WHO IS STRONGER, THE GOD OF THUNDER OR HERCULES?
HA HA HA
EXCUSE ME, LAD, WHILST I REGAIN MY COMPOSURE! SURELY YOU KNOW THAT I AM CALLED THE PRINCE OF POWER! I DID NOT COME BY THAT NAME EASILY!
"NO, TO EARN THAT TITLE, I PERFORMED MANY LABORS, WONDROUS AND FRAUGHT WITH DANGER. SURELY YOU HAVE HEARD OF MY BATTLE 'GAINST THE FEARSOME NINE-HEADED HYDRA. NO!?
"THEN, PERHAPS, YOU HAVE READ OF HOW I DID SUBDUE THE SAVAGE BULL OF CRETE. NOW THERE WAS A MIGHTY STRUGGLE! YOU HAVE NOT?! TRULY, THE LITERACY AMONG MORTAL CHILDREN IS APPALLING, JARVIS!
"SURELY, YOU HAVE HEARD TALES OF MY BATTLE WITH CERBERUS, THE GUARDIAN HOUND OF HADES, THE SHADOW-REALM OF MY UNCLE, PLUTO... BUT I SEE THAT TALE HAS ALSO EVADED YOUR EARS.
"Hmmm, WHAT ABOUT THE TIME I DID RELIEVE ATLAS OF HIS CELESTIAL BURDEN FOR A TIME. TRULY ALL REMEMBER THAT--Heh, heh-- HERCULEAN TASK. BUT STILL I SEE THOU ART UNIMPRESSED!"
I'M SORRY, MR. HERCULES. I'M SURE ALL THAT OLD STUFF IS REAL IMPRESSNE, BUT I JUST GOTTA KNOW --WHO'S STRONGER, YOU OR THOR?
WELL, IF YOU INSIST, CHILD, I SUPPOSE I WILL HAVE TO TELL YOU OF THE LAST CONFRONTATION BETWEEN THE GOD OF THUNDER AND MYSELF. TRULY, IT WAS AN EPIC BATTLE OF WHICH THE POETS SHALL LONG SING!

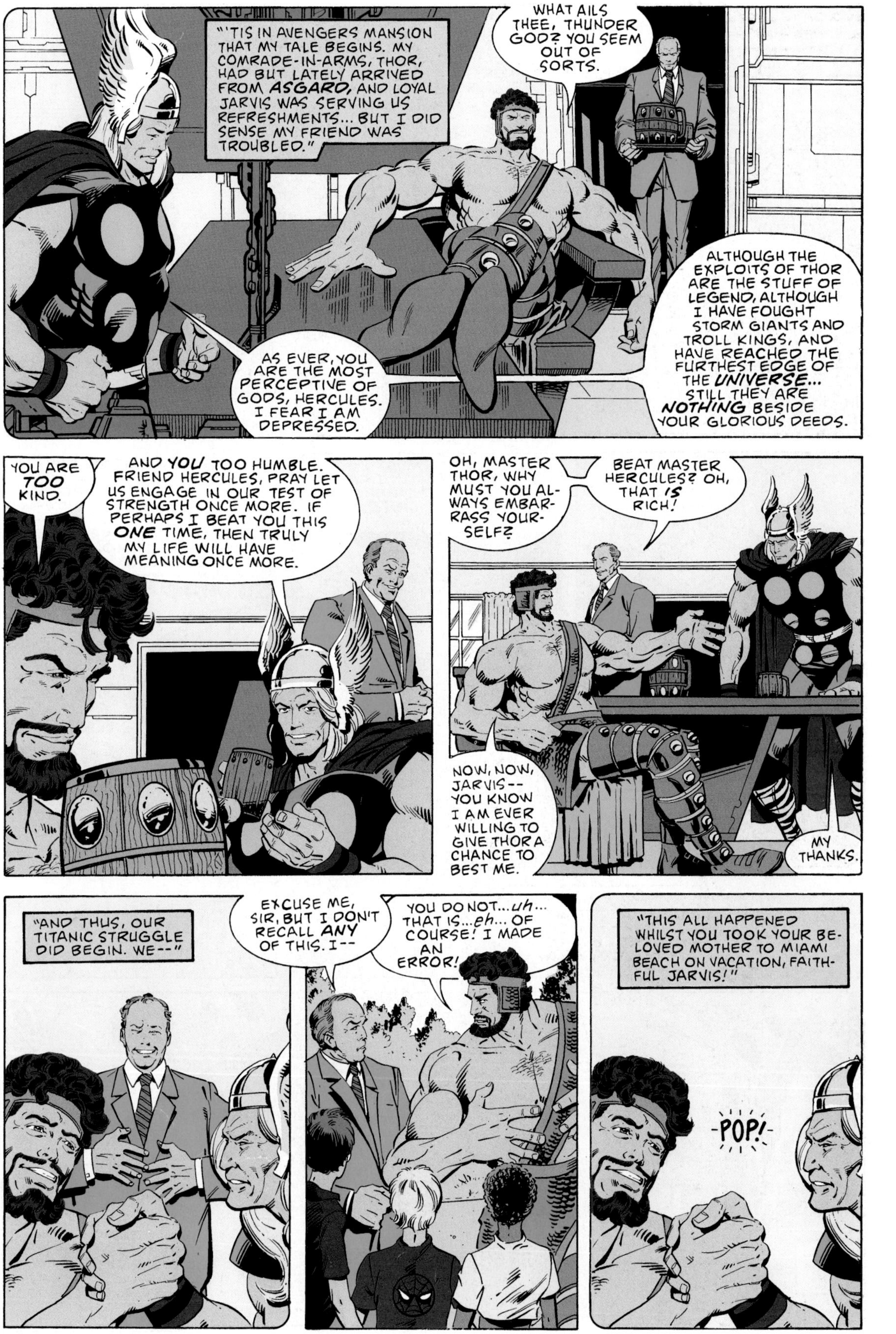
"'TIS IN AVENGERS MANSION THAT MY TALE BEGINS. MY COMRADE-IN-ARMS, THOR, HAD BUT LATELY ARRIVED FROM ASGARD, AND LOYAL JARVIS WAS SERVING US REFRESHMENTS... BUT I DID SENSE MY FRIEND WAS TROUBLED."
WHAT AILS THEE, THUNDER GOD? YOU SEEM OUT OF SORTS.
AS EVER, YOU ARE THE MOST PERCEPTIVE OF GODS, HERCULES. I FEAR I AM DEPRESSED.
ALTHOUGH THE EXPLOITS OF THOR ARE THE STUFF OF LEGEND, ALTHOUGH I HAVE FOUGHT STORM GIANTS AND TROLL KINGS, AND HAVE REACHED THE FURTHEST EDGE OF THE UNIVERSE... STILL THEY ARE NOTHING BESIDE YOUR GLORIOUS DEEDS.
YOU ARE TOO KIND.
AND YOU TOO HUMBLE. FRIEND HERCULES, PRAY LET US ENGAGE IN OUR TEST OF STRENGTH ONCE MORE. IF PERHAPS I BEAT YOU THIS ONE TIME, THEN TRULY MY LIFE WILL HAVE MEANING ONCE MORE.
OH, MASTER THOR, WHY MUST YOU ALWAYS EMBARRASS YOURSELF?
BEAT MASTER HERCULES? OH, THAT IS RICH!
NOW, NOW, JARVIS-- YOU KNOW I AM EVER WILLING TO GIVE THOR A CHANCE TO BEST ME.
MY THANKS.
"AND THUS, OUR TITANIC STRUGGLE DID BEGIN. WE--"
EXCUSE ME, SIR, BUT I DON'T RECALL ANY OF THIS. I--
YOU DO NOT...uh... THAT IS...eh... OF COURSE! I MADE AN ERROR!
"THIS ALL HAPPENED WHILST YOU TOOK YOUR BELOVED MOTHER TO MIAMI BEACH ON VACATION, FAITHFUL JARVIS!"
-POP!-

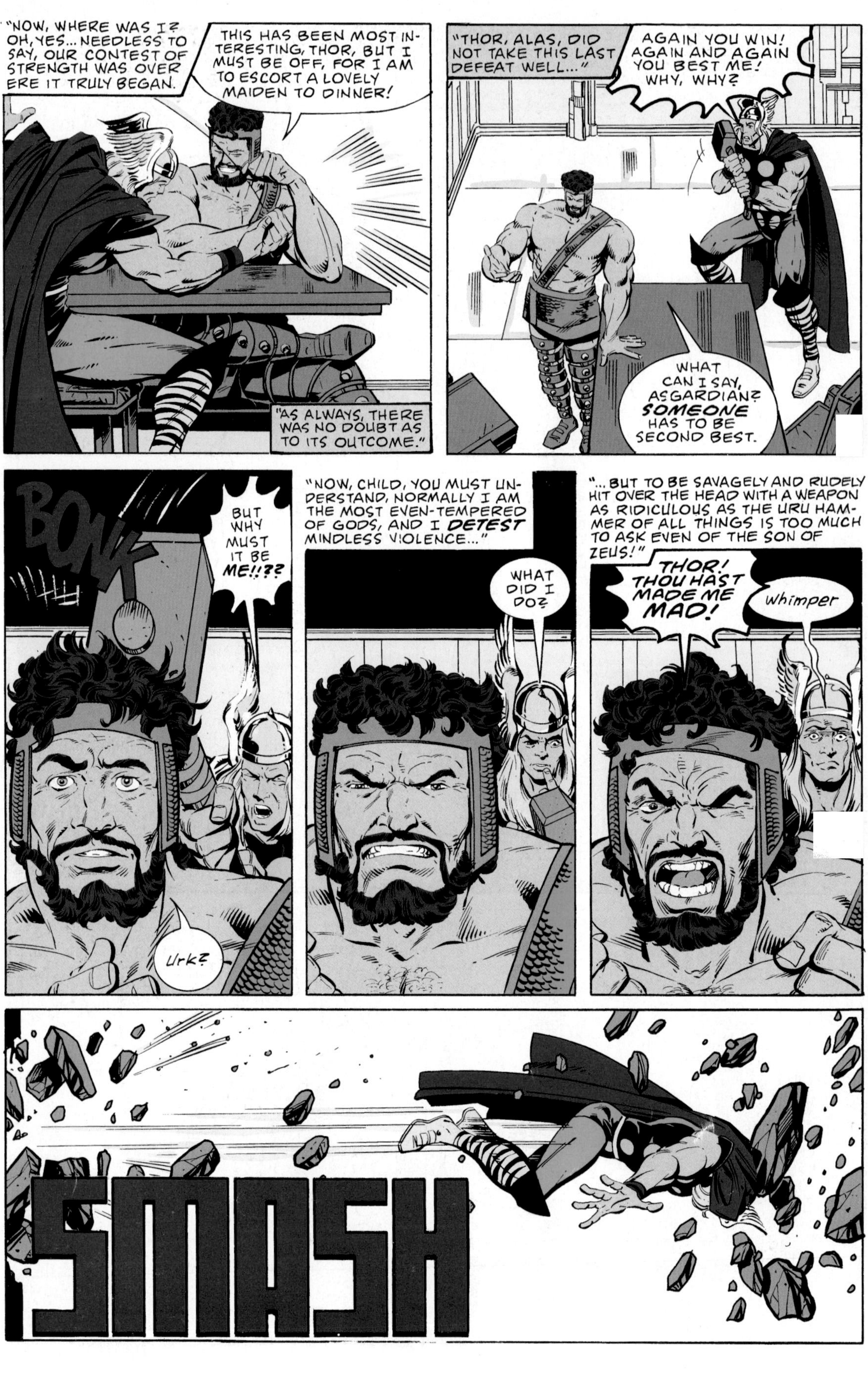

"NOW, WHERE WAS I? OH, YES... NEEDLESS TO SAY, OUR CONTEST OF STRENGTH WAS OVER ERE IT TRULY BEGAN.
THIS HAS BEEN MOST INTERESTING, THOR, BUT I MUST BE OFF, FOR I AM TO ESCORT A LOVELY MAIDEN TO DINNER!
"AS ALWAYS, THERE WAS NO DOUBT AS TO ITS OUTCOME."
"THOR, ALAS, DID NOT TAKE THIS LAST DEFEAT WELL..."
AGAIN YOU WIN! AGAIN AND AGAIN YOU BEST ME! WHY, WHY?
WHAT CAN I SAY, ASGARDIAN? SOMEONE HAS TO BE SECOND BEST.
BONK
BUT WHY MUST IT BE ME!!??
Urk?
"NOW, CHILD, YOU MUST UNDERSTAND, NORMALLY I AM THE MOST EVEN-TEMPERED OF GODS, AND I DETEST MINDLESS VIOLENCE..."
WHAT DID I DO?
"...BUT TO BE SAVAGELY AND RUDELY HIT OVER THE HEAD WITH A WEAPON AS RIDICULOUS AS THE URU HAMMER OF ALL THINGS IS TOO MUCH TO ASK EVEN OF THE SON OF ZEUS!"
THOR! THOU HAST MADE ME MAD!
Whimper
SMASH

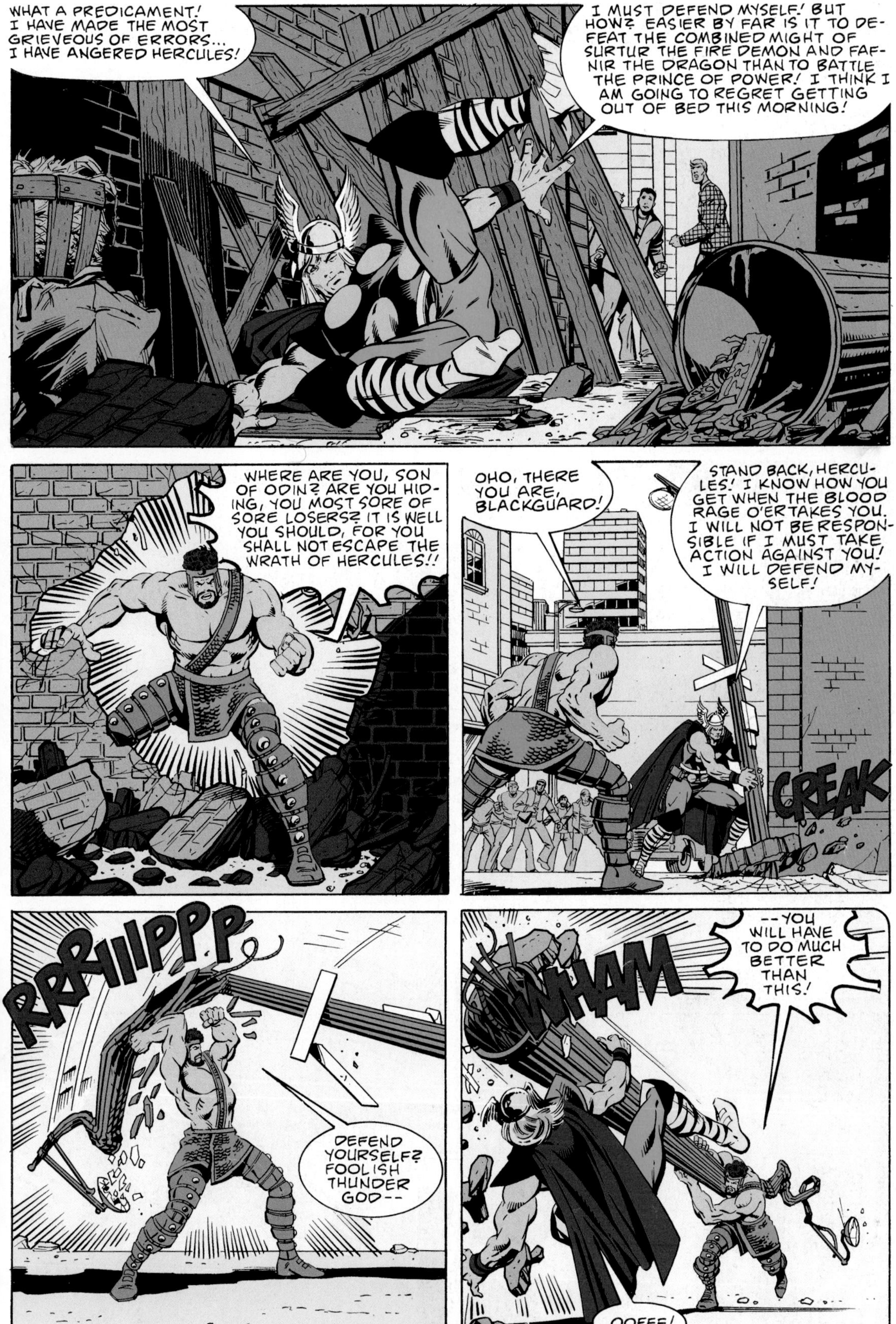

WHAT A PREDICAMENT! I HAVE MADE THE MOST GRIEVEOUS OF ERRORS... I HAVE ANGERED HERCULES!
I MUST DEFEND MYSELF! BUT HOW? EASIER BY FAR IS IT TO DEFEAT THE COMBINED MIGHT OF SURTUR THE FIRE DEMON AND FAFNIR THE DRAGON THAN TO BATTLE THE PRINCE OF POWER! I THINK I AM GOING TO REGRET GETTING OUT OF BED THIS MORNING!
WHERE ARE YOU, SON OF ODIN? ARE YOU HIDING, YOU MOST SORE OF SORE LOSERS? IT IS WELL YOU SHOULD, FOR YOU SHALL NOT ESCAPE THE WRATH OF HERCULES!!
OHO, THERE YOU ARE, BLACKGUARD!
STAND BACK, HERCULES! I KNOW HOW YOU GET WHEN THE BLOOD RAGE O'ERTAKES YOU. I WILL NOT BE RESPONSIBLE IF I MUST TAKE ACTION AGAINST YOU! I WILL DEFEND MYSELF!
CREAK
RRRIIIPPP
DEFEND YOURSELF? FOOLISH THUNDER GOD--
WHAM
--YOU WILL HAVE TO DO MUCH BETTER THAN THIS!
OOFFF!

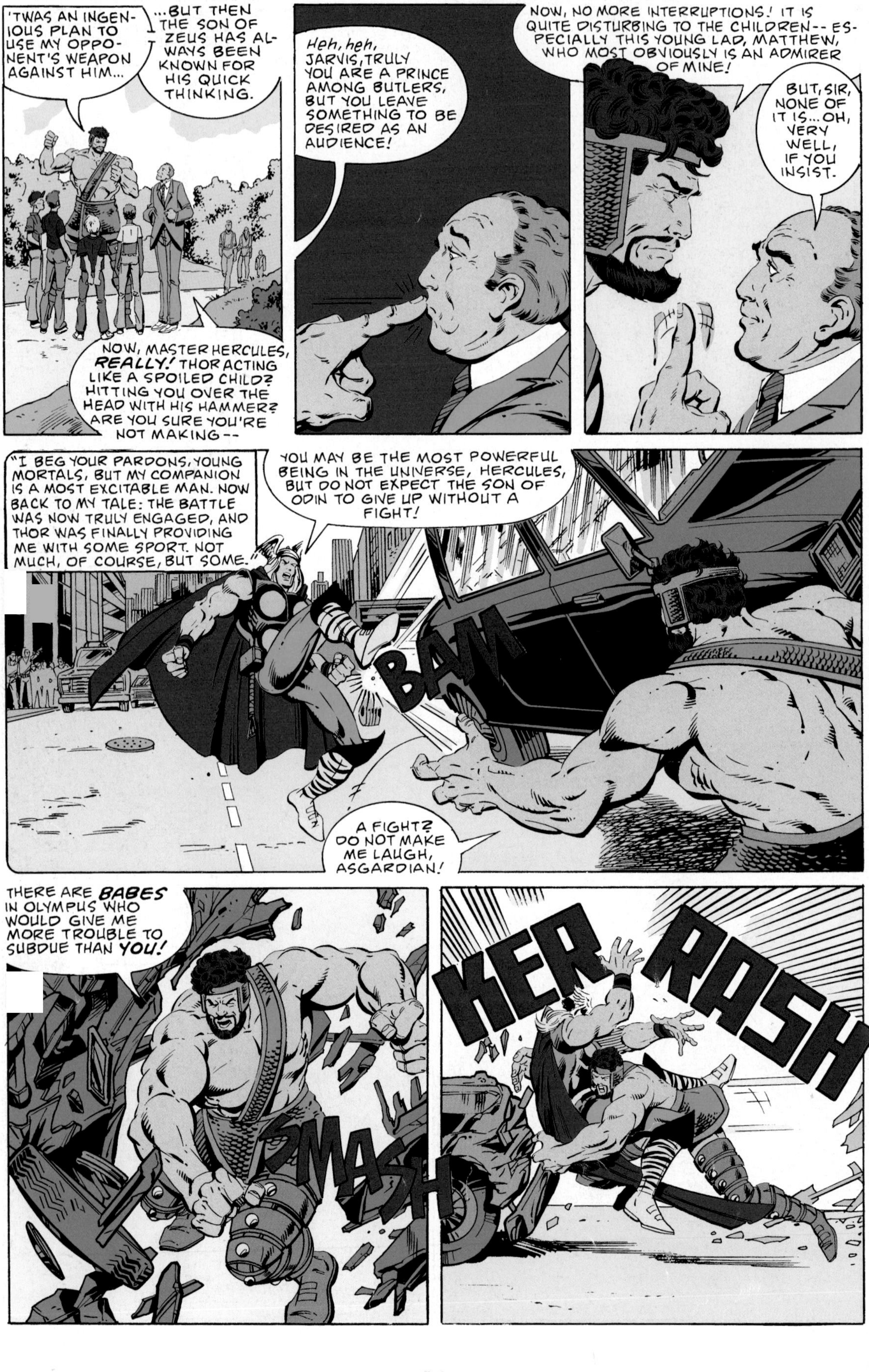
'TWAS AN INGENIOUS PLAN TO USE MY OPPONENT'S WEAPON AGAINST HIM...
...BUT THEN THE SON OF ZEUS HAS ALWAYS BEEN KNOWN FOR HIS QUICK THINKING.
NOW, MASTER HERCULES, REALLY! THOR ACTING LIKE A SPOILED CHILD? HITTING YOU OVER THE HEAD WITH HIS HAMMER? ARE YOU SURE YOU'RE NOT MAKING--
Heh, heh, JARVIS, TRULY YOU ARE A PRINCE AMONG BUTLERS, BUT YOU LEAVE SOMETHING TO BE DESIRED AS AN AUDIENCE!
NOW, NO MORE INTERRUPTIONS! IT IS QUITE DISTURBING TO THE CHILDREN-- ESPECIALLY THIS YOUNG LAD, MATTHEW, WHO MOST OBVIOUSLY IS AN ADMIRER OF MINE!
BUT, SIR, NONE OF IT IS... OH, VERY WELL, IF YOU INSIST.
"I BEG YOUR PARDONS, YOUNG MORTALS, BUT MY COMPANION IS A MOST EXCITABLE MAN. NOW BACK TO MY TALE: THE BATTLE WAS NOW TRULY ENGAGED, AND THOR WAS FINALLY PROVIDING ME WITH SOME SPORT. NOT MUCH, OF COURSE, BUT SOME."
YOU MAY BE THE MOST POWERFUL BEING IN THE UNIVERSE, HERCULES, BUT DO NOT EXPECT THE SON OF ODIN TO GIVE UP WITHOUT A FIGHT!
BAM
A FIGHT? DO NOT MAKE ME LAUGH, ASGARDIAN!
THERE ARE BABES IN OLYMPUS WHO WOULD GIVE ME MORE TROUBLE TO SUBDUE THAN YOU!
SMASH
KER RASH

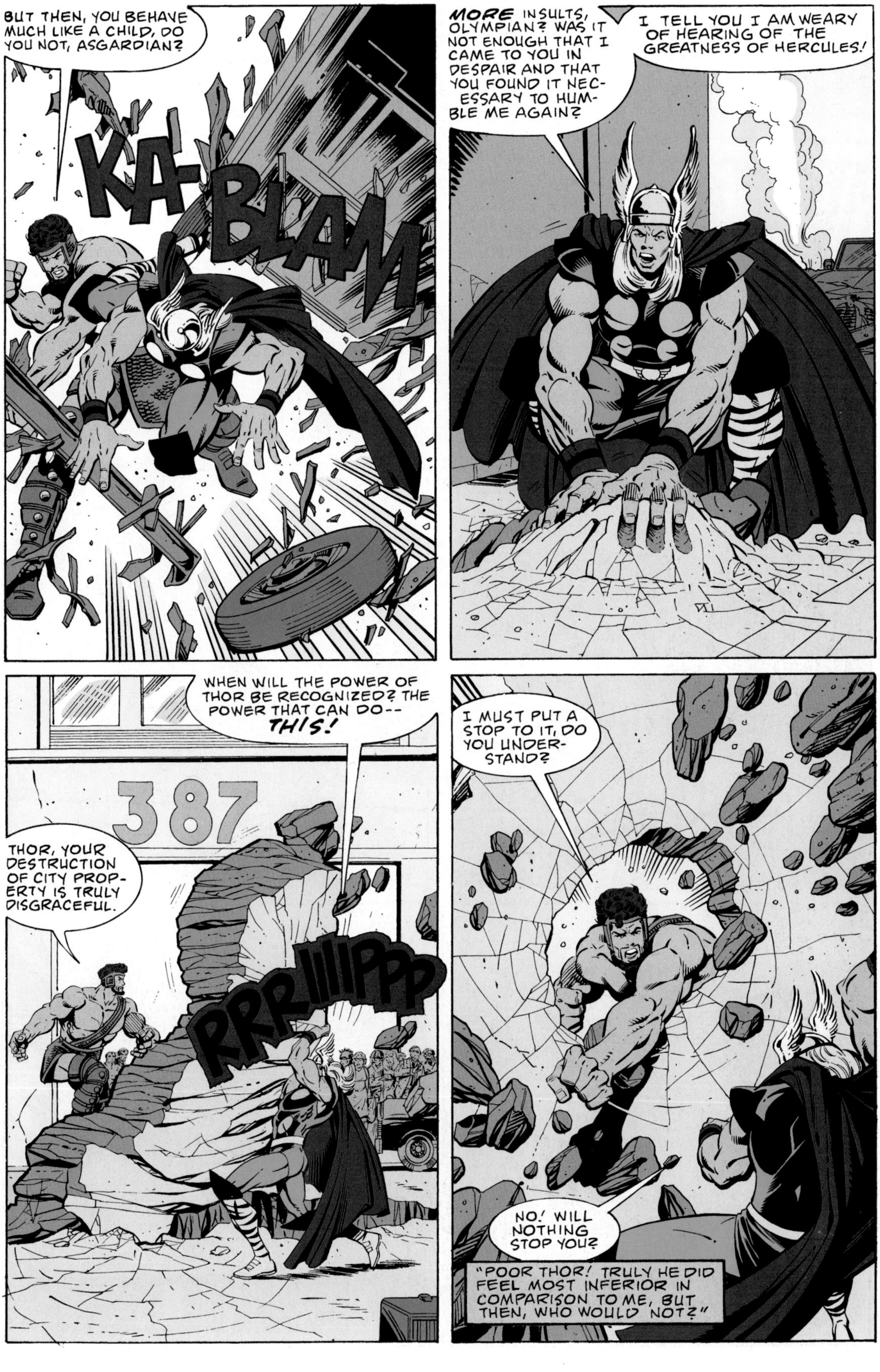
BUT THEN, YOU BEHAVE MUCH LIKE A CHILD, DO YOU NOT, ASGARDIAN?
KA-BLAM
MORE INSULTS, OLYMPIAN? WAS IT NOT ENOUGH THAT I CAME TO YOU IN DESPAIR AND THAT YOU FOUND IT NECESSARY TO HUMBLE ME AGAIN?
I TELL YOU I AM WEARY OF HEARING OF THE GREATNESS OF HERCULES!
WHEN WILL THE POWER OF THOR BE RECOGNIZED? THE POWER THAT CAN DO-- THIS!
387
THOR, YOUR DESTRUCTION OF CITY PROPERTY IS TRULY DISGRACEFUL.
RRRIIIIPPP
I MUST PUT A STOP TO IT, DO YOU UNDERSTAND?
NO! WILL NOTHING STOP YOU?
"POOR THOR! TRULY HE DID FEEL MOST INFERIOR IN COMPARISON TO ME, BUT THEN, WHO WOULD NOT?"

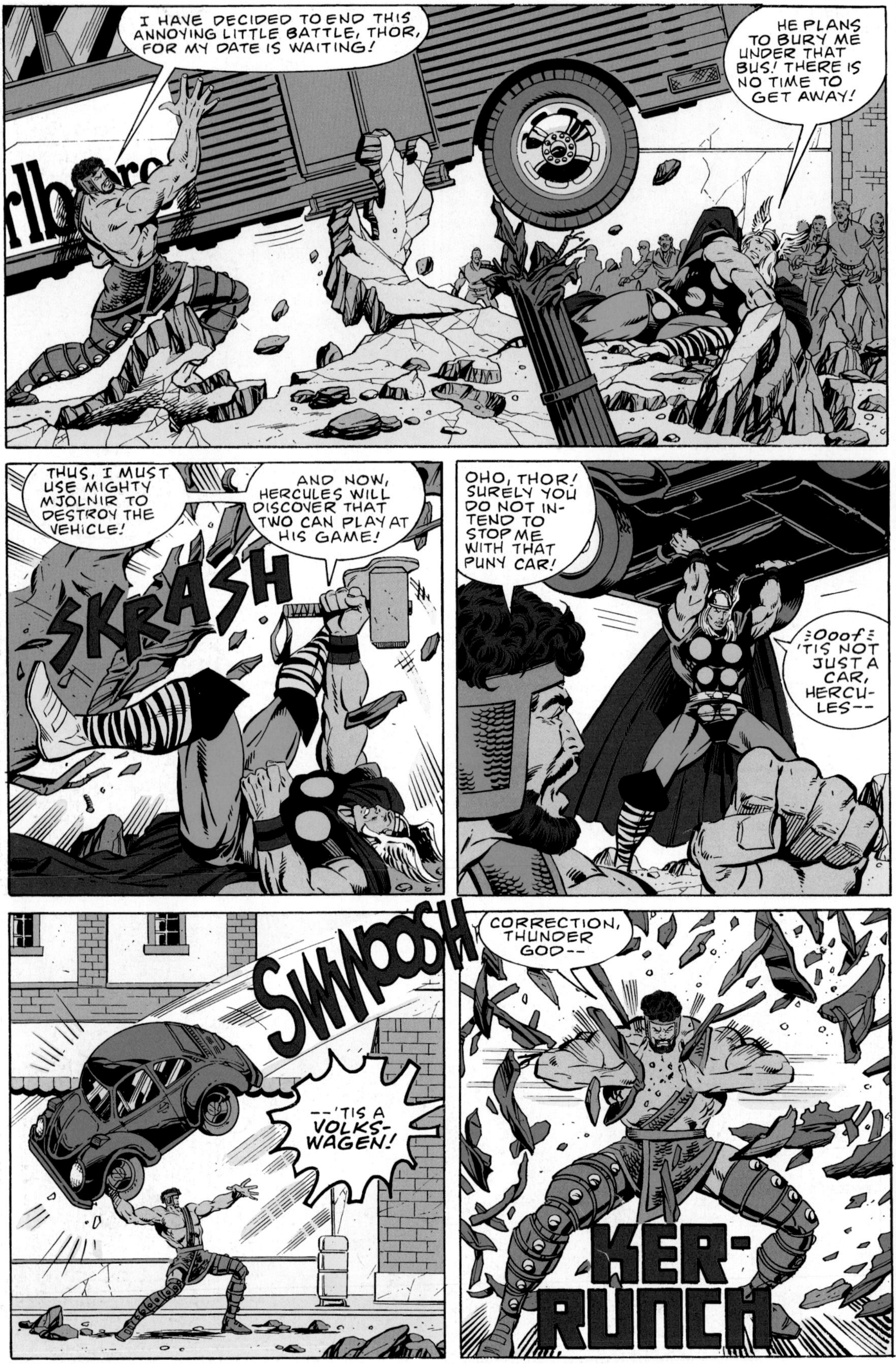
I HAVE DECIDED TO END THIS ANNOYING LITTLE BATTLE, THOR, FOR MY DATE IS WAITING!
HE PLANS TO BURY ME UNDER THAT BUS! THERE IS NO TIME TO GET AWAY!
THUS, I MUST USE MIGHTY MJOLNIR TO DESTROY THE VEHICLE!
AND NOW, HERCULES WILL DISCOVER THAT TWO CAN PLAY AT HIS GAME!
SKRASH
OHO, THOR! SURELY YOU DO NOT INTEND TO STOP ME WITH THAT PUNY CAR!
Ooof! 'TIS NOT JUST A CAR, HERCULES--
SWOOSH
--'TIS A VOLKSWAGEN!
CORRECTION, THUNDER GOD--
KER-RUNCH

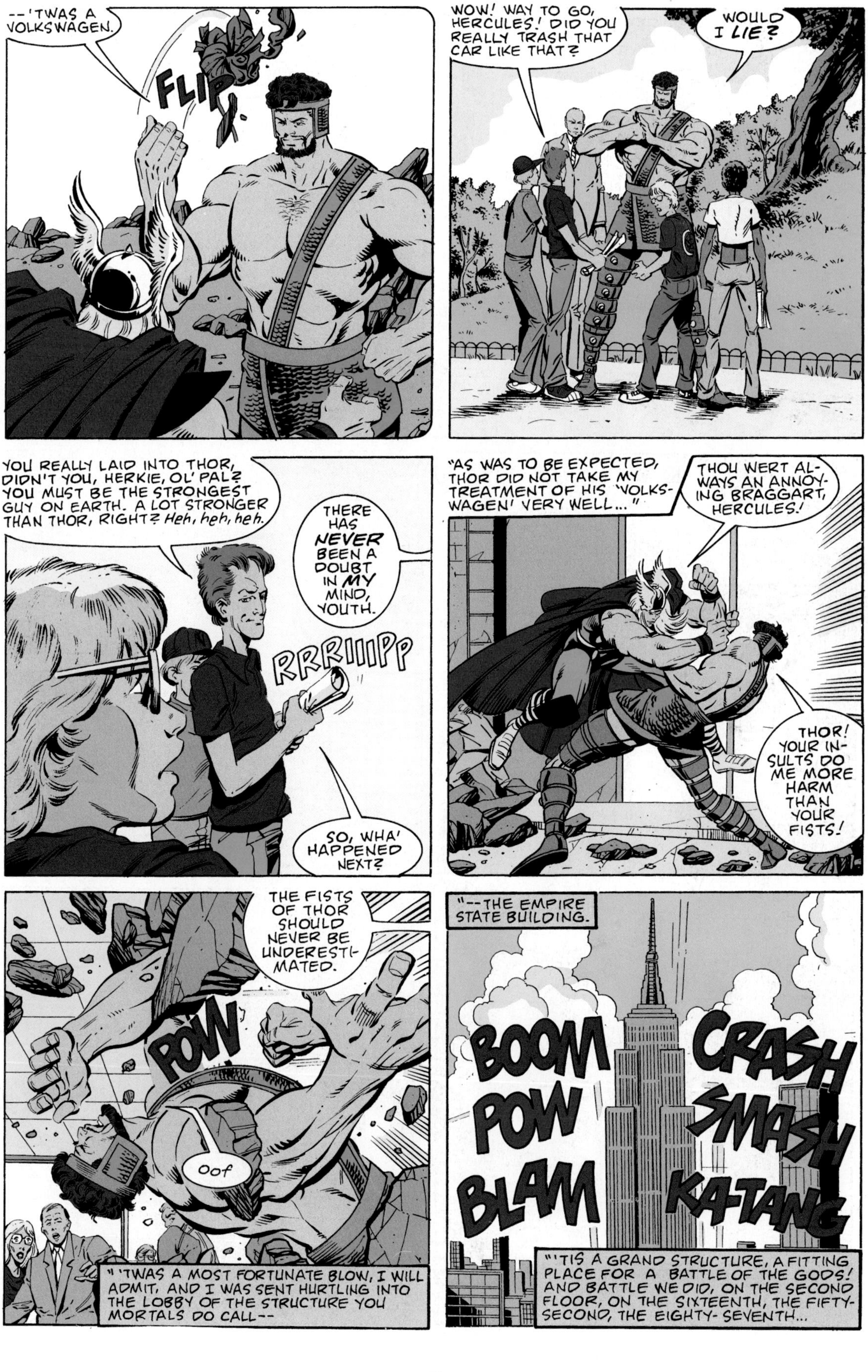
--'TWAS A VOLKSWAGEN.
FLIP
WOW! WAY TO GO, HERCULES! DID YOU REALLY TRASH THAT CAR LIKE THAT?
WOULD I LIE?
YOU REALLY LAID INTO THOR, DIDN'T YOU, HERKIE, OL' PAL? YOU MUST BE THE STRONGEST GUY ON EARTH. A LOT STRONGER THAN THOR, RIGHT? Heh, heh, heh.
THERE HAS NEVER BEEN A DOUBT IN MY MIND, YOUTH.
RRRIIIPP
SO, WHA' HAPPENED NEXT?
"AS WAS TO BE EXPECTED, THOR DID NOT TAKE MY TREATMENT OF HIS 'VOLKSWAGEN' VERY WELL..."
THOU WERT ALWAYS AN ANNOYING BRAGGART, HERCULES!
THOR! YOUR INSULTS DO ME MORE HARM THAN YOUR FISTS!
THE FISTS OF THOR SHOULD NEVER BE UNDERESTIMATED.
POW
Oof
"'TWAS A MOST FORTUNATE BLOW, I WILL ADMIT, AND I WAS SENT HURTLING INTO THE LOBBY OF THE STRUCTURE YOU MORTALS DO CALL--
"--THE EMPIRE STATE BUILDING.
BOOM
POW
BLAM
CRASH
SMASH
KATANG
"'TIS A GRAND STRUCTURE, A FITTING PLACE FOR A BATTLE OF THE GODS! AND BATTLE WE DID, ON THE SECOND FLOOR, ON THE SIXTEENTH, THE FIFTY-SECOND, THE EIGHTY-SEVENTH...

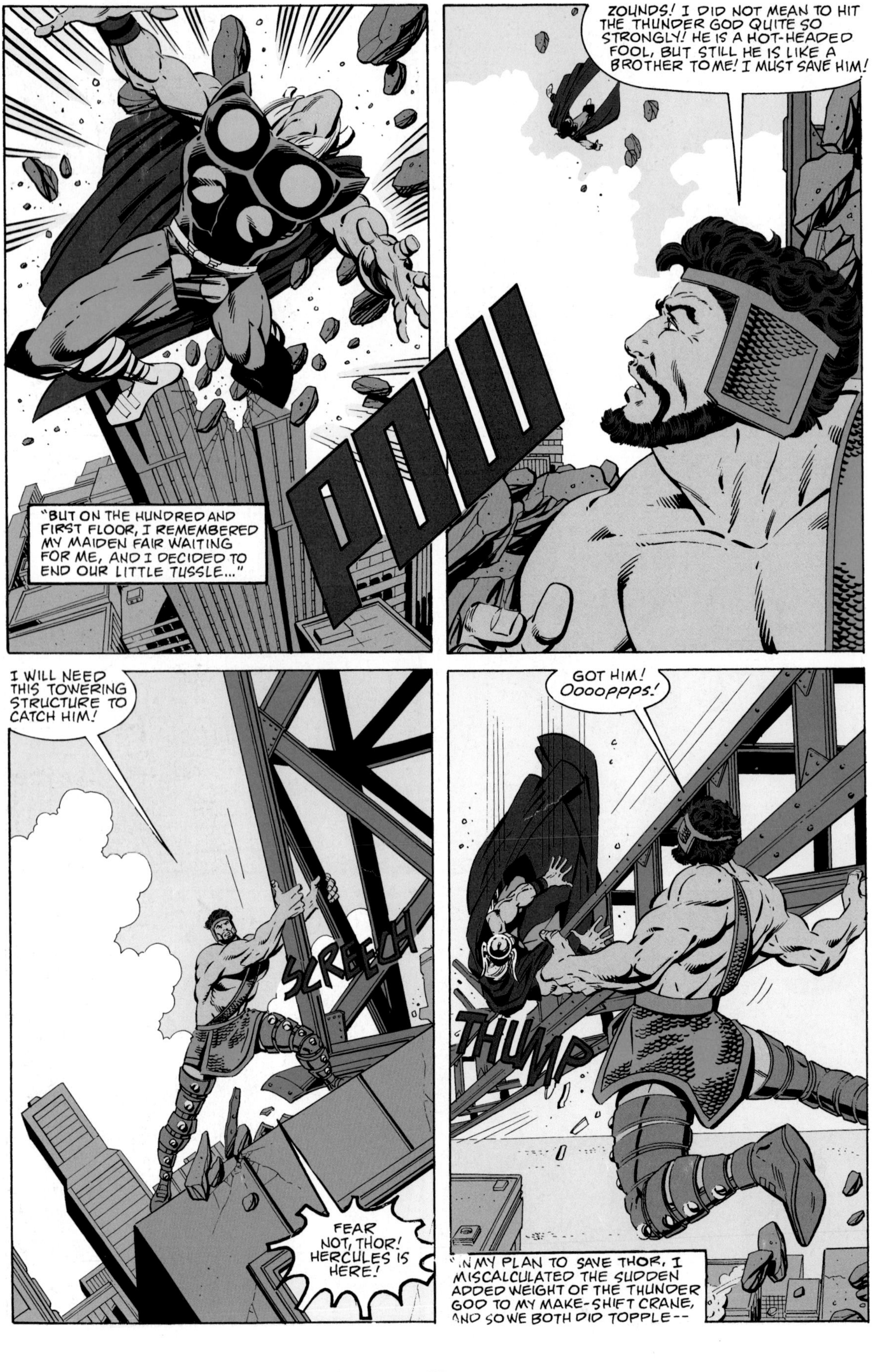
"BUT ON THE HUNDRED AND FIRST FLOOR, I REMEMBERED MY MAIDEN FAIR WAITING FOR ME, AND I DECIDED TO END OUR LITTLE TUSSLE..."
POW
ZOUNDS! I DID NOT MEAN TO HIT THE THUNDER GOD QUITE SO STRONGLY! HE IS A HOT-HEADED FOOL, BUT STILL HE IS LIKE A BROTHER TO ME! I MUST SAVE HIM!
I WILL NEED THIS TOWERING STRUCTURE TO CATCH HIM!
SCREECH
FEAR NOT, THOR! HERCULES IS HERE!
GOT HIM! Ooooppps!
THUMP
IN MY PLAN TO SAVE THOR, I MISCALCULATED THE SUDDEN ADDED WEIGHT OF THE THUNDER GOD TO MY MAKE-SHIFT CRANE, AND SO WE BOTH DID TOPPLE--

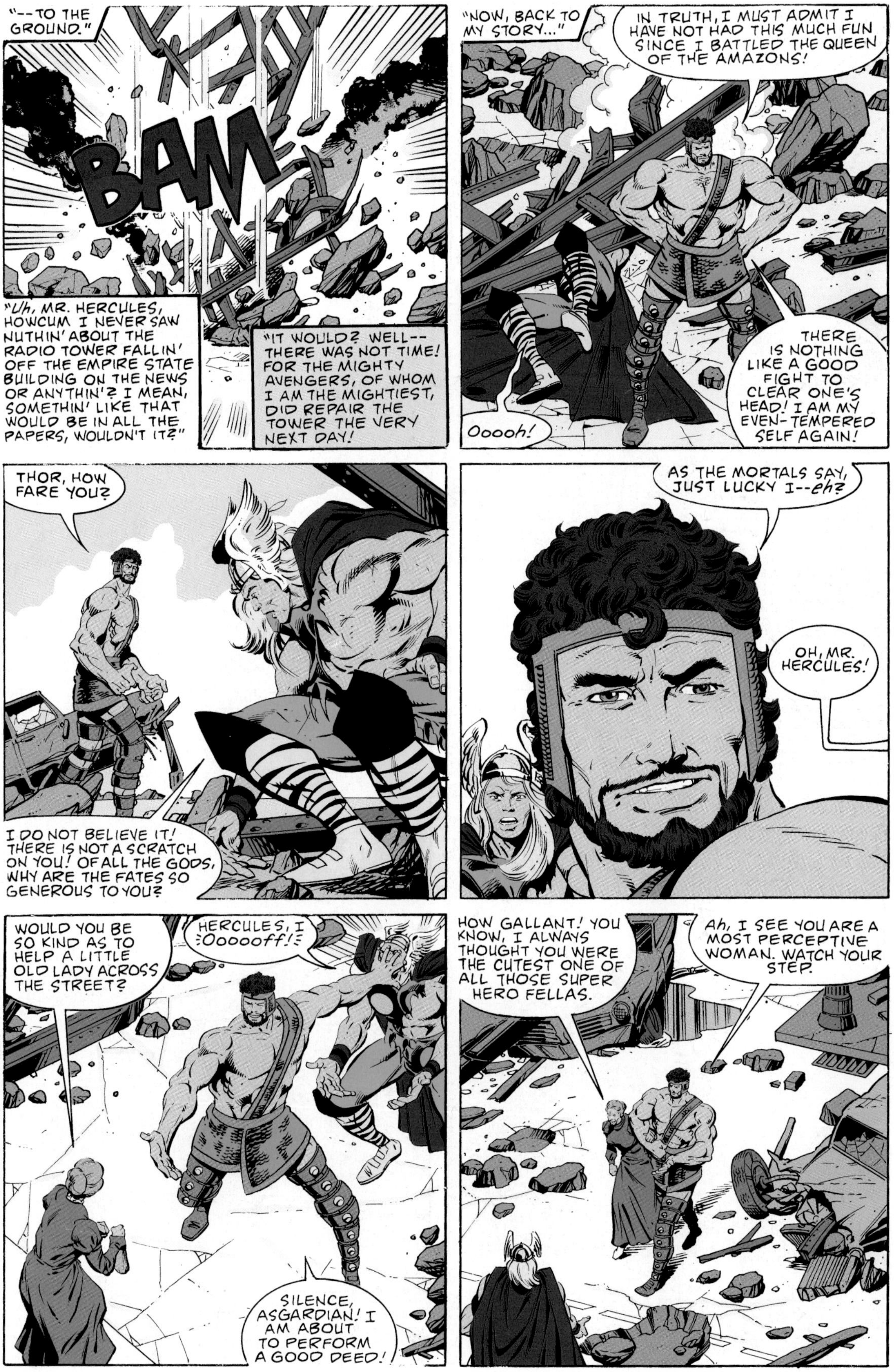
"--TO THE GROUND."
BAM
"Uh, MR. HERCULES, HOWCUM I NEVER SAW NUTHIN' ABOUT THE RADIO TOWER FALLIN' OFF THE EMPIRE STATE BUILDING ON THE NEWS OR ANYTHIN'? I MEAN, SOMETHIN' LIKE THAT WOULD BE IN ALL THE PAPERS, WOULDN'T IT?"
"IT WOULD? WELL-- THERE WAS NOT TIME! FOR THE MIGHTY AVENGERS, OF WHOM I AM THE MIGHTIEST, DID REPAIR THE TOWER THE VERY NEXT DAY!
"NOW, BACK TO MY STORY..."
IN TRUTH, I MUST ADMIT I HAVE NOT HAD THIS MUCH FUN SINCE I BATTLED THE QUEEN OF THE AMAZONS!
THERE IS NOTHING LIKE A GOOD FIGHT TO CLEAR ONE'S HEAD! I AM MY EVEN-TEMPERED SELF AGAIN!
Ooooh!
THOR, HOW FARE YOU?
I DO NOT BELIEVE IT! THERE IS NOT A SCRATCH ON YOU! OF ALL THE GODS, WHY ARE THE FATES SO GENEROUS TO YOU?
AS THE MORTALS SAY, JUST LUCKY I--eh?
OH, MR. HERCULES!
WOULD YOU BE SO KIND AS TO HELP A LITTLE OLD LADY ACROSS THE STREET?
HERCULES, I --Ooooooff!
SILENCE, ASGARDIAN! I AM ABOUT TO PERFORM A GOOD DEED!
HOW GALLANT! YOU KNOW, I ALWAYS THOUGHT YOU WERE THE CUTEST ONE OF ALL THOSE SUPER HERO FELLAS.
Ah, I SEE YOU ARE A MOST PERCEPTIVE WOMAN. WATCH YOUR STEP.

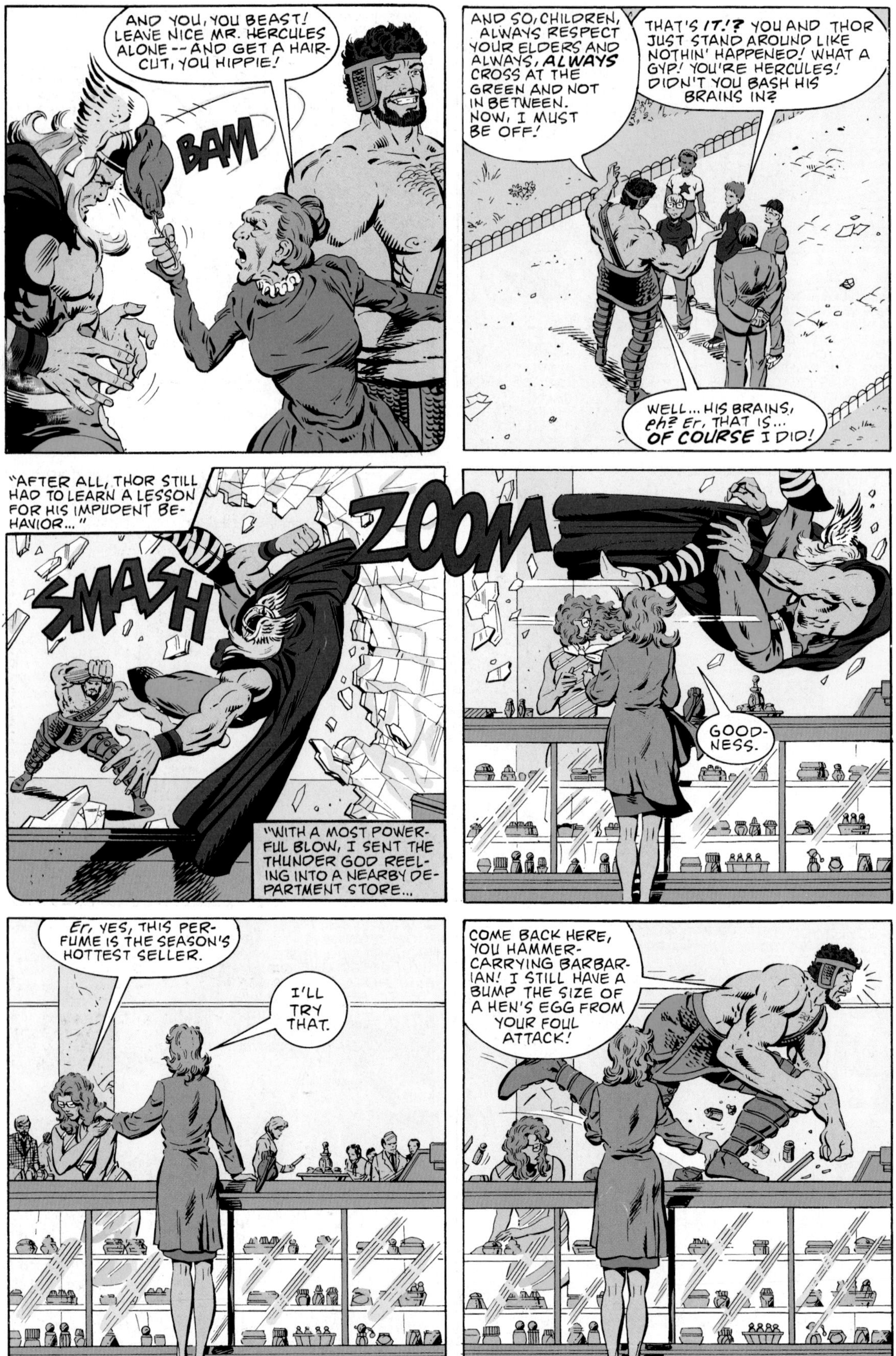
AND YOU, YOU BEAST! LEAVE NICE MR. HERCULES ALONE -- AND GET A HAIR-CUT, YOU HIPPIE!
BAM
AND SO, CHILDREN, ALWAYS RESPECT YOUR ELDERS AND ALWAYS, ALWAYS CROSS AT THE GREEN AND NOT IN BETWEEN. NOW, I MUST BE OFF!
THAT'S IT!? YOU AND THOR JUST STAND AROUND LIKE NOTHIN' HAPPENED! WHAT A GYP! YOU'RE HERCULES! DIDN'T YOU BASH HIS BRAINS IN?
WELL... HIS BRAINS, eh? Er, THAT IS... OF COURSE I DID!
"AFTER ALL, THOR STILL HAD TO LEARN A LESSON FOR HIS IMPUDENT BE-HAVIOR..."
ZOOM
SMASH
"WITH A MOST POWER-FUL BLOW, I SENT THE THUNDER GOD REEL-ING INTO A NEARBY DE-PARTMENT STORE...
GOOD-NESS.
Er, YES, THIS PER-FUME IS THE SEASON'S HOTTEST SELLER.
I'LL TRY THAT.
COME BACK HERE, YOU HAMMER-CARRYING BARBAR-IAN! I STILL HAVE A BUMP THE SIZE OF A HEN'S EGG FROM YOUR FOUL ATTACK!

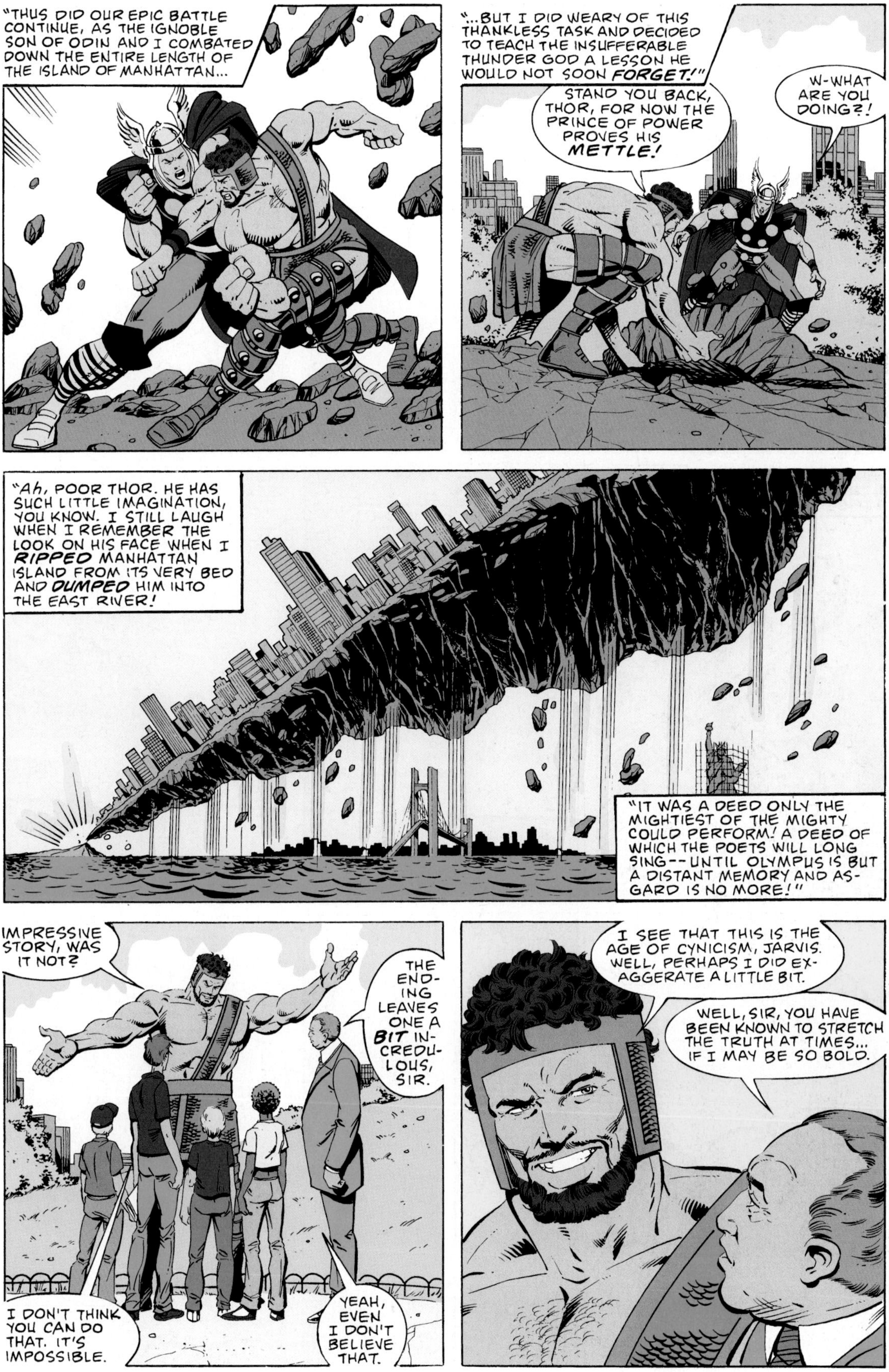
"THUS DID OUR EPIC BATTLE CONTINUE, AS THE IGNOBLE SON OF ODIN AND I COMBATED DOWN THE ENTIRE LENGTH OF THE ISLAND OF MANHATTAN...
"...BUT I DID WEARY OF THIS THANKLESS TASK AND DECIDED TO TEACH THE INSUFFERABLE THUNDER GOD A LESSON HE WOULD NOT SOON FORGET!"
STAND YOU BACK, THOR, FOR NOW THE PRINCE OF POWER PROVES HIS METTLE!
W-WHAT ARE YOU DOING?!
"Ah, POOR THOR. HE HAS SUCH LITTLE IMAGINATION, YOU KNOW. I STILL LAUGH WHEN I REMEMBER THE LOOK ON HIS FACE WHEN I RIPPED MANHATTAN ISLAND FROM ITS VERY BED AND DUMPED HIM INTO THE EAST RIVER!
"IT WAS A DEED ONLY THE MIGHTIEST OF THE MIGHTY COULD PERFORM! A DEED OF WHICH THE POETS WILL LONG SING--UNTIL OLYMPUS IS BUT A DISTANT MEMORY AND AS-GARD IS NO MORE!"
IMPRESSIVE STORY, WAS IT NOT?
THE END-ING LEAVES ONE A BIT IN-CREDU-LOUS, SIR.
I DON'T THINK YOU CAN DO THAT. IT'S IMPOSSIBLE.
YEAH, EVEN I DON'T BELIEVE THAT.
I SEE THAT THIS IS THE AGE OF CYNICISM, JARVIS. WELL, PERHAPS I DID EX-AGGERATE A LITTLE BIT.
WELL, SIR, YOU HAVE BEEN KNOWN TO STRETCH THE TRUTH AT TIMES... IF I MAY BE SO BOLD.

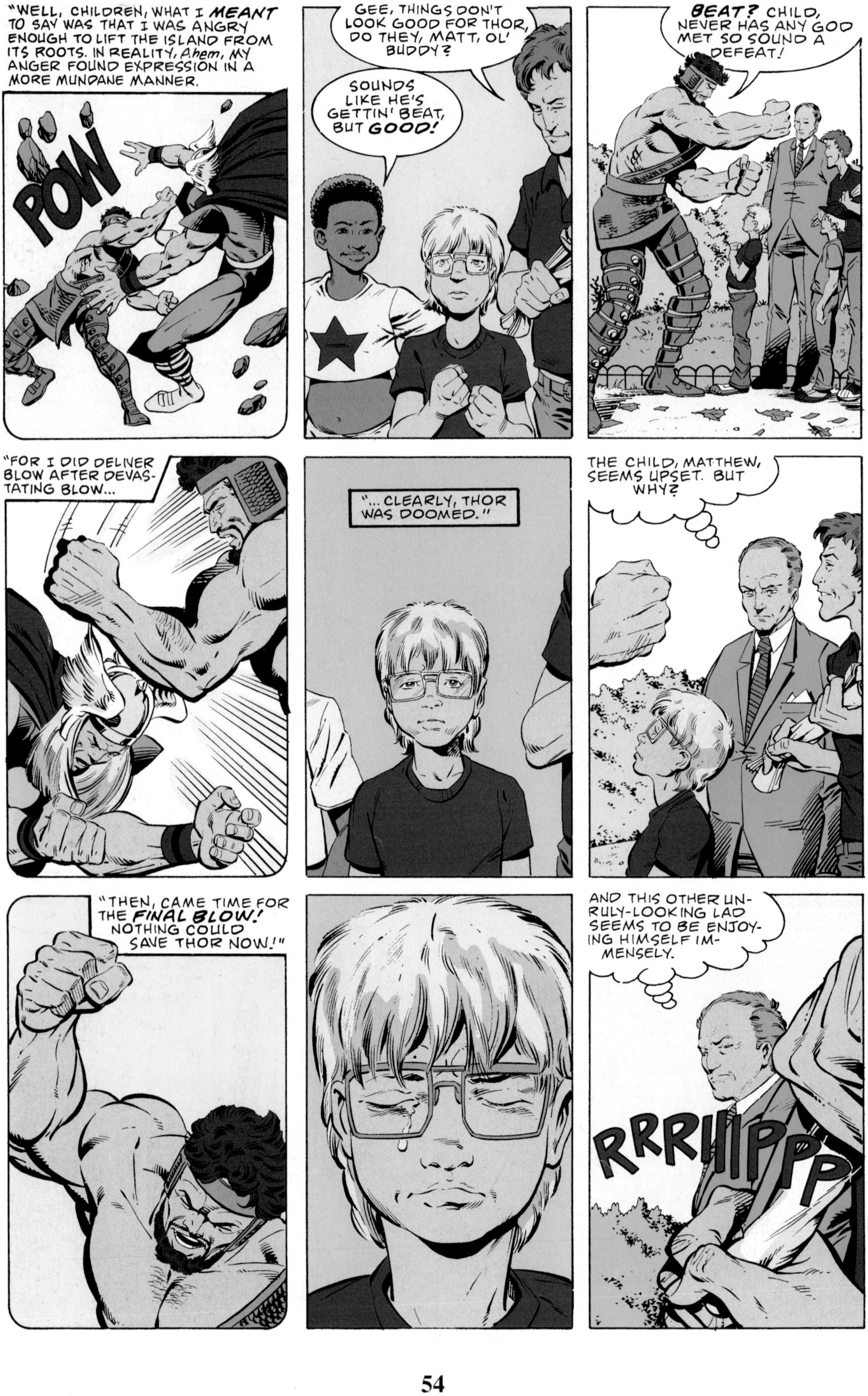
"WELL, CHILDREN, WHAT I MEANT TO SAY WAS THAT I WAS ANGRY ENOUGH TO LIFT THE ISLAND FROM ITS ROOTS. IN REALITY, Ahem, MY ANGER FOUND EXPRESSION IN A MORE MUNDANE MANNER.
POW
GEE, THINGS DON'T LOOK GOOD FOR THOR, DO THEY, MATT, OL' BUDDY?
SOUNDS LIKE HE'S GETTIN' BEAT, BUT GOOD!
BEAT? CHILD, NEVER HAS ANY GOD MET SO SOUND A DEFEAT!
"FOR I DID DELIVER BLOW AFTER DEVASTATING BLOW...
"...CLEARLY, THOR WAS DOOMED."
THE CHILD, MATTHEW, SEEMS UPSET. BUT WHY?
"THEN, CAME TIME FOR THE FINAL BLOW! NOTHING COULD SAVE THOR NOW!"
AND THIS OTHER UNRULY-LOOKING LAD SEEMS TO BE ENJOYING HIMSELF IMMENSELY.
RRRIIIPPP

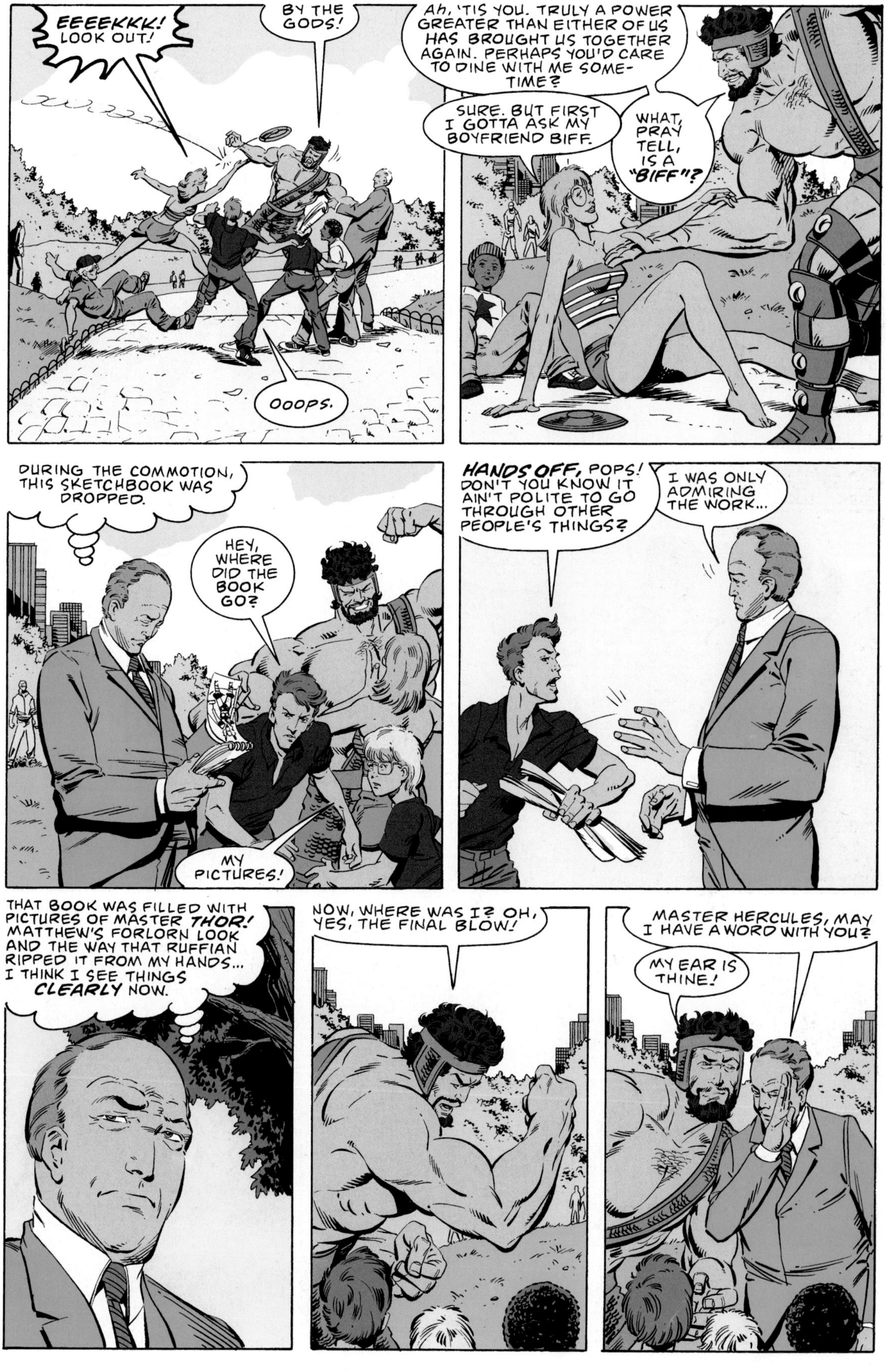
EEEEKKK! LOOK OUT!
BY THE GODS!
OOOPS.
AH, 'TIS YOU. TRULY A POWER GREATER THAN EITHER OF US HAS BROUGHT US TOGETHER AGAIN. PERHAPS YOU'D CARE TO DINE WITH ME SOMETIME?
SURE. BUT FIRST I GOTTA ASK MY BOYFRIEND BIFF.
WHAT, PRAY TELL, IS A "BIFF"?
DURING THE COMMOTION, THIS SKETCHBOOK WAS DROPPED.
HEY, WHERE DID THE BOOK GO?
MY PICTURES!
HANDS OFF, POPS! DON'T YOU KNOW IT AIN'T POLITE TO GO THROUGH OTHER PEOPLE'S THINGS?
I WAS ONLY ADMIRING THE WORK...
THAT BOOK WAS FILLED WITH PICTURES OF MASTER THOR! MATTHEW'S FORLORN LOOK AND THE WAY THAT RUFFIAN RIPPED IT FROM MY HANDS... I THINK I SEE THINGS CLEARLY NOW.
NOW, WHERE WAS I? OH, YES, THE FINAL BLOW!
MASTER HERCULES, MAY I HAVE A WORD WITH YOU?
MY EAR IS THINE!

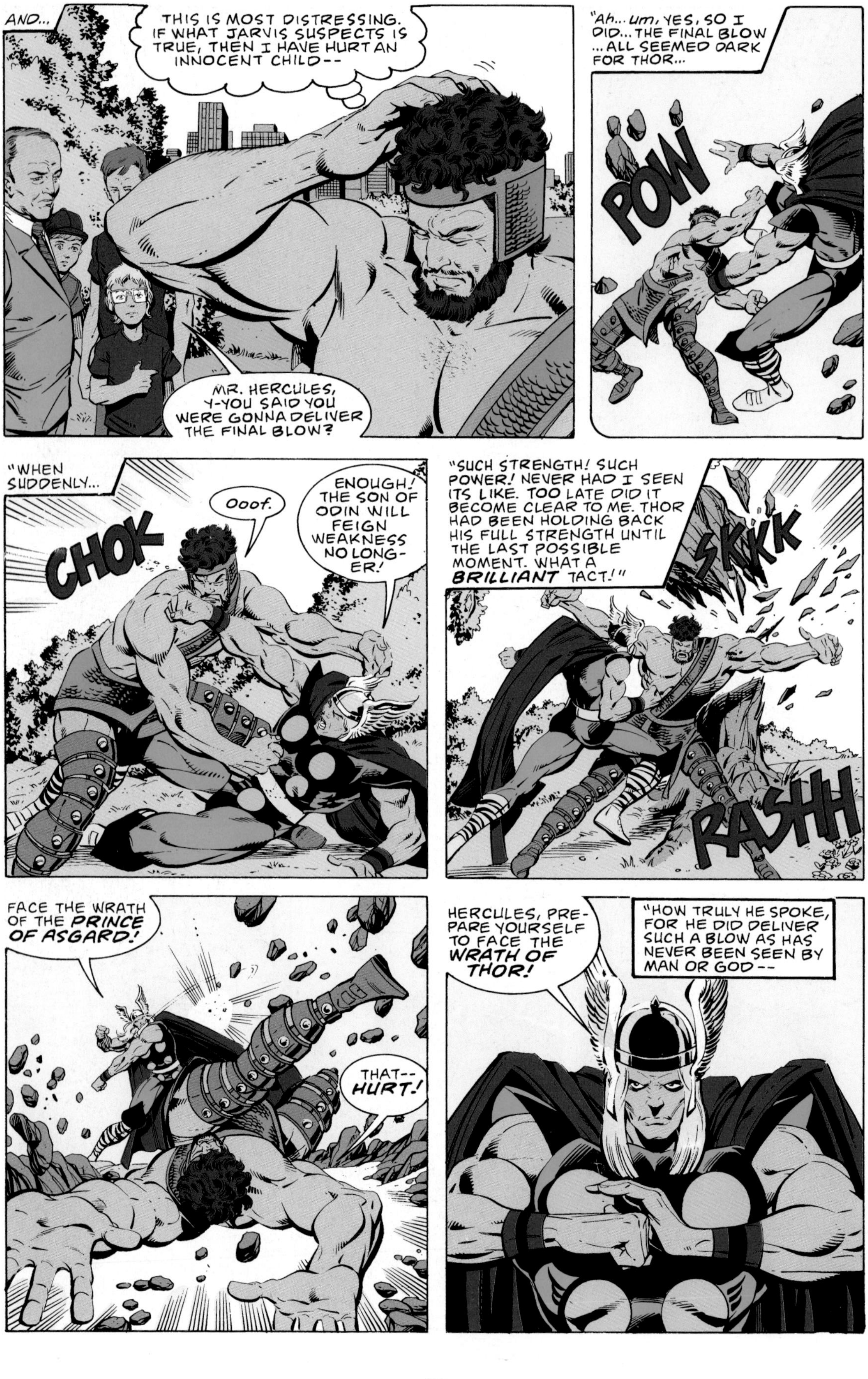
AND...
THIS IS MOST DISTRESSING. IF WHAT JARVIS SUSPECTS IS TRUE, THEN I HAVE HURT AN INNOCENT CHILD--
MR. HERCULES, Y-YOU SAID YOU WERE GONNA DELIVER THE FINAL BLOW?
"Ah... um, YES, SO I DID... THE FINAL BLOW ...ALL SEEMED DARK FOR THOR...
POW
"WHEN SUDDENLY...
CHOK
Ooof.
ENOUGH! THE SON OF ODIN WILL FEIGN WEAKNESS NO LONGER!
"SUCH STRENGTH! SUCH POWER! NEVER HAD I SEEN ITS LIKE. TOO LATE DID IT BECOME CLEAR TO ME. THOR HAD BEEN HOLDING BACK HIS FULL STRENGTH UNTIL THE LAST POSSIBLE MOMENT. WHAT A BRILLIANT TACT!"
SKKK
RASHH
FACE THE WRATH OF THE PRINCE OF ASGARD!
THAT-- HURT!
HERCULES, PREPARE YOURSELF TO FACE THE WRATH OF THOR!
"HOW TRULY HE SPOKE, FOR HE DID DELIVER SUCH A BLOW AS HAS NEVER BEEN SEEN BY MAN OR GOD--

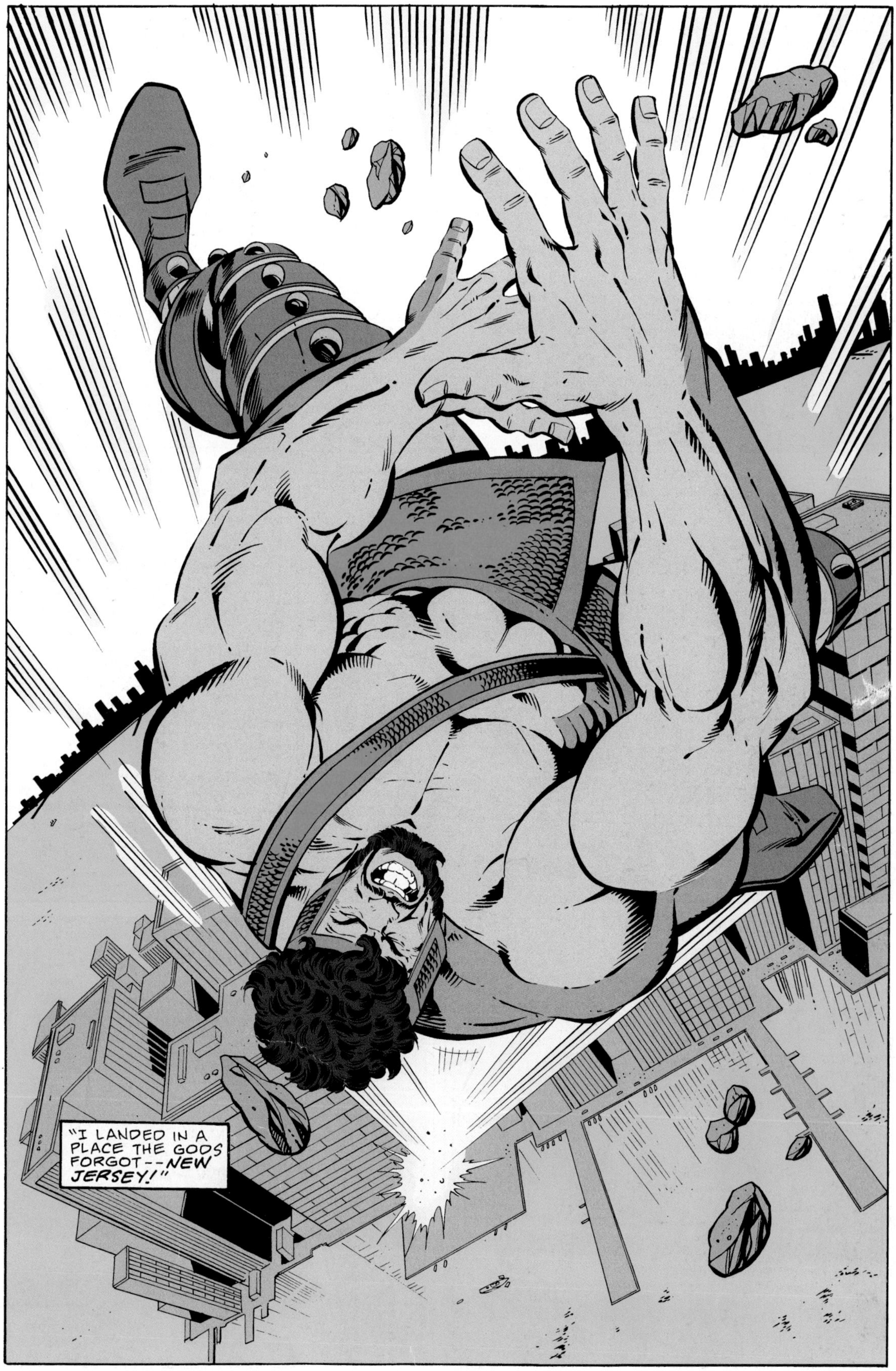
"I LANDED IN A PLACE THE GODS FORGOT--NEW JERSEY!"

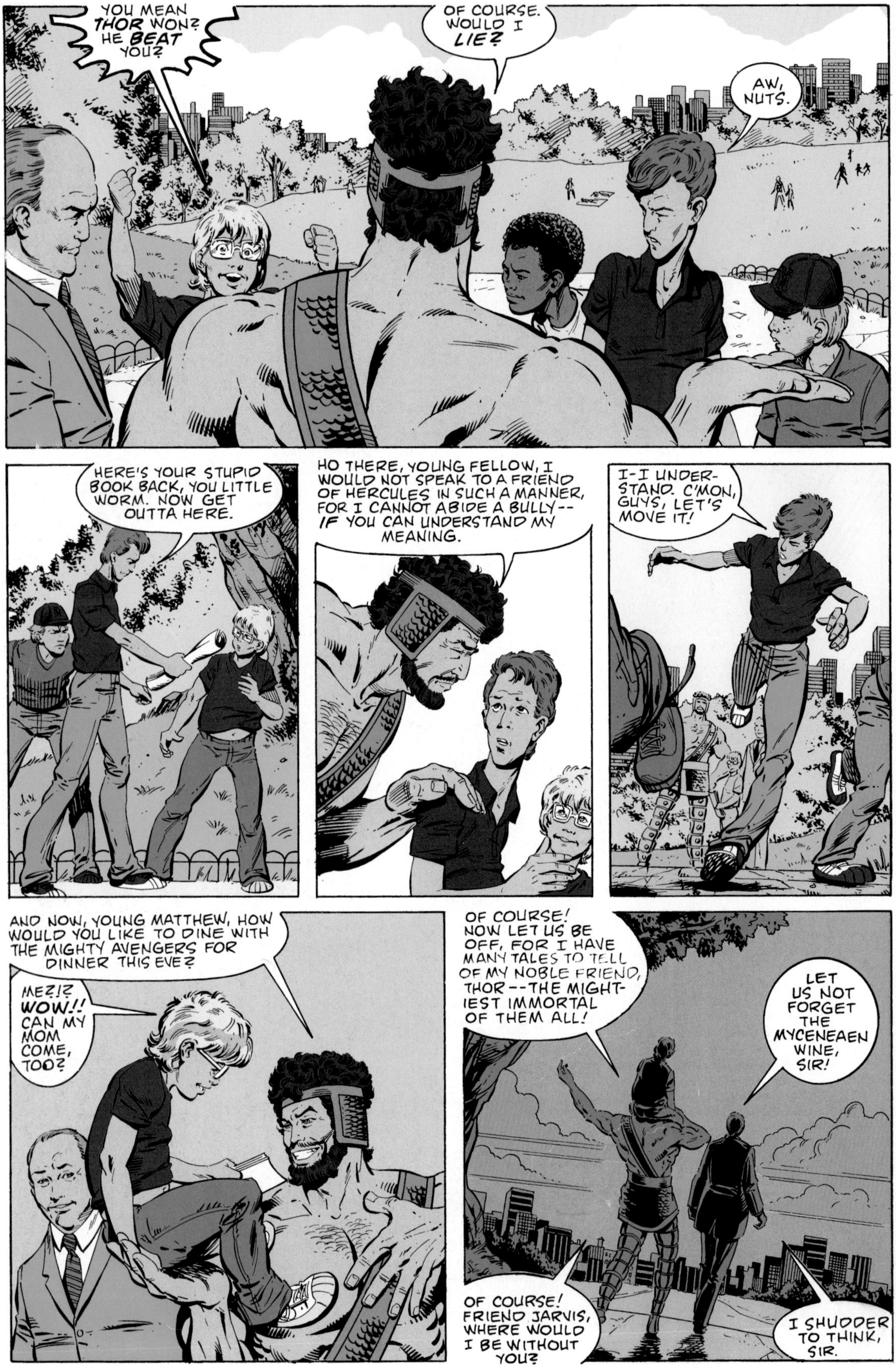
YOU MEAN THOR WON? HE BEAT YOU?
OF COURSE. WOULD I LIE?
AW, NUTS.
HERE'S YOUR STUPID BOOK BACK, YOU LITTLE WORM. NOW GET OUTTA HERE.
HO THERE, YOUNG FELLOW, I WOULD NOT SPEAK TO A FRIEND OF HERCULES IN SUCH A MANNER, FOR I CANNOT ABIDE A BULLY-- IF YOU CAN UNDERSTAND MY MEANING.
I-I UNDER-STAND. C'MON, GUYS, LET'S MOVE IT!
AND NOW, YOUNG MATTHEW, HOW WOULD YOU LIKE TO DINE WITH THE MIGHTY AVENGERS FOR DINNER THIS EVE?
ME?!? WOW!! CAN MY MOM COME, TOO?
OF COURSE! NOW LET US BE OFF, FOR I HAVE MANY TALES TO TELL OF MY NOBLE FRIEND, THOR--THE MIGHT-IEST IMMORTAL OF THEM ALL!
LET US NOT FORGET THE MYCENEAEN WINE, SIR!
OF COURSE! FRIEND JARVIS, WHERE WOULD I BE WITHOUT YOU?
I SHUDDER TO THINK, SIR.

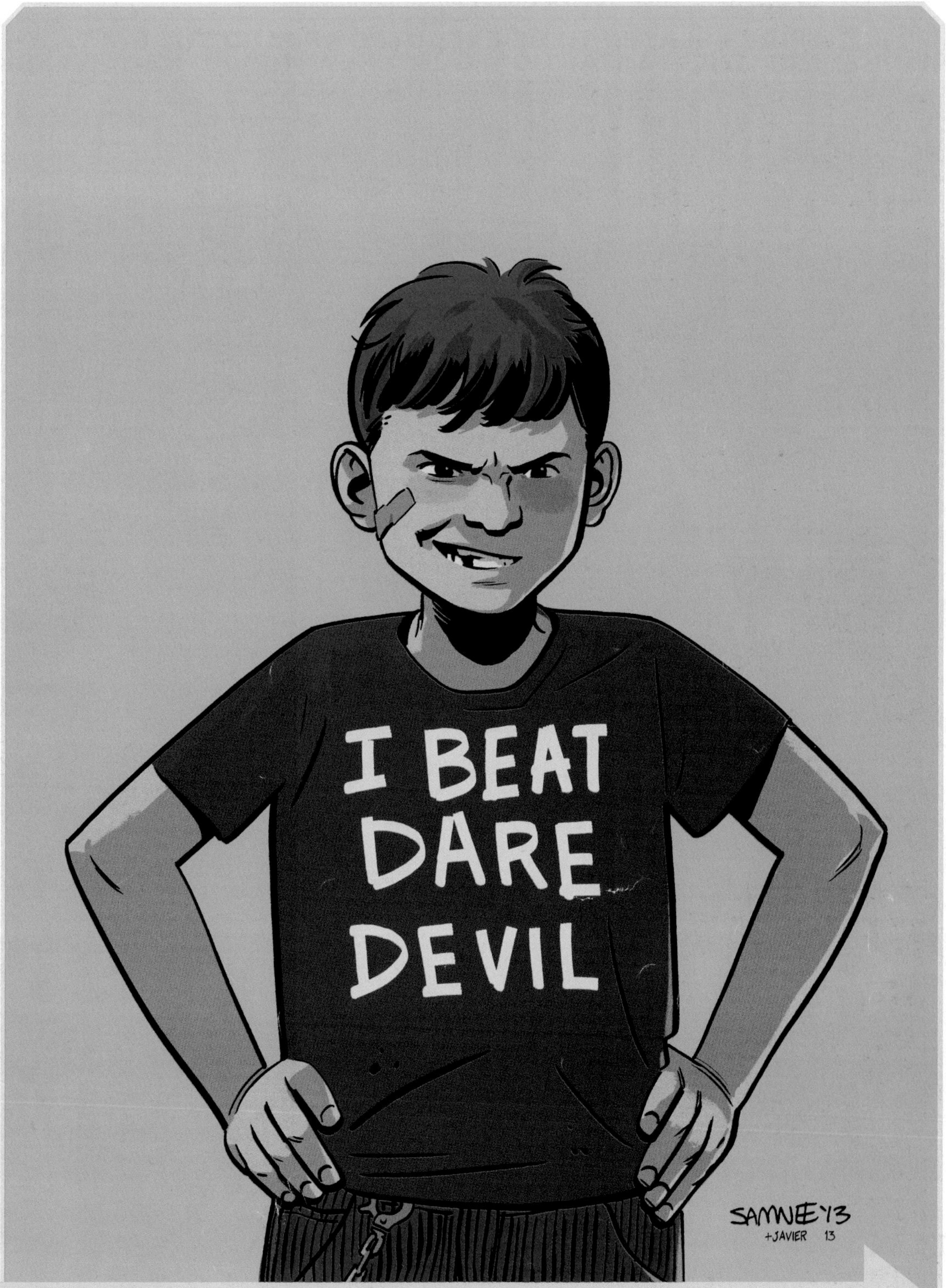
I BEAT DARE DEVIL
SAMNEE '13
+JAVIER 13

DAREDEVIL #28

DAILY ⌇ BUGLE®

NEW YORK'S FINEST DAILY NEWSPAPER

SINCE 1897
$1.00 (in NYC)
$1.50 (outside city)

INSIDE: SPIDER-SLAYER TO BE EXECUTED ABOARD THE RAFT! WHERE ARE THE FANTASTIC FOUR? NEW NOVA! NEW WARRIOR?

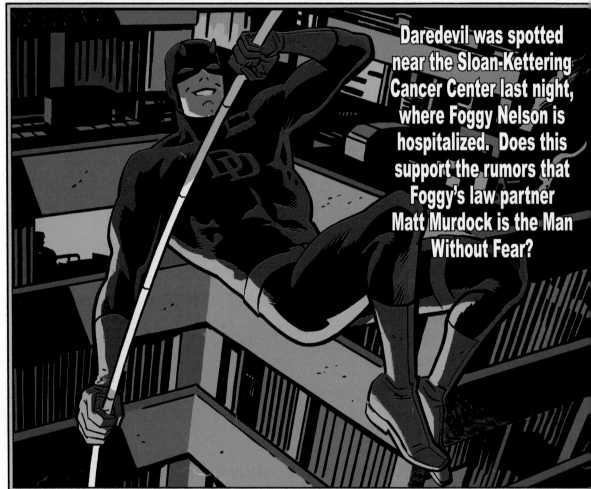

Daredevil was spotted near the Sloan-Kettering Cancer Center last night, where Foggy Nelson is hospitalized. Does this support the rumors that Foggy's law partner Matt Murdock is the Man Without Fear?

HELP WANTED

The Law Firm of Nelson and Murdock seeks an experienced trial lawyer to temporarily handle Mr. Nelson's caseload while he is out for treatment. Min. 5 Years experience required. Public defense background a plus. Must have excellent and verifiable references. Those interested in working with Daredevil need not apply.

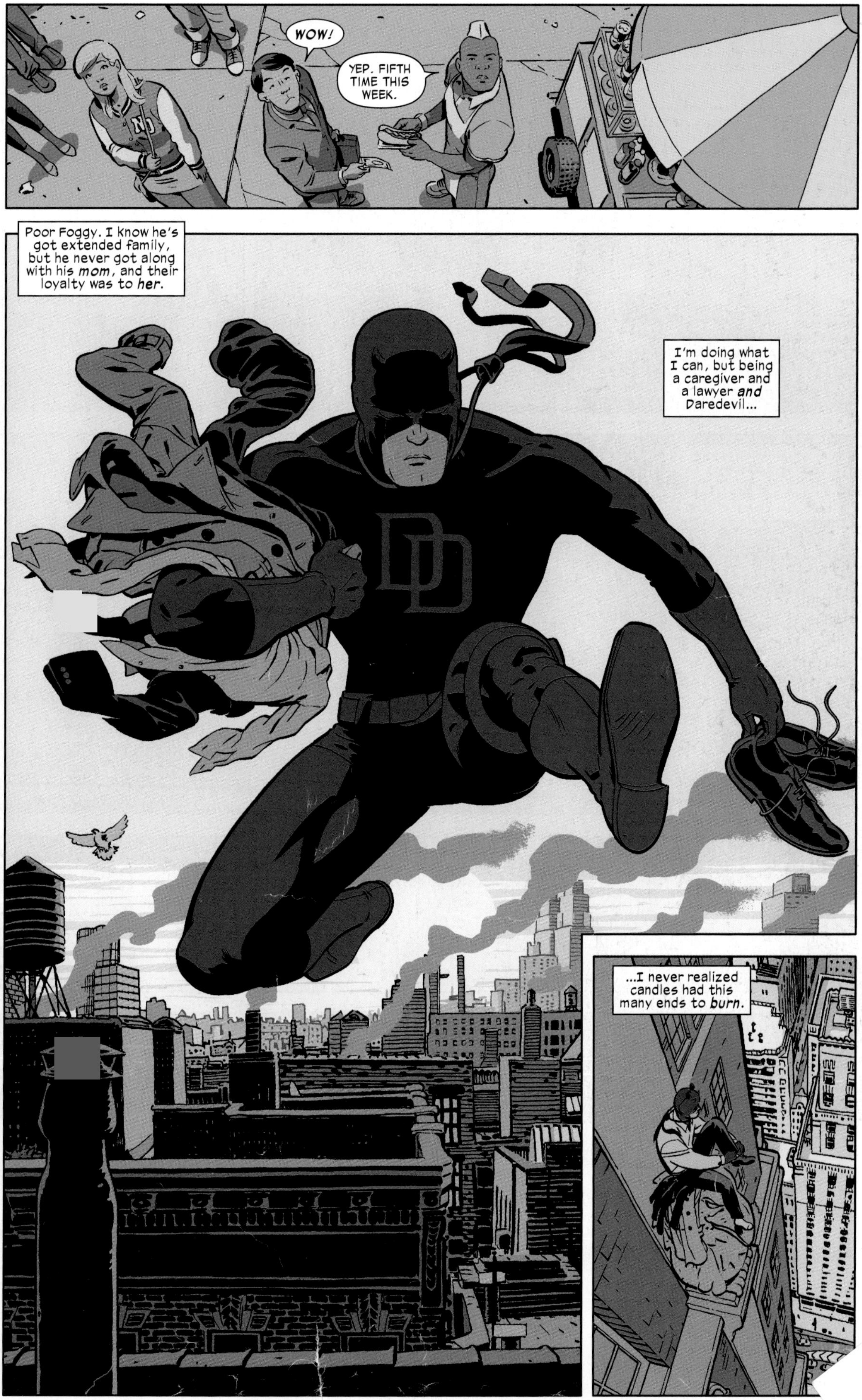
WOW!
YEP. FIFTH TIME THIS WEEK.
Poor Foggy. I know he's got extended family, but he never got along with his *mom*, and their loyalty was to *her*.
I'm doing what I can, but being a caregiver and a lawyer *and* Daredevil...
...I never realized candles had this many ends to *burn*.

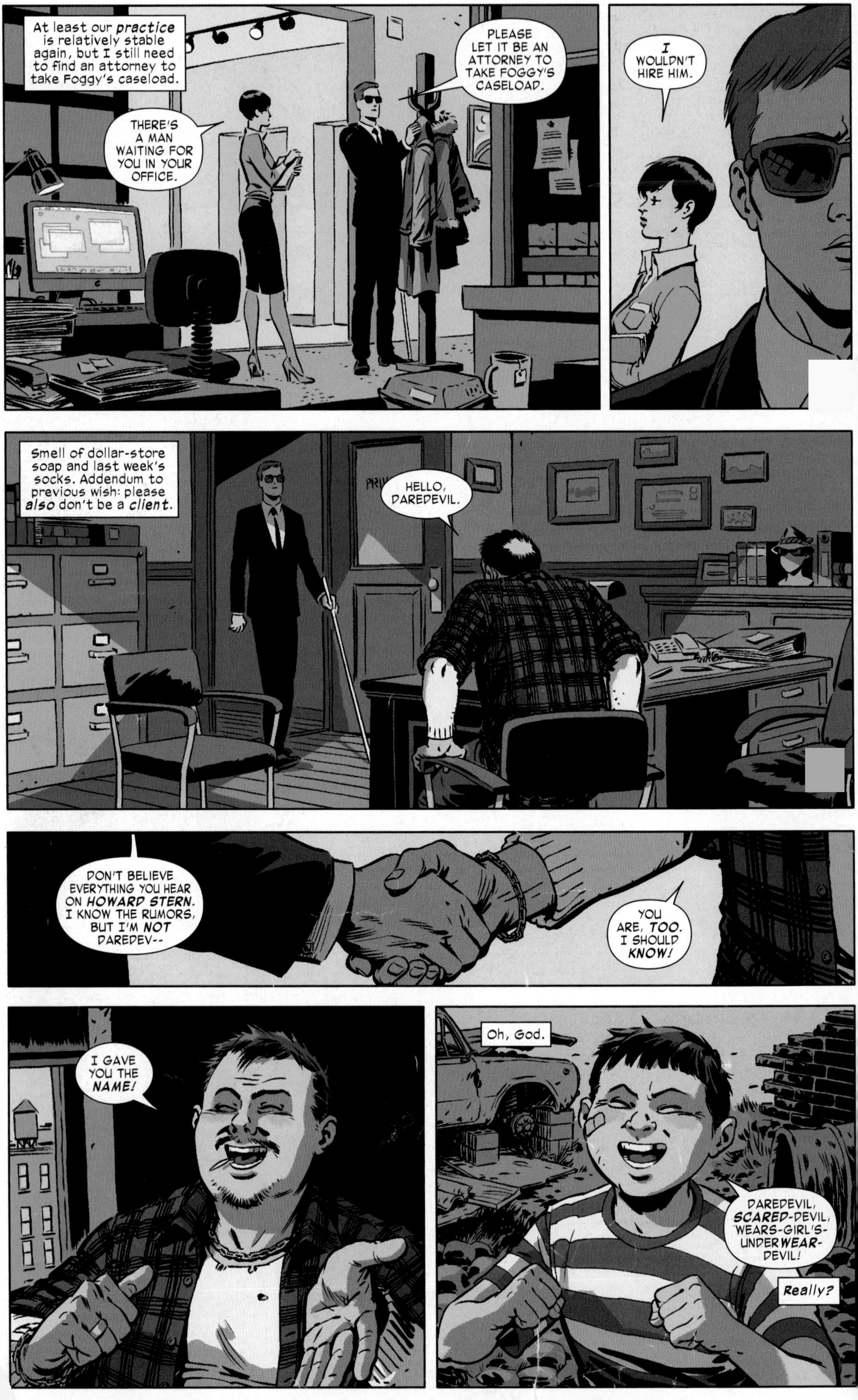
At least our *practice* is relatively stable again, but I still need to find an attorney to take Foggy's caseload.
THERE'S A MAN WAITING FOR YOU IN YOUR OFFICE.
PLEASE LET IT BE AN ATTORNEY TO TAKE FOGGY'S CASELOAD.
I WOULDN'T HIRE HIM.
Smell of dollar-store soap and last week's socks. Addendum to previous wish: please *also* don't be a *client*.
HELLO, DAREDEVIL.
DON'T BELIEVE EVERYTHING YOU HEAR ON ***HOWARD STERN***. I KNOW THE RUMORS, BUT I'M ***NOT*** DAREDEV--
YOU ARE, ***TOO***. I SHOULD ***KNOW!***
I GAVE YOU THE ***NAME!***
Oh, God.
DAREDEVIL, ***SCARED***-DEVIL, WEARS-GIRL'S-UNDER***WEAR***-DEVIL!
Really?

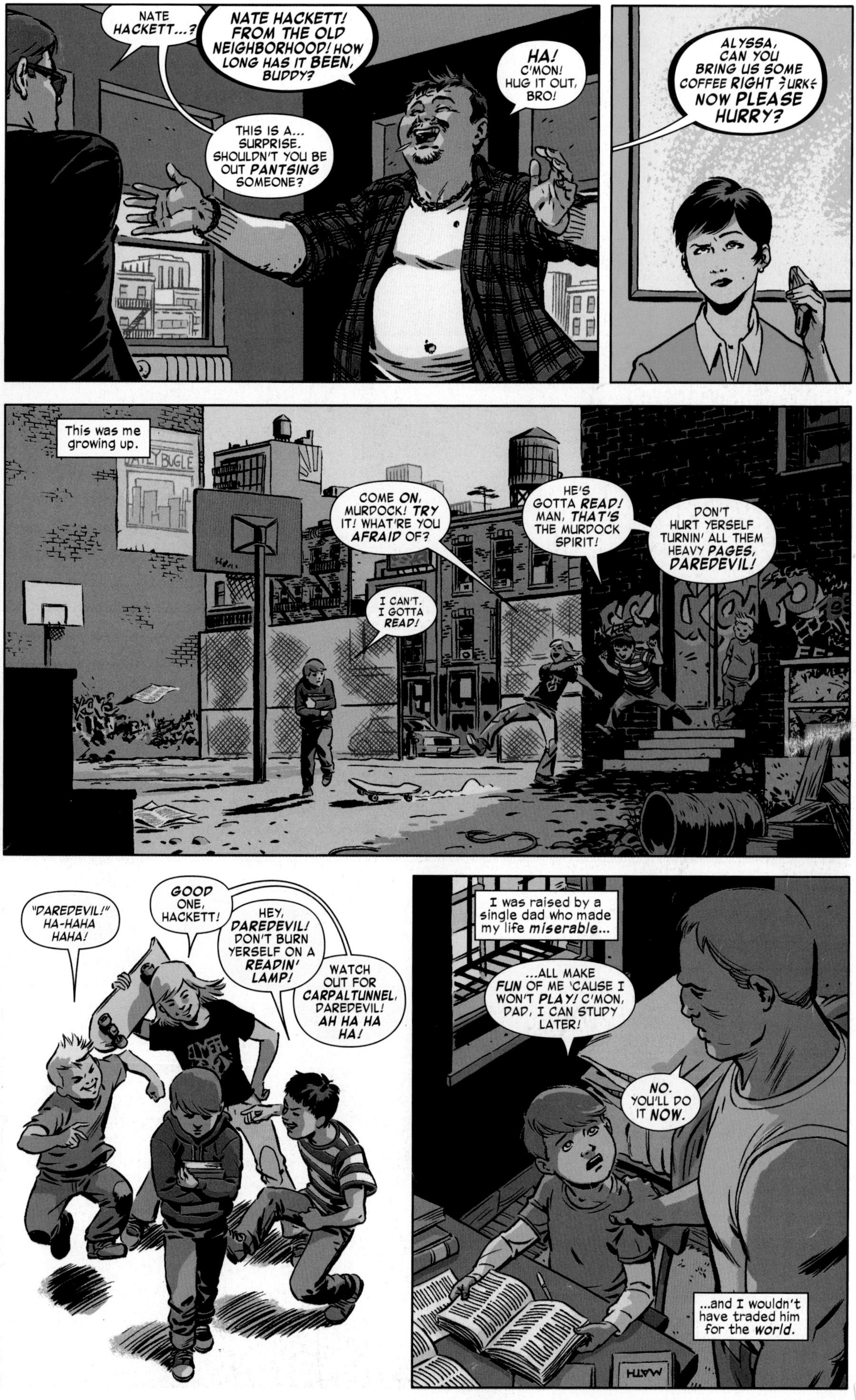
NATE HACKETT...?
NATE HACKETT! FROM THE OLD NEIGHBORHOOD! HOW LONG HAS IT BEEN, BUDDY?
THIS IS A... SURPRISE. SHOULDN'T YOU BE OUT PANTSING SOMEONE?
HA! C'MON! HUG IT OUT, BRO!
ALYSSA, CAN YOU BRING US SOME COFFEE RIGHT ≯URK≮ NOW PLEASE HURRY?
This was me growing up.
COME ON, MURDOCK! TRY IT! WHAT'RE YOU AFRAID OF?
I CAN'T. I GOTTA READ!
HE'S GOTTA READ! MAN, THAT'S THE MURDOCK SPIRIT!
DON'T HURT YERSELF TURNIN' ALL THEM HEAVY PAGES, DAREDEVIL!
"DAREDEVIL!" HA-HAHA HAHA!
GOOD ONE, HACKETT!
HEY, DAREDEVIL! DON'T BURN YERSELF ON A READIN' LAMP!
WATCH OUT FOR CARPALTUNNEL, DAREDEVIL! AH HA HA HA!
I was raised by a single dad who made my life miserable...
...ALL MAKE FUN OF ME 'CAUSE I WON'T PLAY! C'MON, DAD, I CAN STUDY LATER!
NO. YOU'LL DO IT NOW.
...and I wouldn't have traded him for the world.
MATH

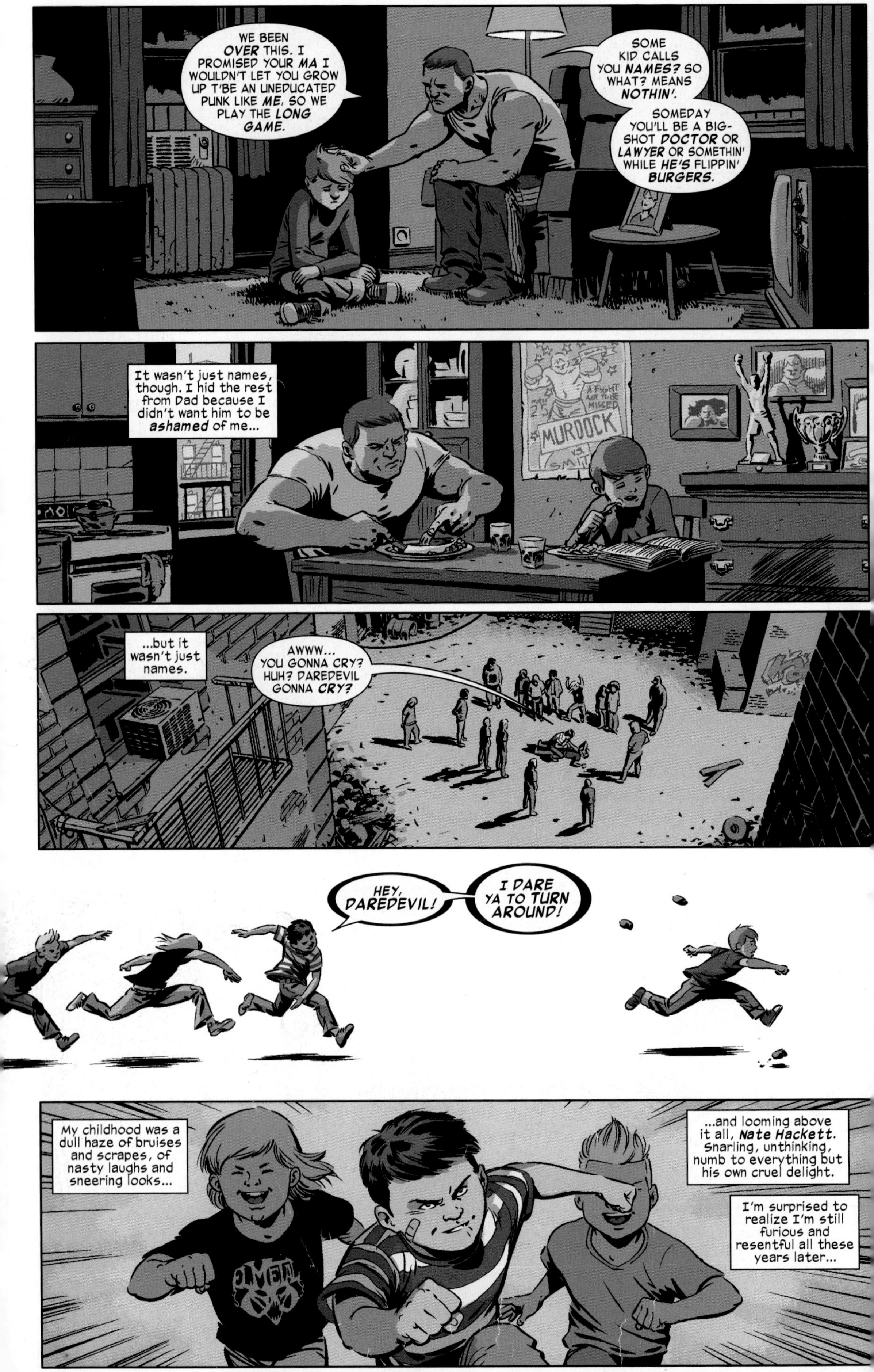

WE BEEN OVER THIS. I PROMISED YOUR MA I WOULDN'T LET YOU GROW UP T'BE AN UNEDUCATED PUNK LIKE ME, SO WE PLAY THE LONG GAME.
SOME KID CALLS YOU NAMES? SO WHAT? MEANS NOTHIN'.
SOMEDAY YOU'LL BE A BIG-SHOT DOCTOR OR LAWYER OR SOMETHIN' WHILE HE'S FLIPPIN' BURGERS.
It wasn't just names, though. I hid the rest from Dad because I didn't want him to be ashamed of me...
A FIGHT NOT TO BE MISSED
MURDOCK VS. SMIT
...but it wasn't just names.
AWWW... YOU GONNA CRY? HUH? DAREDEVIL GONNA CRY?
HEY, DAREDEVIL!
I DARE YA TO TURN AROUND!
My childhood was a dull haze of bruises and scrapes, of nasty laughs and sneering looks...
...and looming above it all, Nate Hackett. Snarling, unthinking, numb to everything but his own cruel delight.
I'm surprised to realize I'm still furious and resentful all these years later...

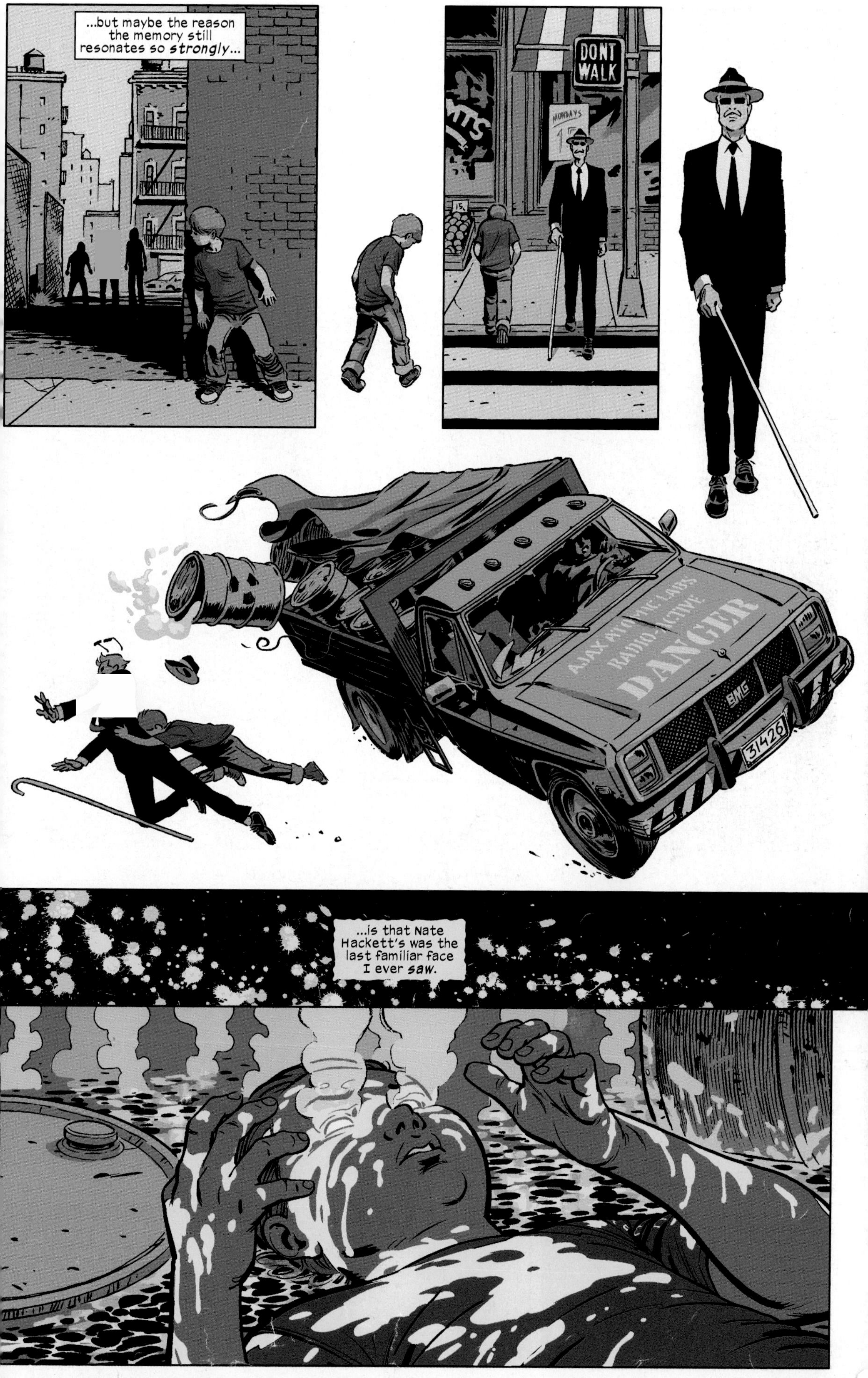
...but maybe the reason the memory still resonates so *strongly*...
DONT WALK
MONDAYS
AJAX ATOMIC LABS
RADIO-ACTIVE
DANGER
BMG
31426
...is that Nate Hackett's was the last familiar face I ever *saw*.

SO, TURNS OUT I NEED YOUR *EAR*, DAREDEV--

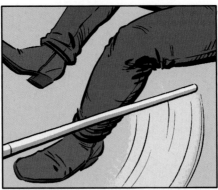

WHOMP

YOU--OF *ALL PEOPLE*-- DO NOT *EVER* GET TO CALL ME THAT.

I--I-- LOOK, I KNOW WE WEREN'T *CLOSE*, BUT--

"*BUT?*"

OH, *FINISH*. I CAN'T *WAIT* TO HEAR WHAT COMES AFTER "*BUT.*"

--BUT IT'S NOT LIKE *YOU* WERE THE EASIEST KID TO LIKE.

WAIT. *WHAT?*

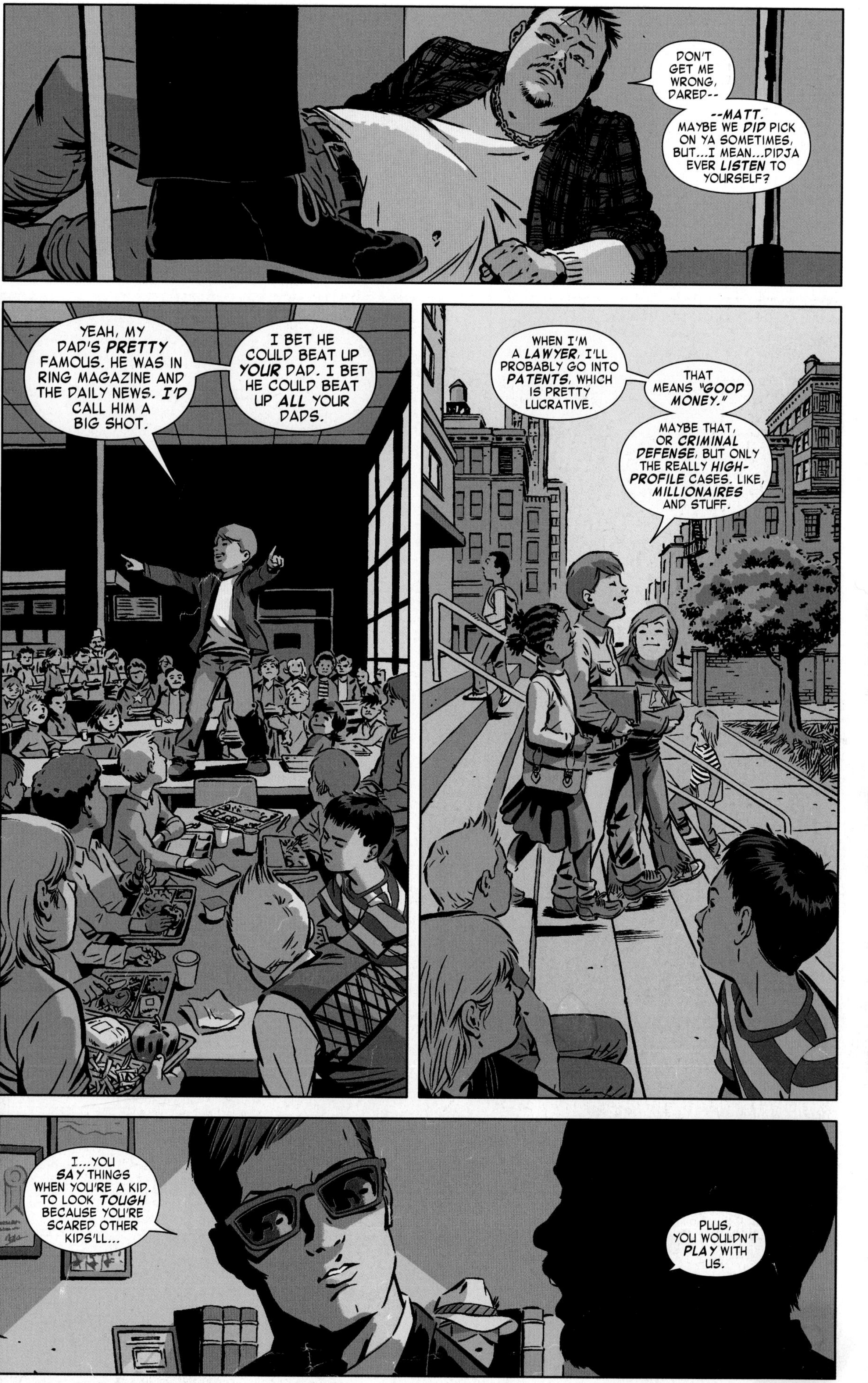

DON'T GET ME WRONG, DARED--
--MATT. MAYBE WE DID PICK ON YA SOMETIMES, BUT...I MEAN...DIDJA EVER LISTEN TO YOURSELF?
YEAH, MY DAD'S PRETTY FAMOUS. HE WAS IN RING MAGAZINE AND THE DAILY NEWS. I'D CALL HIM A BIG SHOT.
I BET HE COULD BEAT UP YOUR DAD. I BET HE COULD BEAT UP ALL YOUR DADS.
WHEN I'M A LAWYER, I'LL PROBABLY GO INTO PATENTS, WHICH IS PRETTY LUCRATIVE.
THAT MEANS "GOOD MONEY."
MAYBE THAT, OR CRIMINAL DEFENSE, BUT ONLY THE REALLY HIGH-PROFILE CASES. LIKE, MILLIONAIRES AND STUFF.
I...YOU SAY THINGS WHEN YOU'RE A KID. TO LOOK TOUGH BECAUSE YOU'RE SCARED OTHER KIDS'LL...
PLUS, YOU WOULDN'T PLAY WITH US.

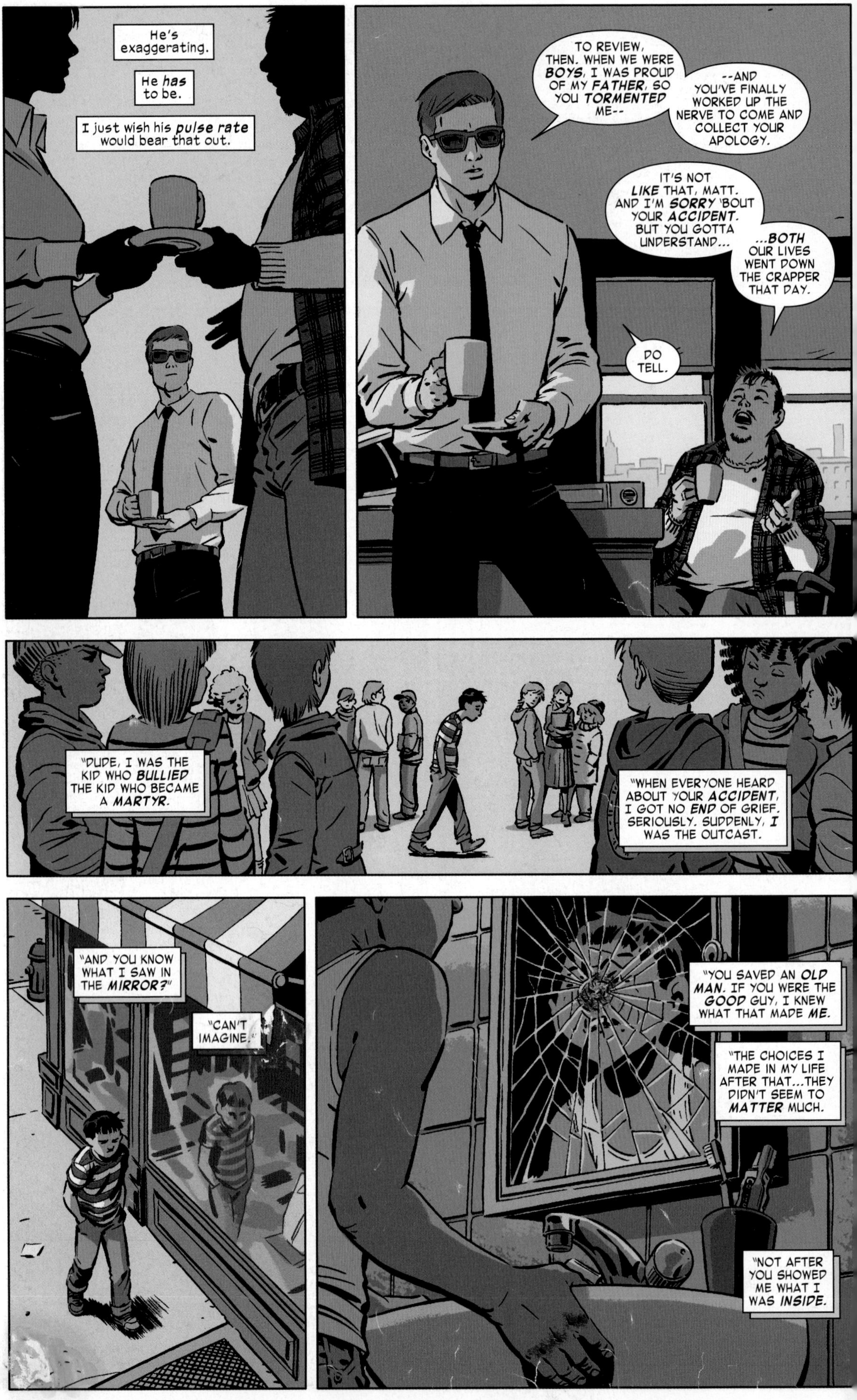

He's exaggerating.
He *has* to be.
I just wish his *pulse rate* would bear that out.
TO REVIEW, THEN. WHEN WE WERE *BOYS*, I WAS PROUD OF MY *FATHER*, SO YOU *TORMENTED* ME--
--AND YOU'VE FINALLY WORKED UP THE NERVE TO COME AND COLLECT YOUR APOLOGY.
IT'S NOT *LIKE* THAT, MATT. AND I'M *SORRY* 'BOUT YOUR *ACCIDENT*. BUT YOU GOTTA UNDERSTAND...
...*BOTH* OUR LIVES WENT DOWN THE CRAPPER THAT DAY.
DO TELL.
"DUDE, I WAS THE KID WHO *BULLIED* THE KID WHO BECAME A *MARTYR*.
"WHEN EVERYONE HEARD ABOUT YOUR *ACCIDENT*, I GOT NO *END* OF GRIEF. SERIOUSLY. SUDDENLY, *I* WAS THE OUTCAST.
"AND YOU KNOW WHAT I SAW IN THE *MIRROR?*"
"CAN'T IMAGINE."
"YOU SAVED AN *OLD MAN*. IF YOU WERE THE *GOOD* GUY, I KNEW WHAT THAT MADE *ME*.
"THE CHOICES I MADE IN MY LIFE AFTER THAT...THEY DIDN'T SEEM TO *MATTER* MUCH.
"NOT AFTER YOU SHOWED ME WHAT I WAS *INSIDE*.

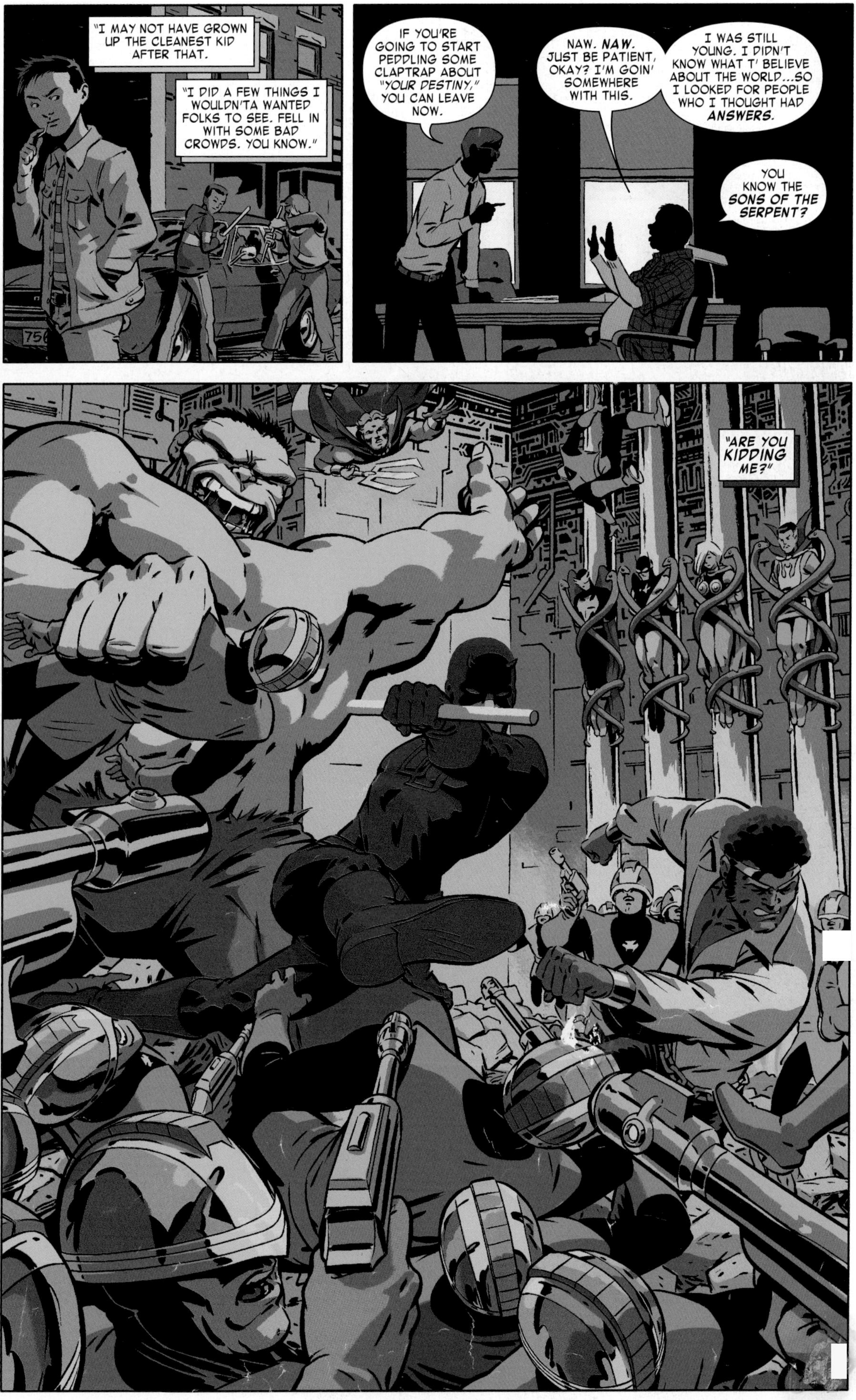

"I MAY NOT HAVE GROWN UP THE CLEANEST KID AFTER THAT.
"I DID A FEW THINGS I WOULDN'TA WANTED FOLKS TO SEE. FELL IN WITH SOME BAD CROWDS. YOU KNOW."
IF YOU'RE GOING TO START PEDDLING SOME CLAPTRAP ABOUT "YOUR DESTINY," YOU CAN LEAVE NOW.
NAW. NAW. JUST BE PATIENT, OKAY? I'M GOIN' SOMEWHERE WITH THIS.
I WAS STILL YOUNG. I DIDN'T KNOW WHAT T' BELIEVE ABOUT THE WORLD...SO I LOOKED FOR PEOPLE WHO I THOUGHT HAD ANSWERS.
YOU KNOW THE SONS OF THE SERPENT?
"ARE YOU KIDDING ME?"

THE *RACIST HATE-GROUP?* **YES,** NATE! NOW YOU'RE TELLING ME YOU'RE A *RACIST,* **TOO--?**

NO!

"LOOK, I SWEAR I DIDN'T KNOW. MY GUYS SAID THEY'D BROKEN OFF AND GONE *INDEPENDENT* A WHILE BACK!"

"THEIR *SALES PITCH* WAS ALL ABOUT *BROTHERHOOD* AND *BELONGING* AND '*PERSONAL EMPOWERMENT*' AND..."

"...AND ALL WE DID WAS *SMOKE* AND *DRINK* AND GO *BOWLIN',* OKAY?"

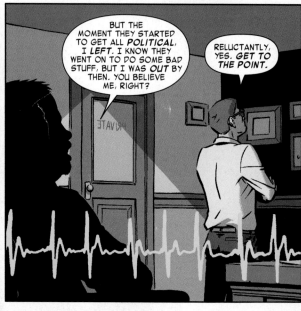

BUT THE MOMENT THEY STARTED TO GET ALL *POLITICAL,* I *LEFT.* I KNOW THEY WENT ON TO DO SOME *BAD STUFF,* BUT I WAS *OUT* BY THEN. YOU BELIEVE ME, RIGHT?

RELUCTANTLY, YES. *GET TO THE POINT.*

"SO WHEN THE *BUGLE* SAID YOU WERE *DAREDEV--*"

"--THAT YOU WERE A *SUPER HERO--*"

"--THAT WAS THE *GREATEST DAY!*"

"IT ALL *LIFTED* FROM ME! ALL THE *GUILT,* ALL THE *WEIGHT*...I HADN'T *RUINED* YOUR LIFE! YOU ENDED UP BETTER OFF THAN *ME!*"

DAILY BUGLE
MURDOCK EXPOSED
REDEVIL

OH, I *GET* IT. I *GET* IT.

YOU DON'T WANT ME TO *APOLOGIZE* FOR ANYTHING. YOU WANT ME TO *THANK YOU?*

NGGHHH...!

NO! NONE OF THIS IS COMIN' OUT RIGHT...

GET. TO. THE. POINT.

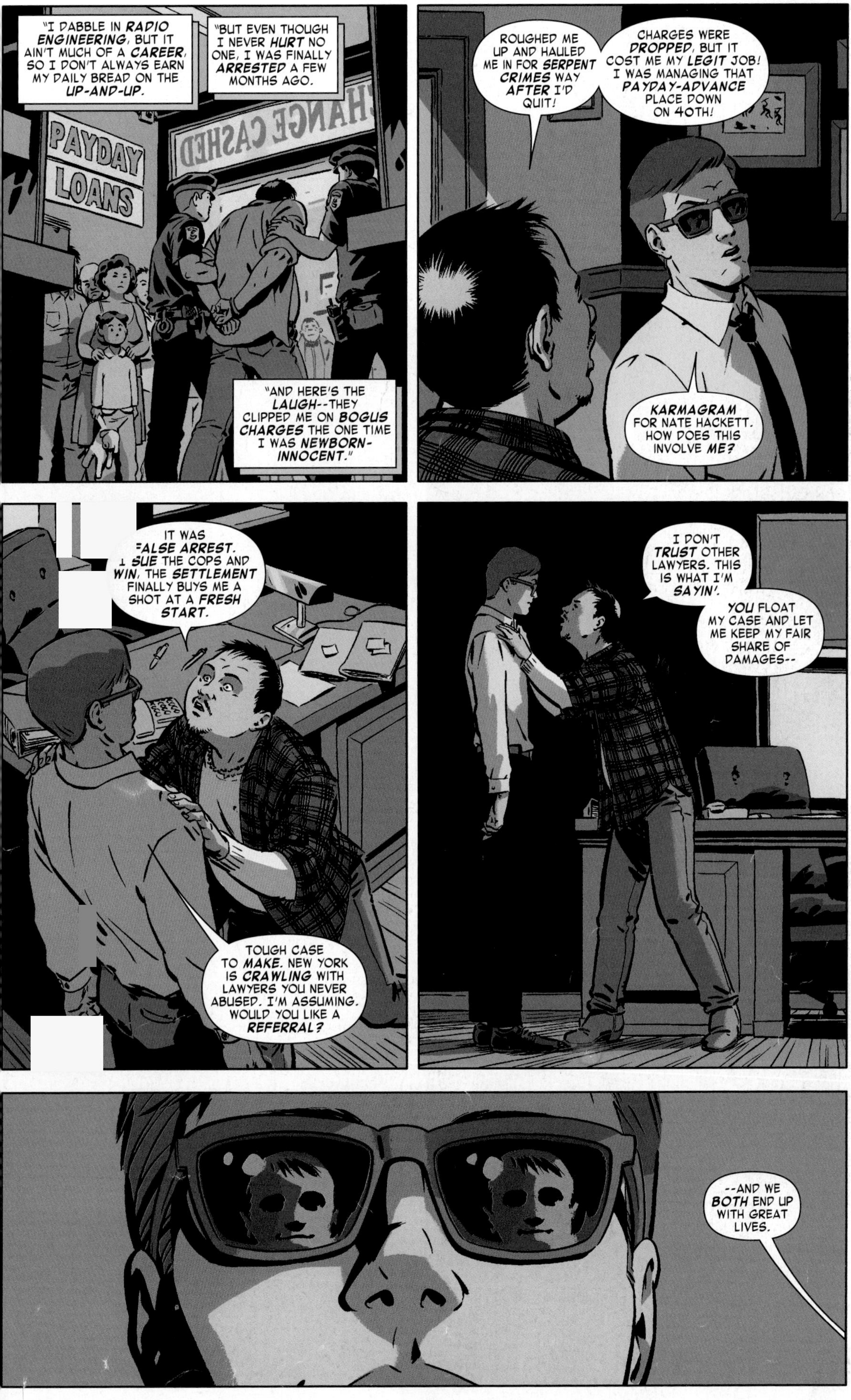

"I DABBLE IN RADIO ENGINEERING, BUT IT AIN'T MUCH OF A CAREER, SO I DON'T ALWAYS EARN MY DAILY BREAD ON THE UP-AND-UP.
"BUT EVEN THOUGH I NEVER HURT NO ONE, I WAS FINALLY ARRESTED A FEW MONTHS AGO.
PAYDAY LOANS
HANGE CASHED
"AND HERE'S THE LAUGH--THEY CLIPPED ME ON BOGUS CHARGES THE ONE TIME I WAS NEWBORN-INNOCENT."
ROUGHED ME UP AND HAULED ME IN FOR SERPENT CRIMES WAY AFTER I'D QUIT!
CHARGES WERE DROPPED, BUT IT COST ME MY LEGIT JOB! I WAS MANAGING THAT PAYDAY-ADVANCE PLACE DOWN ON 40TH!
KARMAGRAM FOR NATE HACKETT. HOW DOES THIS INVOLVE ME?
IT WAS FALSE ARREST. I SUE THE COPS AND WIN, THE SETTLEMENT FINALLY BUYS ME A SHOT AT A FRESH START.
TOUGH CASE TO MAKE. NEW YORK IS CRAWLING WITH LAWYERS YOU NEVER ABUSED. I'M ASSUMING. WOULD YOU LIKE A REFERRAL?
I DON'T TRUST OTHER LAWYERS. THIS IS WHAT I'M SAYIN'.
YOU FLOAT MY CASE AND LET ME KEEP MY FAIR SHARE OF DAMAGES--
--AND WE BOTH END UP WITH GREAT LIVES.

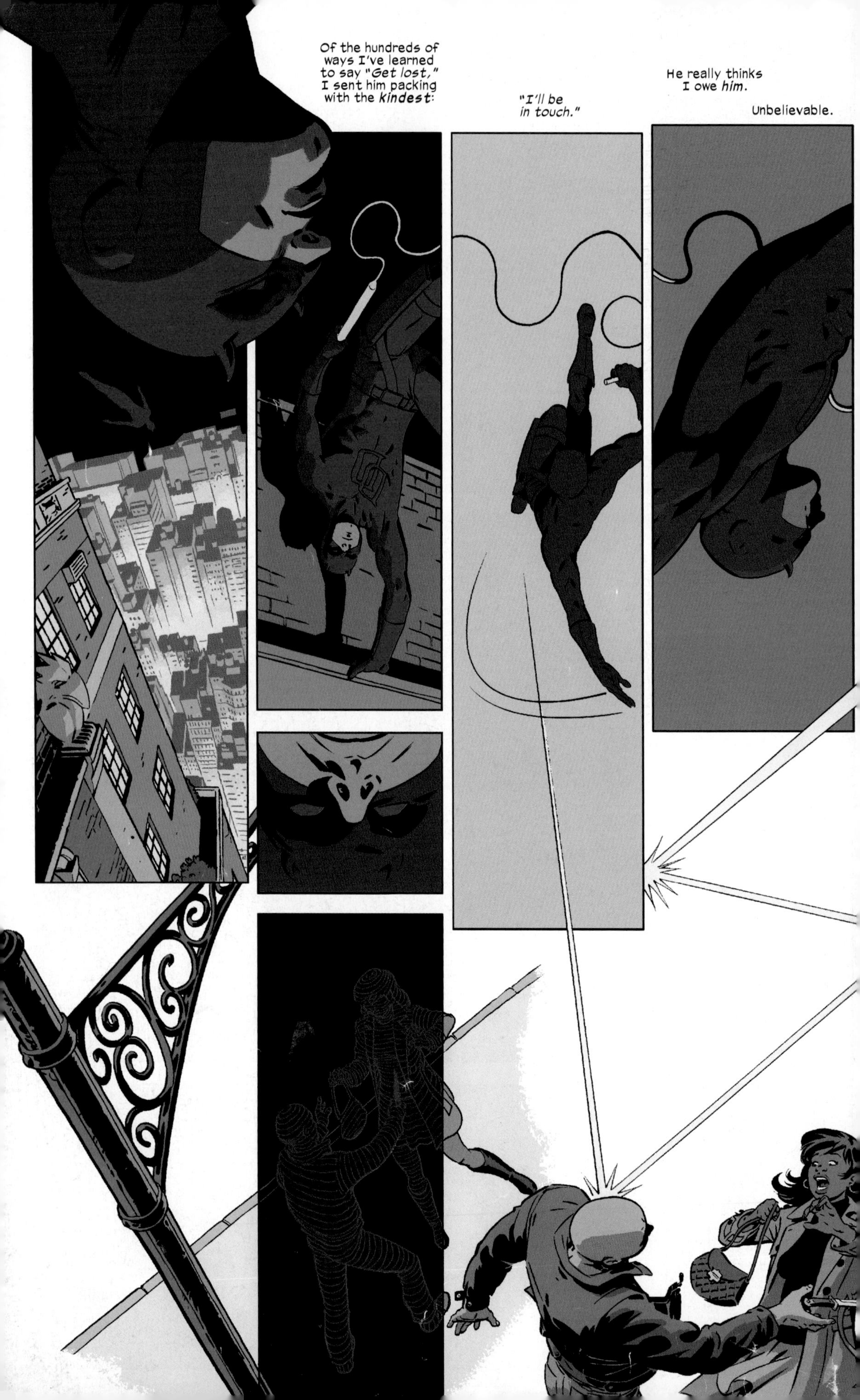
Of the hundreds of ways I've learned to say "Get lost," I sent him packing with the kindest:
"I'll be in touch."
He really thinks I owe him.
Unbelievable.

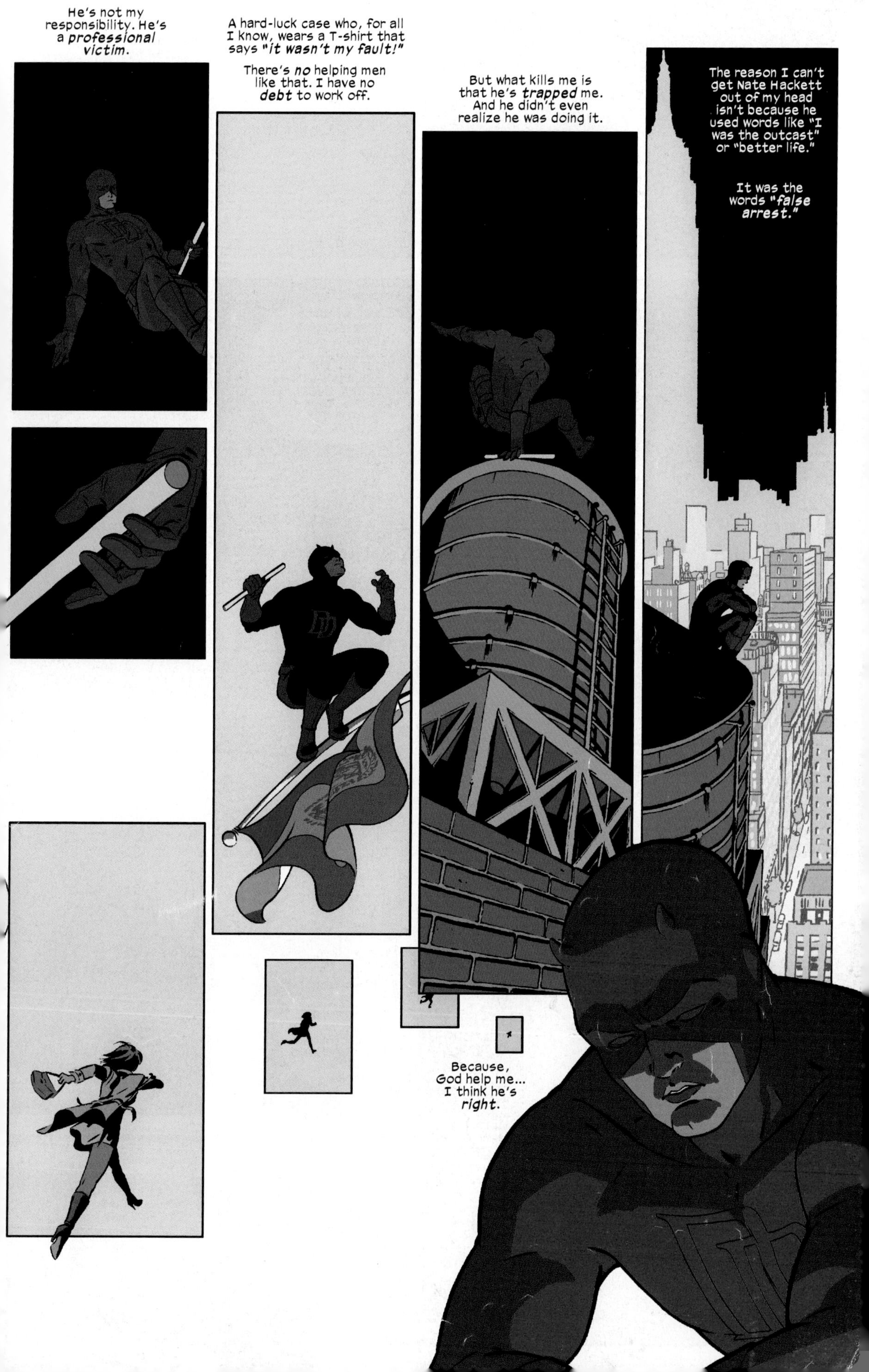
He's not my responsibility. He's a professional victim.
A hard-luck case who, for all I know, wears a T-shirt that says "it wasn't my fault!"
There's no helping men like that. I have no debt to work off.
But what kills me is that he's trapped me. And he didn't even realize he was doing it.
The reason I can't get Nate Hackett out of my head isn't because he used words like "I was the outcast" or "better life."
It was the words "false arrest."
Because, God help me... I think he's right.

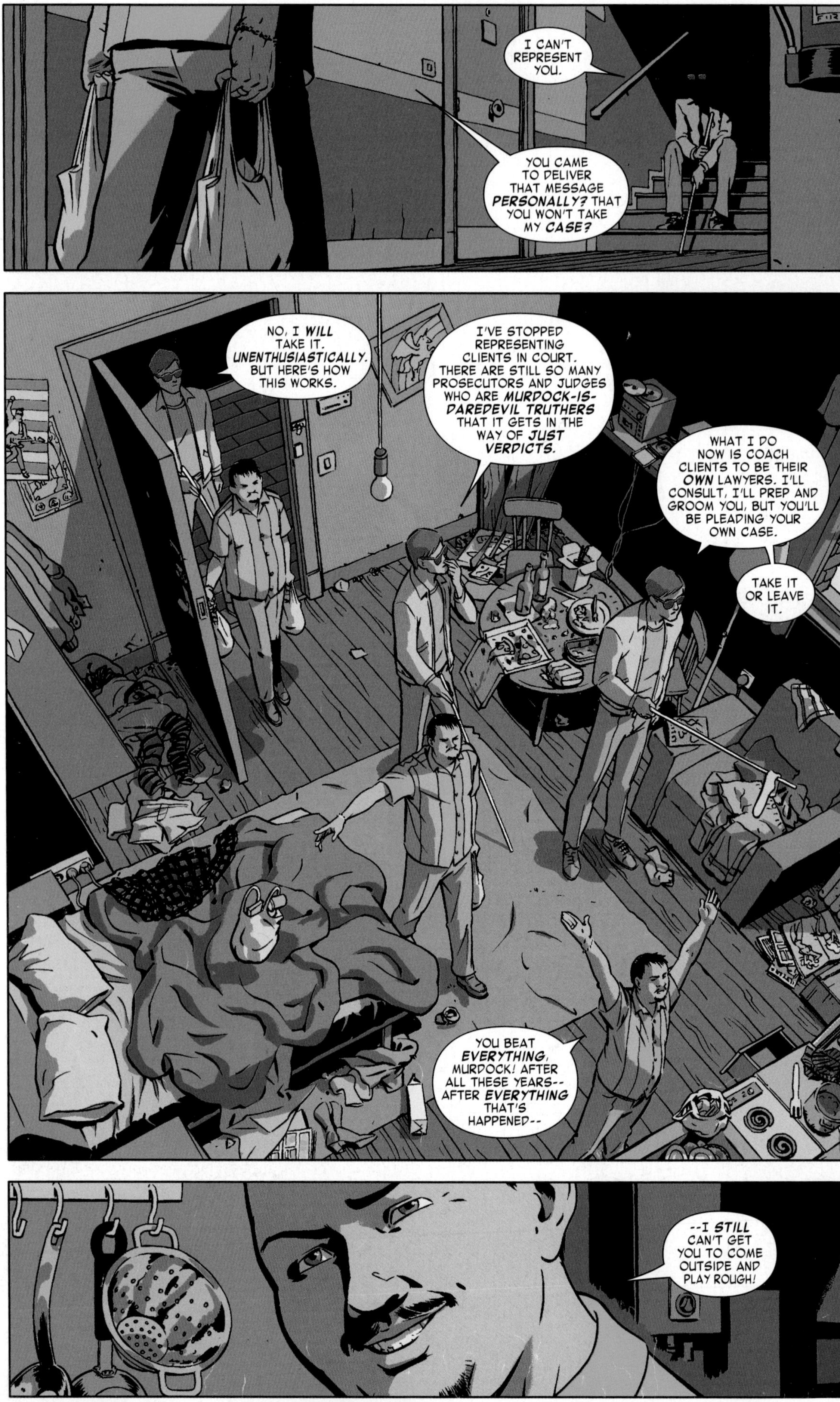
I CAN'T REPRESENT YOU.
YOU CAME TO DELIVER THAT MESSAGE PERSONALLY? THAT YOU WON'T TAKE MY CASE?
NO, I WILL TAKE IT. UNENTHUSIASTICALLY. BUT HERE'S HOW THIS WORKS.
I'VE STOPPED REPRESENTING CLIENTS IN COURT. THERE ARE STILL SO MANY PROSECUTORS AND JUDGES WHO ARE MURDOCK-IS-DAREDEVIL TRUTHERS THAT IT GETS IN THE WAY OF JUST VERDICTS.
WHAT I DO NOW IS COACH CLIENTS TO BE THEIR OWN LAWYERS. I'LL CONSULT, I'LL PREP AND GROOM YOU, BUT YOU'LL BE PLEADING YOUR OWN CASE.
TAKE IT OR LEAVE IT.
YOU BEAT EVERYTHING, MURDOCK! AFTER ALL THESE YEARS-- AFTER EVERYTHING THAT'S HAPPENED--
--I STILL CAN'T GET YOU TO COME OUTSIDE AND PLAY ROUGH!

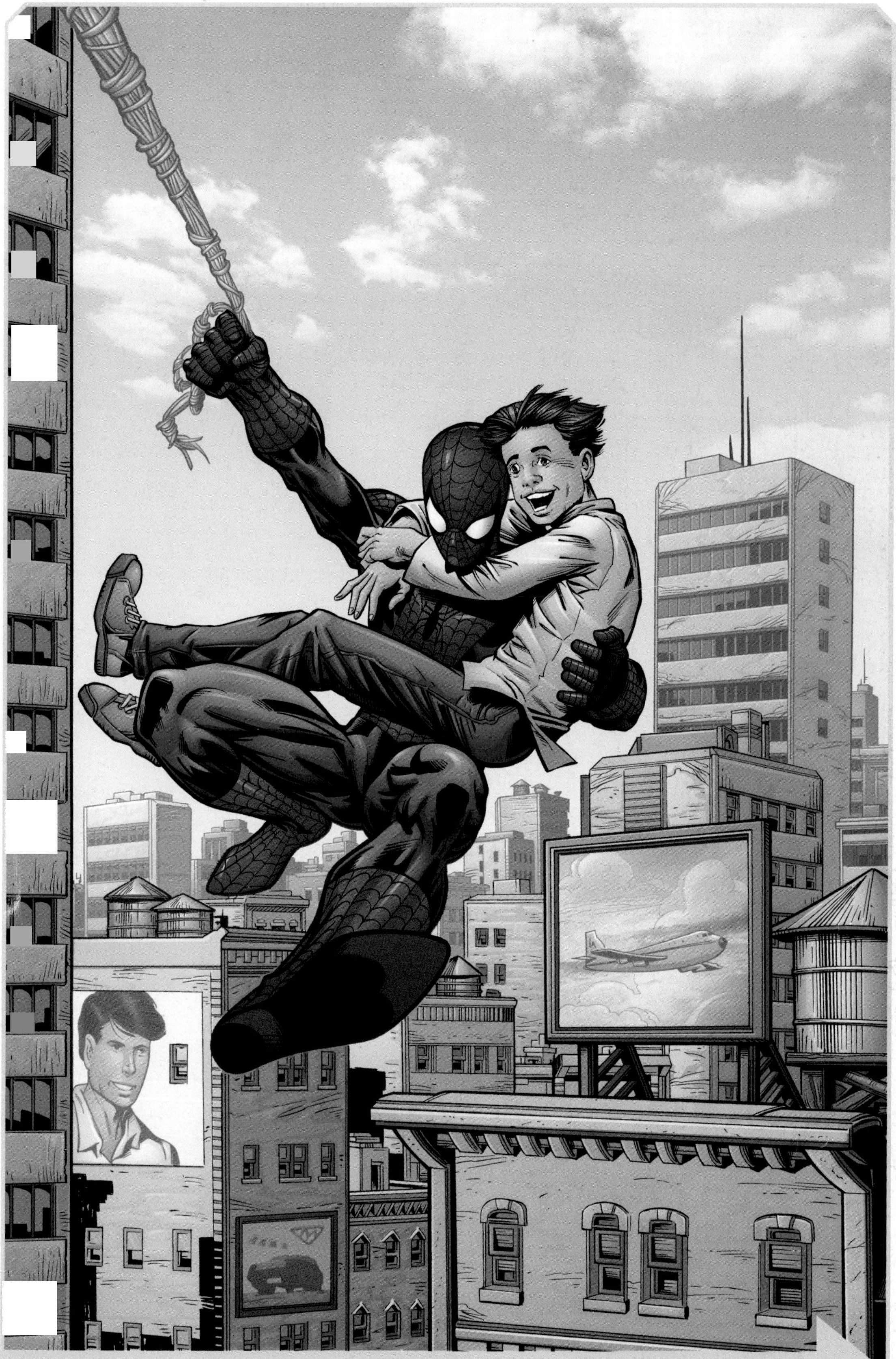

AMAZING SPIDER-MAN ON BULLYING PREVENTION #1

A Message from the President of Prevent Child Abuse America

Name-calling. Hitting. Pinching. Pushing. Stealing money. Threats and intimidation. Intentionally ignoring. Spreading rumors. These examples of bullying can happen to any child, at any time, anywhere.

It is difficult for adults, including teachers and youth leaders, to know when bullying occurs, to say nothing of the difficulty in detecting its symptoms in a bullied child. According to recent studies, much bullying goes unnoticed by adults, *yet many children report they are only too familiar with it as witnesses*. Rather than speak up, children sometimes side with the bully, or laugh at the victims, to protect themselves from possible harm. But having the courage to speak up can help prevent further bullying.

In this story, Spider-Man and The Brace, the villain he is fighting, discover that they share a past as victims of the same school bullies. They come to see how a witness who spoke out against Spider-Man's humiliation helped set the future Super Hero on a path of helping others, while The Brace, who had no ally, became a bully himself. By emphasizing the role and importance of witnesses, Spider-Man suggests that they do not have to feel powerless in the face of bullying.

We hope that this story will inspire and help children of all ages, as well as those adults who wish they could do more to prevent bullying.

Best wishes,

A. Sidney Johnson

A. Sidney Johnson, III
President & CEO
Prevent Child Abuse America

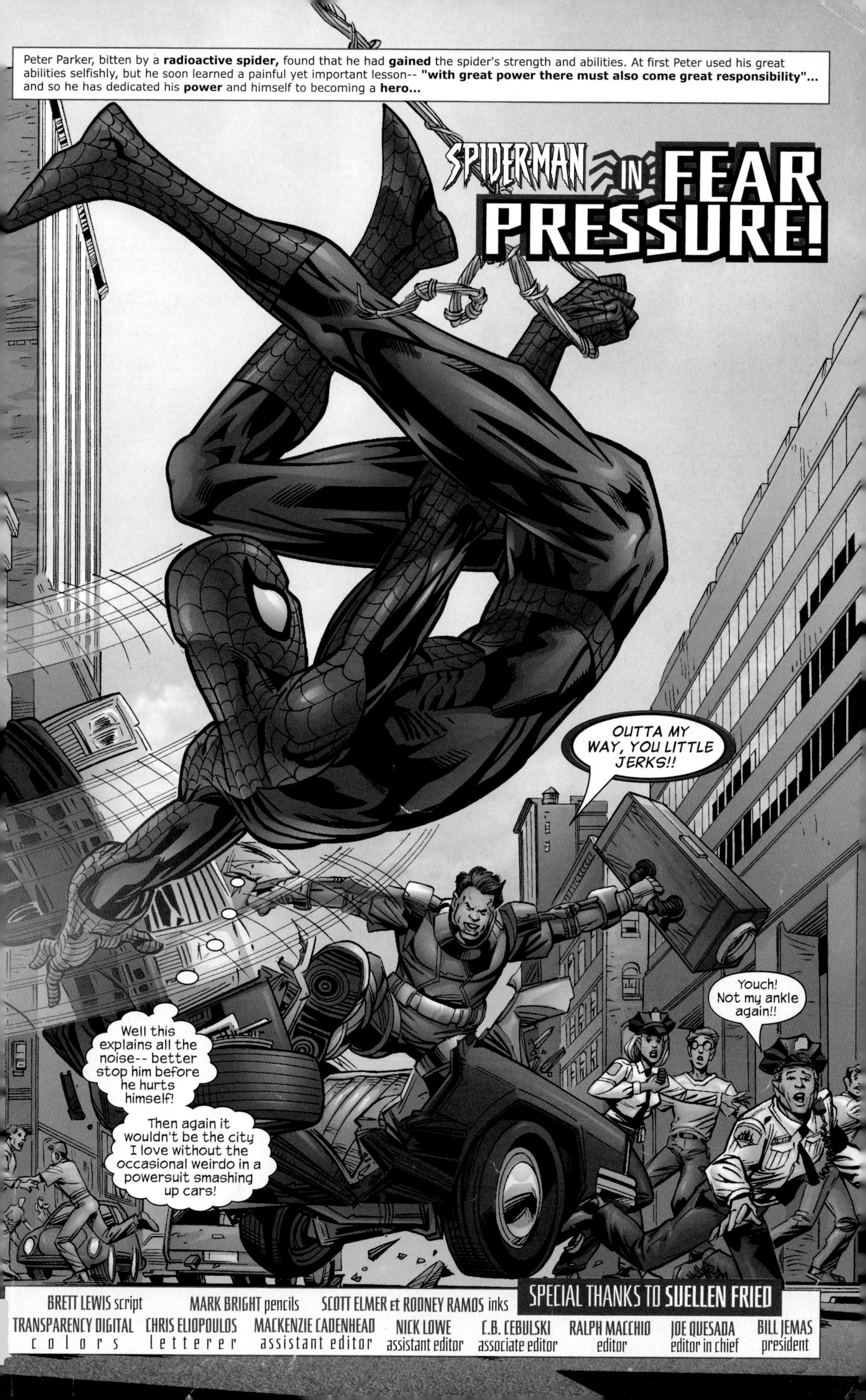
Peter Parker, bitten by a radioactive spider, found that he had gained the spider's strength and abilities. At first Peter used his great abilities selfishly, but he soon learned a painful yet important lesson-- "with great power there must also come great responsibility"... and so he has dedicated his power and himself to becoming a hero...
SPIDER-MAN IN FEAR PRESSURE!
OUTTA MY WAY, YOU LITTLE JERKS!!
Well this explains all the noise-- better stop him before he hurts himself!
Then again it wouldn't be the city I love without the occasional weirdo in a powersuit smashing up cars!
Youch! Not my ankle again!!
BRETT LEWIS script MARK BRIGHT pencils SCOTT ELMER et RODNEY RAMOS inks
SPECIAL THANKS TO SUELLEN FRIED
TRANSPARENCY DIGITAL colors CHRIS ELIOPOULOS letterer MACKENZIE CADENHEAD assistant editor NICK LOWE assistant editor C.B. CEBULSKI associate editor RALPH MACCHIO editor JOE QUESADA editor in chief BILL JEMAS president

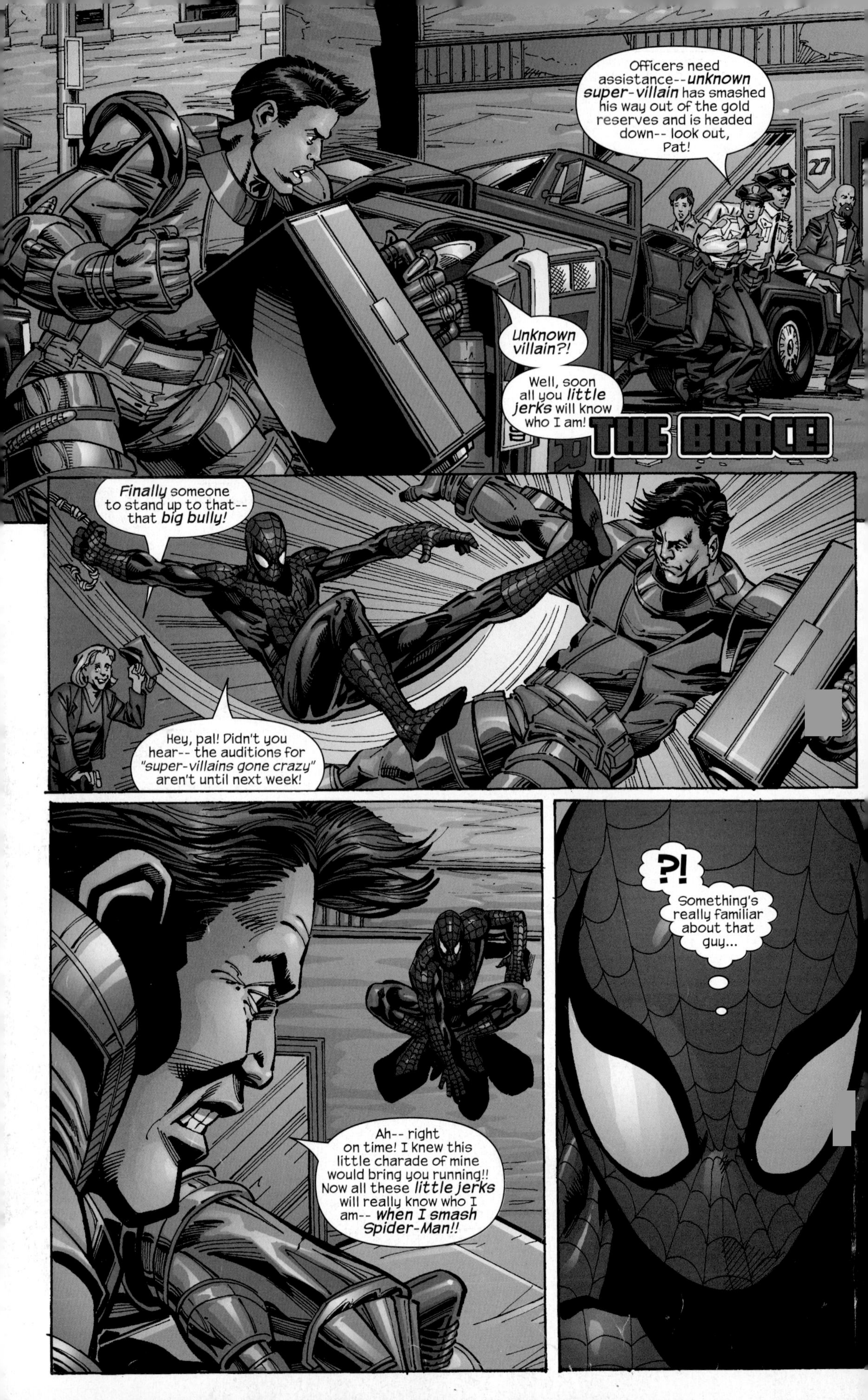
Officers need assistance--*unknown super-villain* has smashed his way out of the gold reserves and is headed down-- look out, Pat!
Unknown villain?!
Well, soon all you *little jerks* will know who I am!
THE BRACE!
Finally someone to stand up to that-- that *big bully!*
Hey, pal! Didn't you hear-- the auditions for *"super-villains gone crazy"* aren't until next week!
Ah-- right on time! I knew this little charade of mine would bring you running!! Now all these *little jerks* will really know who I am-- *when I smash Spider-Man!!*
?!
Something's really familiar about that guy...

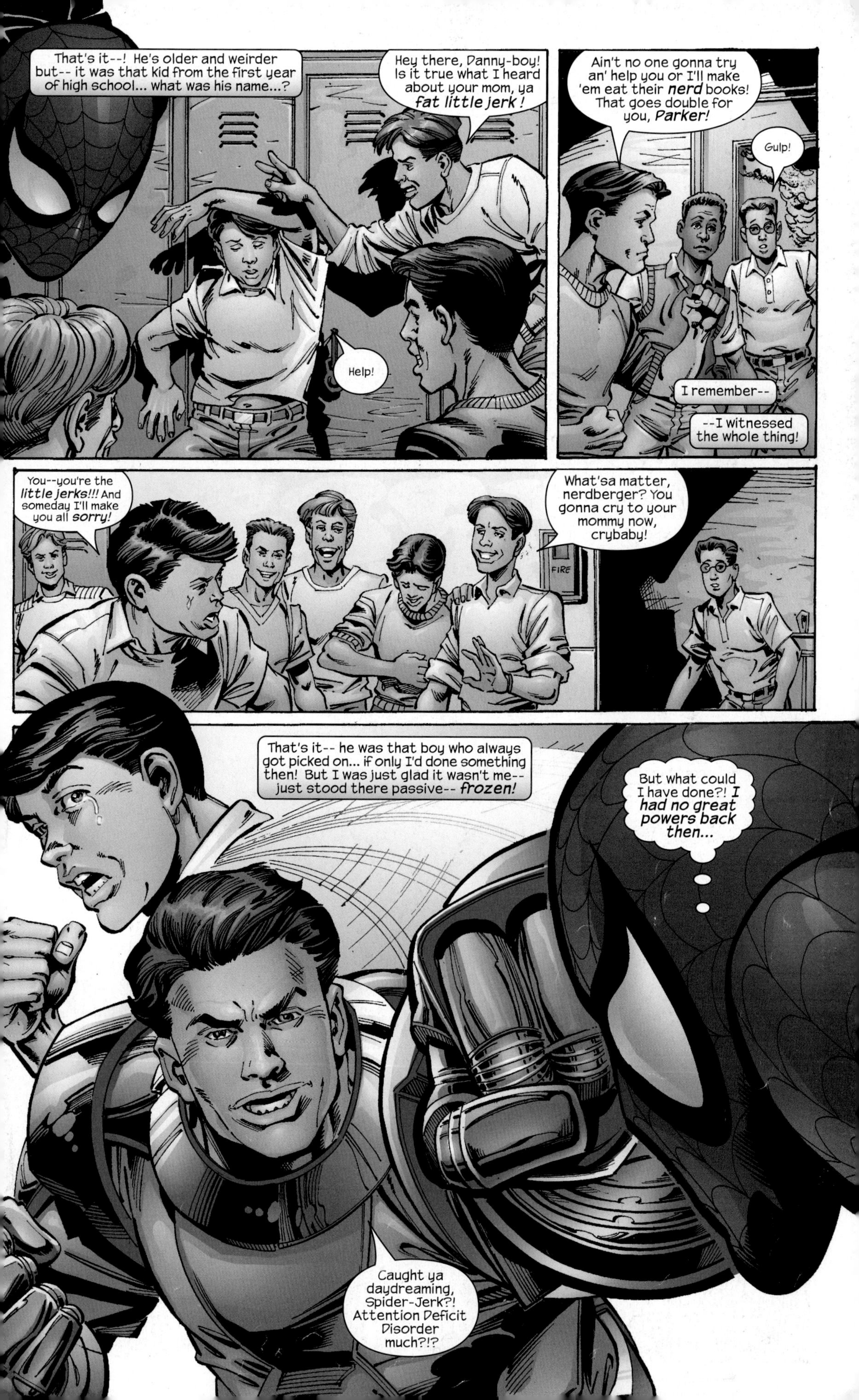
That's it--! He's older and weirder but-- it was that kid from the first year of high school... what was his name...?
Hey there, Danny-boy! Is it true what I heard about your mom, ya fat little jerk!
Help!
Ain't no one gonna try an' help you or I'll make 'em eat their nerd books! That goes double for you, Parker!
Gulp!
I remember--
--I witnessed the whole thing!
You--you're the little jerks!!! And someday I'll make you all sorry!
What'sa matter, nerdberger? You gonna cry to your mommy now, crybaby!
That's it-- he was that boy who always got picked on... if only I'd done something then! But I was just glad it wasn't me-- just stood there passive-- frozen!
But what could I have done?! I had no great powers back then...
Caught ya daydreaming, Spider-Jerk?! Attention Deficit Disorder much?!?

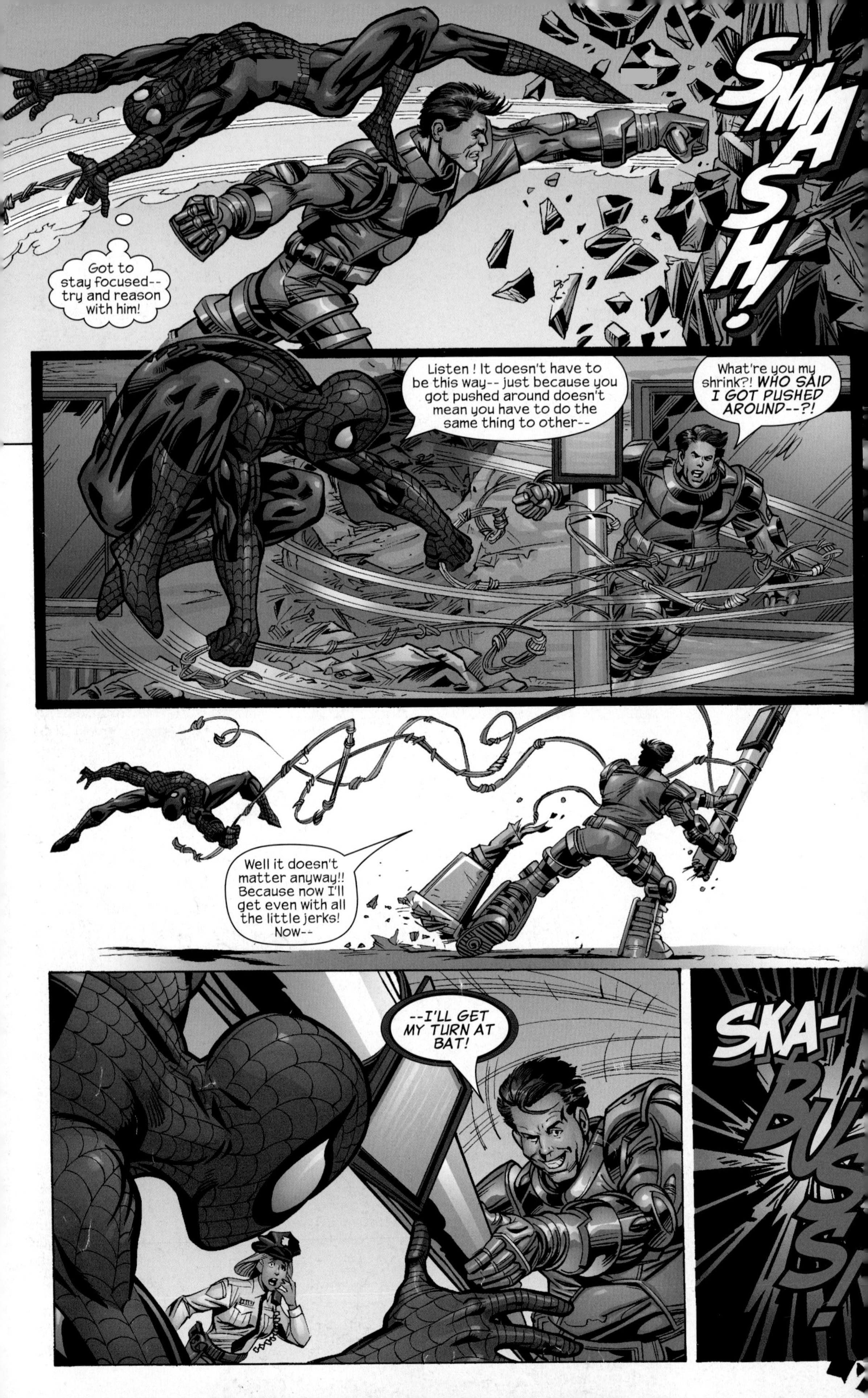
SMASH!
Got to stay focused-- try and reason with him!
Listen! It doesn't have to be this way-- just because you got pushed around doesn't mean you have to do the same thing to other--
What're you my shrink?! WHO SAID I GOT PUSHED AROUND--?!
Well it doesn't matter anyway!! Because now I'll get even with all the little jerks! Now--
--I'LL GET MY TURN AT BAT!
SKA-

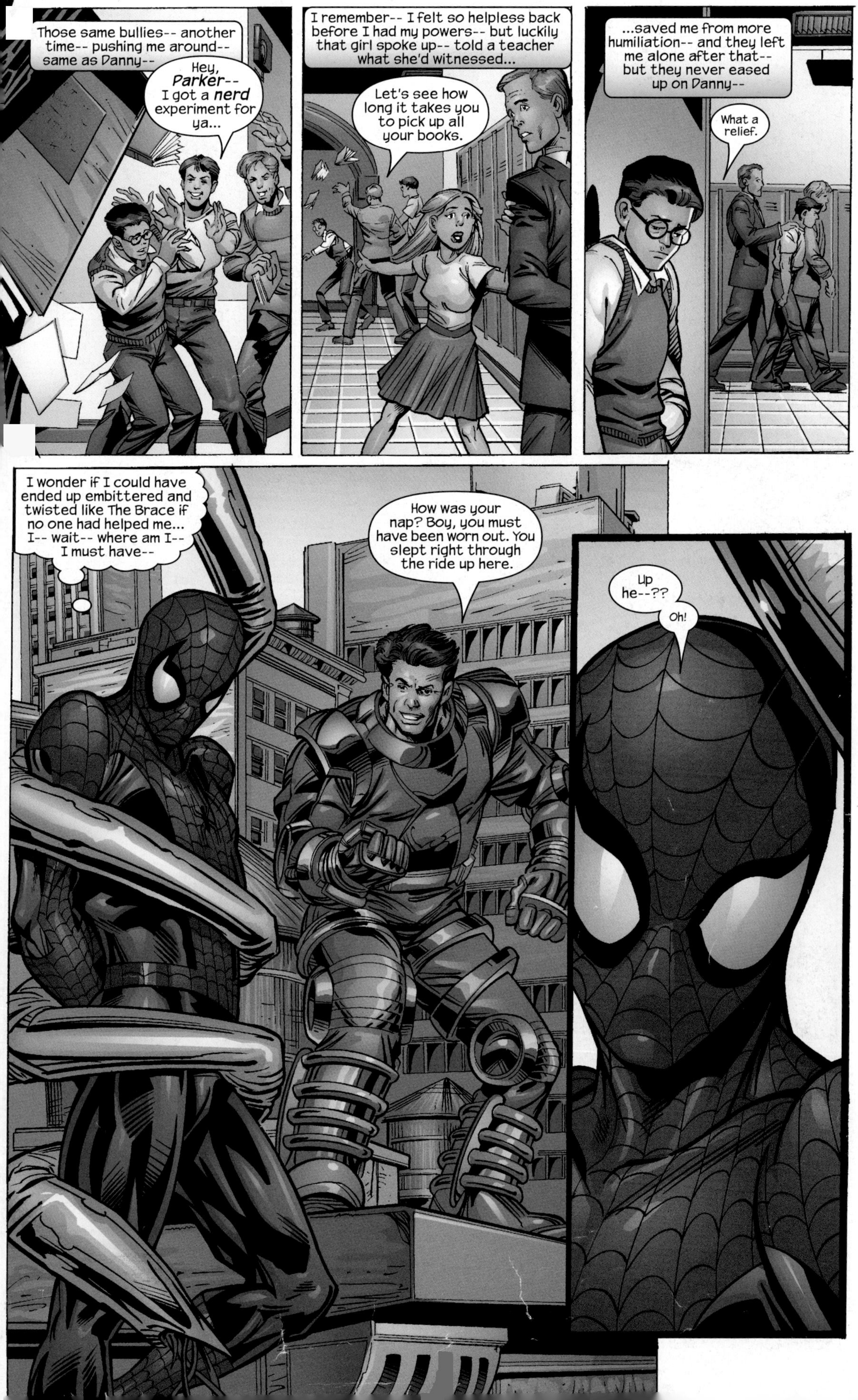
Those same bullies-- another time-- pushing me around-- same as Danny--
Hey, Parker-- I got a nerd experiment for ya...
I remember-- I felt so helpless back before I had my powers-- but luckily that girl spoke up-- told a teacher what she'd witnessed...
Let's see how long it takes you to pick up all your books.
...saved me from more humiliation-- and they left me alone after that-- but they never eased up on Danny--
What a relief.
I wonder if I could have ended up embittered and twisted like The Brace if no one had helped me... I-- wait-- where am I-- I must have--
How was your nap? Boy, you must have been worn out. You slept right through the ride up here.
Up he--??
Oh!

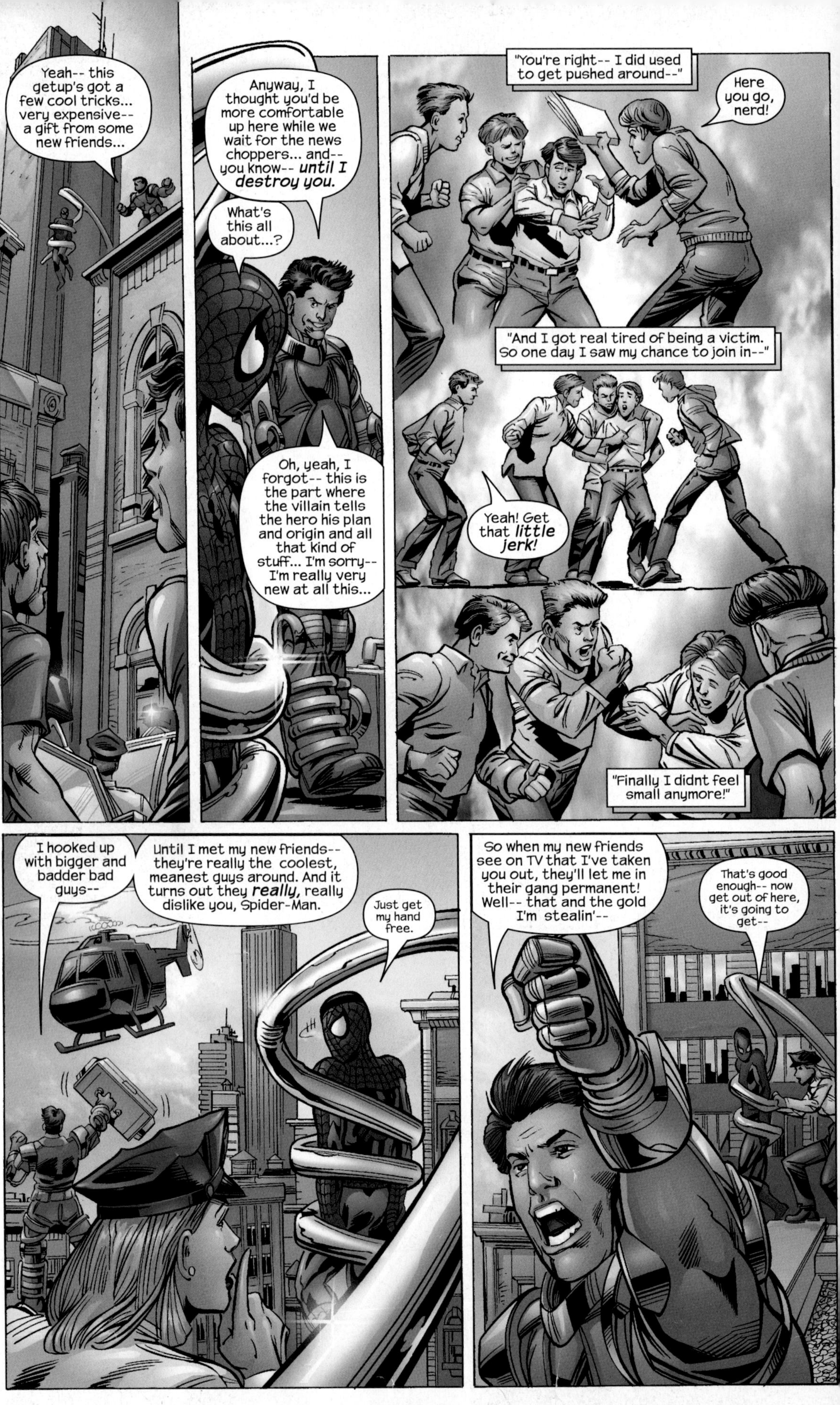
Yeah-- this getup's got a few cool tricks... very expensive-- a gift from some new friends...
Anyway, I thought you'd be more comfortable up here while we wait for the news choppers... and-- you know-- *until I destroy you.*
What's this all about...?
Oh, yeah, I forgot-- this is the part where the villain tells the hero his plan and origin and all that kind of stuff... I'm sorry-- I'm really very new at all this...
"You're right-- I did used to get pushed around--"
Here you go, nerd!
"And I got real tired of being a victim. So one day I saw my chance to join in--"
Yeah! Get that *little jerk!*
"Finally I didnt feel small anymore!"
I hooked up with bigger and badder bad guys--
Until I met my new friends-- they're really the coolest, meanest guys around. And it turns out they *really,* really dislike you, Spider-Man.
Just get my hand free.
So when my new friends see on TV that I've taken you out, they'll let me in their gang permanent! Well-- that and the gold I'm stealin'--
That's good enough-- now get out of here, it's going to get--

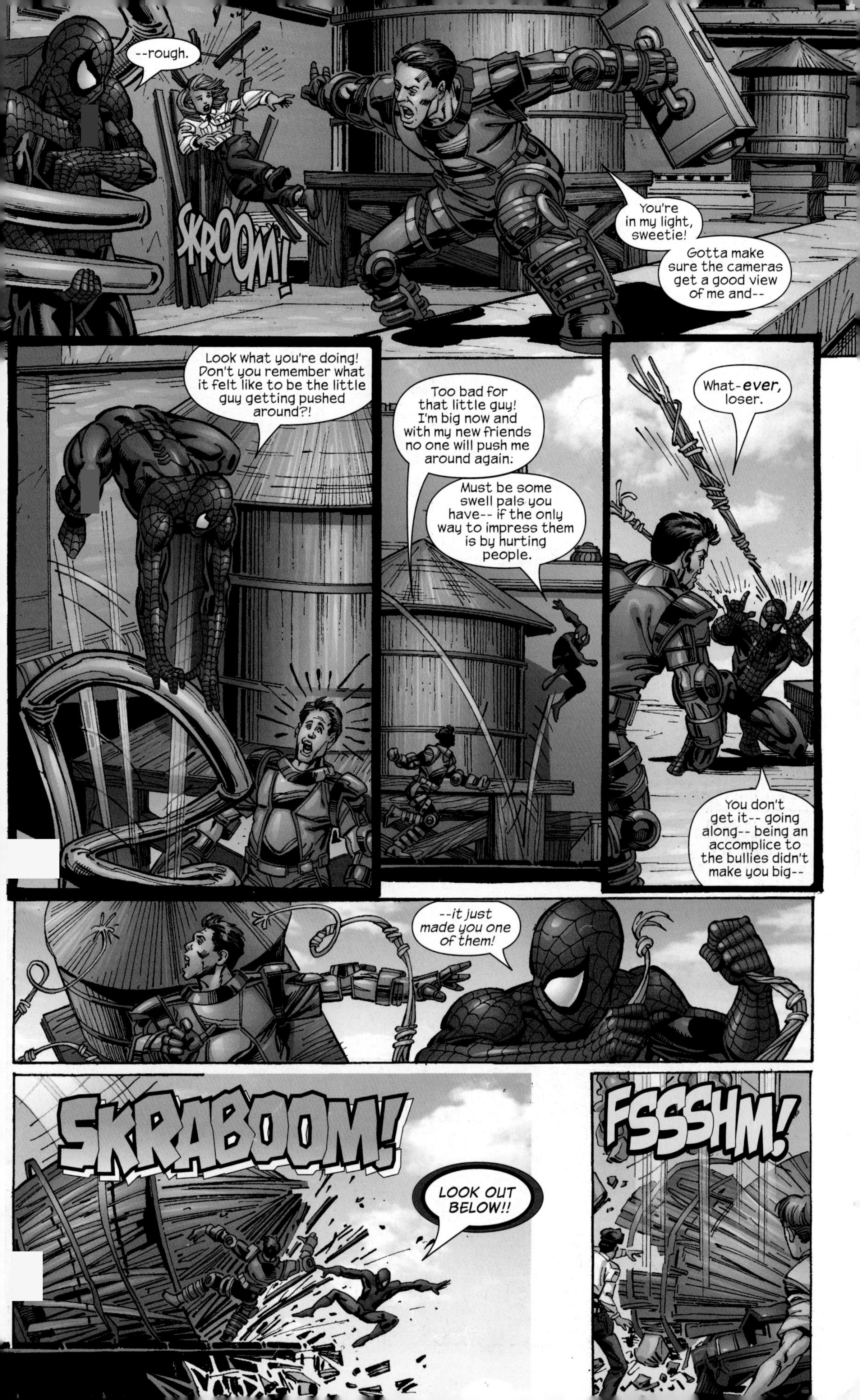
--rough.
SKROOM!
You're in my light, sweetie!
Gotta make sure the cameras get a good view of me and--
Look what you're doing! Don't you remember what it felt like to be the little guy getting pushed around?!
Too bad for that little guy! I'm big now and with my new friends no one will push me around again.
Must be some swell pals you have-- if the only way to impress them is by hurting people.
What-*ever*, loser.
You don't get it-- going along-- being an accomplice to the bullies didn't make you big--
--it just made you one of them!
SKRABOOM!
LOOK OUT BELOW!!
FSSSHM!

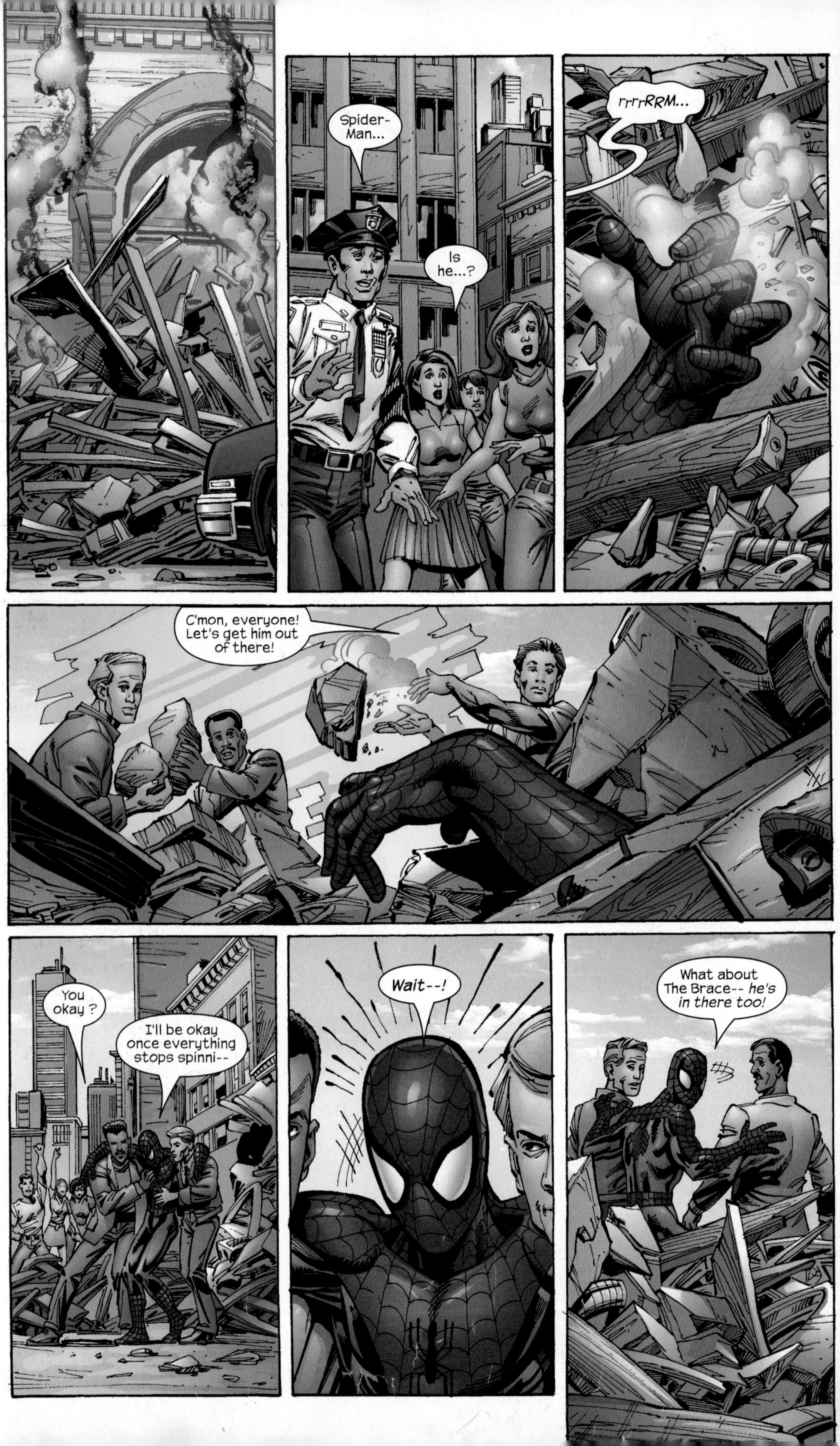
Spider-Man...
Is he...?
rrrrRRM...
C'mon, everyone! Let's get him out of there!
You okay ?
I'll be okay once everything stops spinni--
Wait--!
What about The Brace-- he's in there too!

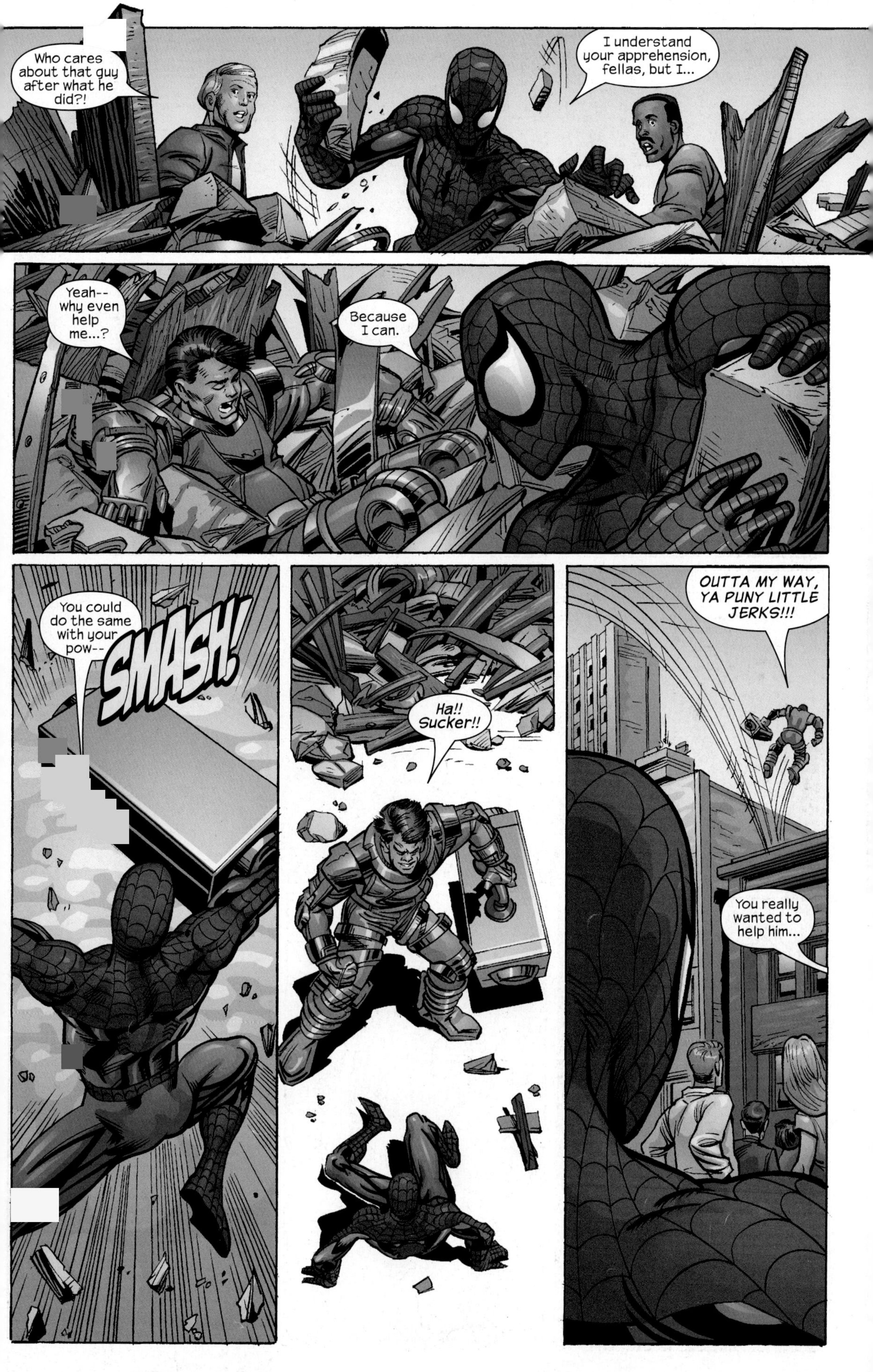

Who cares about that guy after what he did?!
I understand your apprehension, fellas, but I...
Yeah-- why even help me...?
Because I can.
You could do the same with your pow--
SMASH!
Ha!! Sucker!!
OUTTA MY WAY, YA PUNY LITTLE JERKS!!!
You really wanted to help him...

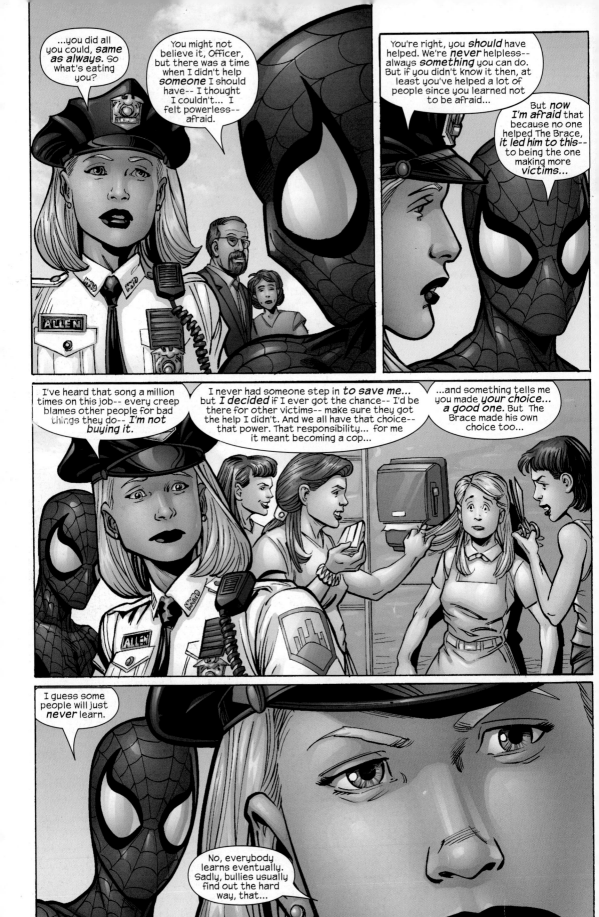

...you did all you could, *same as always.* So what's eating you?

You might not believe it, Officer, but there was a time when I didn't help *someone* I should have-- I thought I couldn't... I felt powerless-- afraid.

You're right, you *should* have helped. We're *never* helpless-- always *something* you can do. But if you didn't know it then, at least you've helped a lot of people since you learned not to be afraid...

But *now* I'm afraid that because no one helped The Brace, *it led him to this*-- to being the one making more *victims...*

I've heard that song a million times on this job-- every creep blames other people for bad things they do-- *I'm not buying it.*

I never had someone step in *to save me...* but *I decided* if I ever got the chance-- I'd be there for other victims-- make sure they got the help I didn't. And we all have that choice-- that power. That responsibility... for me it meant becoming a cop...

...and something tells me you made *your choice...* *a good one.* But The Brace made his own choice too...

I guess some people will just *never* learn.

No, everybody learns eventually. Sadly, bullies usually find out the hard way, that...

"...there's always a bigger bully."

Hey, we was just watching you on TV...

Oh, you guys are here-- I thought we were meeting at the--? I got away with the gold--

Yeah, we'll take that, pip-squeak! For our time and trouble! 'Course-- you didn't really live up to the rest of our bargain...

Yeah, yer violatin' our verbal agreement... we didn't get you that suit for free, y'know.

No-- I did like you guys said-- but Spider-Man--

Yeah, Spider-Man-- he's on to you-- so we gotta take it back, too.

The-- the suit??! But-- it-- doesn't come off--

We'll see about that...

--get involved. Everyone has great power-- use it on the right side-- to help. **Don't be a passive witness to a bully.**

What about you, Spider-Man. Anything to add?

Yes, something someone close to me once reminded me of--

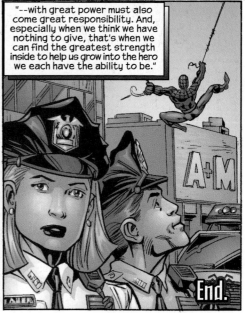

"--with great power must also come great responsibility. And, especially when we think we have nothing to give, that's when we can find the greatest strength inside to help us grow into the hero we each have the ability to be."

End.

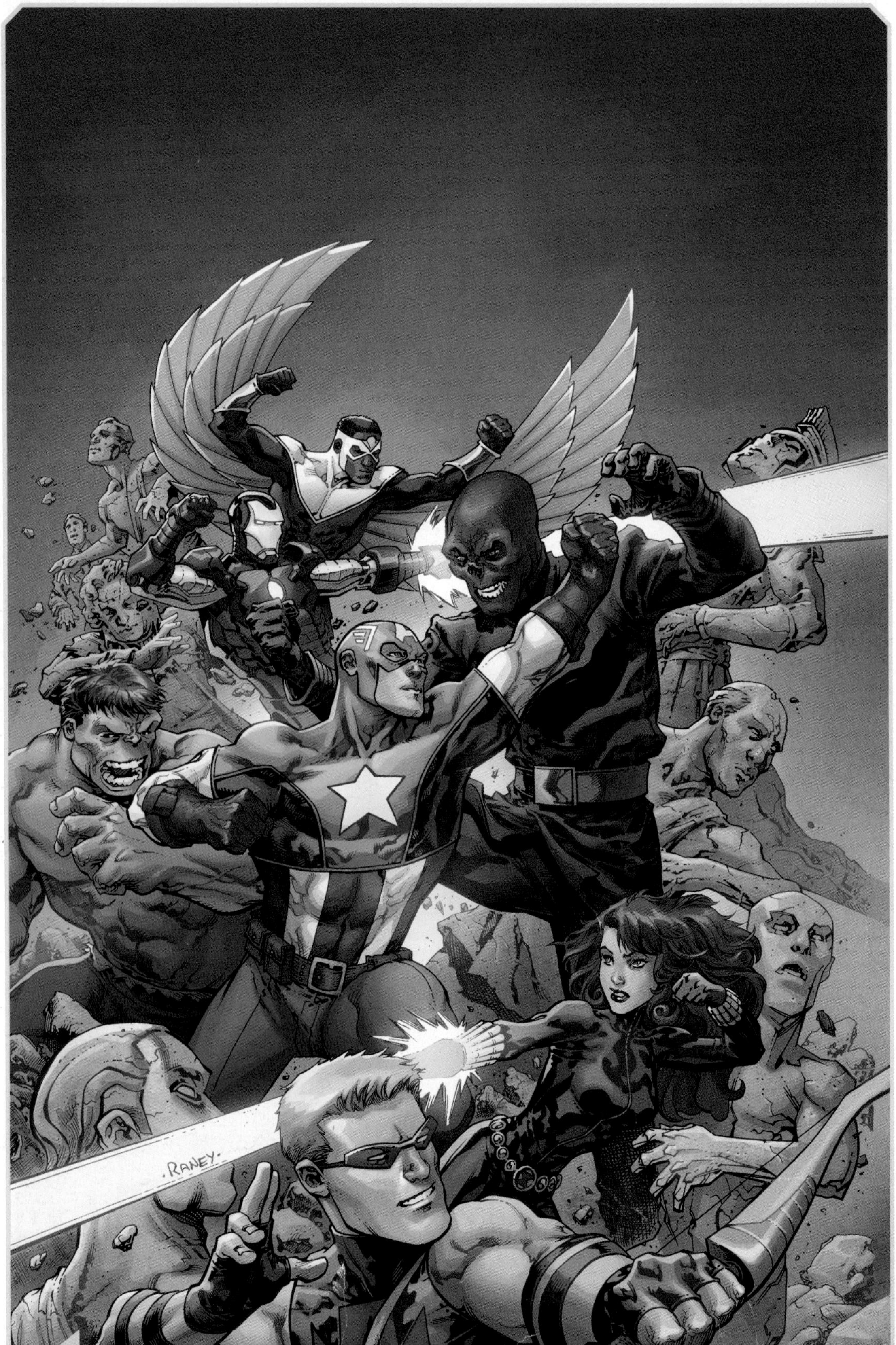
RANEY

AVENGERS VS. #1

IRON MAN, HOW'S IT LOOKING DOWN THERE?

LIKE SOMEONE'S KICKED OVER AN ANT HILL, CAP. PEOPLE ARE SCATTERING IN ALL DIRECTIONS, BUT FROM WHAT, I CAN'T TELL.

THEY JUST STARTED... MOVING!

THEY'RE COMING THIS WAY! THEY'RE ALIVE!

"ALIVE?" WHO'S ALI--?

UHH...CAP? YOU'RE NOT GOING TO BELIEVE THIS.

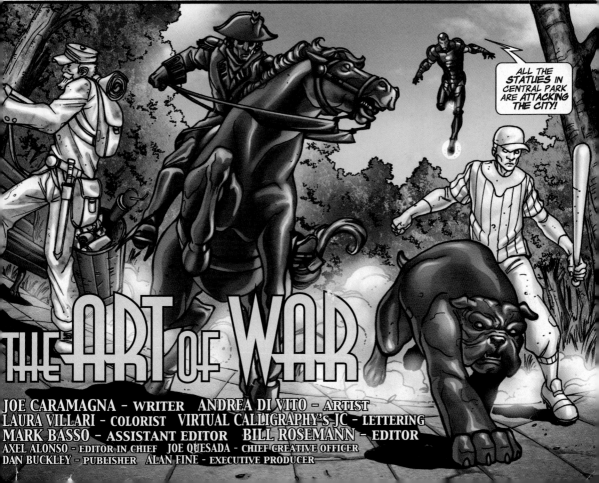

ALL THE STATUES IN CENTRAL PARK ARE ATTACKING THE CITY!

THE ART OF WAR

JOE CARAMAGNA - WRITER   ANDREA DI VITO - ARTIST
LAURA VILLARI - COLORIST   VIRTUAL CALLIGRAPHY'S JC - LETTERING
MARK BASSO - ASSISTANT EDITOR   BILL ROSEMANN - EDITOR
AXEL ALONSO - EDITOR IN CHIEF   JOE QUESADA - CHIEF CREATIVE OFFICER
DAN BUCKLEY - PUBLISHER   ALAN FINE - EXECUTIVE PRODUCER

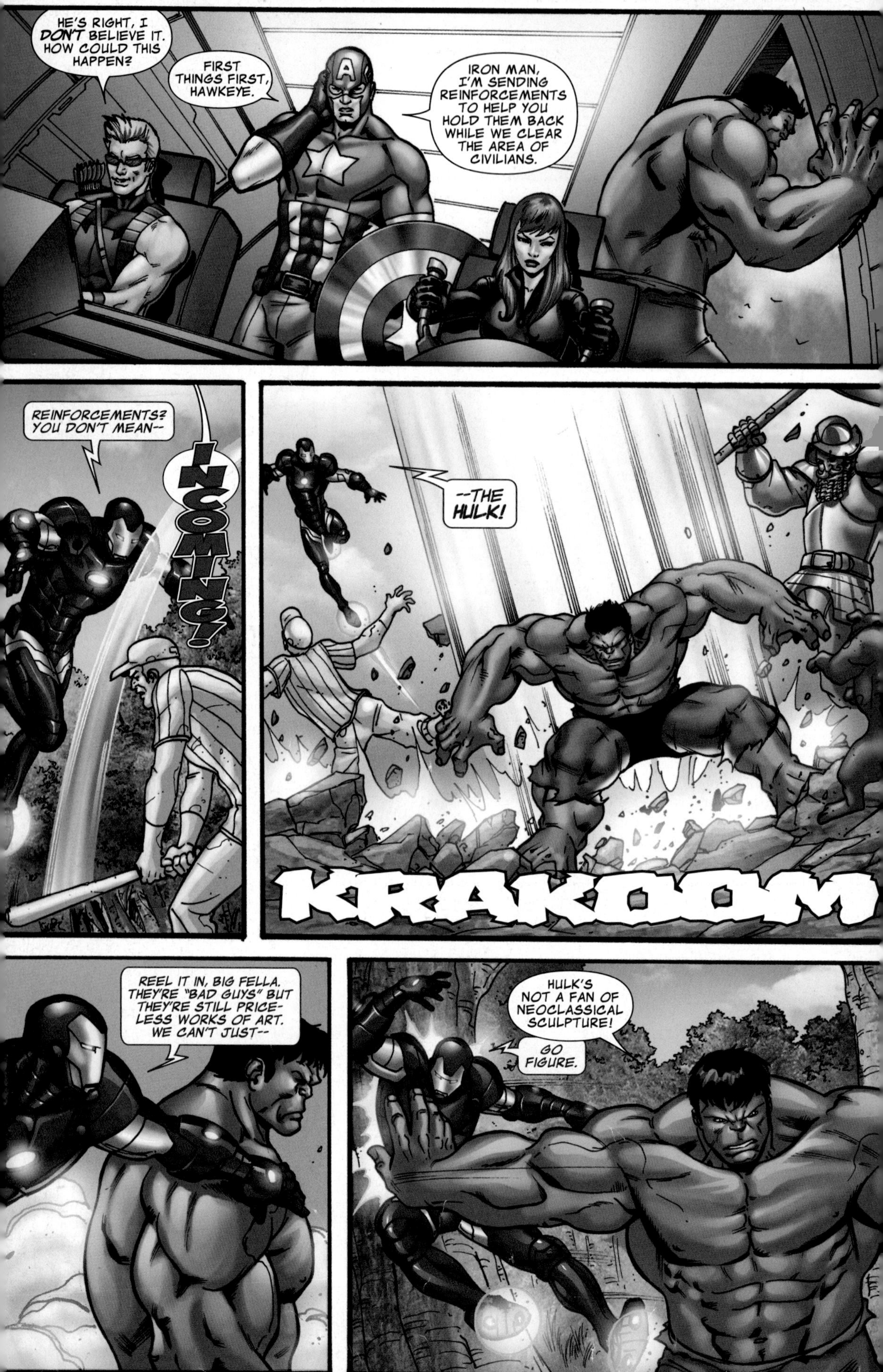

HE'S RIGHT, I DON'T BELIEVE IT. HOW COULD THIS HAPPEN?
FIRST THINGS FIRST, HAWKEYE.
IRON MAN, I'M SENDING REINFORCEMENTS TO HELP YOU HOLD THEM BACK WHILE WE CLEAR THE AREA OF CIVILIANS.
REINFORCEMENTS? YOU DON'T MEAN--
INCOMING!
--THE HULK!
KRAKOOM
REEL IT IN, BIG FELLA. THEY'RE "BAD GUYS" BUT THEY'RE STILL PRICELESS WORKS OF ART. WE CAN'T JUST--
HULK'S NOT A FAN OF NEOCLASSICAL SCULPTURE!
GO FIGURE.

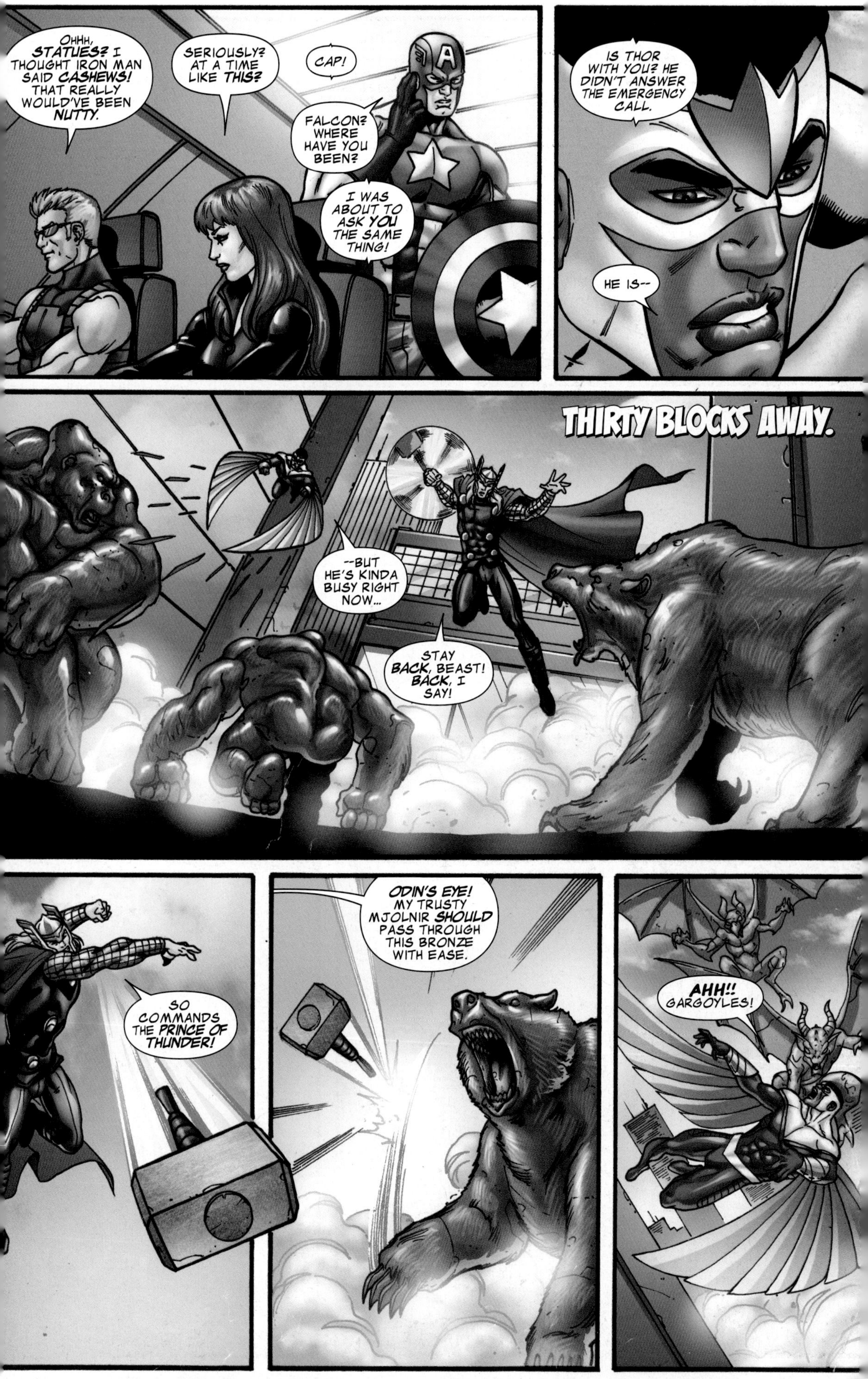
OHHH, STATUES? I THOUGHT IRON MAN SAID CASHEWS! THAT REALLY WOULD'VE BEEN NUTTY.
SERIOUSLY? AT A TIME LIKE THIS?
CAP!
FALCON? WHERE HAVE YOU BEEN?
I WAS ABOUT TO ASK YOU THE SAME THING!
IS THOR WITH YOU? HE DIDN'T ANSWER THE EMERGENCY CALL.
HE IS--
THIRTY BLOCKS AWAY.
--BUT HE'S KINDA BUSY RIGHT NOW...
STAY BACK, BEAST! BACK, I SAY!
SO COMMANDS THE PRINCE OF THUNDER!
ODIN'S EYE! MY TRUSTY MJOLNIR SHOULD PASS THROUGH THIS BRONZE WITH EASE.
AHH!! GARGOYLES!

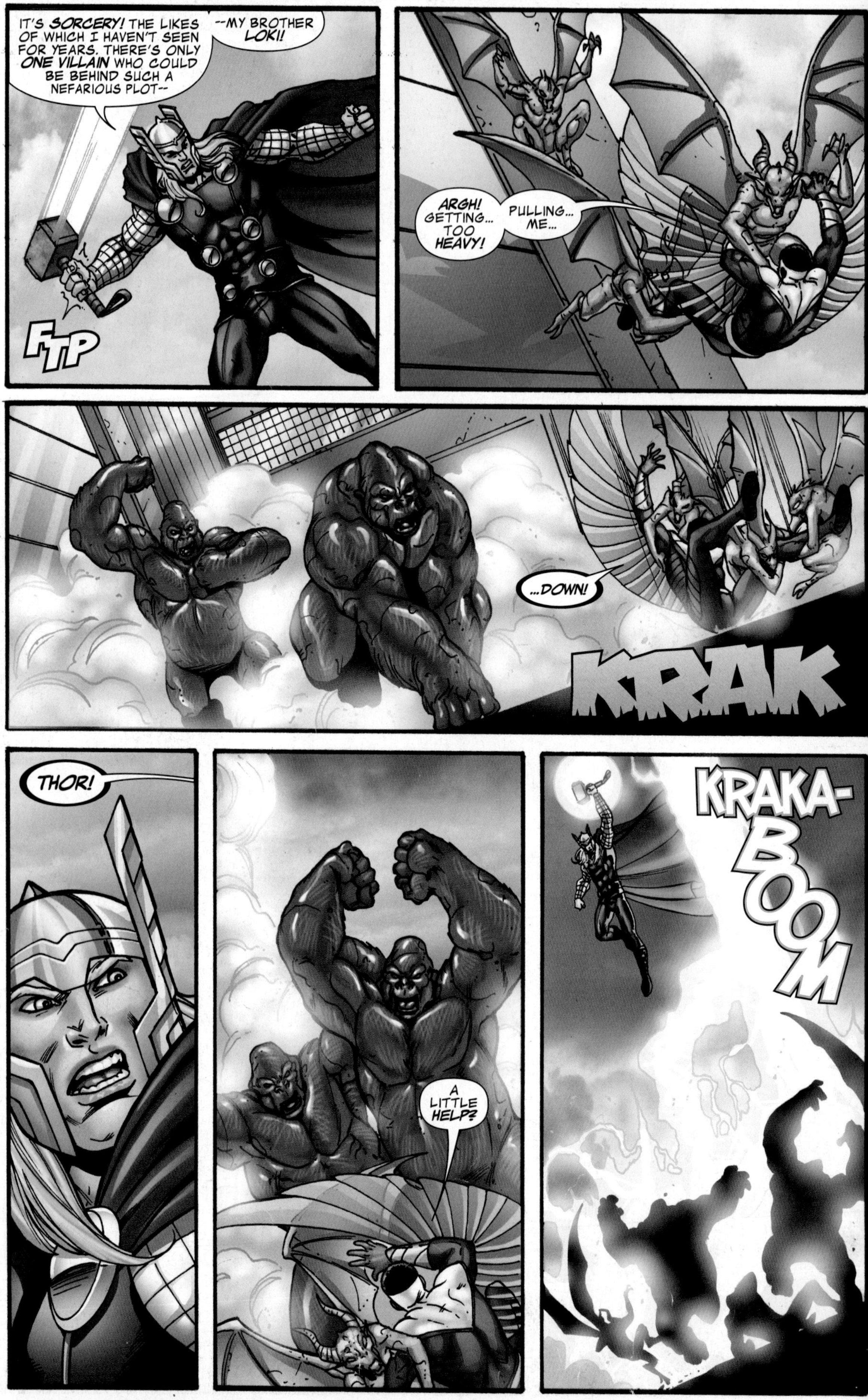
IT'S SORCERY! THE LIKES OF WHICH I HAVEN'T SEEN FOR YEARS. THERE'S ONLY ONE VILLAIN WHO COULD BE BEHIND SUCH A NEFARIOUS PLOT--
--MY BROTHER LOKI!
FTP
ARGH! GETTING... TOO HEAVY!
PULLING... ME...
...DOWN!
KRAK
THOR!
A LITTLE HELP?
KRAKA-BOOM

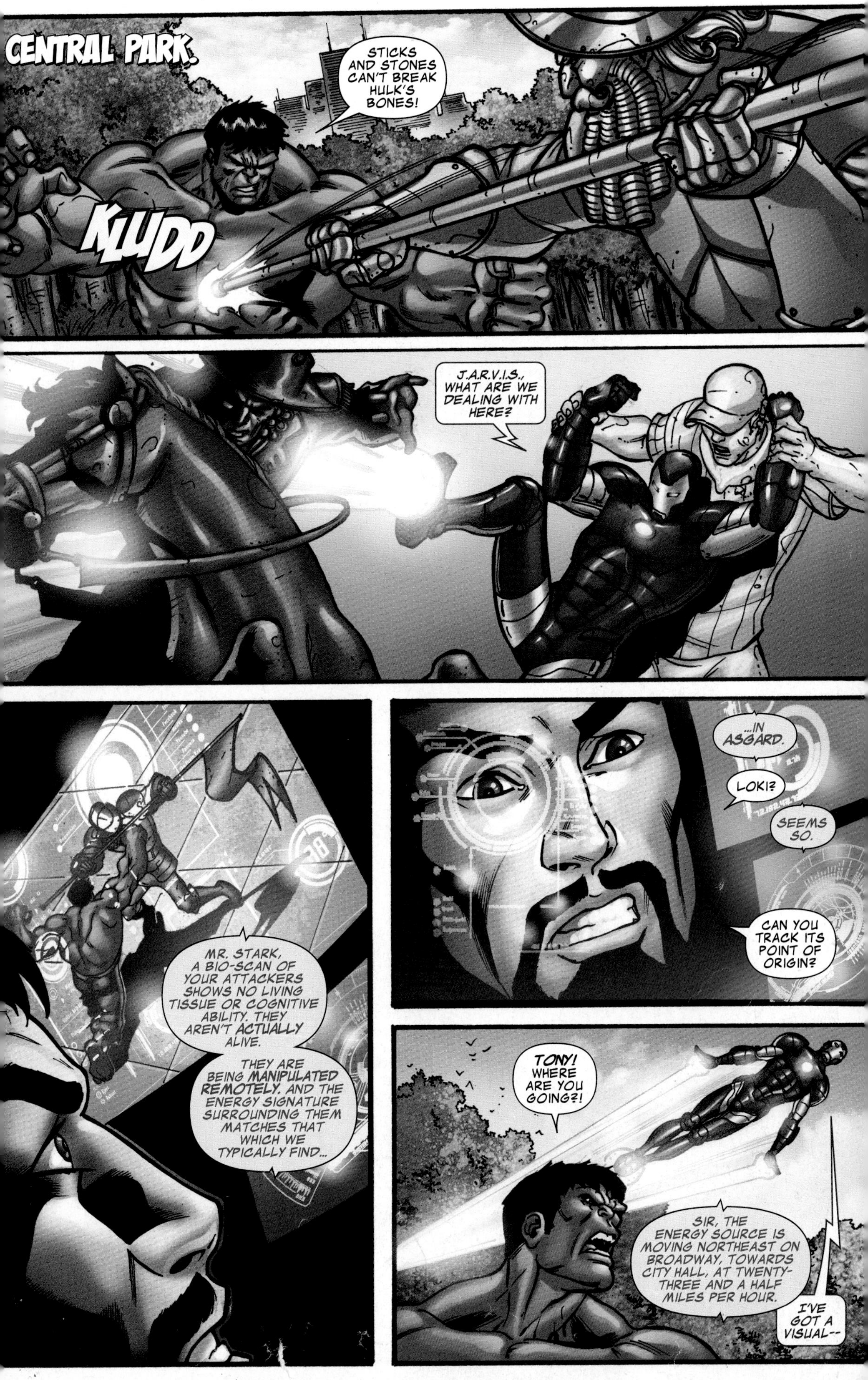
CENTRAL PARK.
STICKS AND STONES CAN'T BREAK HULK'S BONES!
KLUDD
J.A.R.V.I.S., WHAT ARE WE DEALING WITH HERE?
MR. STARK, A BIO-SCAN OF YOUR ATTACKERS SHOWS NO LIVING TISSUE OR COGNITIVE ABILITY. THEY AREN'T ACTUALLY ALIVE.
THEY ARE BEING MANIPULATED REMOTELY. AND THE ENERGY SIGNATURE SURROUNDING THEM MATCHES THAT WHICH WE TYPICALLY FIND...
...IN ASGARD.
LOKI?
SEEMS SO.
CAN YOU TRACK ITS POINT OF ORIGIN?
TONY! WHERE ARE YOU GOING?!
SIR, THE ENERGY SOURCE IS MOVING NORTHEAST ON BROADWAY, TOWARDS CITY HALL, AT TWENTY-THREE AND A HALF MILES PER HOUR.
I'VE GOT A VISUAL--

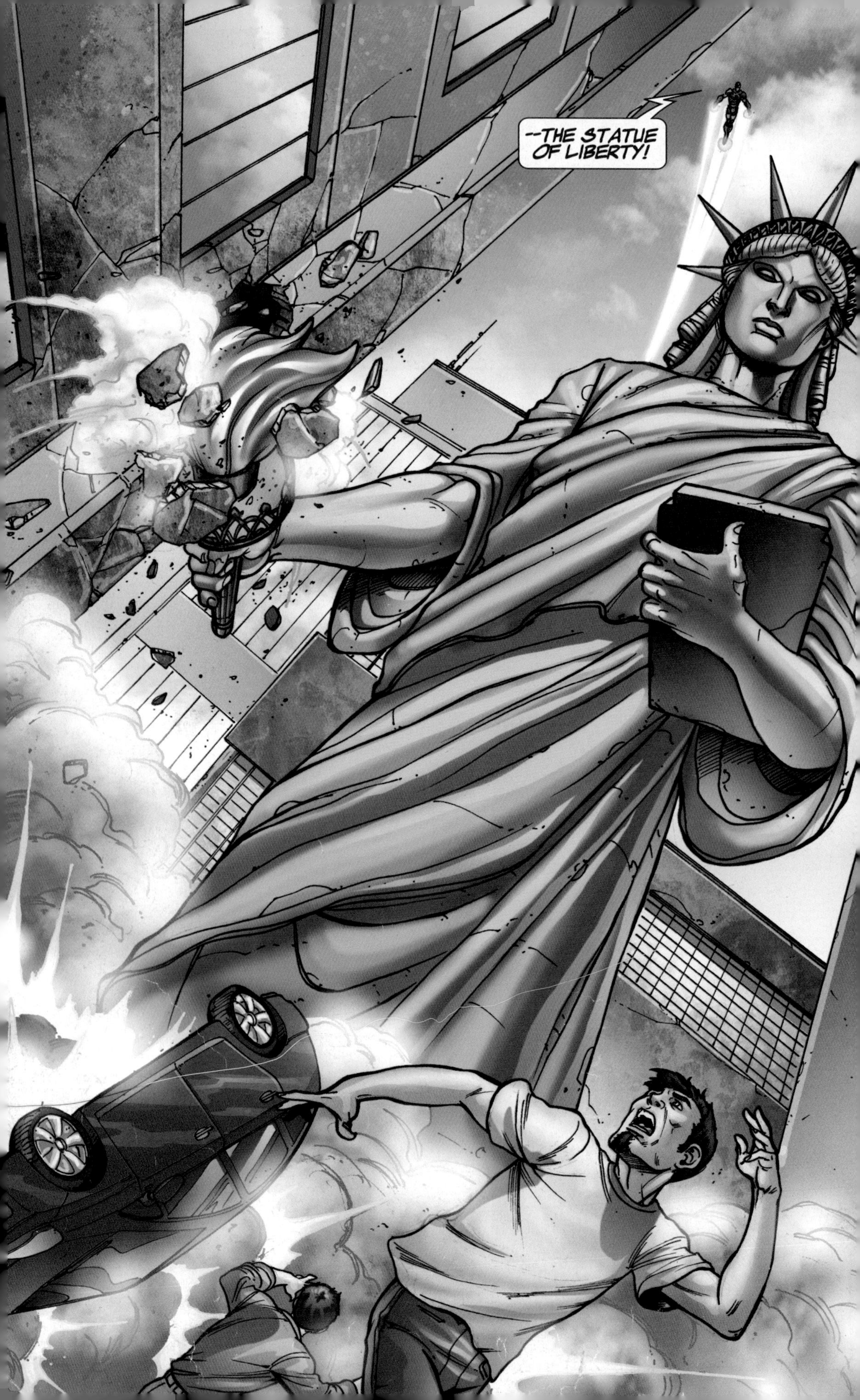
--THE STATUE OF LIBERTY!

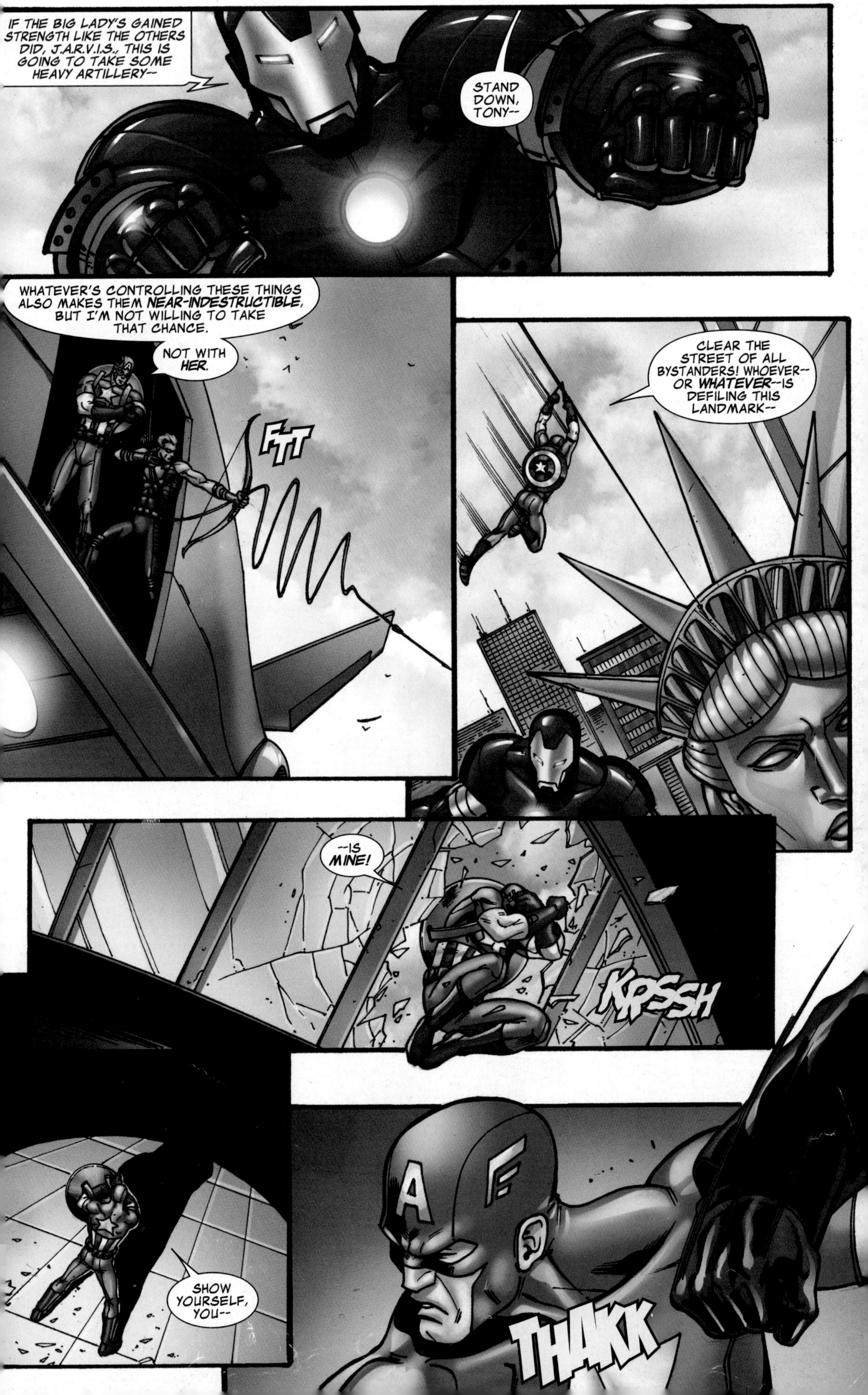
IF THE BIG LADY'S GAINED STRENGTH LIKE THE OTHERS DID, J.A.R.V.I.S., THIS IS GOING TO TAKE SOME HEAVY ARTILLERY--
STAND DOWN, TONY--
WHATEVER'S CONTROLLING THESE THINGS ALSO MAKES THEM NEAR-INDESTRUCTIBLE, BUT I'M NOT WILLING TO TAKE THAT CHANCE.
NOT WITH HER.
FTT
CLEAR THE STREET OF ALL BYSTANDERS! WHOEVER-- OR WHATEVER--IS DEFILING THIS LANDMARK--
--IS MINE!
KRSSH
SHOW YOURSELF, YOU--
THAKK

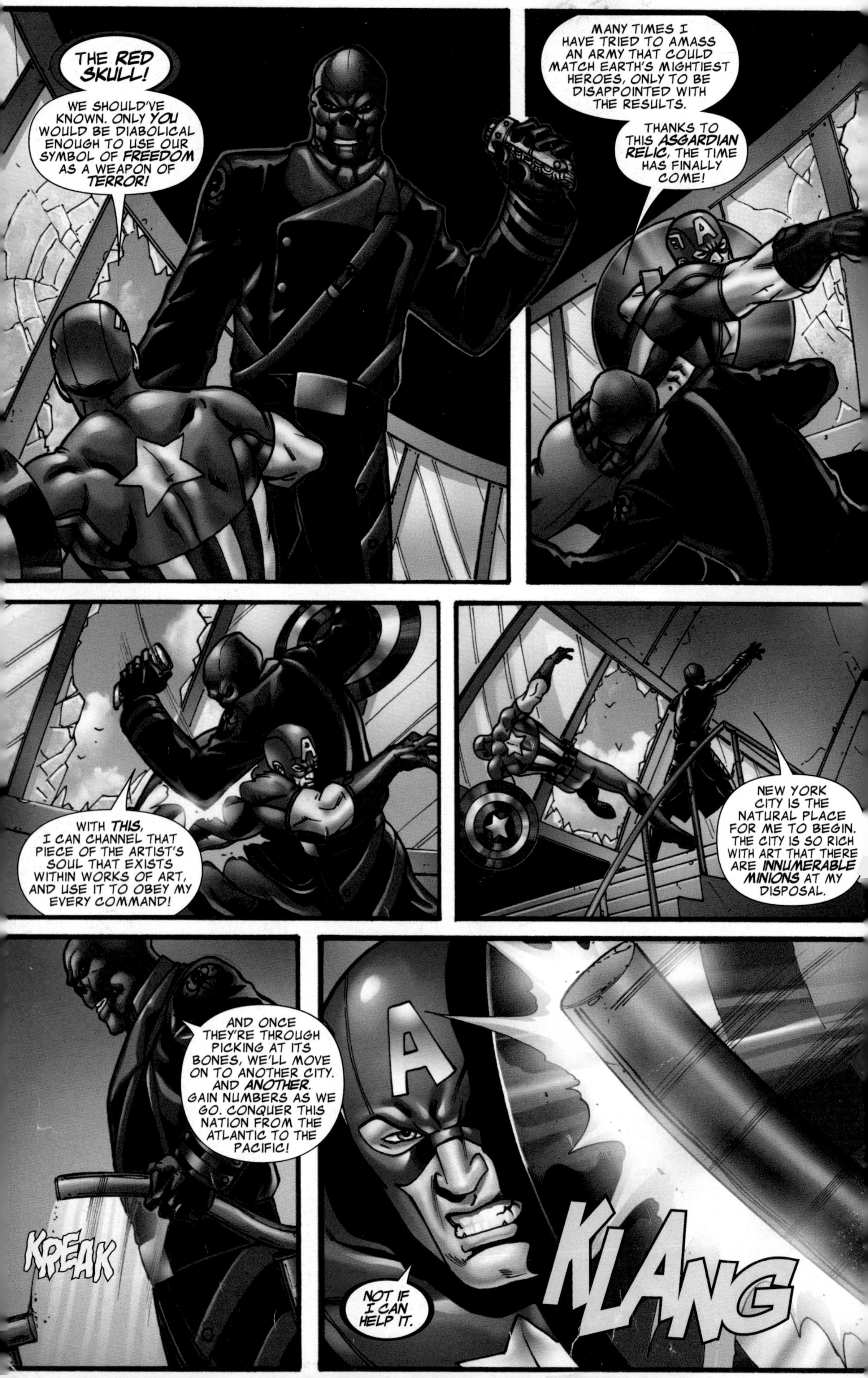

THE RED SKULL!
WE SHOULD'VE KNOWN. ONLY YOU WOULD BE DIABOLICAL ENOUGH TO USE OUR SYMBOL OF FREEDOM AS A WEAPON OF TERROR!
MANY TIMES I HAVE TRIED TO AMASS AN ARMY THAT COULD MATCH EARTH'S MIGHTIEST HEROES, ONLY TO BE DISAPPOINTED WITH THE RESULTS.
THANKS TO THIS ASGARDIAN RELIC, THE TIME HAS FINALLY COME!
WITH THIS, I CAN CHANNEL THAT PIECE OF THE ARTIST'S SOUL THAT EXISTS WITHIN WORKS OF ART, AND USE IT TO OBEY MY EVERY COMMAND!
NEW YORK CITY IS THE NATURAL PLACE FOR ME TO BEGIN. THE CITY IS SO RICH WITH ART THAT THERE ARE INNUMERABLE MINIONS AT MY DISPOSAL.
AND ONCE THEY'RE THROUGH PICKING AT ITS BONES, WE'LL MOVE ON TO ANOTHER CITY. AND ANOTHER. GAIN NUMBERS AS WE GO. CONQUER THIS NATION FROM THE ATLANTIC TO THE PACIFIC!
KREAK
NOT IF I CAN HELP IT.
KLANG

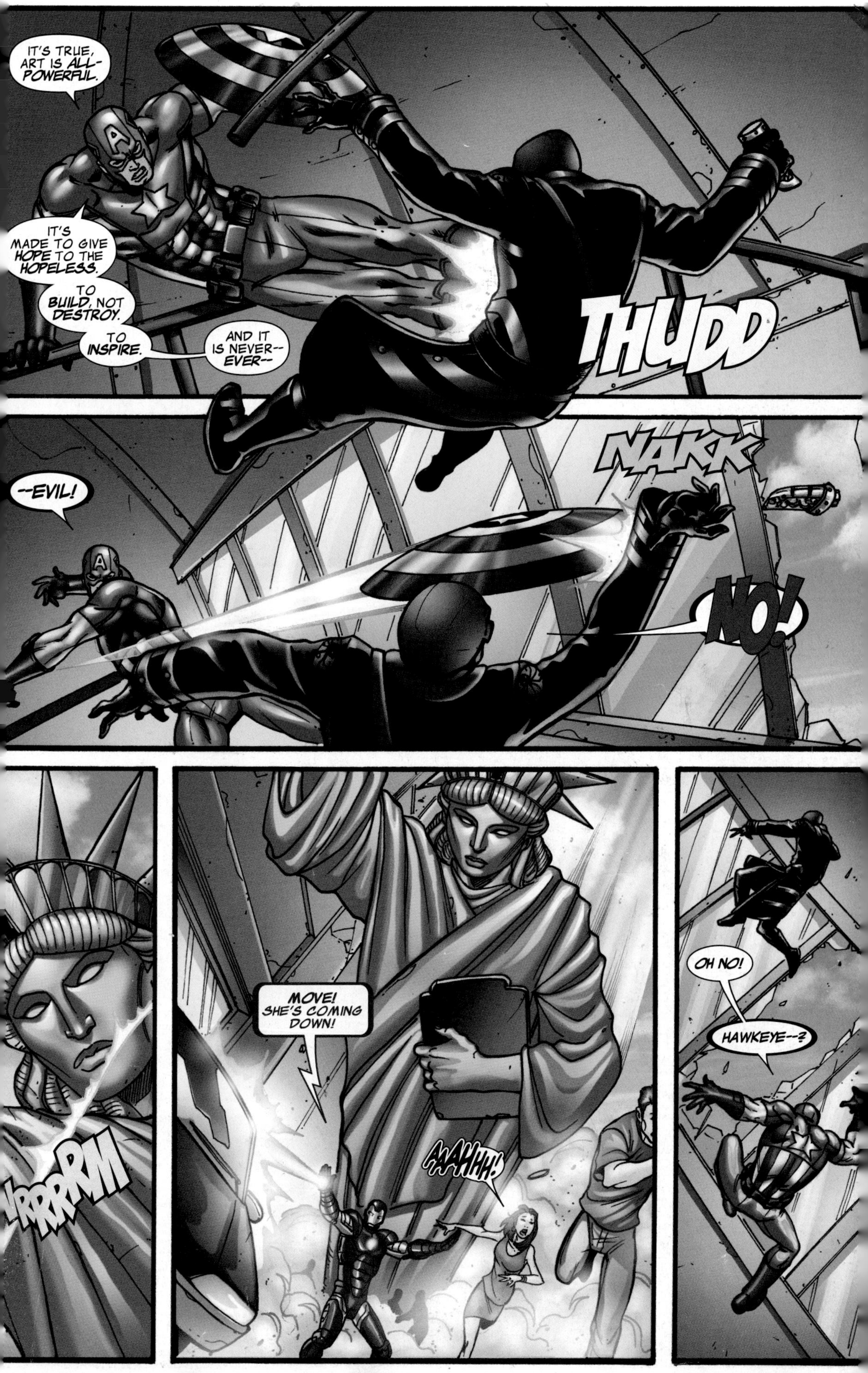
IT'S TRUE, ART IS ALL-POWERFUL.
IT'S MADE TO GIVE HOPE TO THE HOPELESS.
TO BUILD, NOT DESTROY.
TO INSPIRE.
AND IT IS NEVER-- EVER--
THUDD
NAKK
--EVIL!
NO!
RRRRRM
MOVE! SHE'S COMING DOWN!
AAHHH!
OH NO!
HAWKEYE--?

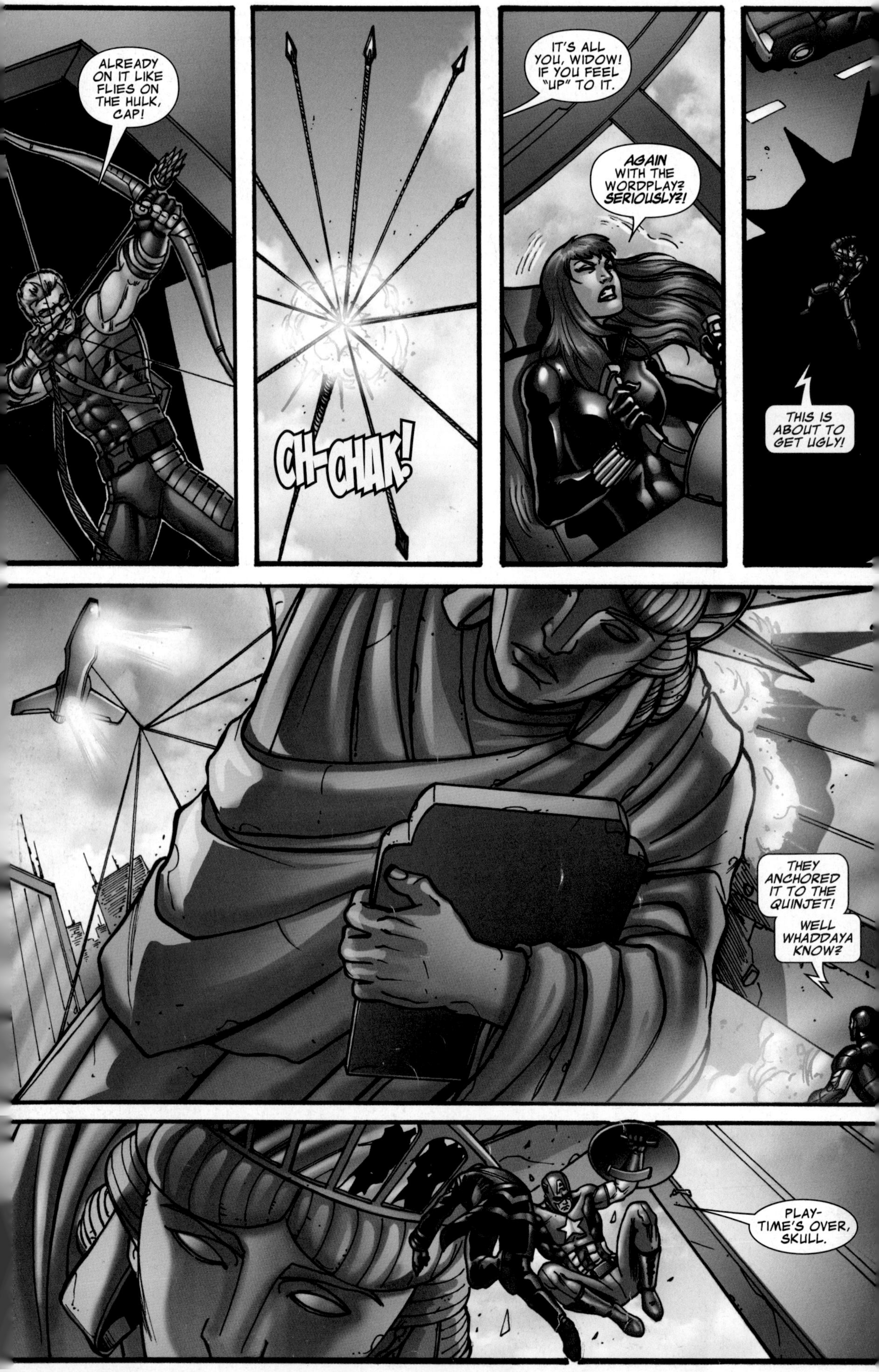
ALREADY ON IT LIKE FLIES ON THE HULK, CAP!
CH-CHAK!
IT'S ALL YOU, WIDOW! IF YOU FEEL "UP" TO IT.
AGAIN WITH THE WORDPLAY? SERIOUSLY?!
THIS IS ABOUT TO GET UGLY!
THEY ANCHORED IT TO THE QUINJET!
WELL WHADDAYA KNOW?
PLAY-TIME'S OVER, SKULL.

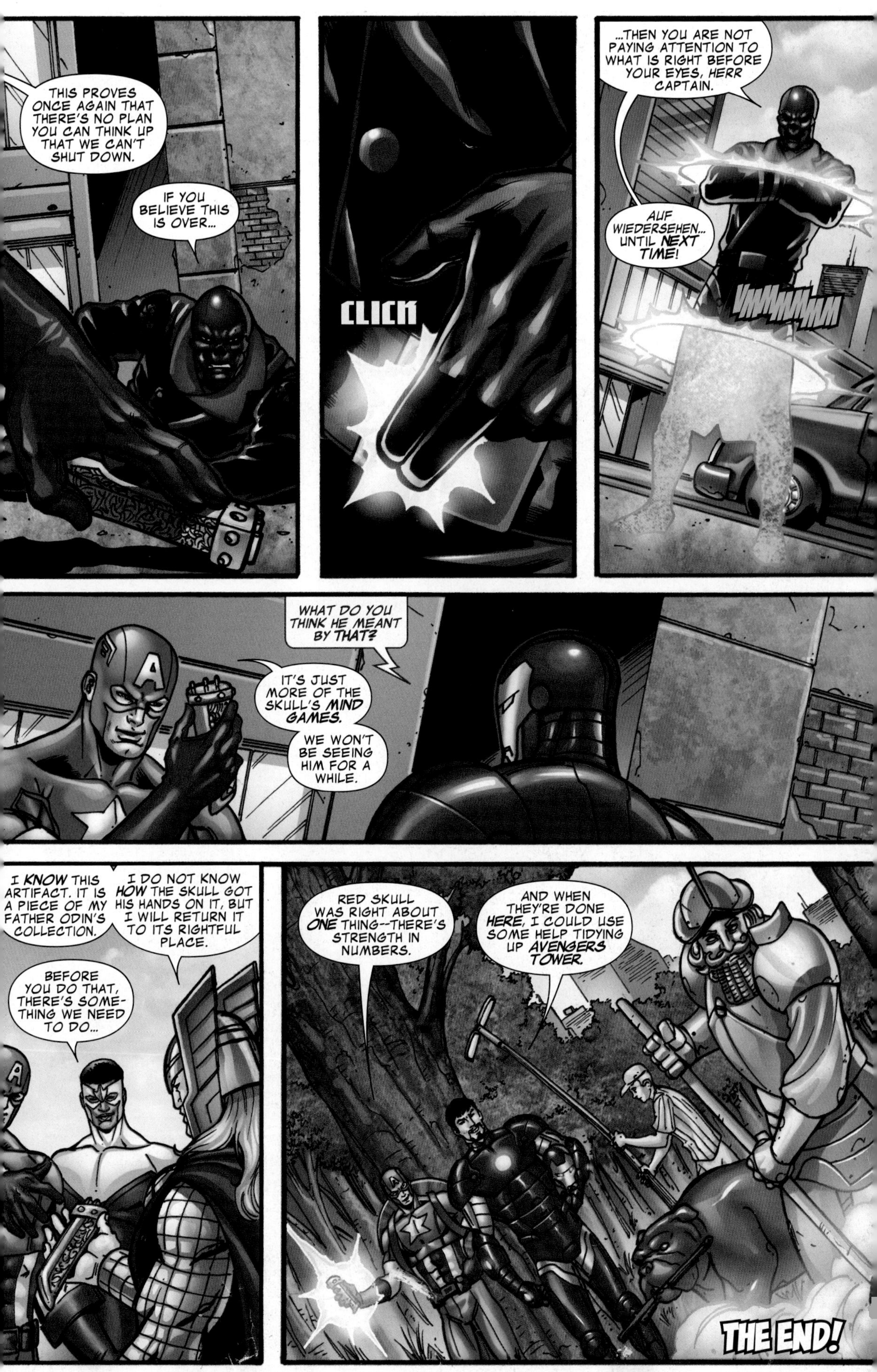
THIS PROVES ONCE AGAIN THAT THERE'S NO PLAN YOU CAN THINK UP THAT WE CAN'T SHUT DOWN.
IF YOU BELIEVE THIS IS OVER...
CLICK
...THEN YOU ARE NOT PAYING ATTENTION TO WHAT IS RIGHT BEFORE YOUR EYES, HERR CAPTAIN.
AUF WIEDERSEHEN... UNTIL NEXT TIME!
VMMMMMM
WHAT DO YOU THINK HE MEANT BY THAT?
IT'S JUST MORE OF THE SKULL'S MIND GAMES.
WE WON'T BE SEEING HIM FOR A WHILE.
I KNOW THIS ARTIFACT. IT IS A PIECE OF MY FATHER ODIN'S COLLECTION.
I DO NOT KNOW HOW THE SKULL GOT HIS HANDS ON IT, BUT I WILL RETURN IT TO ITS RIGHTFUL PLACE.
BEFORE YOU DO THAT, THERE'S SOMETHING WE NEED TO DO...
RED SKULL WAS RIGHT ABOUT ONE THING--THERE'S STRENGTH IN NUMBERS.
AND WHEN THEY'RE DONE HERE, I COULD USE SOME HELP TIDYING UP AVENGERS TOWER.
THE END!

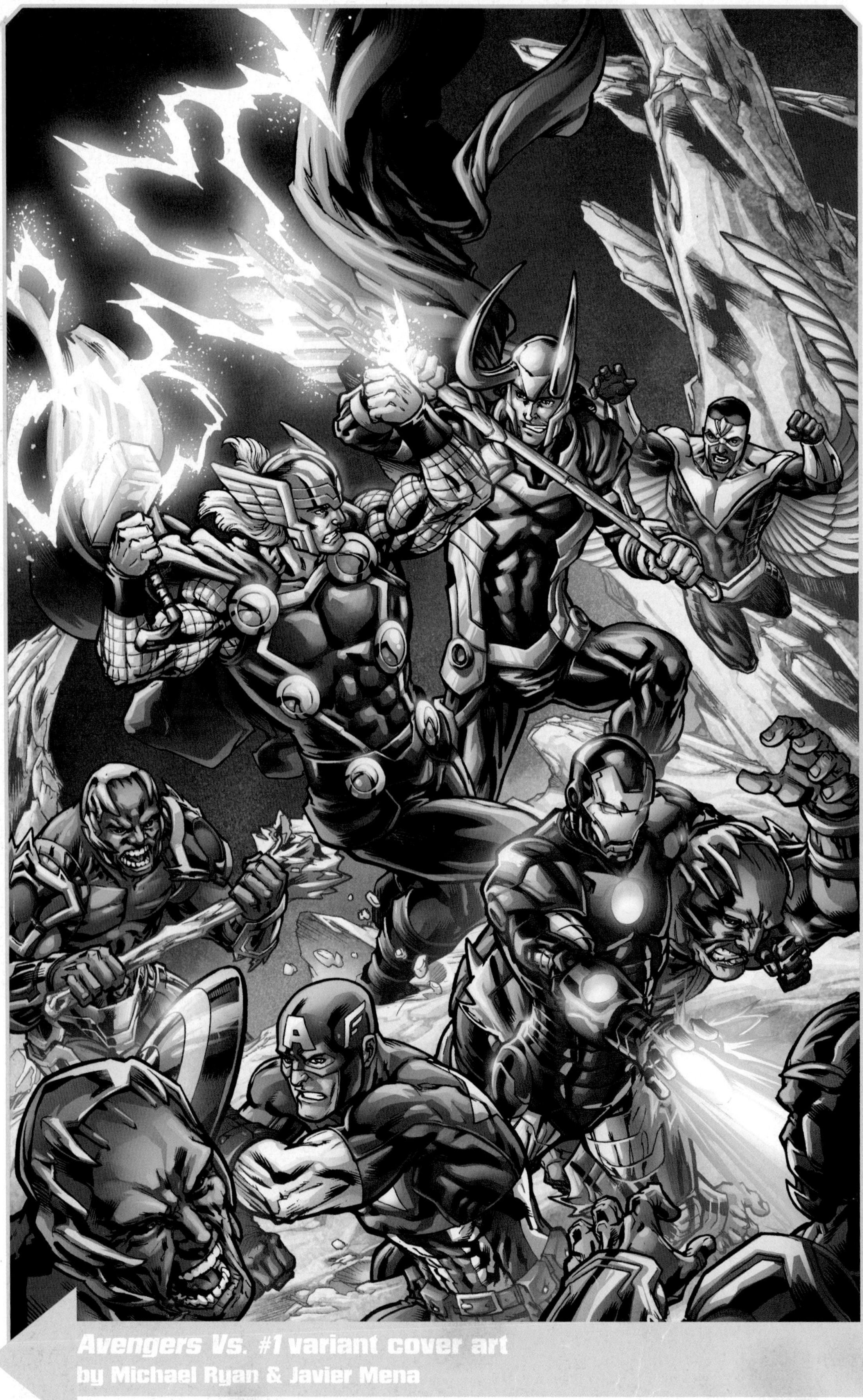

***Avengers Vs. #1* variant cover art**
by Michael Ryan & Javier Mena

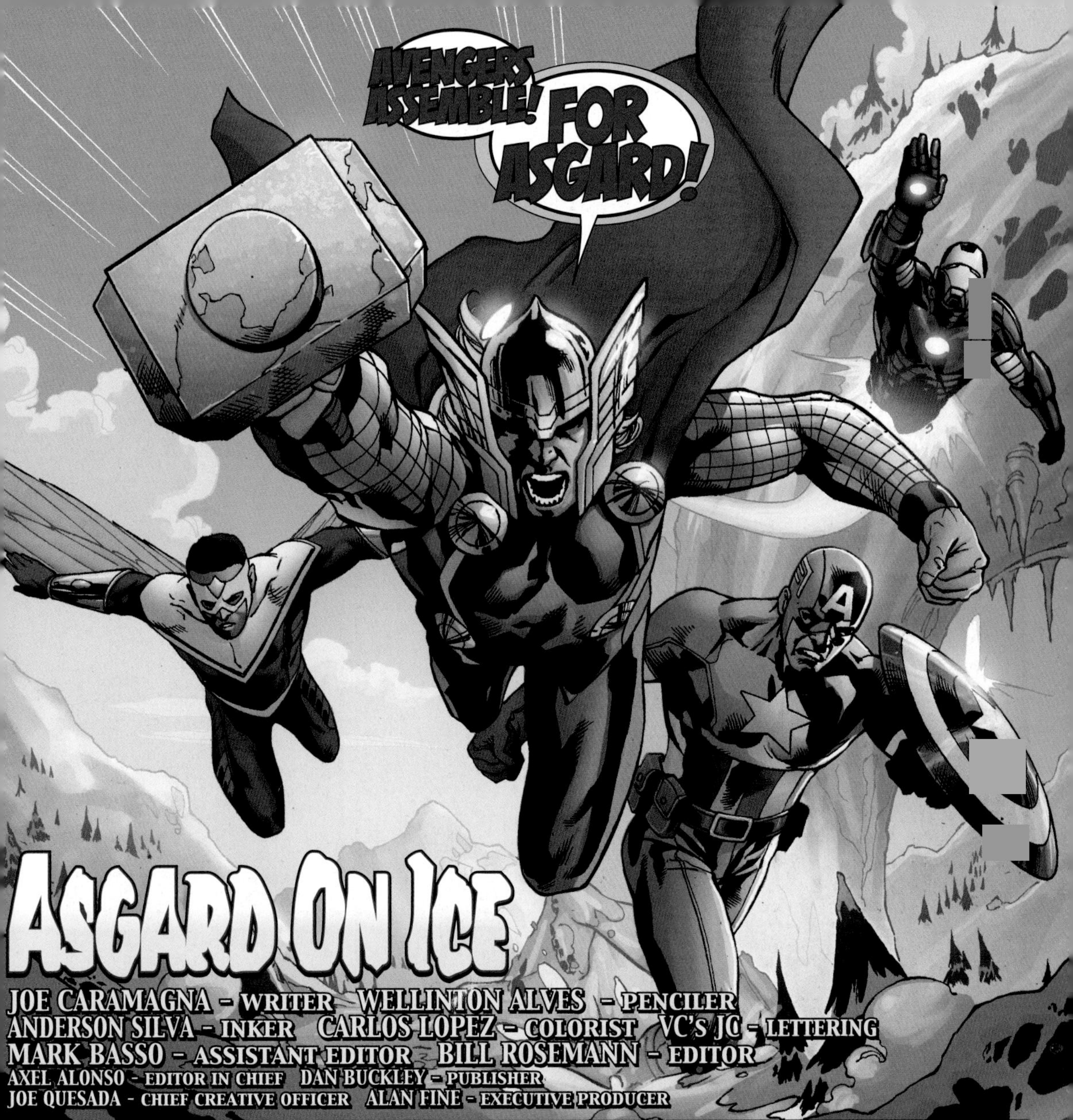
AVENGERS ASSEMBLE!
FOR ASGARD!
ASGARD ON ICE
JOE CARAMAGNA - WRITER WELLINTON ALVES - PENCILER
ANDERSON SILVA - INKER CARLOS LOPEZ - COLORIST VC'S JC - LETTERING
MARK BASSO - ASSISTANT EDITOR BILL ROSEMANN - EDITOR
AXEL ALONSO - EDITOR IN CHIEF DAN BUCKLEY - PUBLISHER
JOE QUESADA - CHIEF CREATIVE OFFICER ALAN FINE - EXECUTIVE PRODUCER

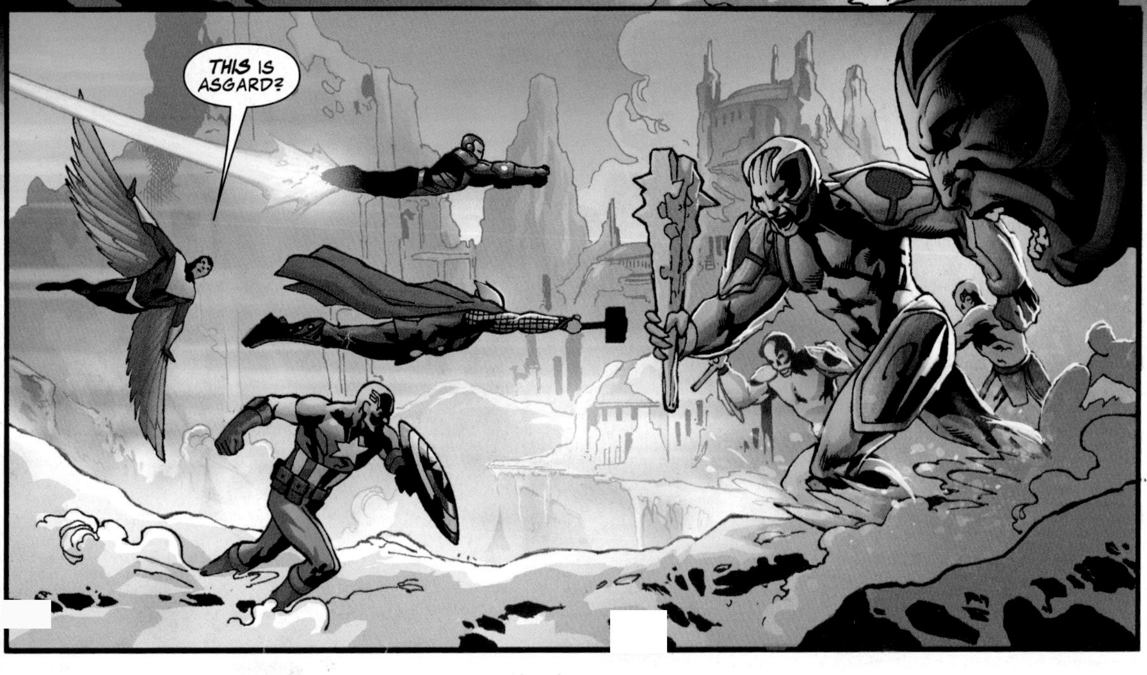
THIS IS ASGARD?

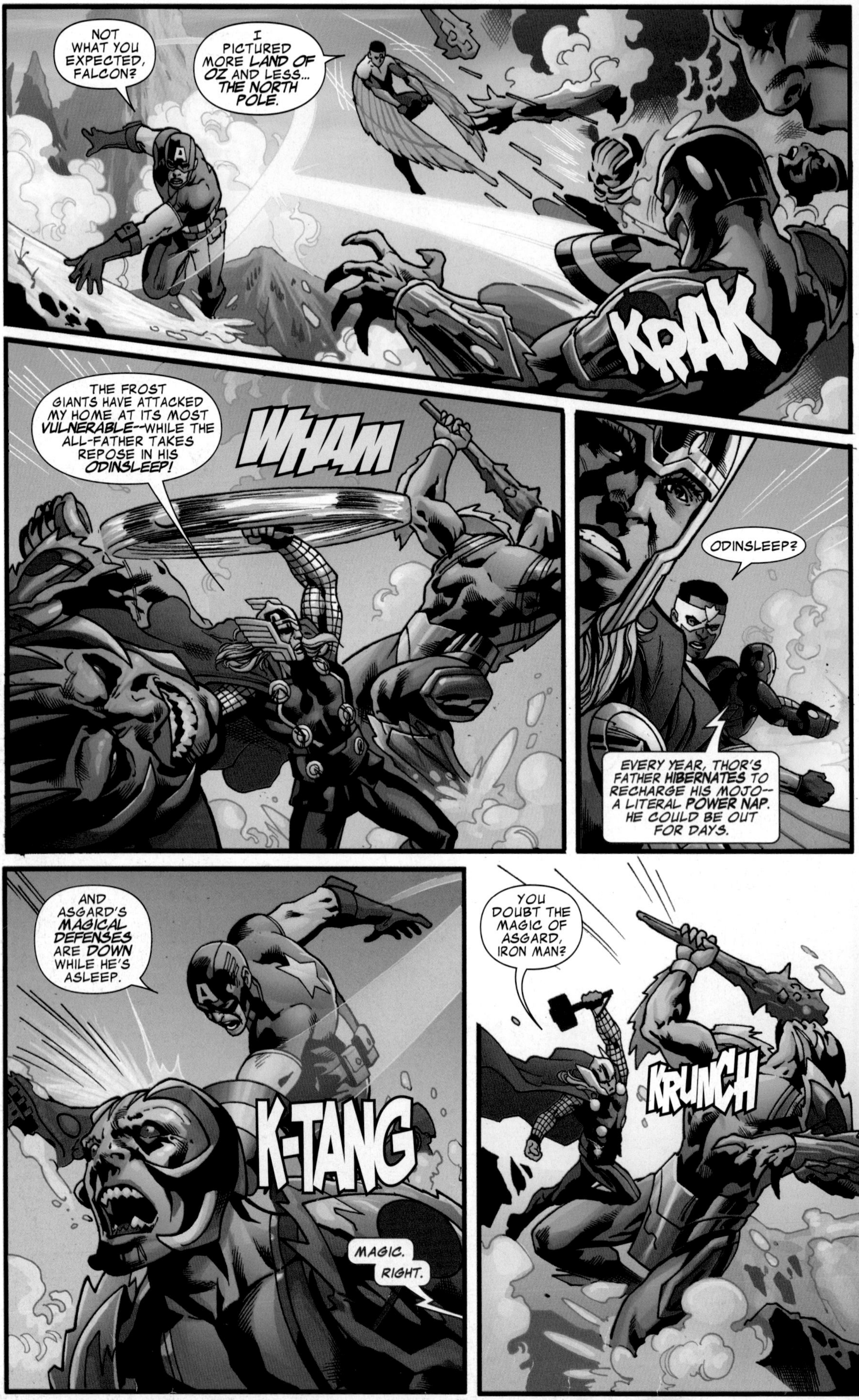
NOT WHAT YOU EXPECTED, FALCON?
I PICTURED MORE LAND OF OZ AND LESS... THE NORTH POLE.
KRAK
THE FROST GIANTS HAVE ATTACKED MY HOME AT ITS MOST VULNERABLE--WHILE THE ALL-FATHER TAKES REPOSE IN HIS ODINSLEEP!
WHAM
ODINSLEEP?
EVERY YEAR, THOR'S FATHER HIBERNATES TO RECHARGE HIS MOJO-- A LITERAL POWER NAP. HE COULD BE OUT FOR DAYS.
AND ASGARD'S MAGICAL DEFENSES ARE DOWN WHILE HE'S ASLEEP.
K-TANG
MAGIC. RIGHT.
YOU DOUBT THE MAGIC OF ASGARD, IRON MAN?
KRUNCH

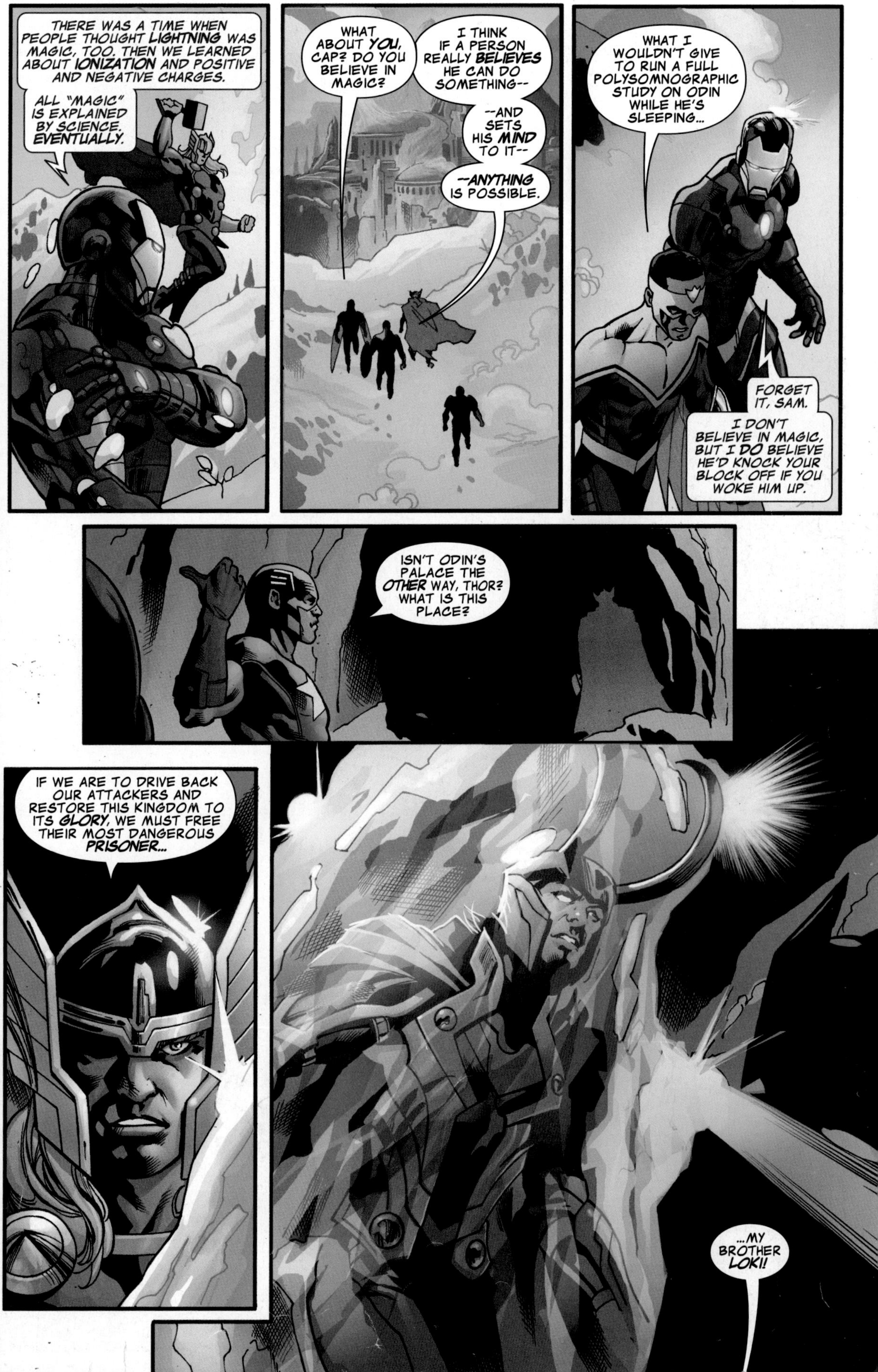
THERE WAS A TIME WHEN PEOPLE THOUGHT LIGHTNING WAS MAGIC, TOO. THEN WE LEARNED ABOUT IONIZATION AND POSITIVE AND NEGATIVE CHARGES.
ALL "MAGIC" IS EXPLAINED BY SCIENCE. EVENTUALLY.
WHAT ABOUT YOU, CAP? DO YOU BELIEVE IN MAGIC?
I THINK IF A PERSON REALLY BELIEVES HE CAN DO SOMETHING--
--AND SETS HIS MIND TO IT--
--ANYTHING IS POSSIBLE.
WHAT I WOULDN'T GIVE TO RUN A FULL POLYSOMNOGRAPHIC STUDY ON ODIN WHILE HE'S SLEEPING...
FORGET IT, SAM.
I DON'T BELIEVE IN MAGIC, BUT I DO BELIEVE HE'D KNOCK YOUR BLOCK OFF IF YOU WOKE HIM UP.
ISN'T ODIN'S PALACE THE OTHER WAY, THOR? WHAT IS THIS PLACE?
IF WE ARE TO DRIVE BACK OUR ATTACKERS AND RESTORE THIS KINGDOM TO ITS GLORY, WE MUST FREE THEIR MOST DANGEROUS PRISONER...
...MY BROTHER LOKI!

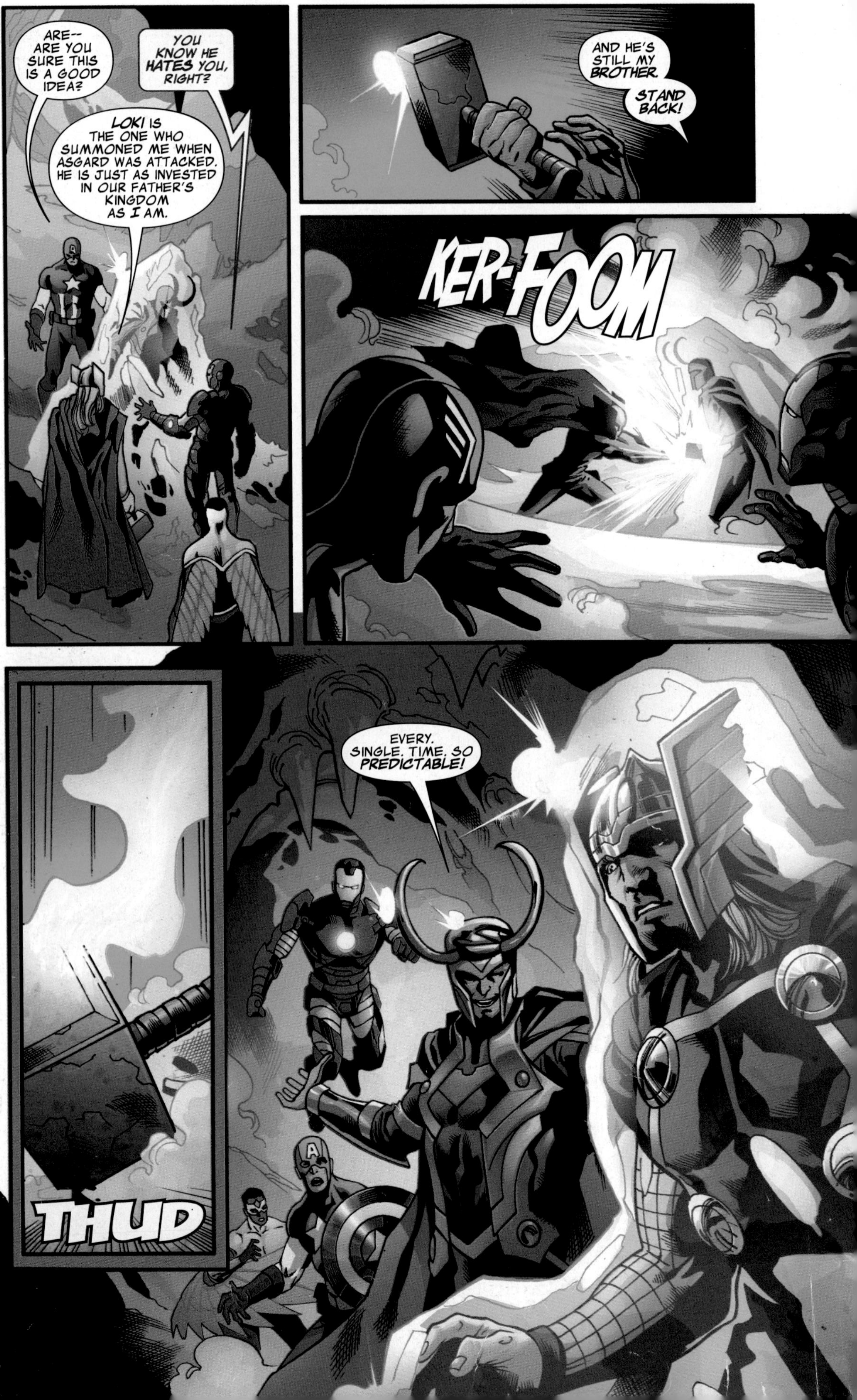
ARE--
ARE YOU SURE THIS IS A GOOD IDEA?
YOU KNOW HE HATES YOU, RIGHT?
LOKI IS THE ONE WHO SUMMONED ME WHEN ASGARD WAS ATTACKED. HE IS JUST AS INVESTED IN OUR FATHER'S KINGDOM AS I AM.
AND HE'S STILL MY BROTHER.
STAND BACK!
KER-FOOM
THUD
EVERY. SINGLE. TIME. SO PREDICTABLE!

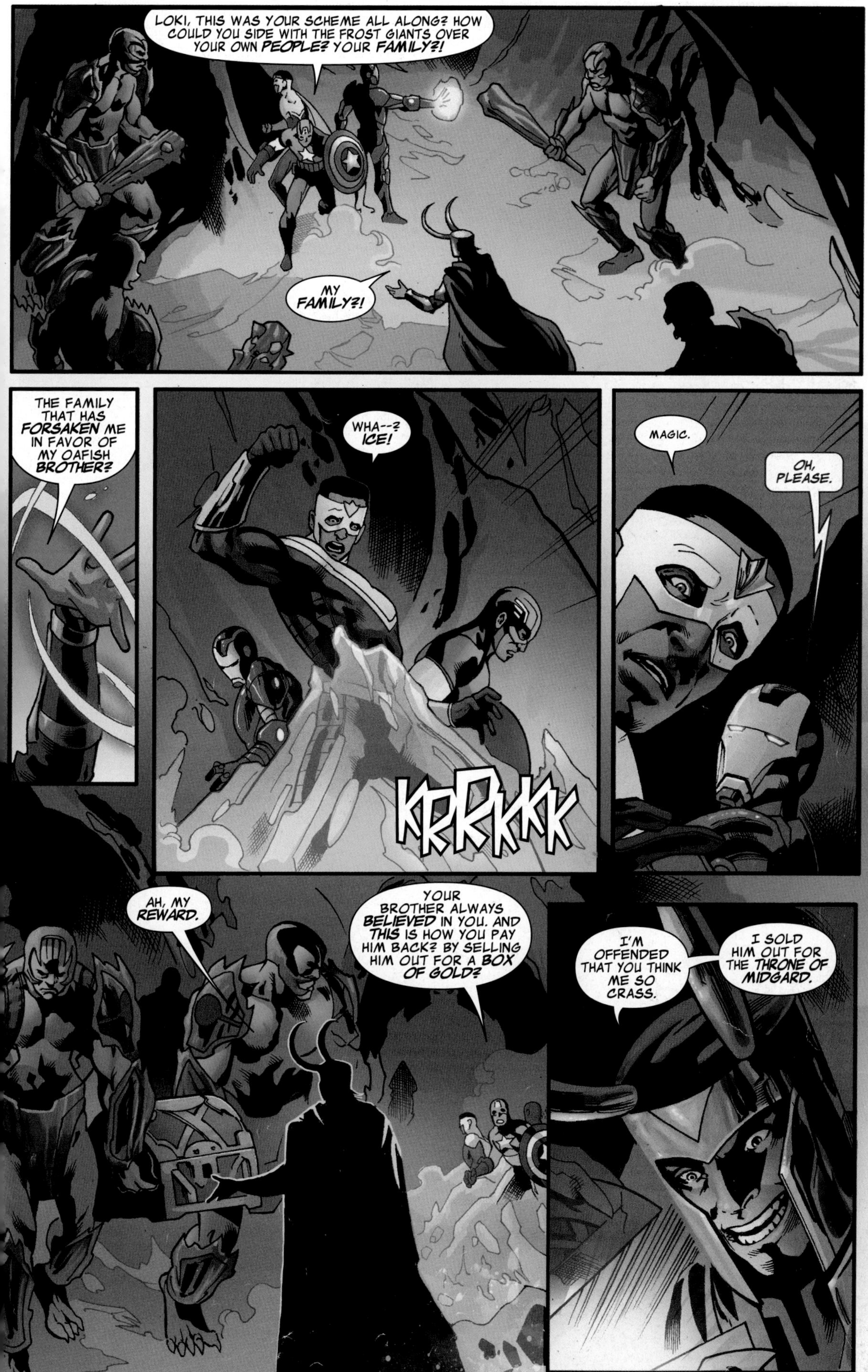
LOKI, THIS WAS YOUR SCHEME ALL ALONG? HOW COULD YOU SIDE WITH THE FROST GIANTS OVER YOUR OWN PEOPLE? YOUR FAMILY?!
MY FAMILY?!
THE FAMILY THAT HAS FORSAKEN ME IN FAVOR OF MY OAFISH BROTHER?
WHA--? ICE!
KRRKKK
MAGIC.
OH, PLEASE.
AH, MY REWARD.
YOUR BROTHER ALWAYS BELIEVED IN YOU. AND THIS IS HOW YOU PAY HIM BACK? BY SELLING HIM OUT FOR A BOX OF GOLD?
I'M OFFENDED THAT YOU THINK ME SO CRASS.
I SOLD HIM OUT FOR THE THRONE OF MIDGARD.

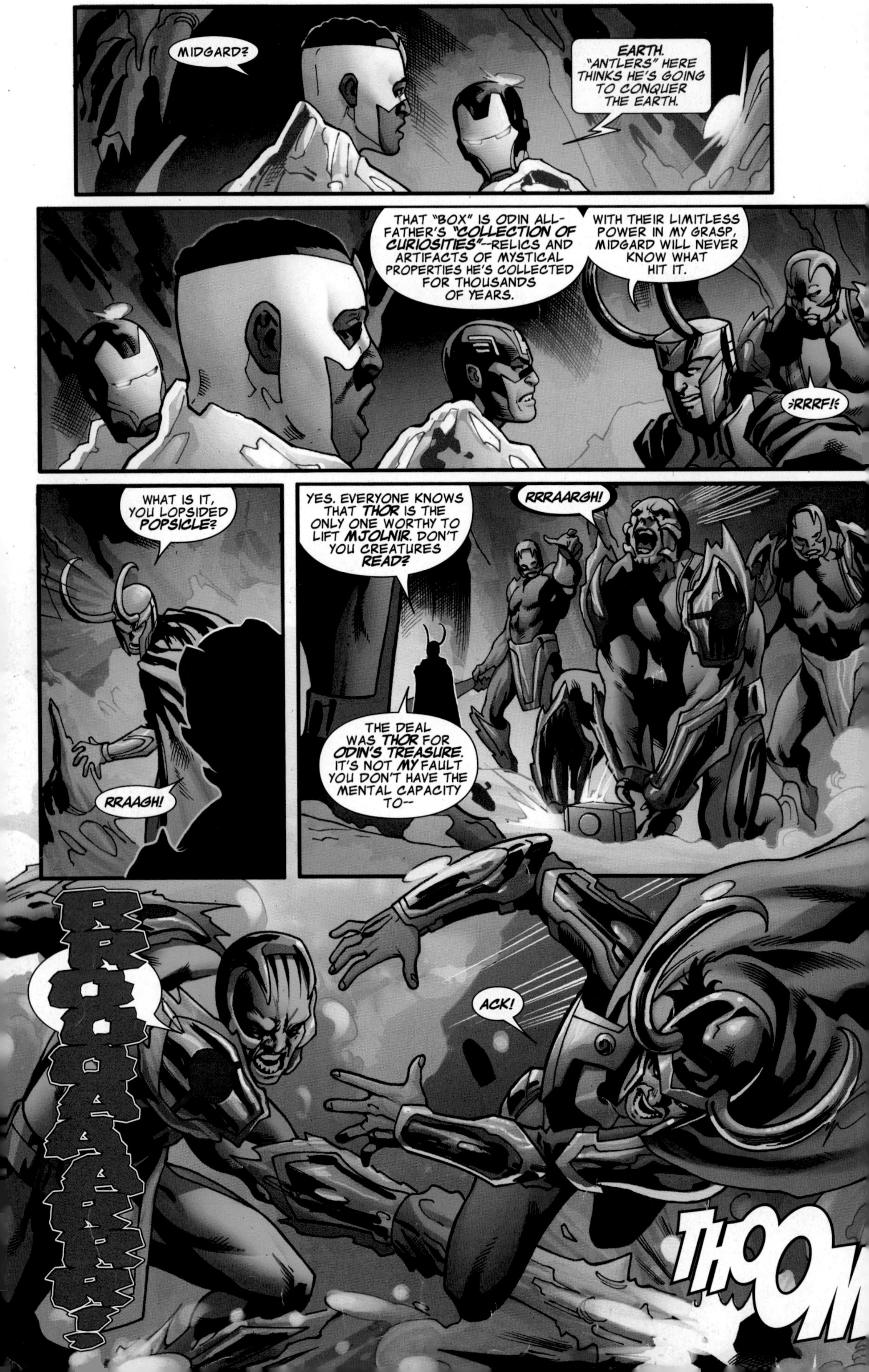
MIDGARD?
EARTH. "ANTLERS" HERE THINKS HE'S GOING TO CONQUER THE EARTH.
THAT "BOX" IS ODIN ALL-FATHER'S "COLLECTION OF CURIOSITIES"--RELICS AND ARTIFACTS OF MYSTICAL PROPERTIES HE'S COLLECTED FOR THOUSANDS OF YEARS.
WITH THEIR LIMITLESS POWER IN MY GRASP, MIDGARD WILL NEVER KNOW WHAT HIT IT.
RRRF!
WHAT IS IT, YOU LOPSIDED POPSICLE?
RRAAGH!
YES. EVERYONE KNOWS THAT THOR IS THE ONLY ONE WORTHY TO LIFT MJOLNIR. DON'T YOU CREATURES READ?
RRRAARGH!
THE DEAL WAS THOR FOR ODIN'S TREASURE. IT'S NOT MY FAULT YOU DON'T HAVE THE MENTAL CAPACITY TO--
ACK!
THOOM

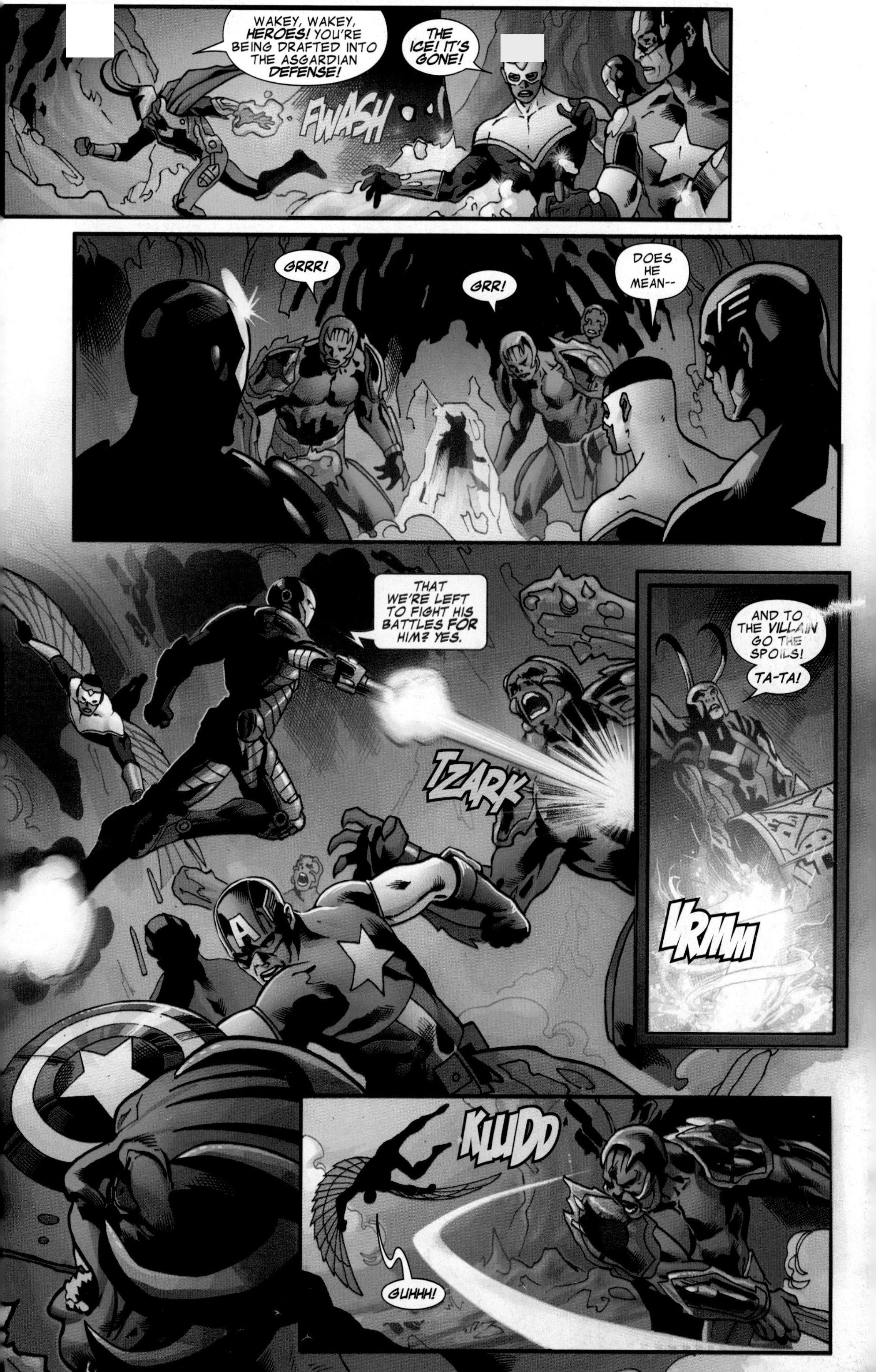

WAKEY, WAKEY, HEROES! YOU'RE BEING DRAFTED INTO THE ASGARDIAN DEFENSE!
FWASH
THE ICE! IT'S GONE!
GRRR!
GRR!
DOES HE MEAN--
THAT WE'RE LEFT TO FIGHT HIS BATTLES FOR HIM? YES.
TZARK
AND TO THE VILLAIN GO THE SPOILS!
TA-TA!
VRMMM
KLUDD
GUHHH!

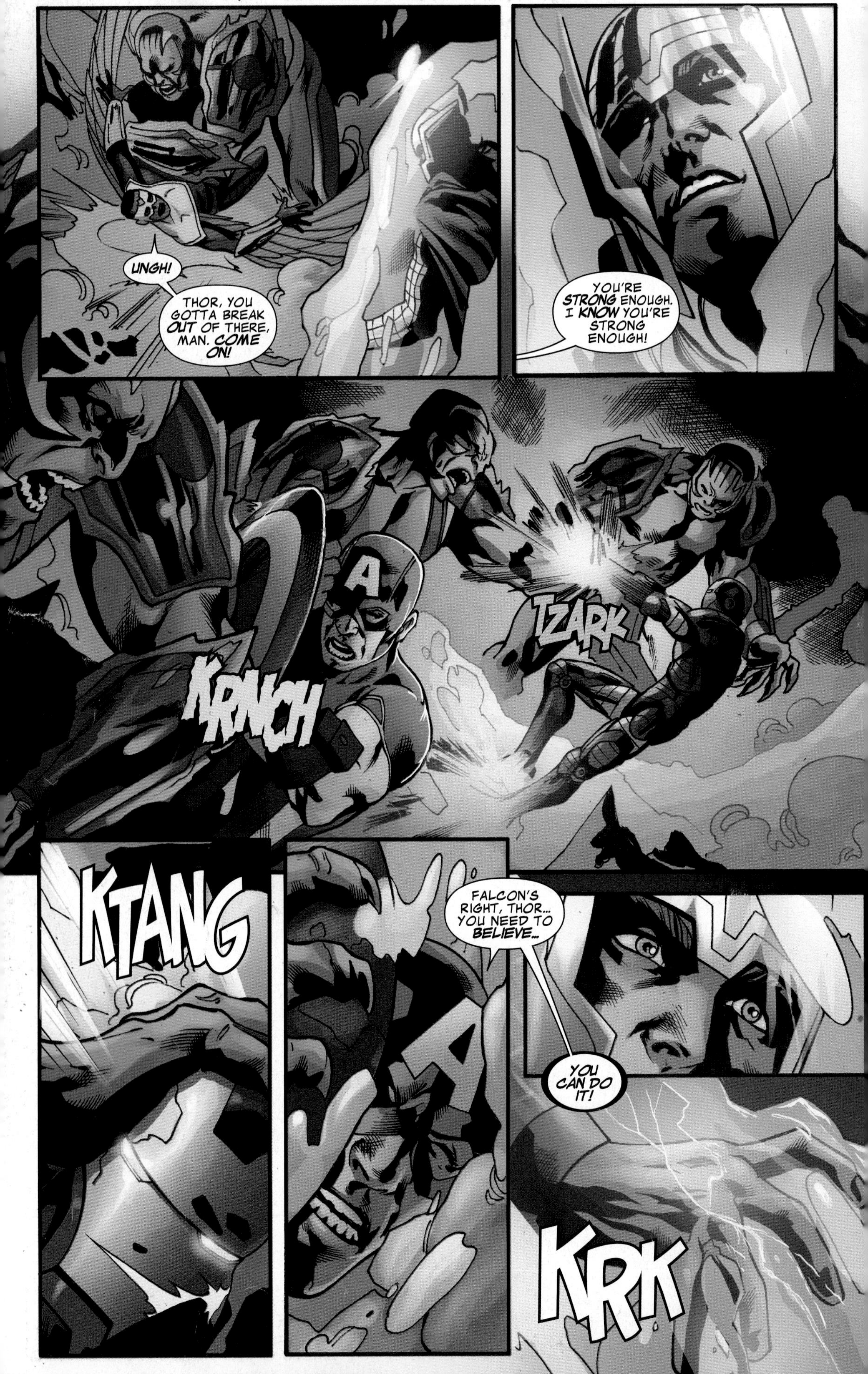
UNGH!
THOR, YOU GOTTA BREAK OUT OF THERE, MAN. COME ON!
YOU'RE STRONG ENOUGH. I KNOW YOU'RE STRONG ENOUGH!
KRNCH
TZARK
KTANG
FALCON'S RIGHT, THOR... YOU NEED TO BELIEVE...
YOU CAN DO IT!
KRK

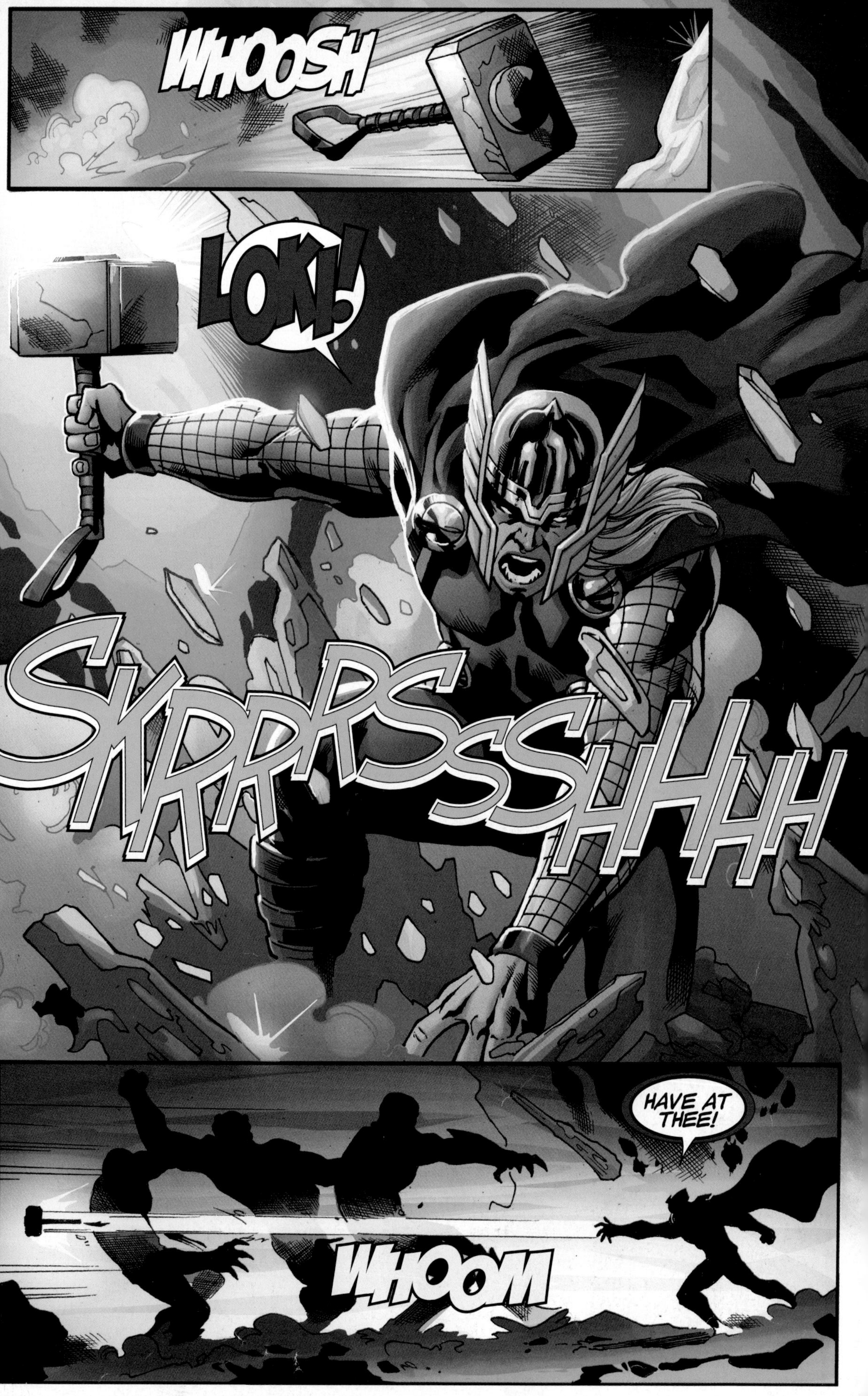
WHOOSH
LOKI!
SKRRRSSSHHHH
HAVE AT THEE!
WHOOM

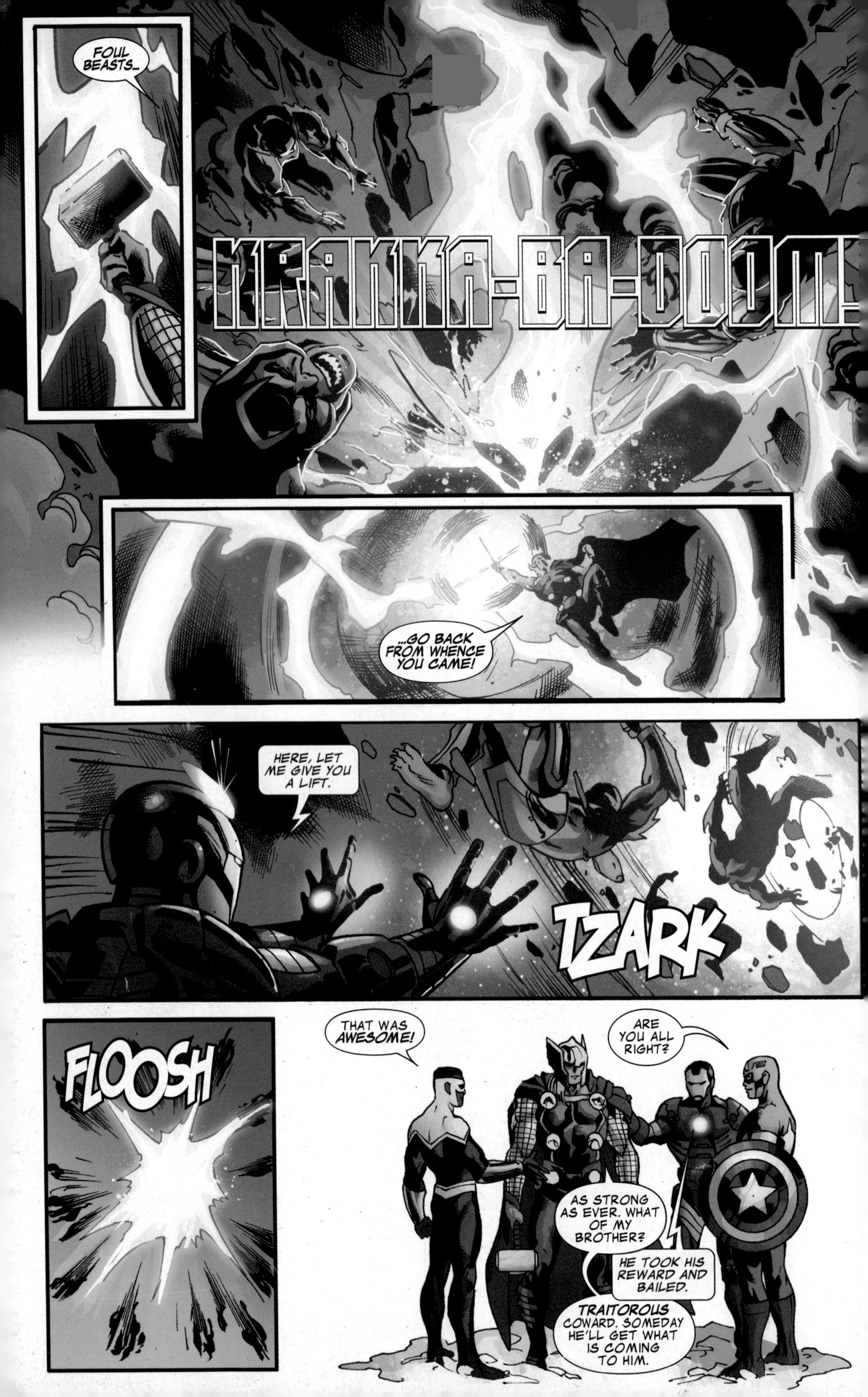
FOUL BEASTS...
KRAKKA-BA-DOOM!
...GO BACK FROM WHENCE YOU CAME!
HERE, LET ME GIVE YOU A LIFT.
TZARK
FLOOSH
THAT WAS AWESOME!
ARE YOU ALL RIGHT?
AS STRONG AS EVER. WHAT OF MY BROTHER?
HE TOOK HIS REWARD AND BAILED.
TRAITOROUS COWARD. SOMEDAY HE'LL GET WHAT IS COMING TO HIM.

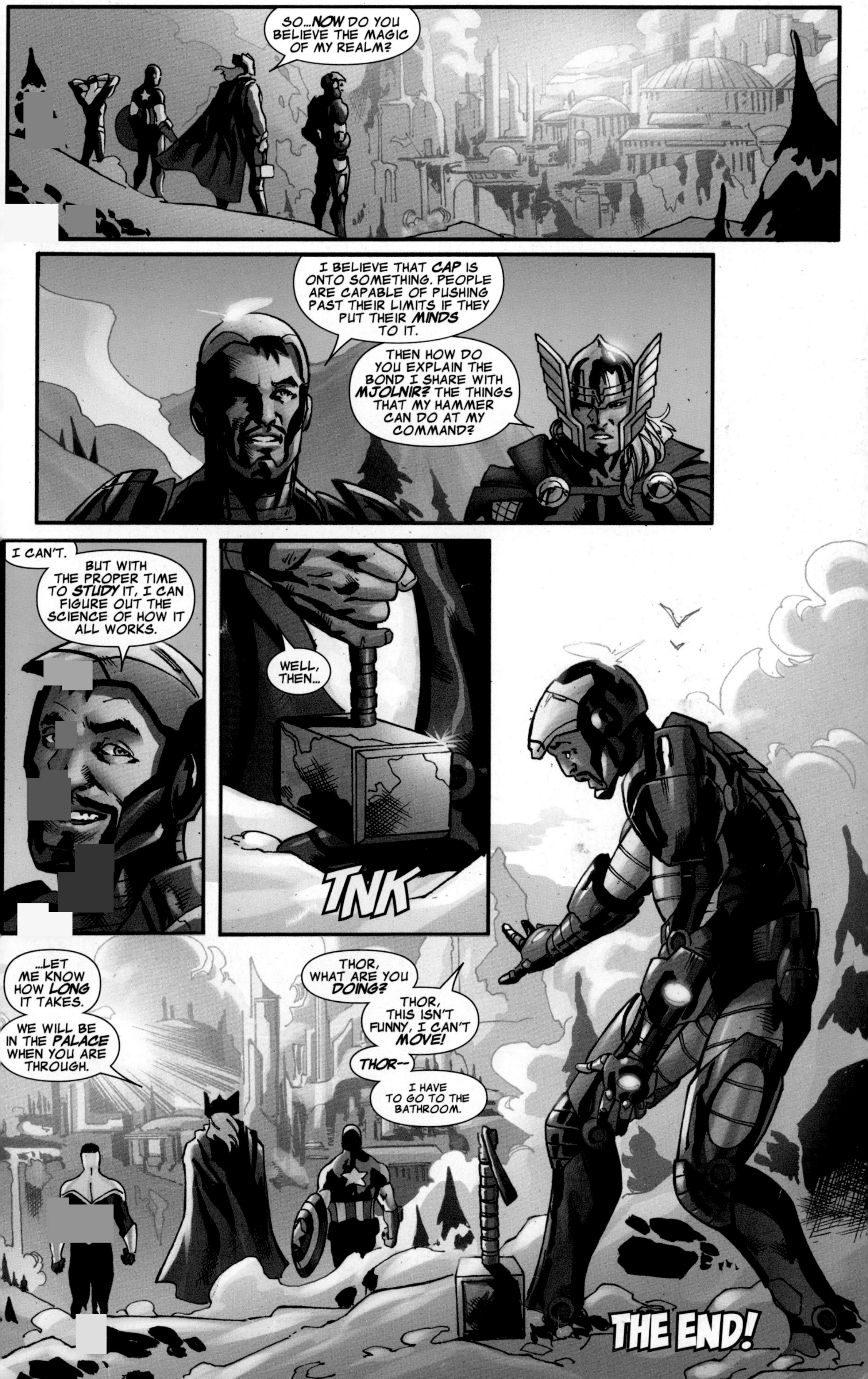
SO...NOW DO YOU BELIEVE THE MAGIC OF MY REALM?
I BELIEVE THAT CAP IS ONTO SOMETHING. PEOPLE ARE CAPABLE OF PUSHING PAST THEIR LIMITS IF THEY PUT THEIR MINDS TO IT.
THEN HOW DO YOU EXPLAIN THE BOND I SHARE WITH MJOLNIR? THE THINGS THAT MY HAMMER CAN DO AT MY COMMAND?
I CAN'T.
BUT WITH THE PROPER TIME TO STUDY IT, I CAN FIGURE OUT THE SCIENCE OF HOW IT ALL WORKS.
WELL, THEN...
TNK
...LET ME KNOW HOW LONG IT TAKES.
WE WILL BE IN THE PALACE WHEN YOU ARE THROUGH.
THOR, WHAT ARE YOU DOING?
THOR, THIS ISN'T FUNNY, I CAN'T MOVE!
THOR--
I HAVE TO GO TO THE BATHROOM.
THE END!

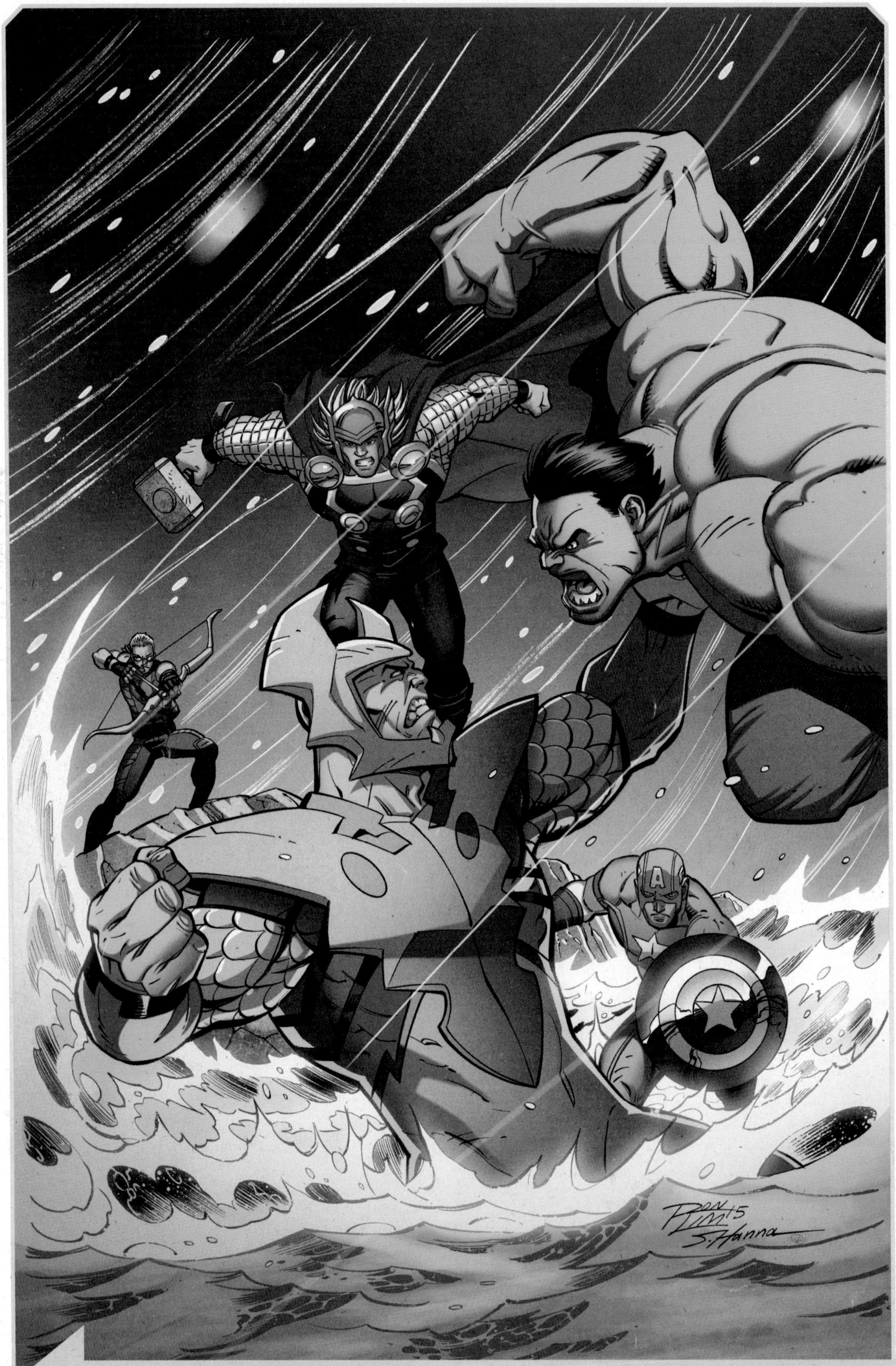

***Avengers Vs. #1* variant cover art**
by Ron Lim, Scott Hanna & Wil Quintana

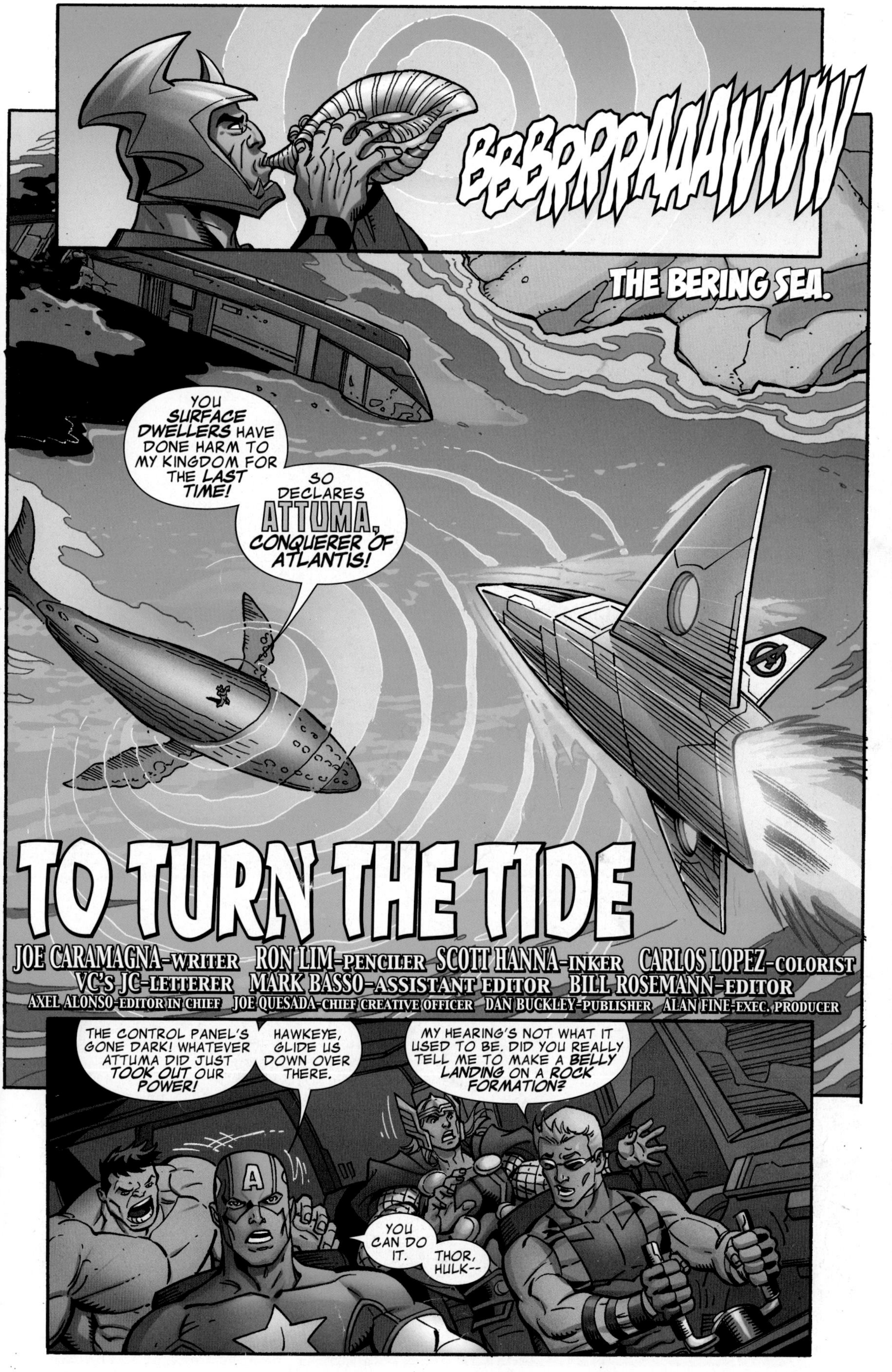
BBBRPRAAAWWW
THE BERING SEA.
YOU SURFACE DWELLERS HAVE DONE HARM TO MY KINGDOM FOR THE LAST TIME!
SO DECLARES ATTUMA, CONQUERER OF ATLANTIS!
TO TURN THE TIDE
JOE CARAMAGNA-WRITER RON LIM-PENCILER SCOTT HANNA-INKER CARLOS LOPEZ-COLORIST
VC'S JC-LETTERER MARK BASSO-ASSISTANT EDITOR BILL ROSEMANN-EDITOR
AXEL ALONSO-EDITOR IN CHIEF JOE QUESADA-CHIEF CREATIVE OFFICER DAN BUCKLEY-PUBLISHER ALAN FINE-EXEC. PRODUCER
THE CONTROL PANEL'S GONE DARK! WHATEVER ATTUMA DID JUST TOOK OUT OUR POWER!
HAWKEYE, GLIDE US DOWN OVER THERE.
MY HEARING'S NOT WHAT IT USED TO BE. DID YOU REALLY TELL ME TO MAKE A BELLY LANDING ON A ROCK FORMATION?
YOU CAN DO IT.
THOR, HULK--

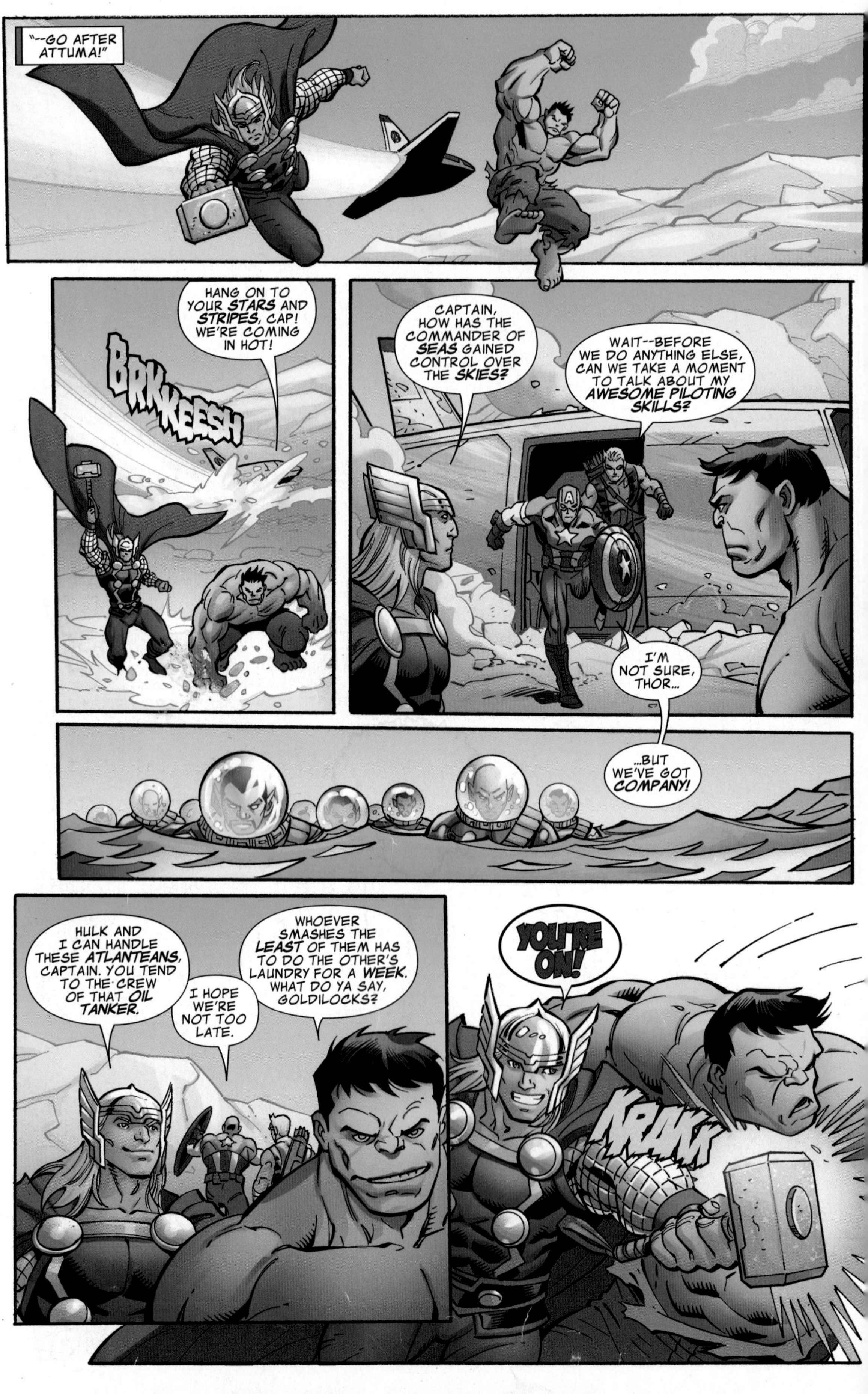
"--GO AFTER ATTUMA!"
HANG ON TO YOUR STARS AND STRIPES, CAP! WE'RE COMING IN HOT!
BRKKEESH
CAPTAIN, HOW HAS THE COMMANDER OF SEAS GAINED CONTROL OVER THE SKIES?
WAIT--BEFORE WE DO ANYTHING ELSE, CAN WE TAKE A MOMENT TO TALK ABOUT MY AWESOME PILOTING SKILLS?
I'M NOT SURE, THOR...
...BUT WE'VE GOT COMPANY!
HULK AND I CAN HANDLE THESE ATLANTEANS, CAPTAIN. YOU TEND TO THE CREW OF THAT OIL TANKER.
I HOPE WE'RE NOT TOO LATE.
WHOEVER SMASHES THE LEAST OF THEM HAS TO DO THE OTHER'S LAUNDRY FOR A WEEK. WHAT DO YA SAY, GOLDILOCKS?
YOU'RE ON!
KRAKK

I OUGHTTA PUT A FIVE-KNUCKLE DENT IN YOUR HELMET FOR THAT! BUT YOU DID ME A FAVOR.

THE ANGRIER I GET, THE STRONGER I GET. THE STRONGER I GET--

--THE MORE I SMASH!

SLAM

KRAKKK

YOUR TURN.

NEARBY.

IT'S NO USE, CAPTAIN, IT'S BROKEN!

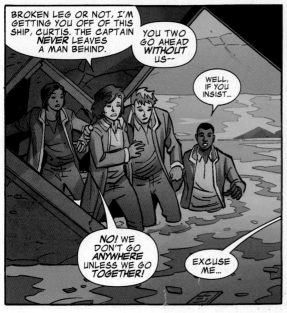

BROKEN LEG OR NOT, I'M GETTING YOU OFF OF THIS SHIP, CURTIS. THE CAPTAIN NEVER LEAVES A MAN BEHIND.

YOU TWO GO AHEAD WITHOUT US--

WELL, IF YOU INSIST...

NO! WE DON'T GO ANYWHERE UNLESS WE GO TOGETHER!

EXCUSE ME...

...DID SOMEONE ORDER A PIZZA?

CAPTAIN AMERICA!

AND HAWK GUY!

WHAT HAPPENED HERE?

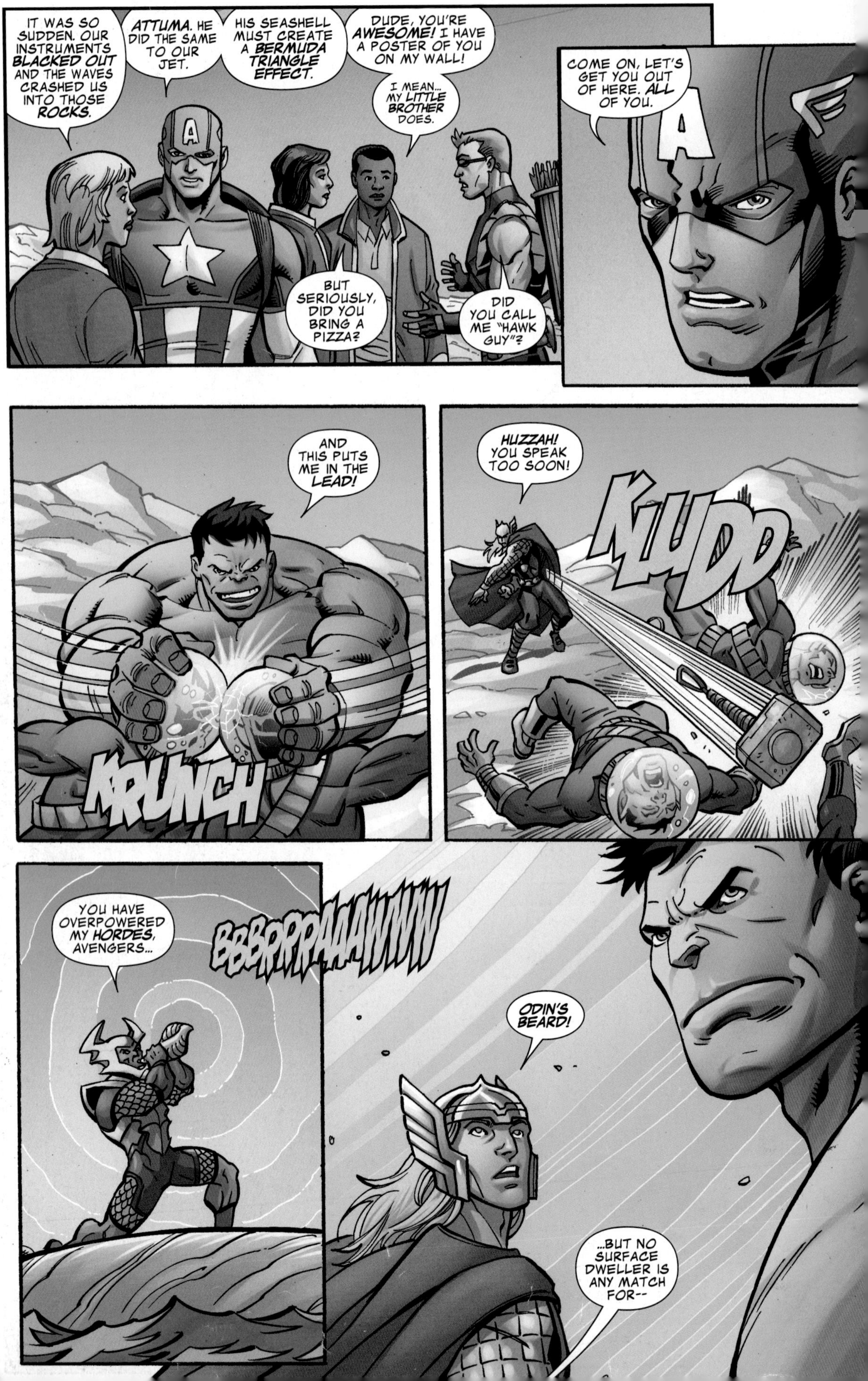
IT WAS SO SUDDEN. OUR INSTRUMENTS BLACKED OUT AND THE WAVES CRASHED US INTO THOSE ROCKS.
ATTUMA. HE DID THE SAME TO OUR JET.
HIS SEASHELL MUST CREATE A BERMUDA TRIANGLE EFFECT.
DUDE, YOU'RE AWESOME! I HAVE A POSTER OF YOU ON MY WALL!
I MEAN... MY LITTLE BROTHER DOES.
BUT SERIOUSLY, DID YOU BRING A PIZZA?
DID YOU CALL ME "HAWK GUY"?
COME ON, LET'S GET YOU OUT OF HERE. ALL OF YOU.
AND THIS PUTS ME IN THE LEAD!
KRUNCH
HUZZAH! YOU SPEAK TOO SOON!
KLUDD
YOU HAVE OVERPOWERED MY HORDES, AVENGERS...
BBBRRRAAAWWW
ODIN'S BEARD!
...BUT NO SURFACE DWELLER IS ANY MATCH FOR--

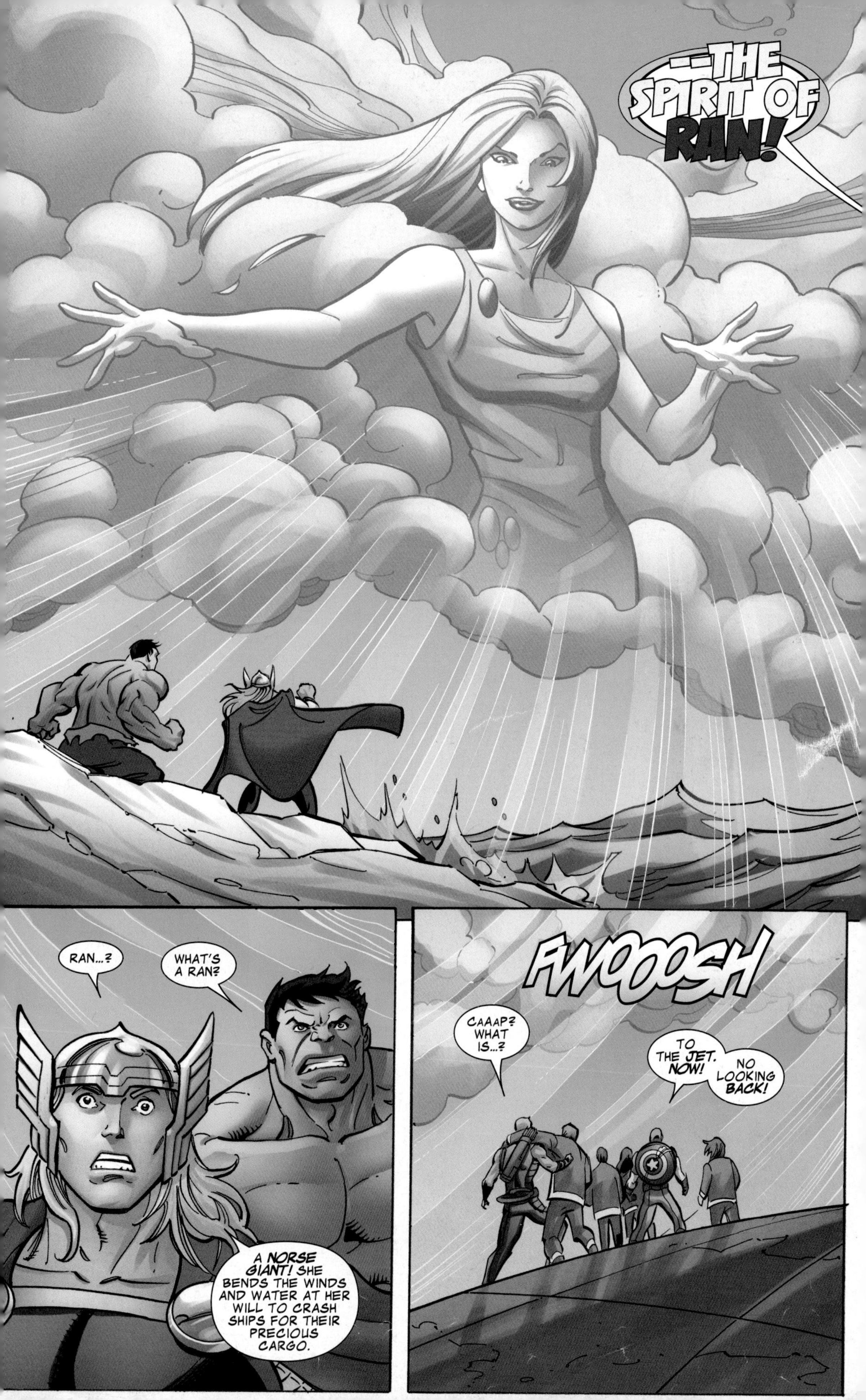
--THE SPIRIT OF RAN!
RAN...?
WHAT'S A RAN?
A NORSE GIANT! SHE BENDS THE WINDS AND WATER AT HER WILL TO CRASH SHIPS FOR THEIR PRECIOUS CARGO.
FWOOOSH
CAAAP? WHAT IS...?
TO THE JET. NOW!
NO LOOKING BACK!

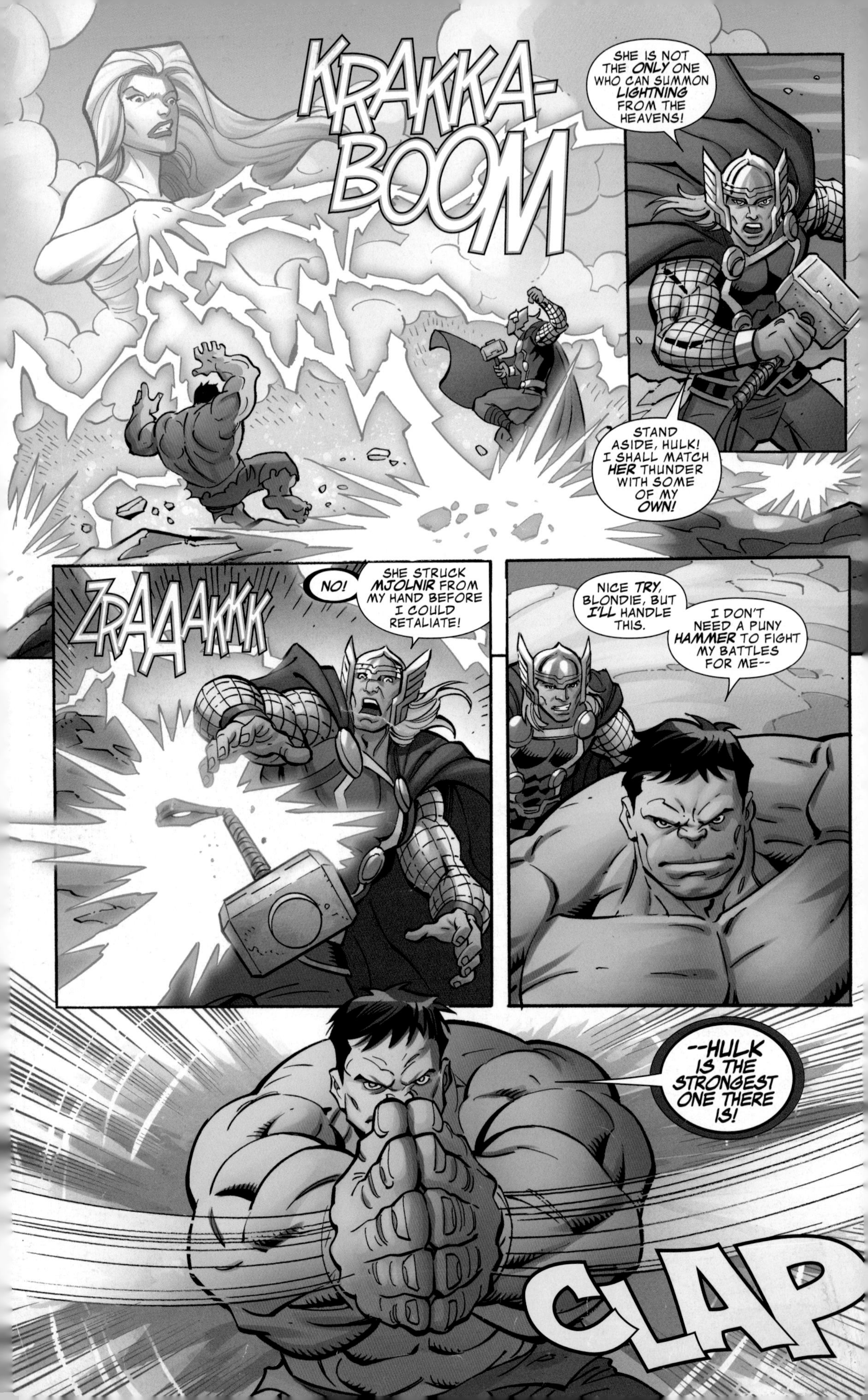
KRAKKA-BOOM
SHE IS NOT THE ONLY ONE WHO CAN SUMMON LIGHTNING FROM THE HEAVENS!
STAND ASIDE, HULK! I SHALL MATCH HER THUNDER WITH SOME OF MY OWN!
ZRAAAKKK
NO!
SHE STRUCK MJOLNIR FROM MY HAND BEFORE I COULD RETALIATE!
NICE TRY, BLONDIE, BUT I'LL HANDLE THIS.
I DON'T NEED A PUNY HAMMER TO FIGHT MY BATTLES FOR ME--
--HULK IS THE STRONGEST ONE THERE IS!
CLAP

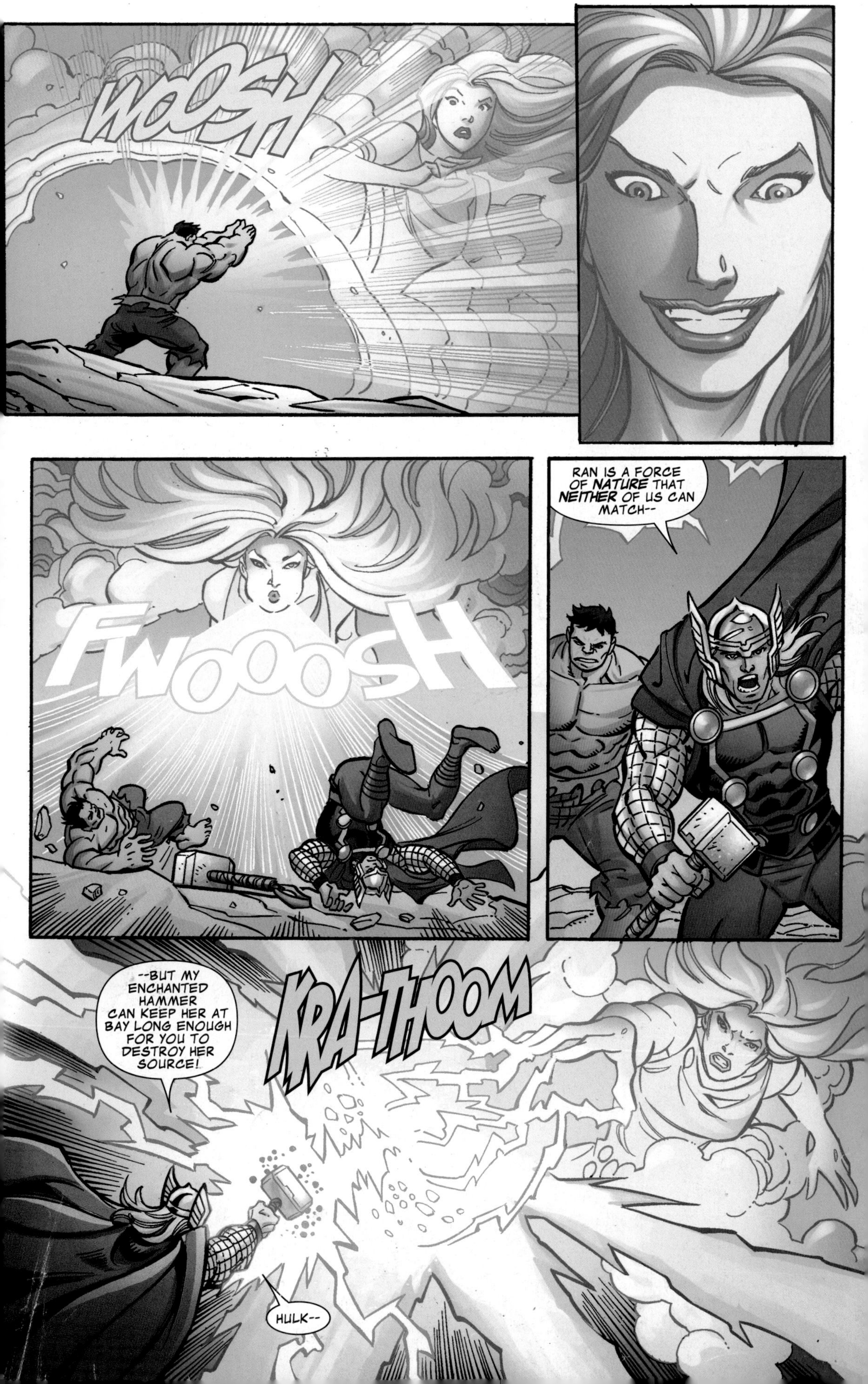
WOOSH
FWOOOSH
RAN IS A FORCE OF NATURE THAT NEITHER OF US CAN MATCH--
--BUT MY ENCHANTED HAMMER CAN KEEP HER AT BAY LONG ENOUGH FOR YOU TO DESTROY HER SOURCE!
KRA-THOOM
HULK--

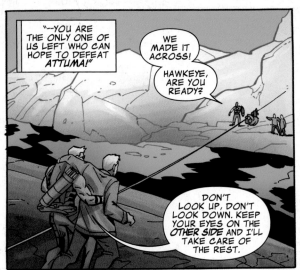

"--YOU ARE THE ONLY ONE OF US LEFT WHO CAN HOPE TO DEFEAT ATTUMA!"

WE MADE IT ACROSS!

HAWKEYE, ARE YOU READY?

DON'T LOOK UP, DON'T LOOK DOWN. KEEP YOUR EYES ON THE OTHER SIDE AND I'LL TAKE CARE OF THE REST.

TYPICAL SURFACE-DWELLER ARROGANCE! DEFENDING THOSE WHO WOULD DESTROY YOUR WORLD'S RESOURCES WITH THEIR PRECIOUS CRUDE!

IT'S YOUR ARROGANCE THAT CAUSED THIS MESS IN THE FIRST PLACE, ATTUMA!

LIES!

FLRSSH

ME AND MY MOUTH!

WHAT DID YOU DO?!

I STUPIDLY FORGOT THAT ATTUMA HAS CONTROL OVER THE OCEAN WATERS!

WE'RE FINISHED!

NOT YET!

FTT

KRIK

SPRSSSHHH

HANG ON!

DRAT.

HEY, ATTUMA!

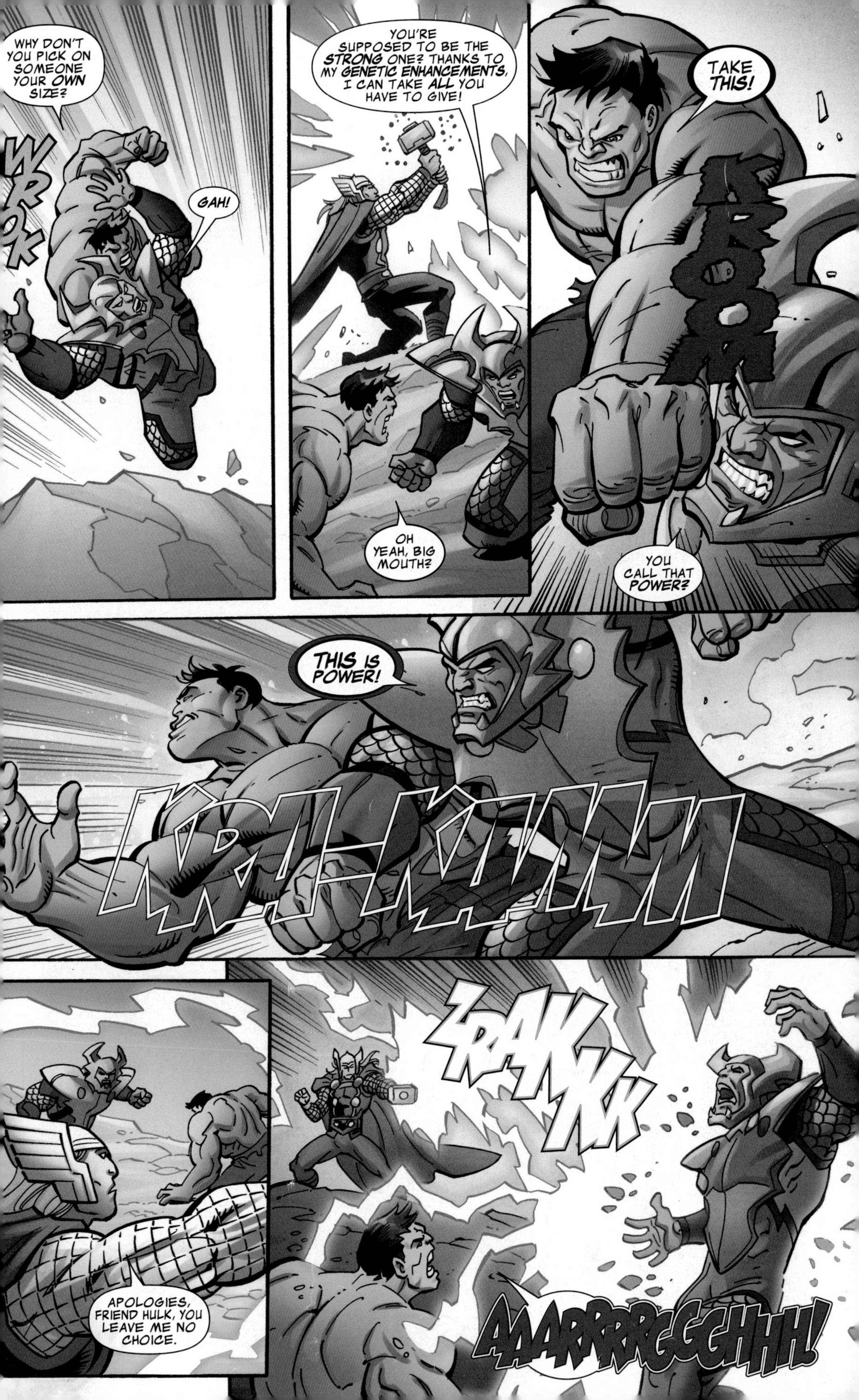
WHY DON'T YOU PICK ON SOMEONE YOUR OWN SIZE?
WROK
GAH!
YOU'RE SUPPOSED TO BE THE STRONG ONE? THANKS TO MY GENETIC ENHANCEMENTS, I CAN TAKE ALL YOU HAVE TO GIVE!
OH YEAH, BIG MOUTH?
TAKE THIS!
KROOM
YOU CALL THAT POWER?
THIS IS POWER!
APOLOGIES, FRIEND HULK, YOU LEAVE ME NO CHOICE.
ZRAKKKK
AAARRRRGGHHH!

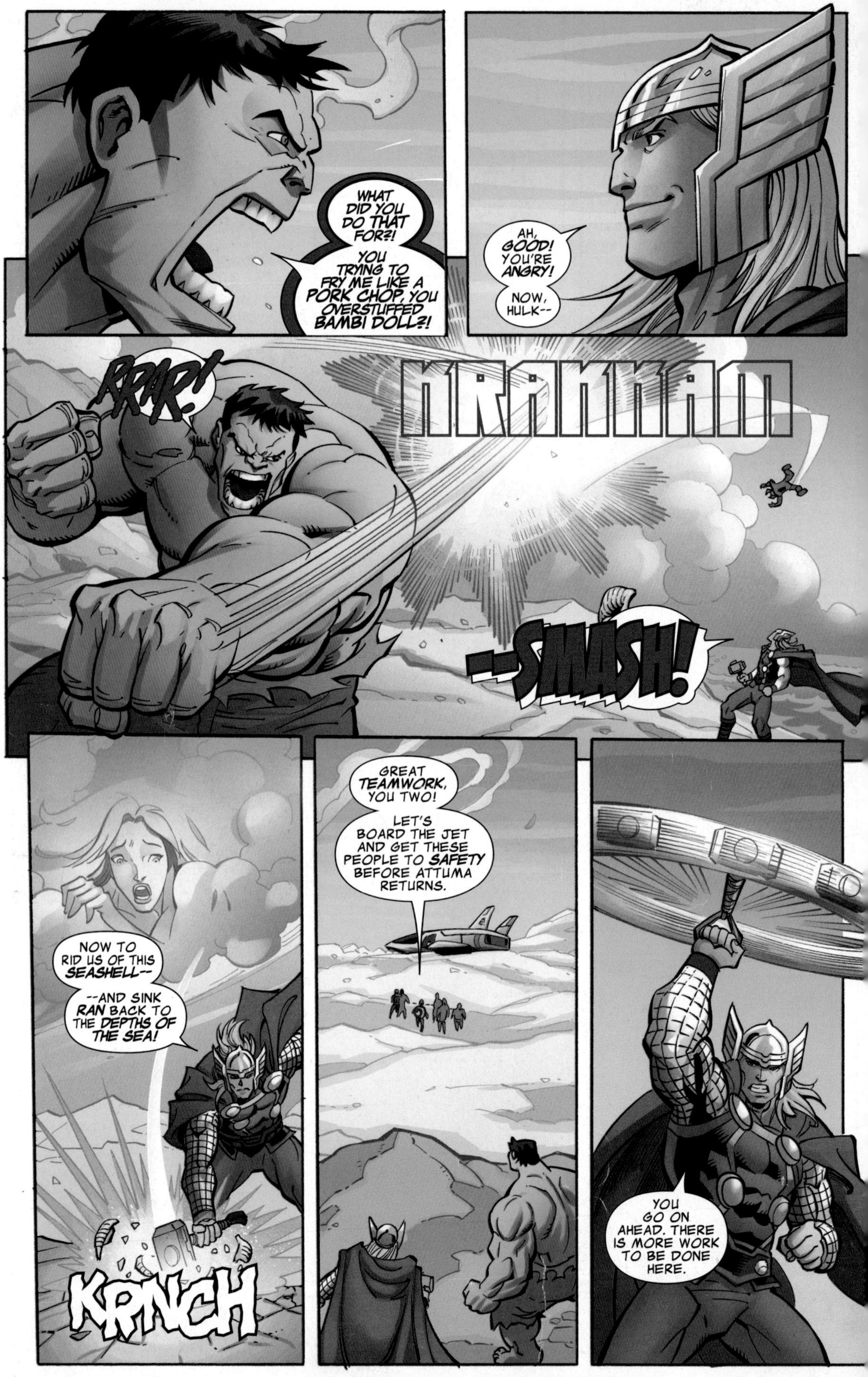

WHAT DID YOU DO THAT FOR?! YOU TRYING TO FRY ME LIKE A PORK CHOP, YOU OVERSTUFFED BAMBI DOLL?!
AH, GOOD! YOU'RE ANGRY!
NOW, HULK--
RRAR!
KRAKKAM
--SMASH!
NOW TO RID US OF THIS SEASHELL--
--AND SINK RAN BACK TO THE DEPTHS OF THE SEA!
KRNCH
GREAT TEAMWORK, YOU TWO!
LET'S BOARD THE JET AND GET THESE PEOPLE TO SAFETY BEFORE ATTUMA RETURNS.
YOU GO ON AHEAD. THERE IS MORE WORK TO BE DONE HERE.

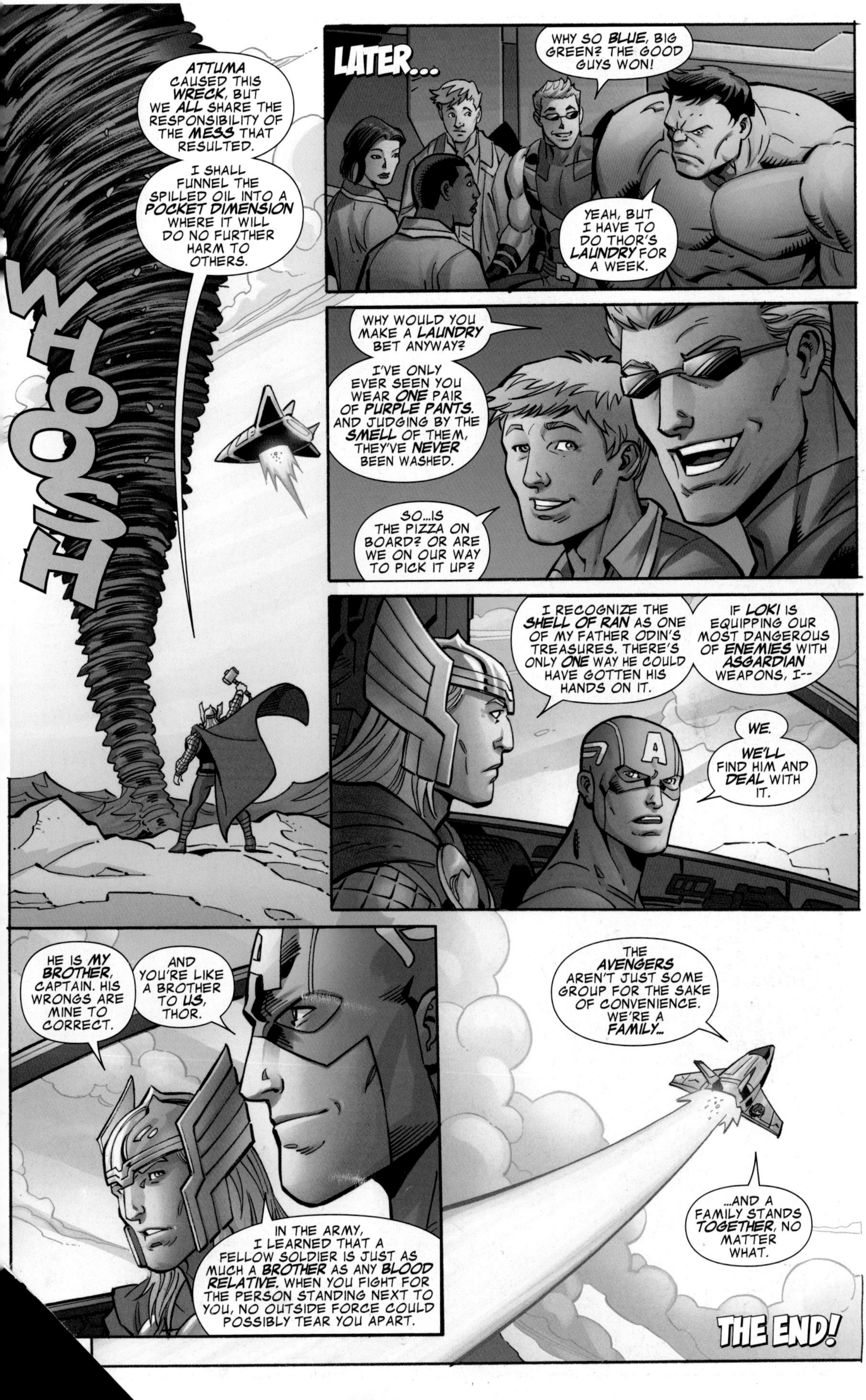
ATTUMA CAUSED THIS WRECK, BUT WE ALL SHARE THE RESPONSIBILITY OF THE MESS THAT RESULTED.
I SHALL FUNNEL THE SPILLED OIL INTO A POCKET DIMENSION WHERE IT WILL DO NO FURTHER HARM TO OTHERS.
WHOOSH
LATER...
WHY SO BLUE, BIG GREEN? THE GOOD GUYS WON!
YEAH, BUT I HAVE TO DO THOR'S LAUNDRY FOR A WEEK.
WHY WOULD YOU MAKE A LAUNDRY BET ANYWAY?
I'VE ONLY EVER SEEN YOU WEAR ONE PAIR OF PURPLE PANTS. AND JUDGING BY THE SMELL OF THEM, THEY'VE NEVER BEEN WASHED.
SO...IS THE PIZZA ON BOARD? OR ARE WE ON OUR WAY TO PICK IT UP?
I RECOGNIZE THE SHELL OF RAN AS ONE OF MY FATHER ODIN'S TREASURES. THERE'S ONLY ONE WAY HE COULD HAVE GOTTEN HIS HANDS ON IT.
IF LOKI IS EQUIPPING OUR MOST DANGEROUS OF ENEMIES WITH ASGARDIAN WEAPONS, I--
WE.
WE'LL FIND HIM AND DEAL WITH IT.
HE IS MY BROTHER, CAPTAIN. HIS WRONGS ARE MINE TO CORRECT.
AND YOU'RE LIKE A BROTHER TO US, THOR.
IN THE ARMY, I LEARNED THAT A FELLOW SOLDIER IS JUST AS MUCH A BROTHER AS ANY BLOOD RELATIVE. WHEN YOU FIGHT FOR THE PERSON STANDING NEXT TO YOU, NO OUTSIDE FORCE COULD POSSIBLY TEAR YOU APART.
THE AVENGERS AREN'T JUST SOME GROUP FOR THE SAKE OF CONVENIENCE. WE'RE A FAMILY...
...AND A FAMILY STANDS TOGETHER, NO MATTER WHAT.
THE END!

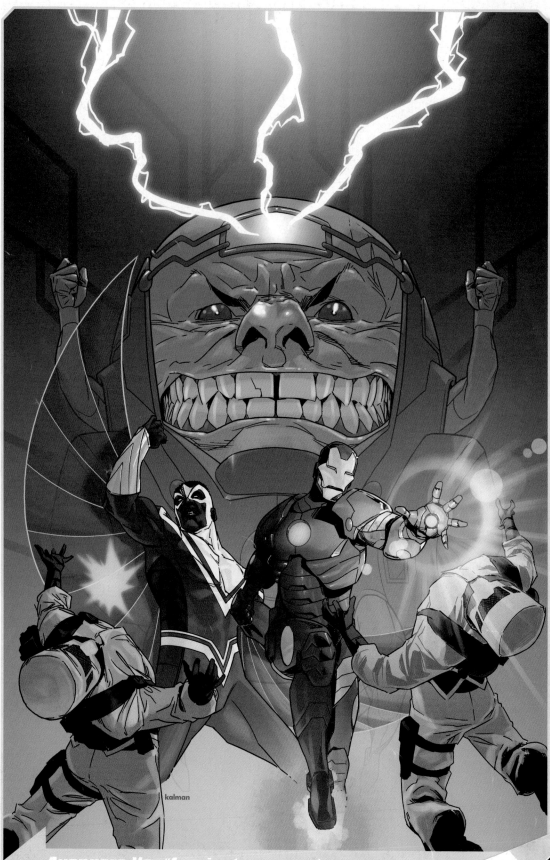

Avengers Vs. #1 variant cover art
by Kalman Andrasofszky

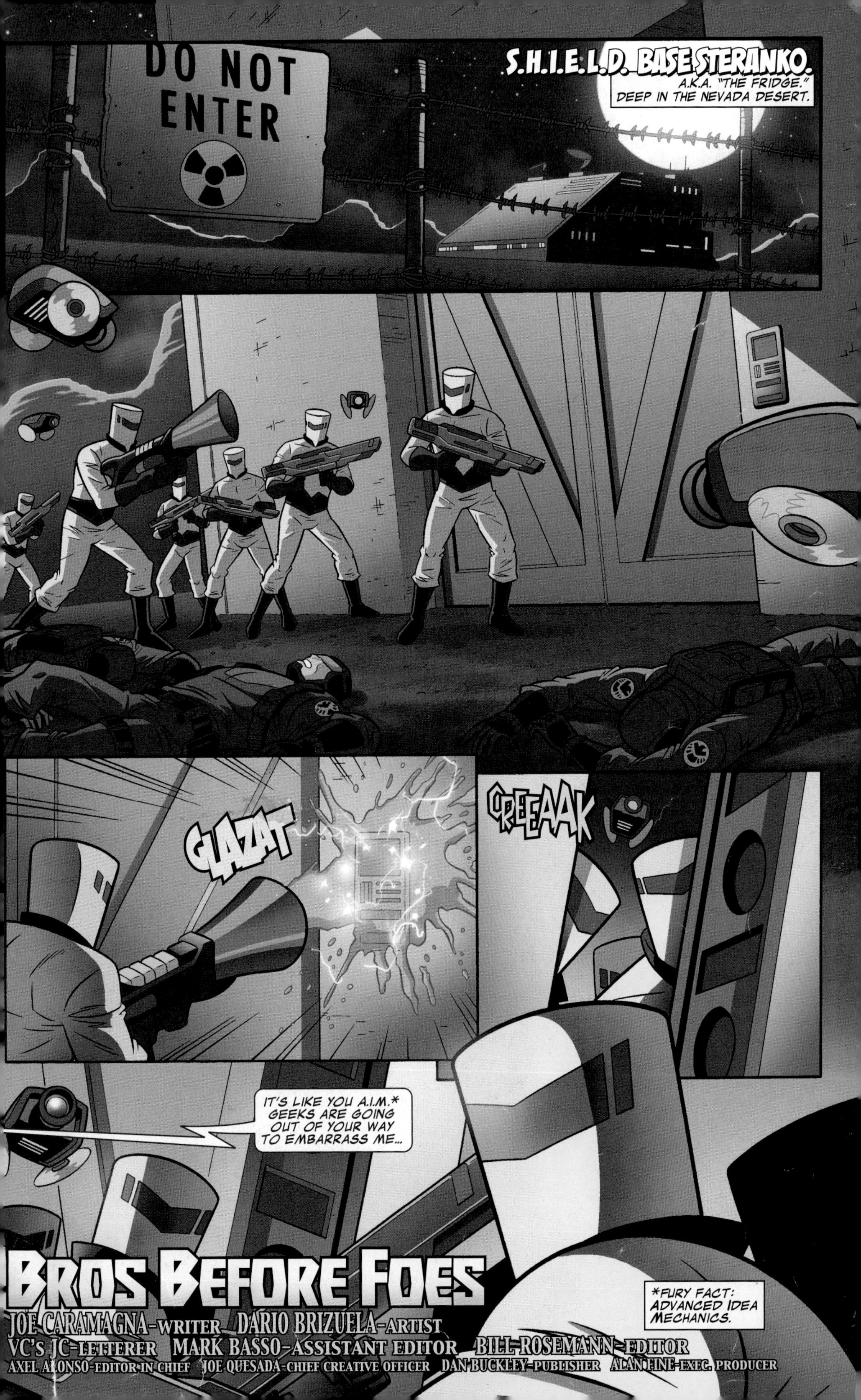
DO NOT ENTER
S.H.I.E.L.D. BASE STERANKO.
A.K.A. "THE FRIDGE." DEEP IN THE NEVADA DESERT.
GLAZAT
CREEAAK
IT'S LIKE YOU A.I.M.* GEEKS ARE GOING OUT OF YOUR WAY TO EMBARRASS ME...
BROS BEFORE FOES
JOE CARAMAGNA-WRITER DARIO BRIZUELA-ARTIST
VC's JC-LETTERER MARK BASSO-ASSISTANT EDITOR BILL ROSEMANN-EDITOR
AXEL ALONSO-EDITOR IN CHIEF JOE QUESADA-CHIEF CREATIVE OFFICER DAN BUCKLEY-PUBLISHER ALAN FINE-EXEC. PRODUCER
*FURY FACT: ADVANCED IDEA MECHANICS.

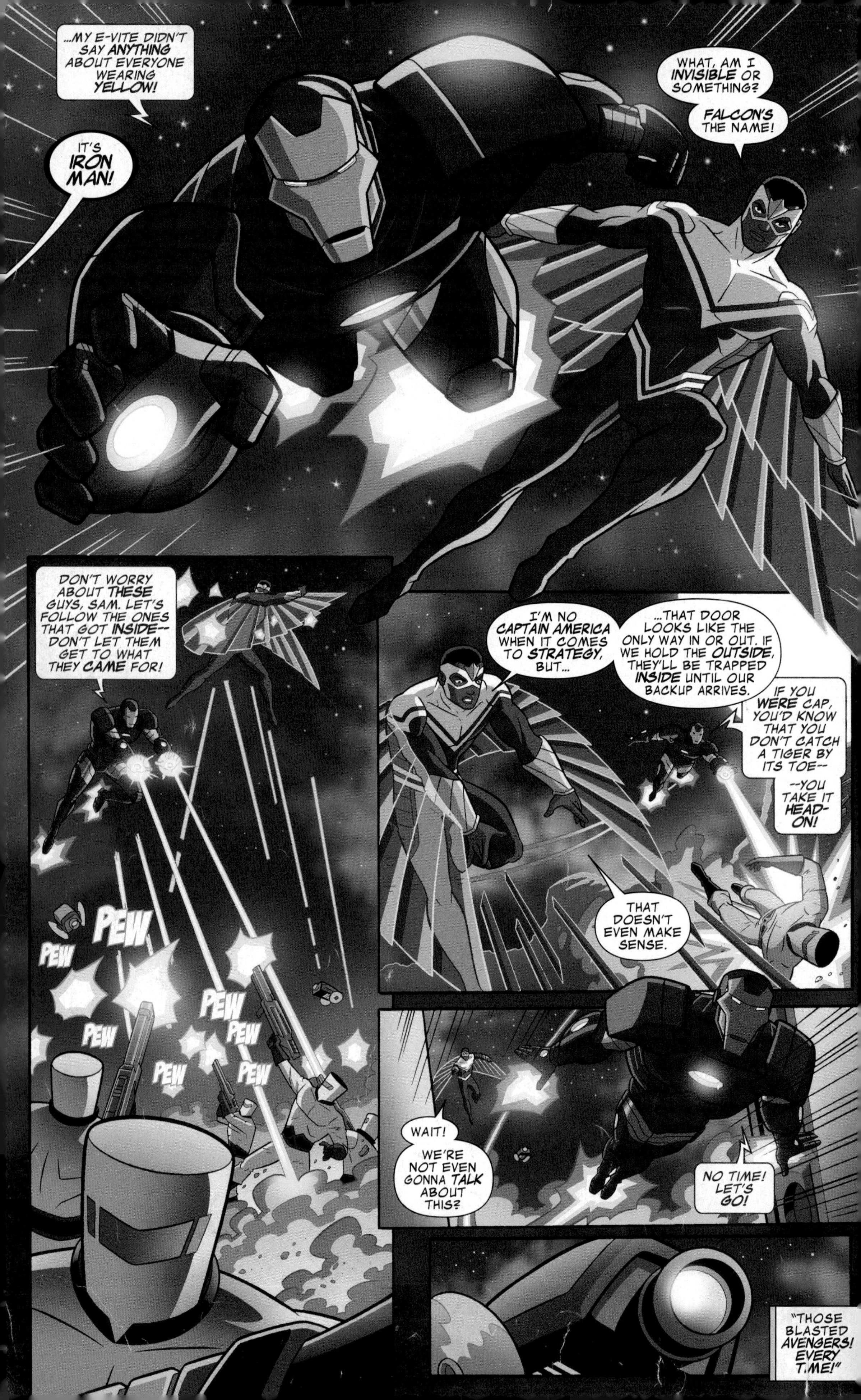

...MY E-VITE DIDN'T SAY ANYTHING ABOUT EVERYONE WEARING YELLOW!
IT'S IRON MAN!
WHAT, AM I INVISIBLE OR SOMETHING?
FALCON'S THE NAME!
DON'T WORRY ABOUT THESE GUYS, SAM. LET'S FOLLOW THE ONES THAT GOT INSIDE-- DON'T LET THEM GET TO WHAT THEY CAME FOR!
PEW
PEW
PEW
PEW
PEW
PEW
PEW
I'M NO CAPTAIN AMERICA WHEN IT COMES TO STRATEGY, BUT...
...THAT DOOR LOOKS LIKE THE ONLY WAY IN OR OUT. IF WE HOLD THE OUTSIDE, THEY'LL BE TRAPPED INSIDE UNTIL OUR BACKUP ARRIVES.
IF YOU WERE CAP, YOU'D KNOW THAT YOU DON'T CATCH A TIGER BY ITS TOE--
--YOU TAKE IT HEAD-ON!
THAT DOESN'T EVEN MAKE SENSE.
WAIT! WE'RE NOT EVEN GONNA TALK ABOUT THIS?
NO TIME! LET'S GO!
"THOSE BLASTED AVENGERS! EVERY TIME!"

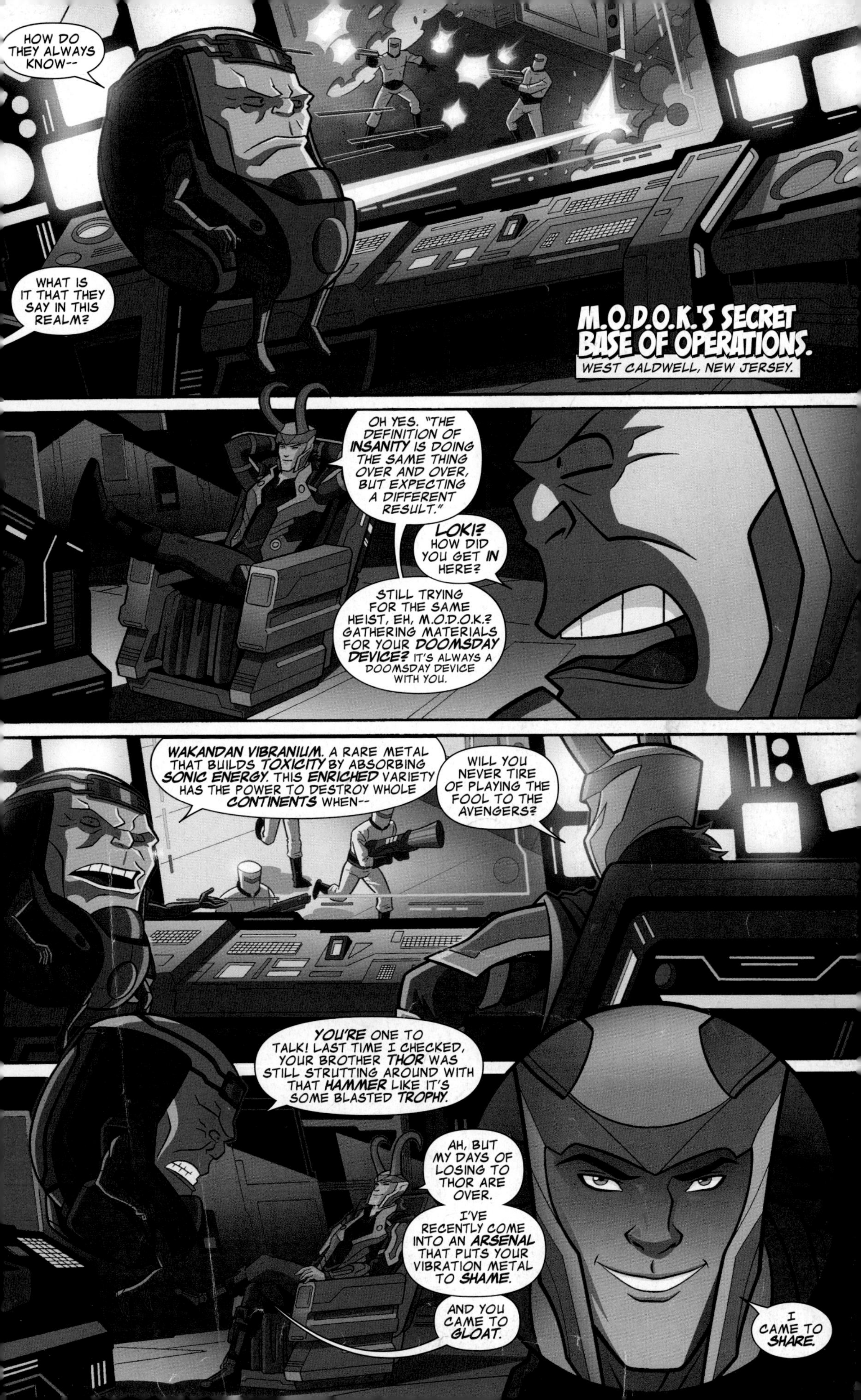

HOW DO THEY ALWAYS KNOW--
WHAT IS IT THAT THEY SAY IN THIS REALM?
M.O.D.O.K.'S SECRET BASE OF OPERATIONS.
WEST CALDWELL, NEW JERSEY.
OH YES. "THE DEFINITION OF INSANITY IS DOING THE SAME THING OVER AND OVER, BUT EXPECTING A DIFFERENT RESULT."
LOKI? HOW DID YOU GET IN HERE?
STILL TRYING FOR THE SAME HEIST, EH, M.O.D.O.K.? GATHERING MATERIALS FOR YOUR DOOMSDAY DEVICE? IT'S ALWAYS A DOOMSDAY DEVICE WITH YOU.
WAKANDAN VIBRANIUM. A RARE METAL THAT BUILDS TOXICITY BY ABSORBING SONIC ENERGY. THIS ENRICHED VARIETY HAS THE POWER TO DESTROY WHOLE CONTINENTS WHEN--
WILL YOU NEVER TIRE OF PLAYING THE FOOL TO THE AVENGERS?
YOU'RE ONE TO TALK! LAST TIME I CHECKED, YOUR BROTHER THOR WAS STILL STRUTTING AROUND WITH THAT HAMMER LIKE IT'S SOME BLASTED TROPHY.
AH, BUT MY DAYS OF LOSING TO THOR ARE OVER.
I'VE RECENTLY COME INTO AN ARSENAL THAT PUTS YOUR VIBRATION METAL TO SHAME.
AND YOU CAME TO GLOAT.
I CAME TO SHARE.

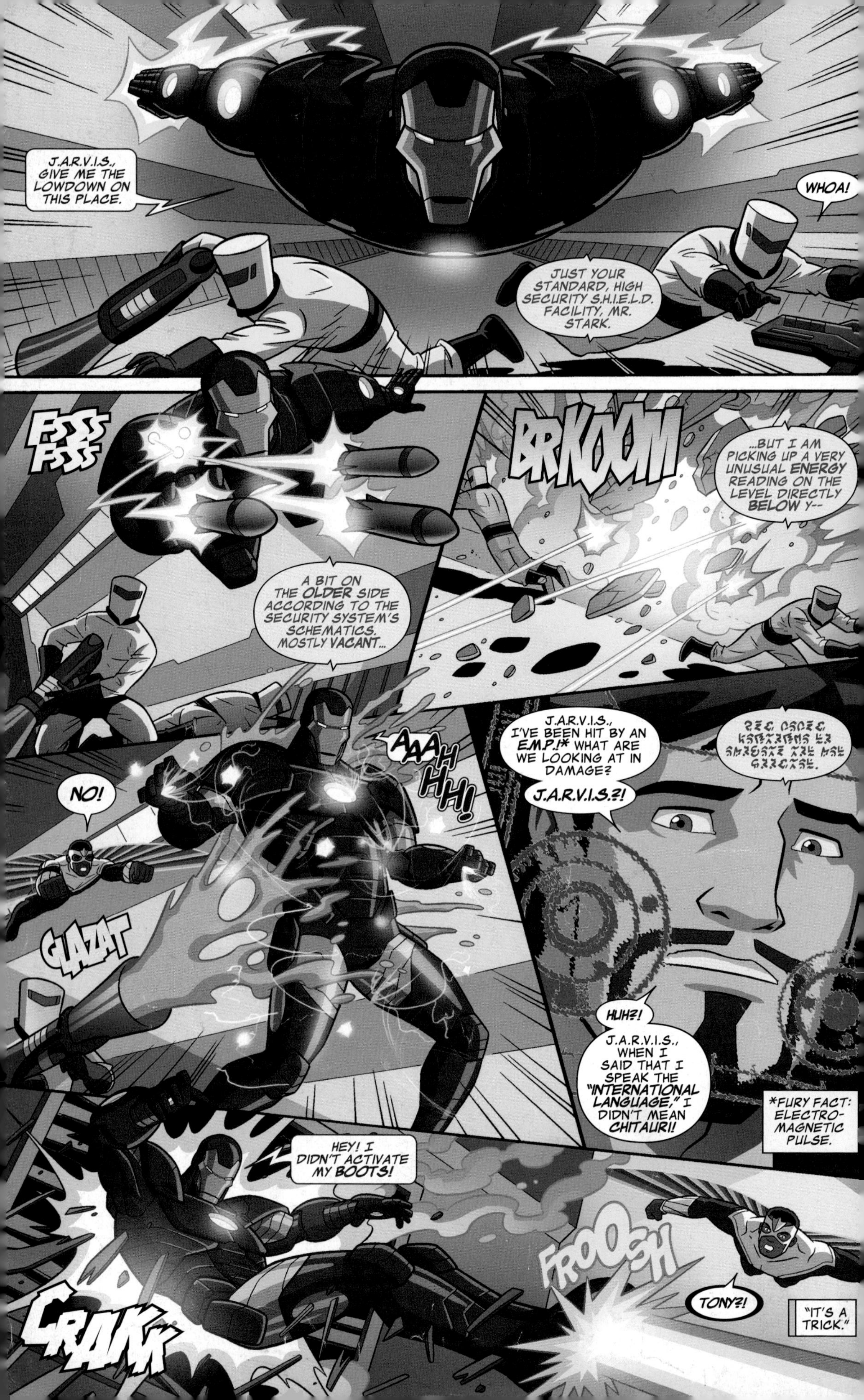

J.A.R.V.I.S., GIVE ME THE LOWDOWN ON THIS PLACE.
WHOA!
JUST YOUR STANDARD, HIGH SECURITY S.H.I.E.L.D. FACILITY, MR. STARK.
FSSS FSSS
A BIT ON THE OLDER SIDE ACCORDING TO THE SECURITY SYSTEM'S SCHEMATICS. MOSTLY VACANT...
BRKOOM
...BUT I AM PICKING UP A VERY UNUSUAL ENERGY READING ON THE LEVEL DIRECTLY BELOW Y--
NO!
AAAHHH!
GLAZAT
J.A.R.V.I.S., I'VE BEEN HIT BY AN E.M.P.!* WHAT ARE WE LOOKING AT IN DAMAGE?
J.A.R.V.I.S.?!
HUH?!
J.A.R.V.I.S., WHEN I SAID THAT I SPEAK THE "INTERNATIONAL LANGUAGE," I DIDN'T MEAN CHITAURI!
*FURY FACT: ELECTRO-MAGNETIC PULSE.
HEY! I DIDN'T ACTIVATE MY BOOTS!
CRANK
FROOSH
TONY?!
"IT'S A TRICK."

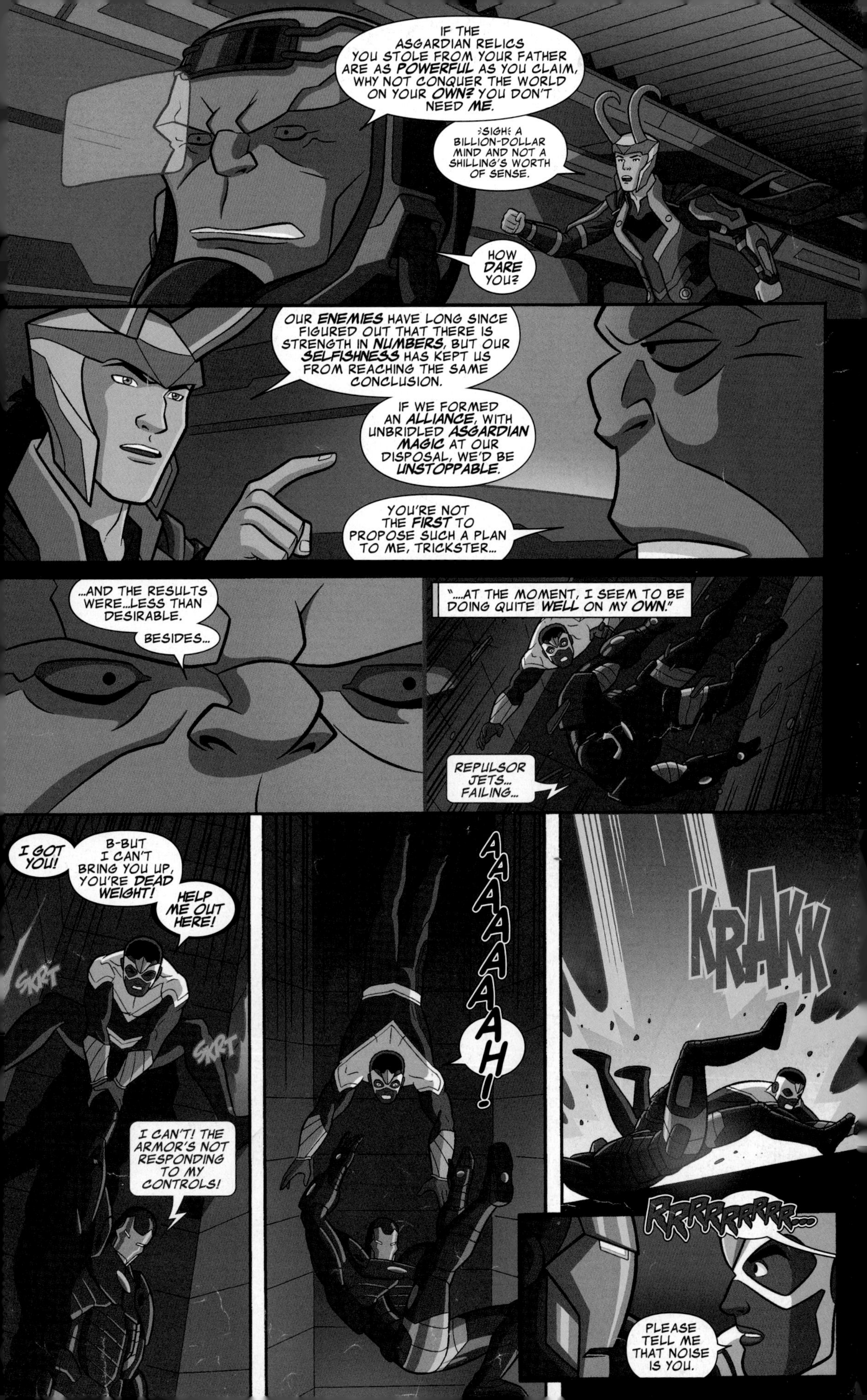
IF THE ASGARDIAN RELICS YOU STOLE FROM YOUR FATHER ARE AS POWERFUL AS YOU CLAIM, WHY NOT CONQUER THE WORLD ON YOUR OWN? YOU DON'T NEED ME.
SIGH A BILLION-DOLLAR MIND AND NOT A SHILLING'S WORTH OF SENSE.
HOW DARE YOU?
OUR ENEMIES HAVE LONG SINCE FIGURED OUT THAT THERE IS STRENGTH IN NUMBERS, BUT OUR SELFISHNESS HAS KEPT US FROM REACHING THE SAME CONCLUSION.
IF WE FORMED AN ALLIANCE, WITH UNBRIDLED ASGARDIAN MAGIC AT OUR DISPOSAL, WE'D BE UNSTOPPABLE.
YOU'RE NOT THE FIRST TO PROPOSE SUCH A PLAN TO ME, TRICKSTER...
...AND THE RESULTS WERE...LESS THAN DESIRABLE.
BESIDES...
"...AT THE MOMENT, I SEEM TO BE DOING QUITE WELL ON MY OWN."
REPULSOR JETS... FAILING...
I GOT YOU!
B-BUT I CAN'T BRING YOU UP, YOU'RE DEAD WEIGHT!
HELP ME OUT HERE!
SKRT
SKRT
I CAN'T! THE ARMOR'S NOT RESPONDING TO MY CONTROLS!
AAAAAAAH!
KRAKK
RRRRRRRRR...
PLEASE TELL ME THAT NOISE IS YOU.

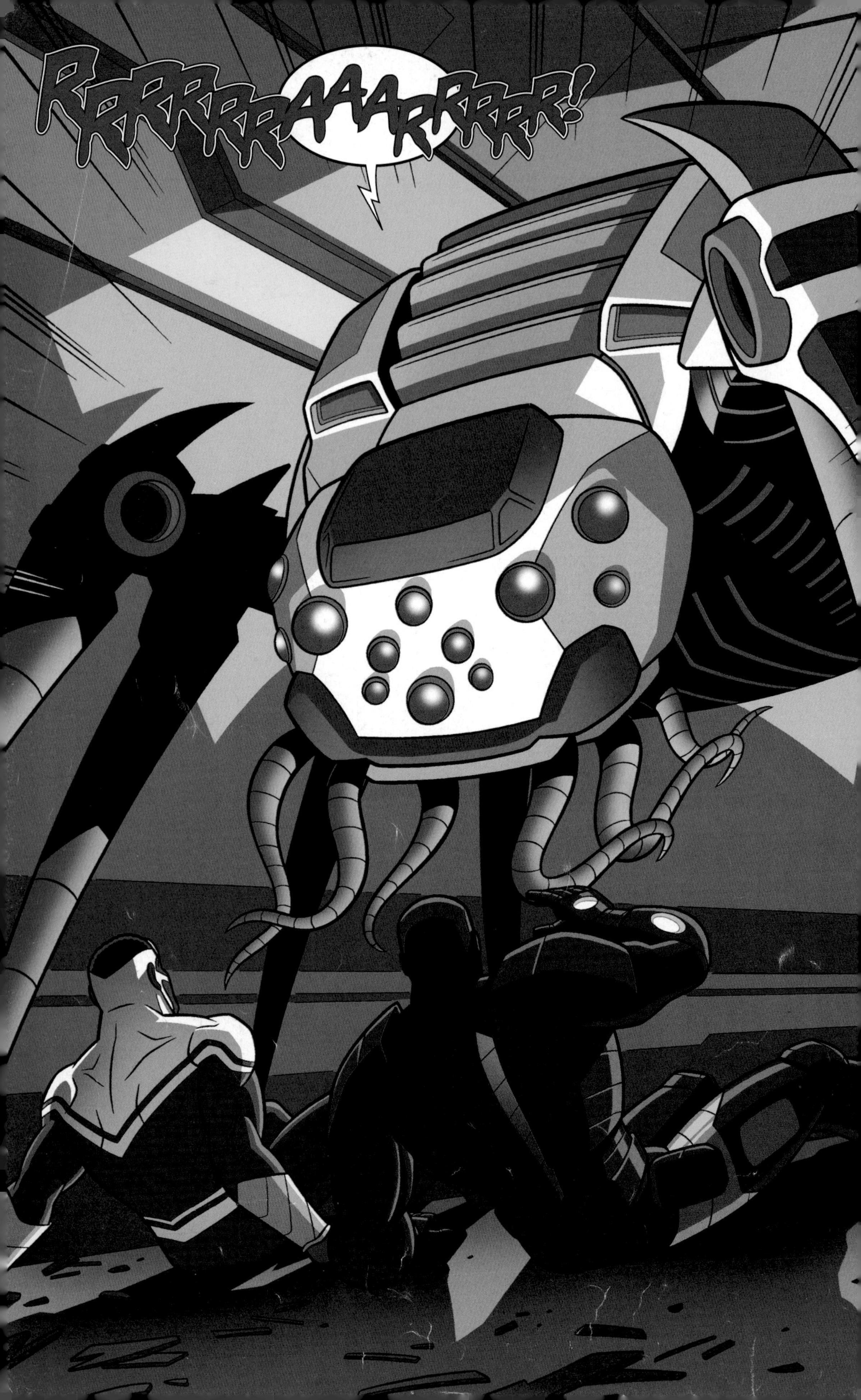
RRRRRRAAARRRRR!

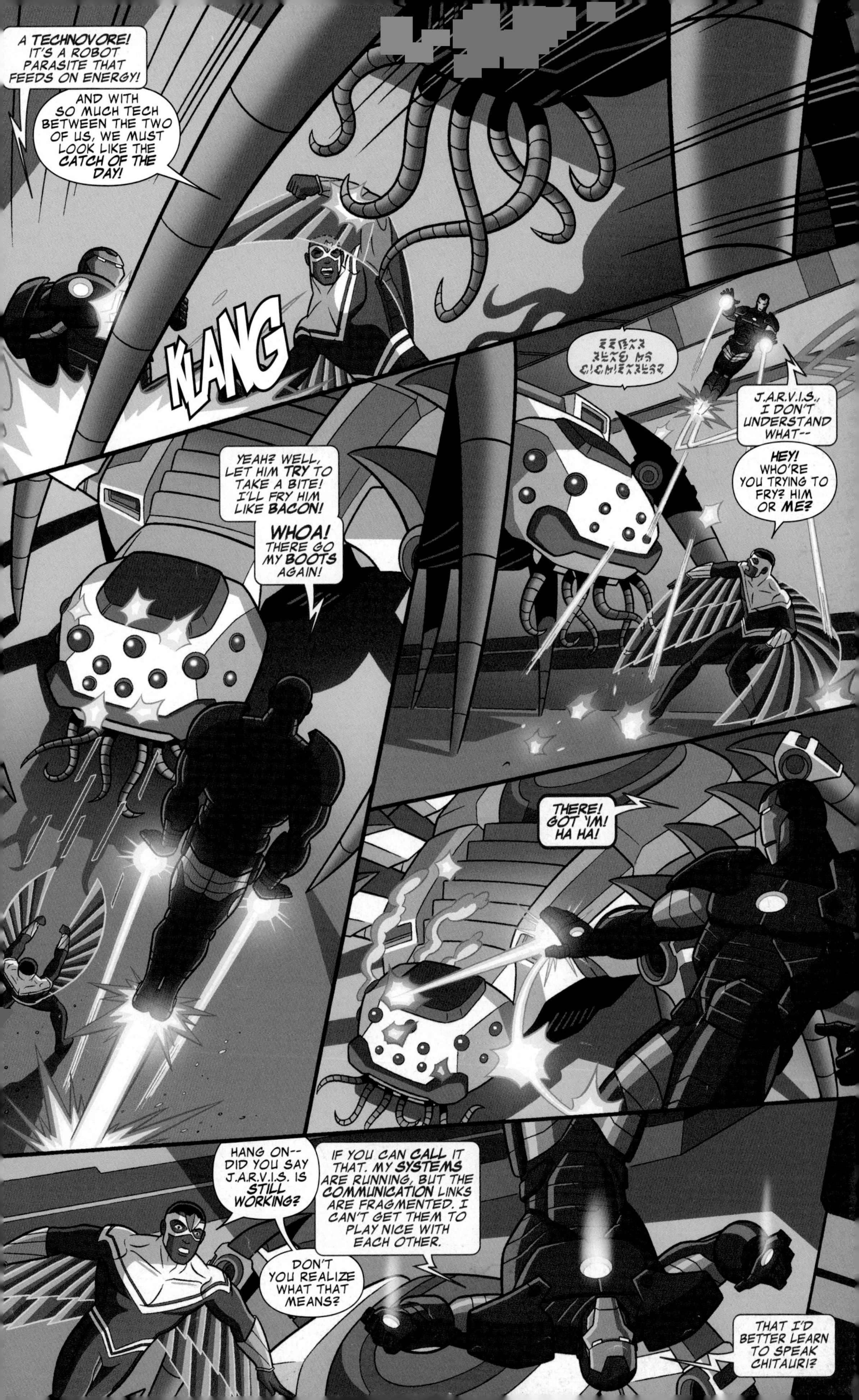
A TECHNOVORE! IT'S A ROBOT PARASITE THAT FEEDS ON ENERGY!
AND WITH SO MUCH TECH BETWEEN THE TWO OF US, WE MUST LOOK LIKE THE CATCH OF THE DAY!
KLANG
YEAH? WELL, LET HIM TRY TO TAKE A BITE! I'LL FRY HIM LIKE BACON!
WHOA! THERE GO MY BOOTS AGAIN!
J.A.R.V.I.S., I DON'T UNDERSTAND WHAT--
HEY! WHO'RE YOU TRYING TO FRY? HIM OR ME?
THERE! GOT 'IM! HA HA!
HANG ON-- DID YOU SAY J.A.R.V.I.S. IS STILL WORKING?
IF YOU CAN CALL IT THAT. MY SYSTEMS ARE RUNNING, BUT THE COMMUNICATION LINKS ARE FRAGMENTED. I CAN'T GET THEM TO PLAY NICE WITH EACH OTHER.
DON'T YOU REALIZE WHAT THAT MEANS?
THAT I'D BETTER LEARN TO SPEAK CHITAURI?

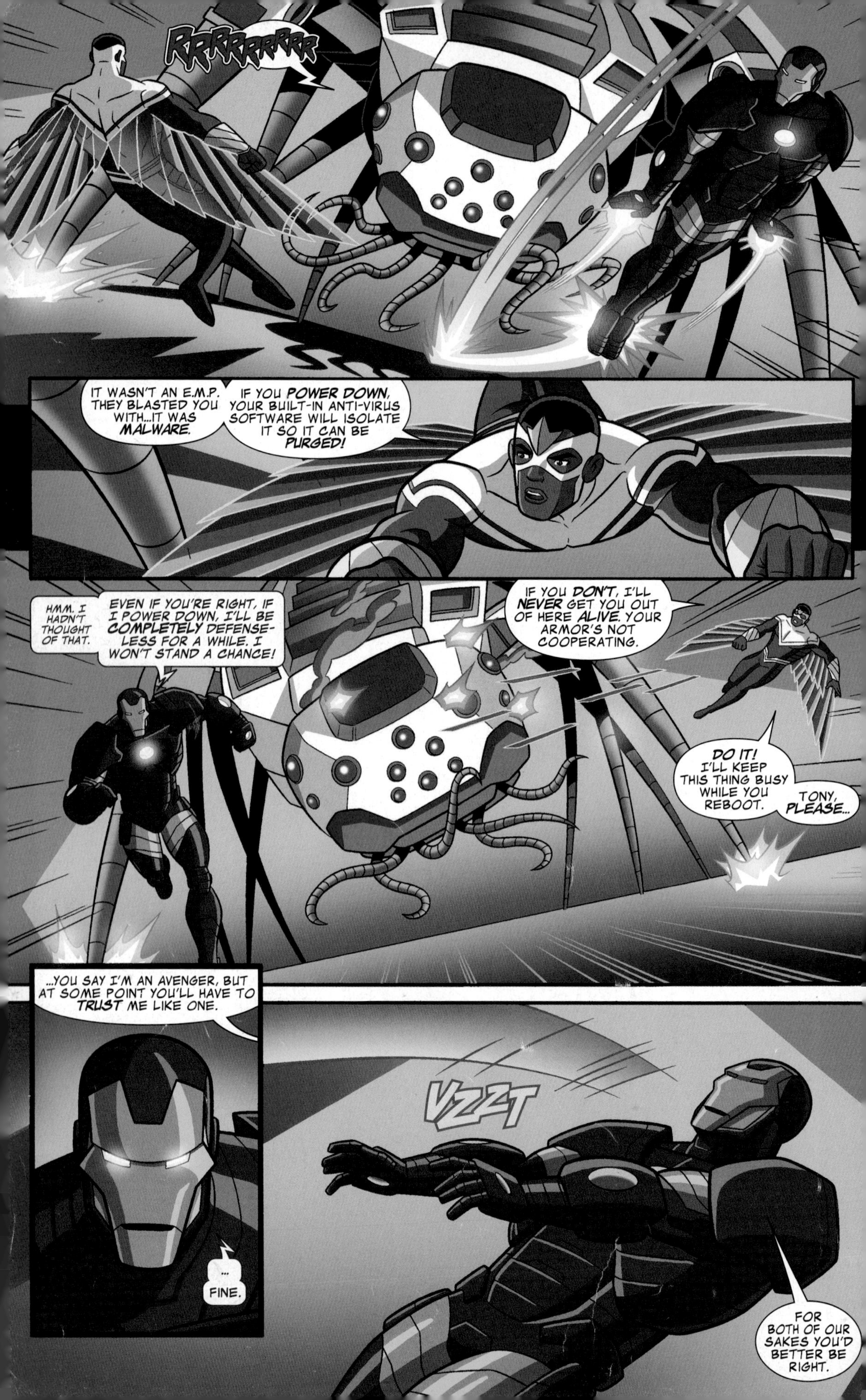
RRRRRRRRR
IT WASN'T AN E.M.P. THEY BLASTED YOU WITH...IT WAS MALWARE.
IF YOU POWER DOWN, YOUR BUILT-IN ANTI-VIRUS SOFTWARE WILL ISOLATE IT SO IT CAN BE PURGED!
HMM. I HADN'T THOUGHT OF THAT.
EVEN IF YOU'RE RIGHT, IF I POWER DOWN, I'LL BE COMPLETELY DEFENSE-LESS FOR A WHILE. I WON'T STAND A CHANCE!
IF YOU DON'T, I'LL NEVER GET YOU OUT OF HERE ALIVE. YOUR ARMOR'S NOT COOPERATING.
DO IT! I'LL KEEP THIS THING BUSY WHILE YOU REBOOT.
TONY, PLEASE...
...YOU SAY I'M AN AVENGER, BUT AT SOME POINT YOU'LL HAVE TO TRUST ME LIKE ONE.
... FINE.
VZZT
FOR BOTH OF OUR SAKES YOU'D BETTER BE RIGHT.

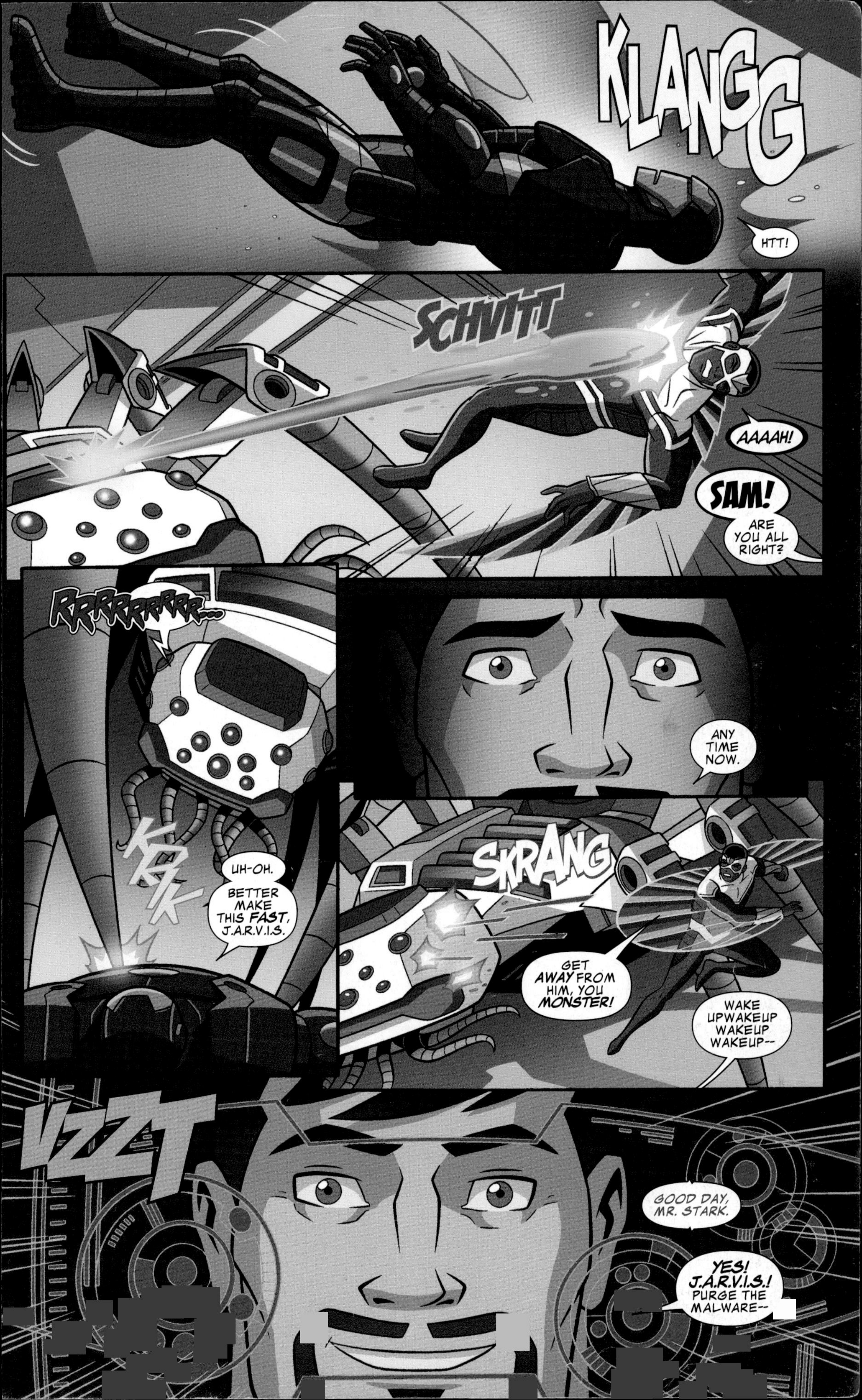
KLANGG
HTT!
SCHVITT
AAAAH!
SAM! ARE YOU ALL RIGHT?
UH-OH. BETTER MAKE THIS FAST, J.A.R.V.I.S.
ANY TIME NOW.
SKRANG
GET AWAY FROM HIM, YOU MONSTER!
WAKE UPWAKEUP WAKEUP WAKEUP--
VZZT
GOOD DAY, MR. STARK.
YES! J.A.R.V.I.S.! PURGE THE MALWARE--

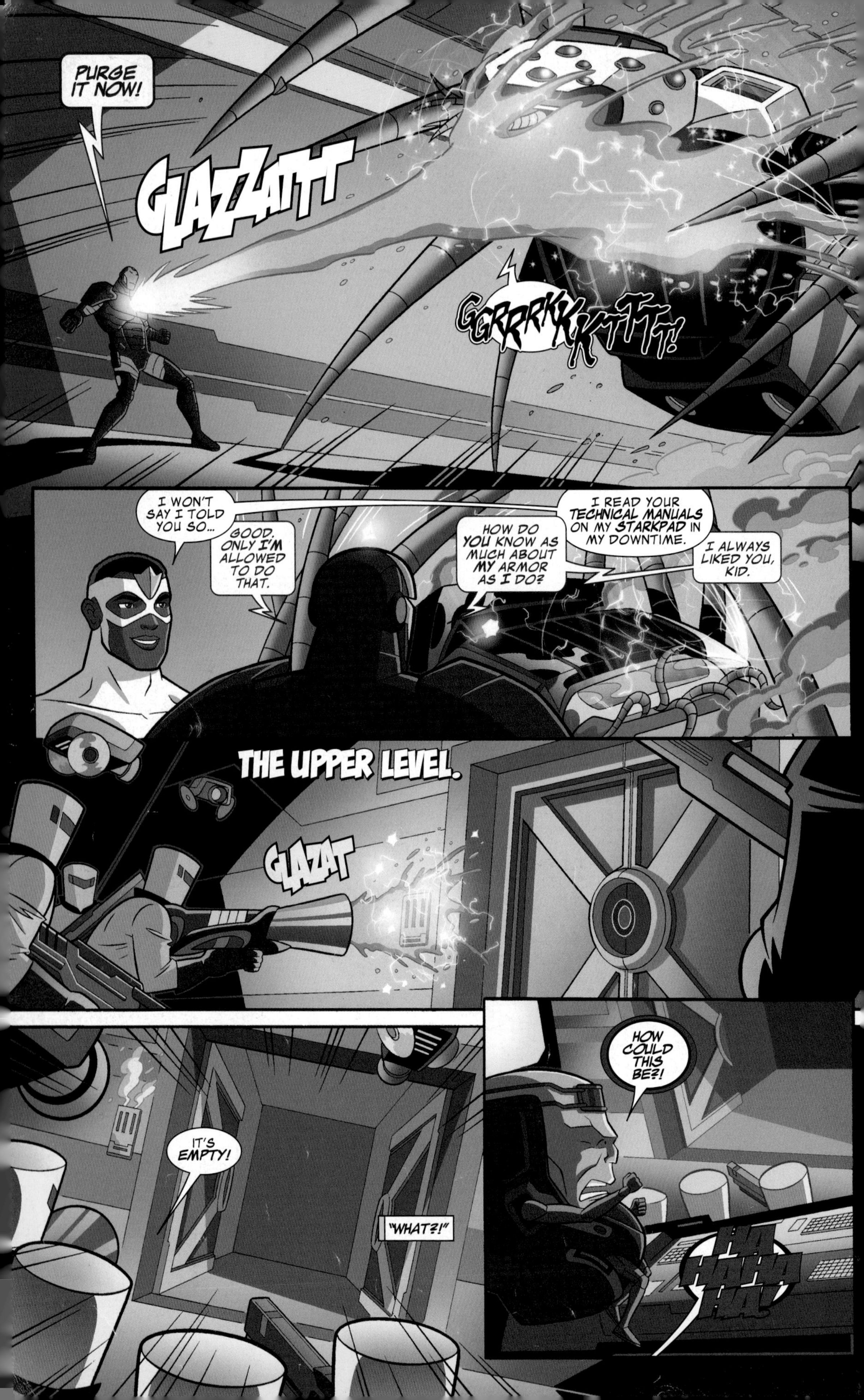
PURGE IT NOW!
GLAZZATTT
GGRRRKKKTTTT!
I WON'T SAY I TOLD YOU SO...
GOOD. ONLY I'M ALLOWED TO DO THAT.
HOW DO YOU KNOW AS MUCH ABOUT MY ARMOR AS I DO?
I READ YOUR TECHNICAL MANUALS ON MY STARKPAD IN MY DOWNTIME.
I ALWAYS LIKED YOU, KID.
THE UPPER LEVEL.
GLAZAT
IT'S EMPTY!
"WHAT?!"
HOW COULD THIS BE?!
HA HAHA HA!

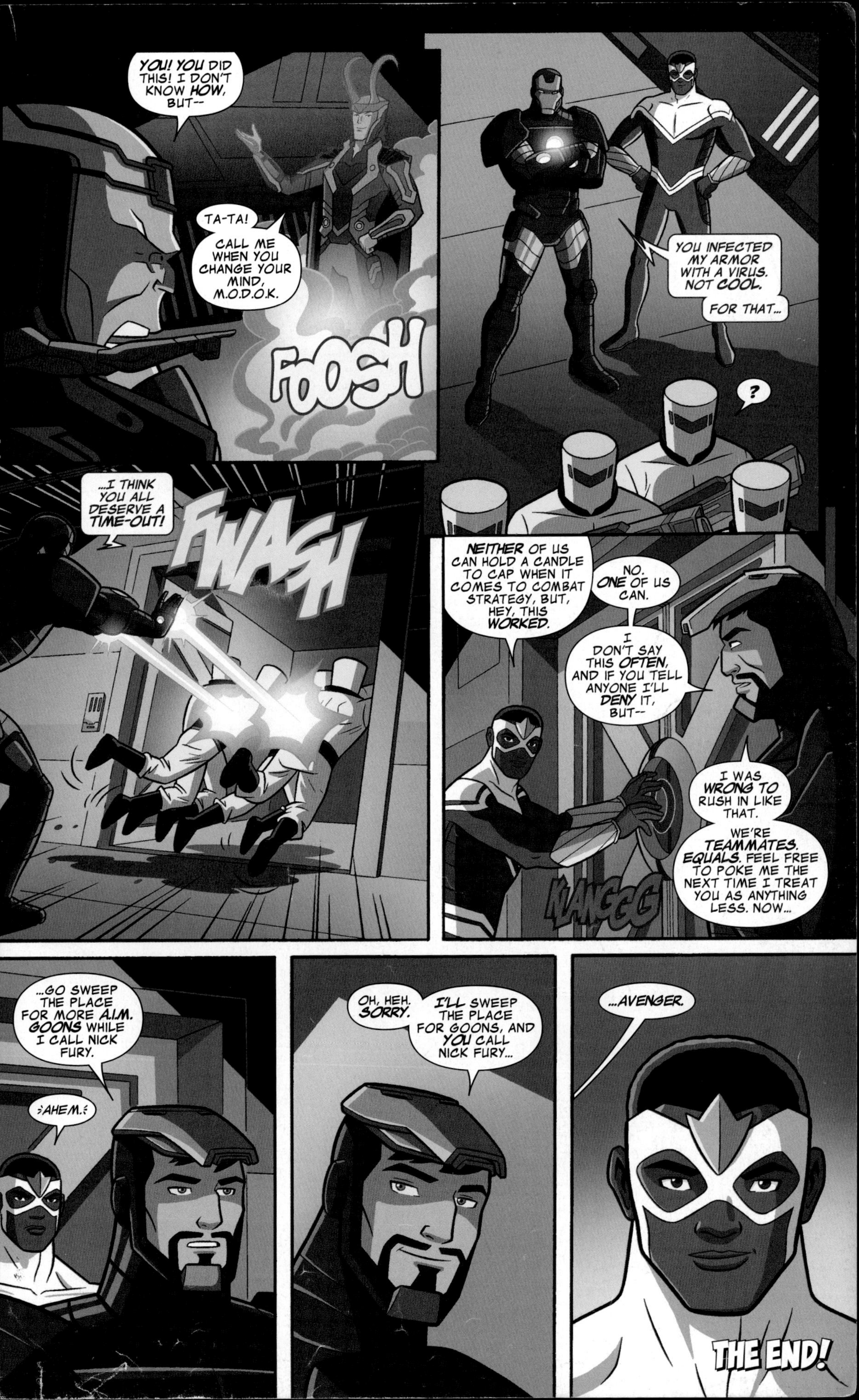

YOU! YOU DID THIS! I DON'T KNOW HOW, BUT--
TA-TA!
CALL ME WHEN YOU CHANGE YOUR MIND, M.O.D.O.K.
FOOSH
YOU INFECTED MY ARMOR WITH A VIRUS. NOT COOL.
FOR THAT...
?
...I THINK YOU ALL DESERVE A TIME-OUT!
FWASH
NEITHER OF US CAN HOLD A CANDLE TO CAP WHEN IT COMES TO COMBAT STRATEGY, BUT, HEY, THIS WORKED.
NO. ONE OF US CAN.
I DON'T SAY THIS OFTEN, AND IF YOU TELL ANYONE I'LL DENY IT, BUT--
I WAS WRONG TO RUSH IN LIKE THAT.
WE'RE TEAMMATES. EQUALS. FEEL FREE TO POKE ME THE NEXT TIME I TREAT YOU AS ANYTHING LESS. NOW...
KLANGGG
...GO SWEEP THE PLACE FOR MORE A.I.M. GOONS WHILE I CALL NICK FURY.
AHEM.
OH, HEH. SORRY.
I'LL SWEEP THE PLACE FOR GOONS, AND YOU CALL NICK FURY...
...AVENGER.
THE END!

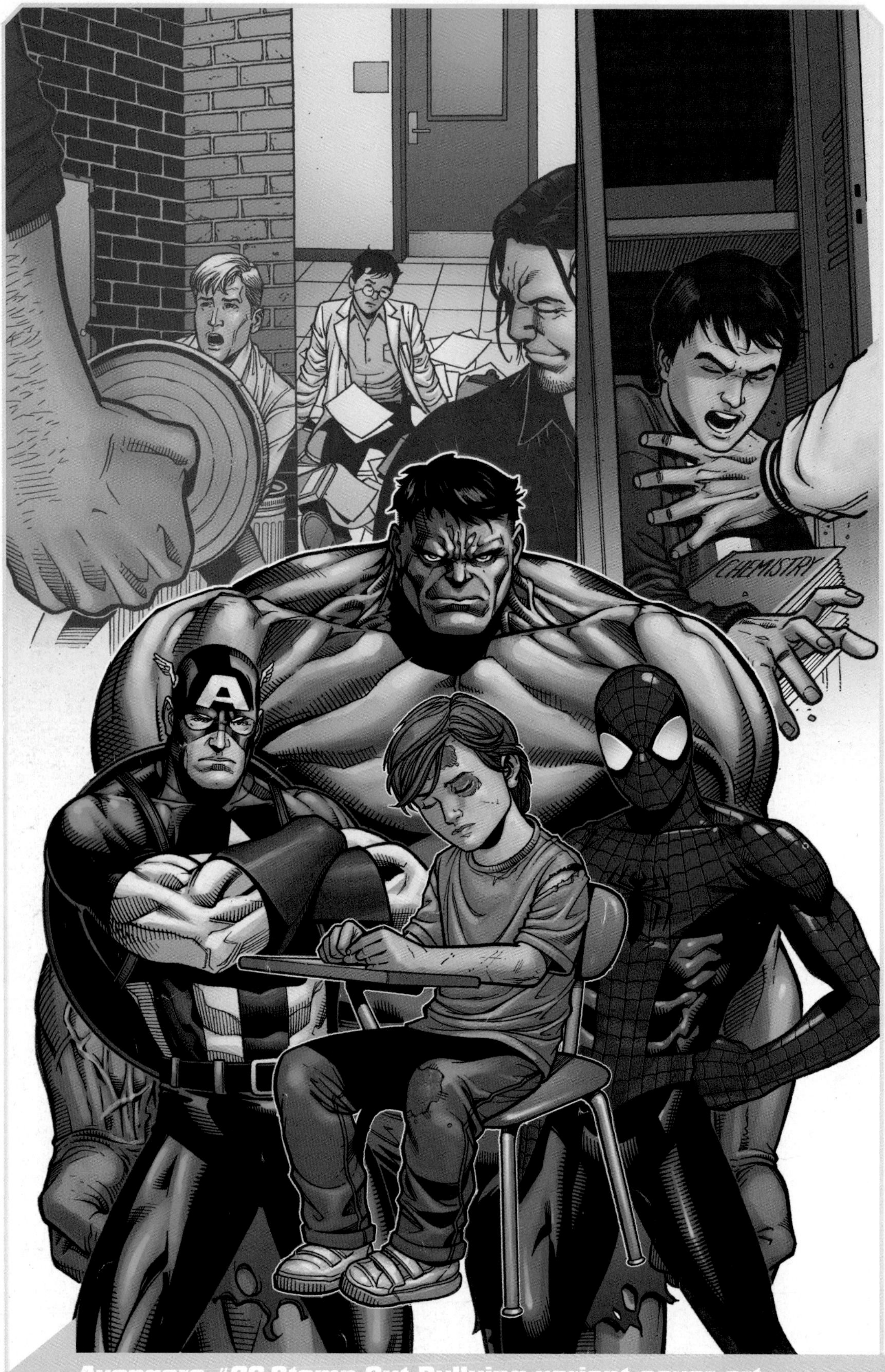
CHEMISTRY

Avengers #36 Stomp Out Bullying variant cover art
by Sean Chen, Mark Morales & Chris Sotomayor

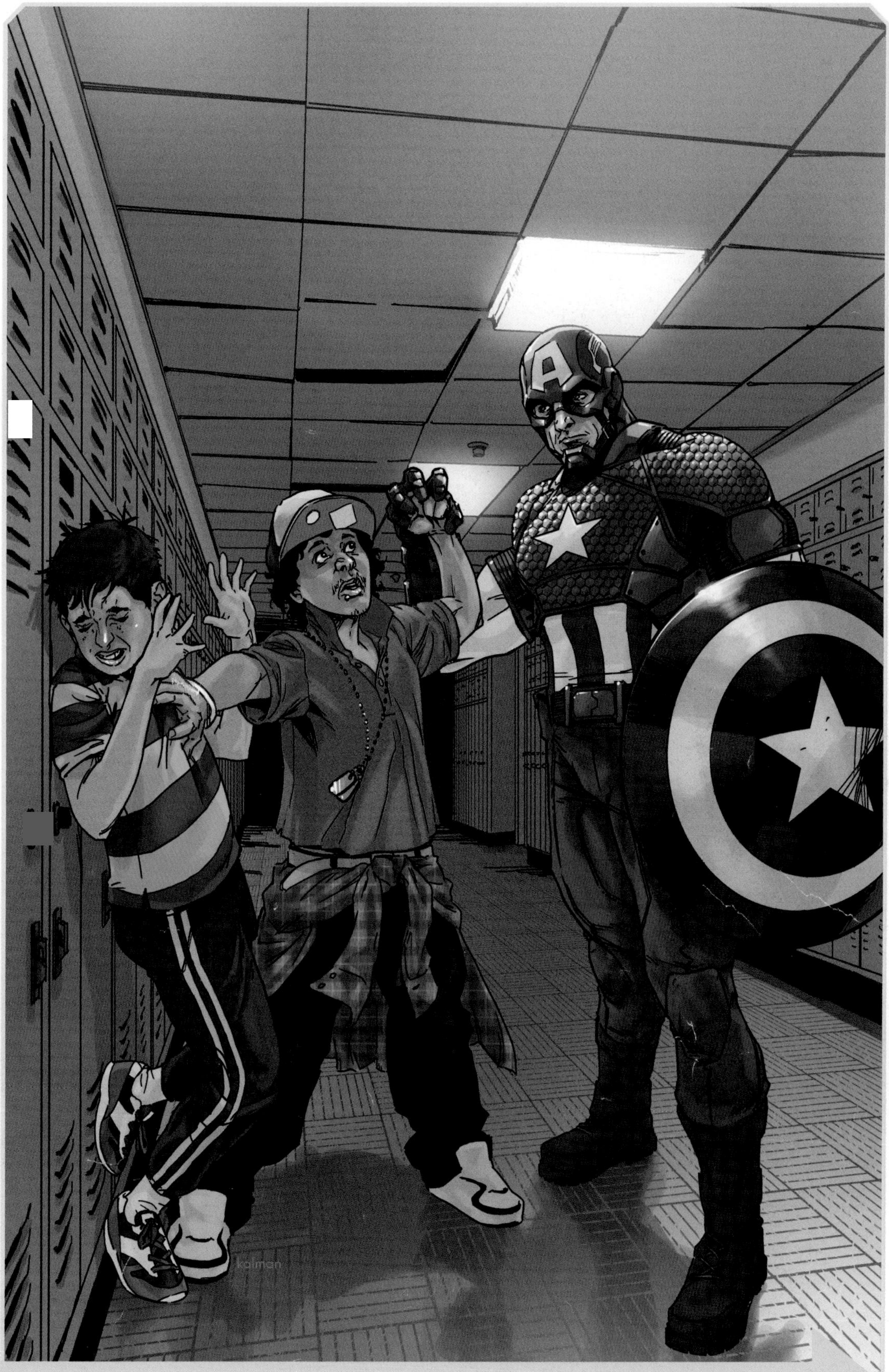

Captain America #25 **Stomp Out Bullying variant cover art by Kalman Andrasofszky**

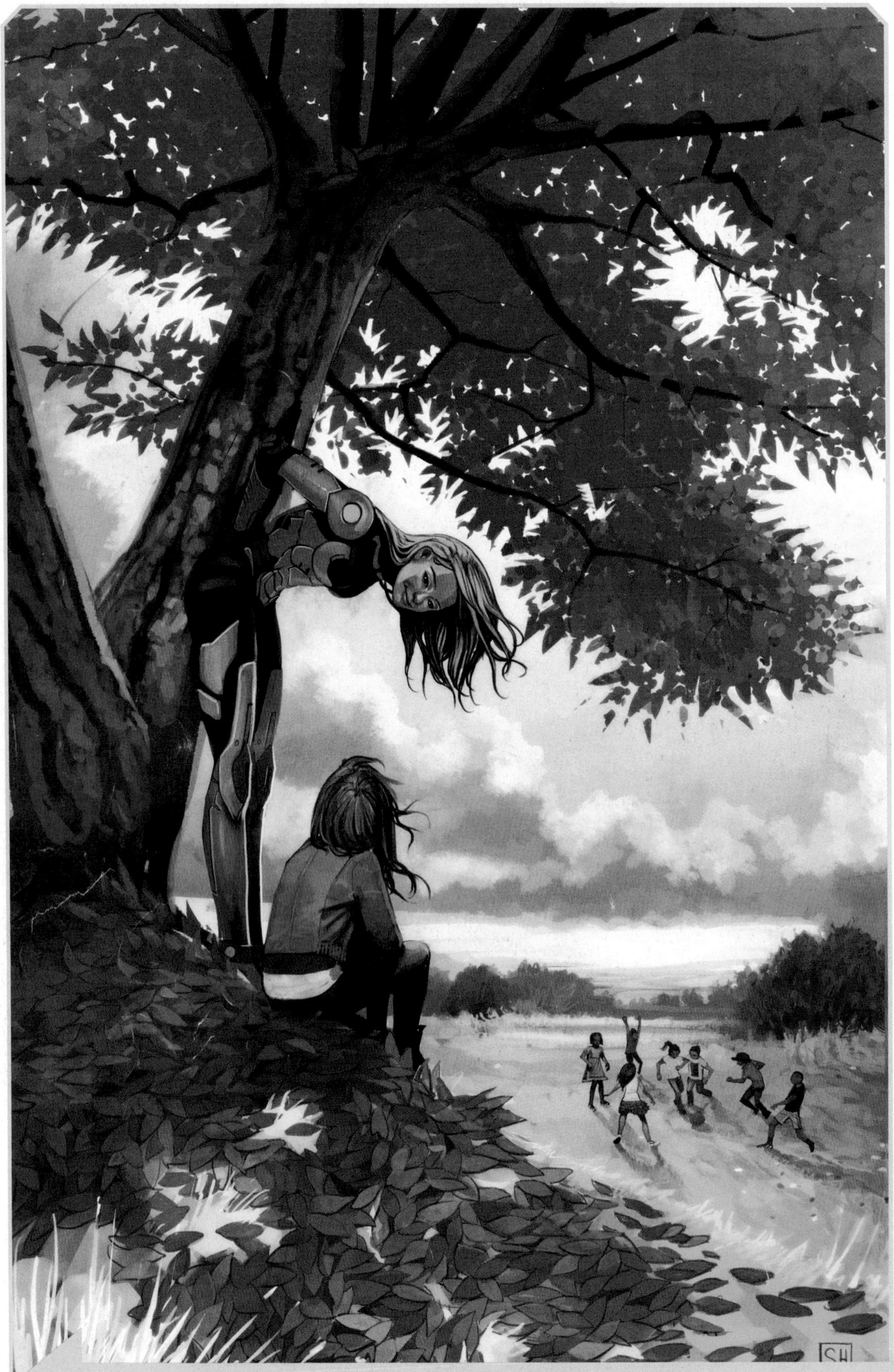
SH

Guardians of the Galaxy #20 Stomp Out Bullying variant cover art by Stephanie Hans

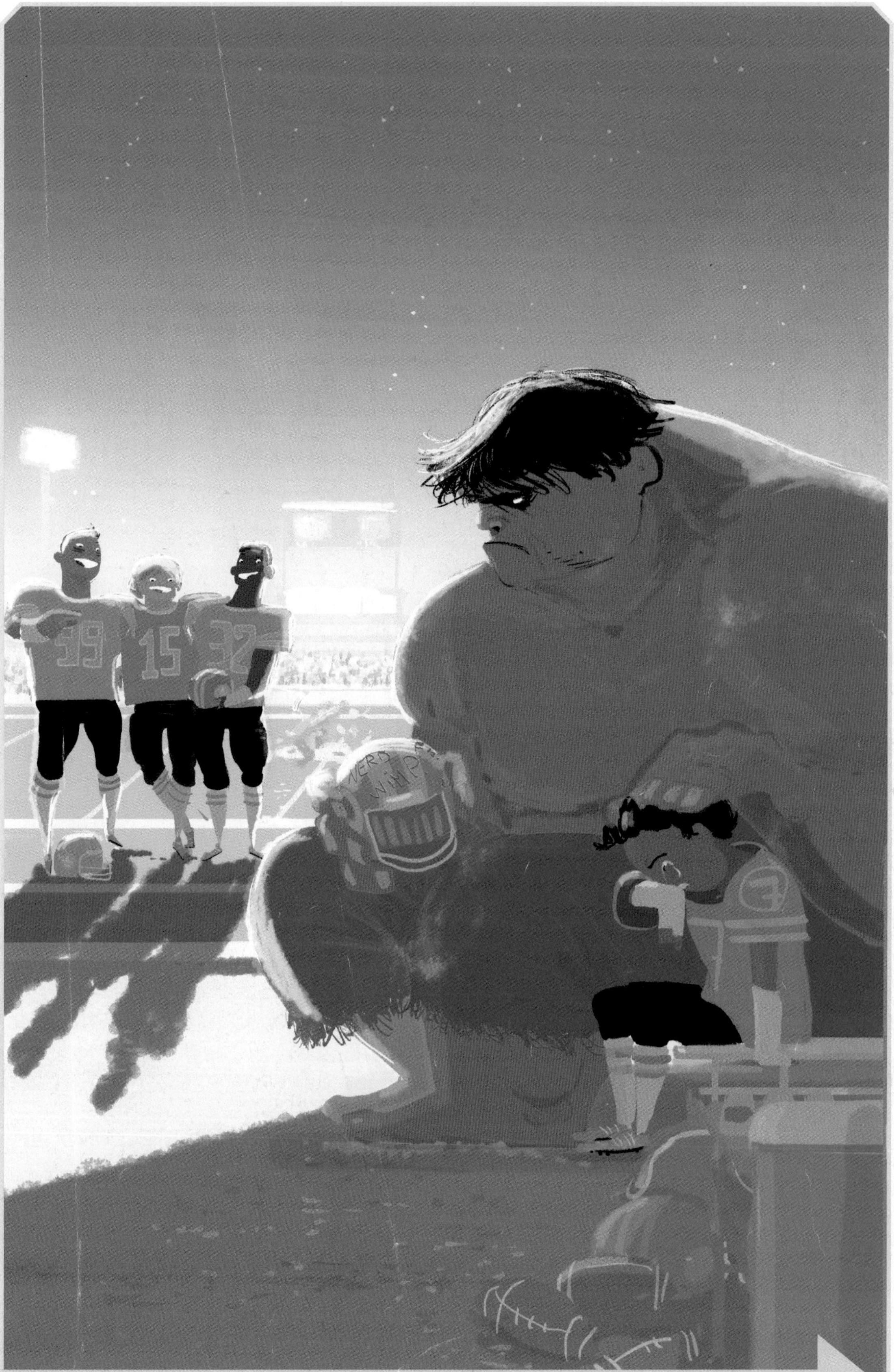
NERD
WIMP

***Hulk* #7 Stomp Out Bullying variant cover art**
by Pascal Campion

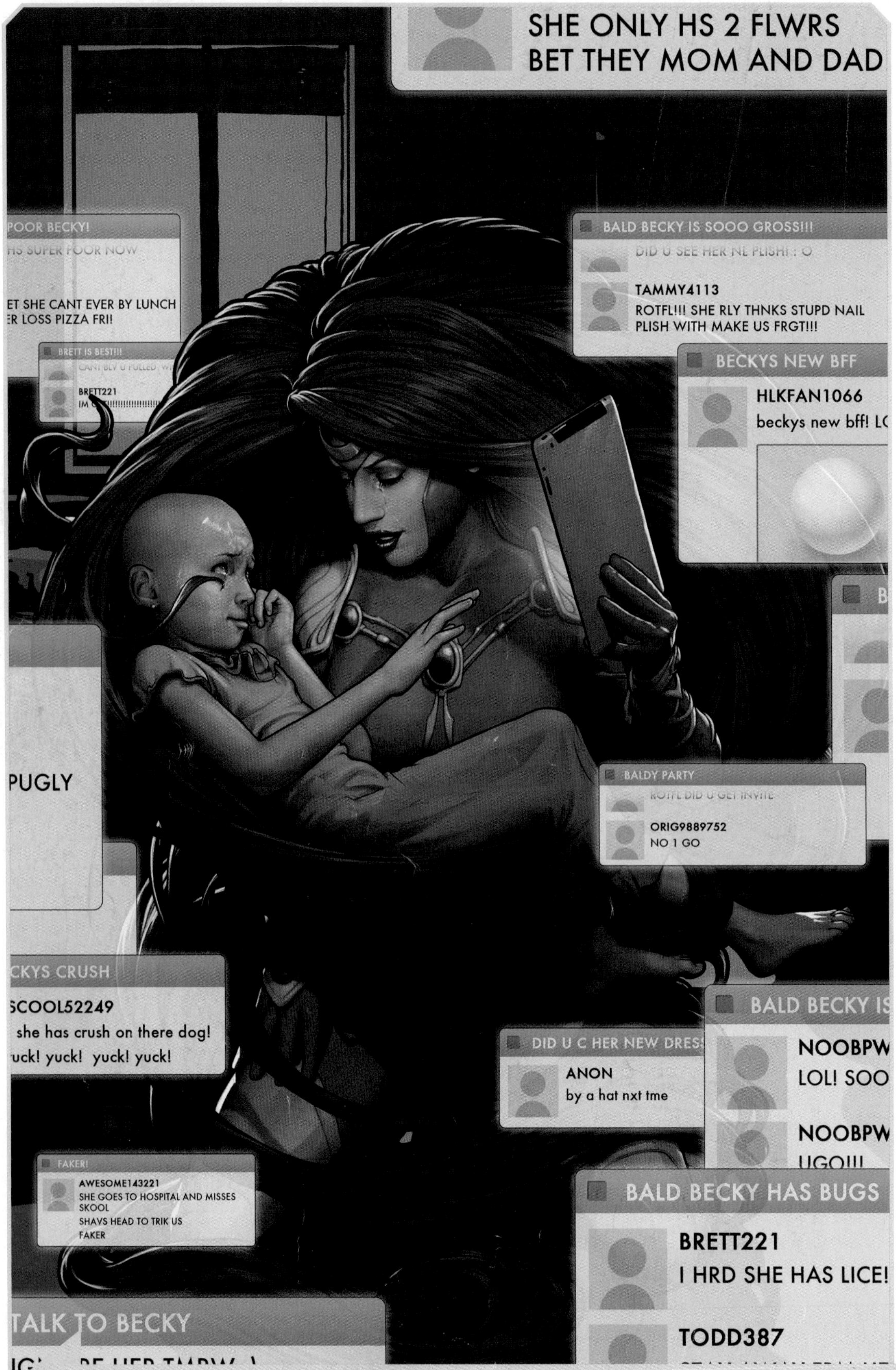
SHE ONLY HS 2 FLWRS
BET THEY MOM AND DAD
POOR BECKY!
HS SUPER POOR NOW
ET SHE CANT EVER BY LUNCH
ER LOSS PIZZA FRI!
BRETT IS BEST!!!
BRETT221
BALD BECKY IS SOOO GROSS!!!
DID U SEE HER NL PLISH! : O
TAMMY4113
ROTFL!!! SHE RLY THNKS STUPD NAIL
PLISH WITH MAKE US FRGT!!!
BECKYS NEW BFF
HLKFAN1066
beckys new bff! L
PUGLY
BALDY PARTY
ROTFL DID U GET INVITE
ORIG9889752
NO 1 GO
CKYS CRUSH
SCOOL52249
she has crush on there dog!
uck! yuck! yuck! yuck!
BALD BECKY IS
NOOBPW
LOL! SOO
NOOBPW
UGO!!!
DID U C HER NEW DRESS
ANON
by a hat nxt tme
FAKER!
AWESOME143221
SHE GOES TO HOSPITAL AND MISSES SKOOL
SHAVS HEAD TO TRIK US
FAKER
BALD BECKY HAS BUGS
BRETT221
I HRD SHE HAS LICE!
TODD387
TALK TO BECKY

***Inhuman* #7 Stomp Out Bullying variant cover art**
by John Tyler Christopher

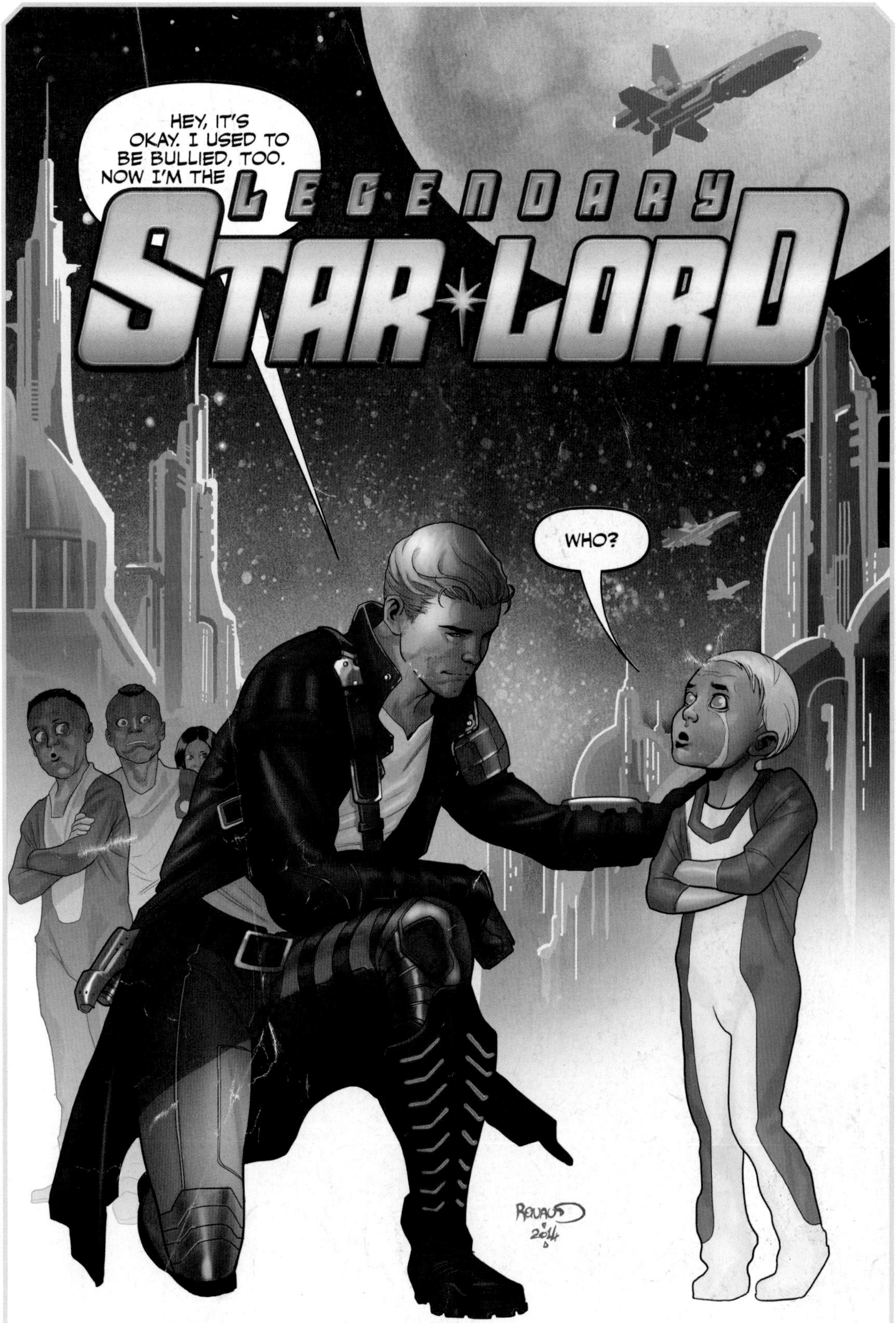
HEY, IT'S OKAY. I USED TO BE BULLIED, TOO. NOW I'M THE
LEGENDARY STAR-LORD
WHO?

Legendary Star-Lord #4 Stomp Out Bullying variant cover art
by Paul Renaud

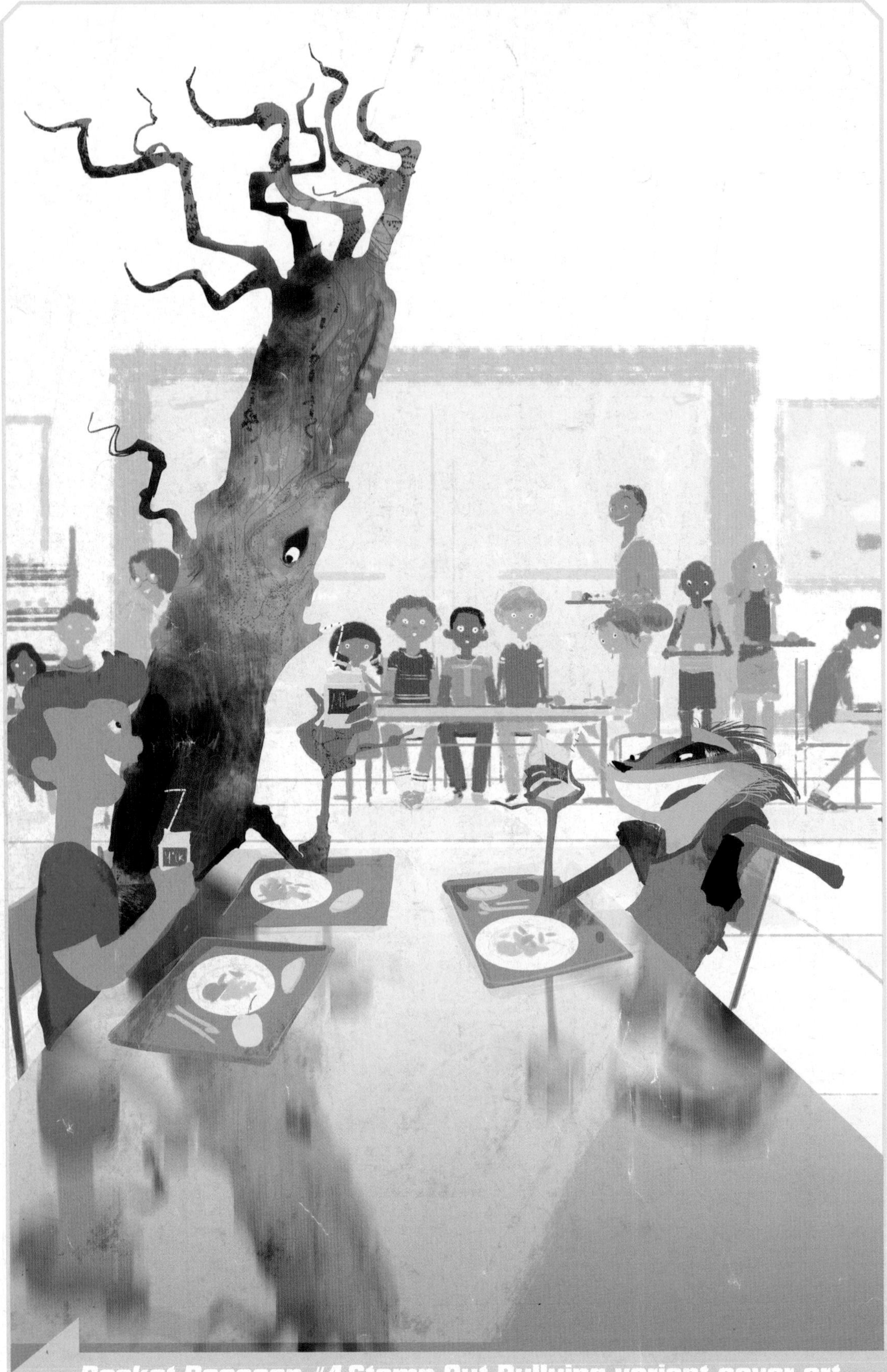

Rocket Raccoon #4 Stomp Out Bullying variant cover art
by Pascal Campion